D0847939

DOUBLE
TAKE

By the Same Author:

MURDER IN MELLINGHAM

DOUBLE TAKE

A Mellingham Mystery

SUSAN OLEKSIW

CHARLES SCRIBNER'S SONS
NEW YORK

MAXWELL MACMILLAN CANADA
TORONTO

MAXWELL MACMILLAN INTERNATIONAL
NEW YORK   OXFORD   SINGAPORE   SYDNEY

Copyright © 1994 by Susan Prince Oleksiw

Charles Scribner's Sons   Maxwell Macmillan Canada, Inc.
Macmillan Publishing Company   1200 Eglinton Avenue East
866 Third Avenue   Suite 200
New York, NY 10022   Don Mills, Ontario M3C 3N1

Macmillan Publishing Company is part of the Maxwell Communication
Group of Companies.

Library of Congress Cataloging-in-Publication Data
Oleksiw, Susan.
Double take:a Mellingham mystery/Susan Oleksiw
p.   cm.
ISBN 0-684-19656-5
1. Police—New England—Fiction.   I. Title.
PS3565.L42D6   1994
813'.54—dc20   93-26111   CIP

Macmillan books are available at special discounts for bulk purchases for sales promo-
tions, premiums, fund-raising, or educational use. For details, contact:

Special Sales Director
Macmillan Publishing Company
866 Third Avenue
New York, NY 10022

10 9 8 7 6 5 4 3 2 1
Printed in the United States of America

To Rae Francoeur and the Tuesday Night Storytellers

DOUBLE
TAKE

THE CHARACTERS

EVAN GOLDMAN—*Dean of Massasoit College of Art*
PRESTON MATTSON—*Chairman of the Painting Department*
ELLEN MATTSON—*his wife*
LARRY SEGAL—*drawing teacher*
BETTY LANE—*academic secretary*
KAREN MEGHAN—*student affairs secretary*
BUDDY LECROIX—*head of maintenance*
CHICKIE MORELLI—*work-study student*
HANK VINNIO—*work-study student*
GREGORY STEWART—*greenhouse owner*
MIKE RABKIN—*owner of the Whimsy Gallery*
HENRY MUIR—*local sculptor*
ED CORRELL—*local bank officer*
LISA HUNT—*resident and part-time art student*

CHIEF JOE SILVA—*chief of police in Mellingham*
SERGEANT KEN DUPOULIS—*a member of the police force*

and other residents of Mellingham and students of the college

1
A MONDAY IN THE FALL

FROM AN EARLY AGE Preston H. Mattson was good at getting people to do what he wanted them to do—and he knew it. Preston was not an evil man, for he never used this knack for anything he adjudged evil. His talent for manipulating people was perhaps more noticeable in the career that had opened before him. A man of mediocre talents, he had risen quickly to the position of chairman of the painting department at the Massasoit College of Art in Mellingham, and there he had stayed for almost twenty years, directing students to the threshold of their careers and keeping an eye on the local community of artists.

For the most part that was about as close as he got to them, for Preston was also something of a squire. Always well dressed, even when drawing or painting, he had a high forehead and a patrician nose that on a lawyer or businessman would have advanced his career considerably, but on an artist in his forties, combined with his attire, gave other artists pause. The exceptions, of course, were students, and they never failed to gratify his ego. This accounted for his willingness to take on the added chore this year of presiding over the committee of students planning the spring art show. Gathered now in the gallery, five students sat on chairs and tables, and even on the floor. The first meeting had gone well, for without a word spoken directly by Preston, the students had decided to make his work the center of the spring show.

There were times when Preston thought his life was just about perfect. The village of Mellingham had that effect on people. The small art college, one of the oldest in the country, rested among groves beyond the residential neighborhoods, ensconced on the grounds of an old estate yet so modest in its posture among the trees that a mindless driver on the highway nearby would miss it. No matter. The college had the warm support of the local residents. With fewer than three thousand people, the village of Mellingham—perched on the rocky New England coast north of Boston—boasted not only artistic talent and pure white sandy beaches free of oil lumps and trash, but also a broad lake of clear water and just about any other amenity a resident could want. All of this crinkled and sparkled in pure sea air and bright sunshine, and yet most of it Preston ignored. He much preferred the sparkling adulation in the eyes of his students, particularly the newer ones.

"I'm sure we could get everything hung on the afternoon before," a pimply-faced but ardent young man said.

Preston nodded and murmured something about dedication, trying to remain suitably aloof and restrained. He surveyed the eager faces turned up at him, choosing bland expressions that would not disturb their emotional focus on him or engage their minds in a challenging thought. The low rumbling timbre of his voice, schooled to emphasize his every mood, vibrated around the students. He liked the sound of it in the stark white gallery with its black ceiling and concrete floor. The richness of his tenor grew by the contrast with the white planes surrounding him. Pleased, he glanced around the room, then wished he hadn't. A student leaning on the door jamb, just outside the group, stared back at him. Preston felt self-conscious, then resentful of Chickie for ruining his mood. Chickie—if that was his real name, Preston pondered spitefully—hung back from the other students, his arms folded across his chest. Chickie was older and felt uncomfortable with the younger students, Preston rationalized; that's why he didn't join in. The teacher went back to nodding his approval as the students seated around him listed the many things they wanted to do to promote the show. Preston was again warmed by the glowing faces of youth.

"Each person is going to have to take one," Chickie broke in, his voice a soft rebuke. "Posters, brochures, program guides, radio announcements, opening night party. That all adds up to a lot of work."

"We didn't have radio announcements," another student said, making a note.

"And then raising money for it all," Chickie said, "that won't be easy."

Preston moved in his chair, hoping he wouldn't have to interrupt Chickie's comments, but he was growing uneasy at the bleak picture the older student was painting of the task ahead and he didn't want Chickie derailing the eager ones. He drew his foot along the floor, scraping it just loud enough to draw the students' eyes away from Chickie's pose in the doorway back to the teacher sitting opposite.

"Don't worry," one said, again looking toward Preston and the other students. "We can handle it."

"Yeah," the apparent student leader agreed. "How about you, Chickie? Which one will you take?"

"Not me," Chickie said easily. "I'm too new here. I've barely figured out how to get around the area."

"How about getting some of your friends from the West Coast to donate money?" another one said, a serious-looking young woman with long dark hair. "To help a fellow artist?" Preston winced at the students' plaintive requests; they seemed to reduce his stature somehow.

Chickie laughed lightly. "I'll have to ask, but don't count on it."

"I know someone who works at a radio station," another student said, giving the call letters of a station that served northeast Massachusetts and southern New Hampshire. "I'll ask about getting some free time for announcements." This offer broke the dam of reserve and each student eagerly claimed one of the many jobs in promoting the show; only Chickie stood quietly aside, his face a study of indifference.

"Shall I make a list of who's doing what?" Preston asked with a slight hesitation. His open hand gestured toward the students. "Or do I leave that up to—" He paused and looked around in mild confusion. As expected, a student replied; the one who had boldly tried to draw in Chickie answered. Preston might cultivate a certain professorial absentness, but only up to a point; it would never do for a man of his position to allow a situation to drift beyond his direction.

"I've got them down." The student waved a sheet of paper in the air to confirm this.

"Should I schedule another meeting in here?" Preston nodded vaguely at the gallery.

"Sure," several students said together, looking back and forth from teacher to students. Preston raised a languid hand to the breast pocket of his tweed jacket and removed a gold ballpoint pen, holding it poised over a leather-bound pocket calendar. "Shall we say four weeks from today?" He lowered the pen to the appropriate block on the page, not waiting for anyone to reply. The students assented eagerly, as expected, and he noted the time and purpose of the meeting in his calendar. He watched out of the corner of his eye as several students wrote down the date on the covers of their notebooks, a practice that repelled him for its riskiness. He also noted that Chickie remained in the doorway, hands in his pockets, eyes on the students.

The group was breaking up now and the pimply-faced boy was rapidly scribbling notes about the show. One of the new women students made a couple of whispered suggestions as she glanced excitedly at Preston. The boy wrote them down and gathered up his bag. He stuffed the list into the pocket with a tube of paint and shuffled toward Preston.

"We're going to have a complete outline of our schedule for the whole thing by next week, we hope."

"You're bringing this along nicely, young man." Preston stood up slowly. "Doug, isn't it?" He continued without letting the student answer yes or no, since Preston rarely made the gaffe of misaddressing someone he wanted something from. "This is the first show you've put together?"

"Yes, sir. The director is giving me a lot of pointers, but I've got some ideas of my own I want to try out."

"Of course." Preston nodded his approval. "And the director will be a great help. This is not the time for anything to go wrong. Your first effort to hang a show must be good."

"Yes, sir."

"And we'll see that it is," Preston said, patting the boy on the arm though the student was a good six inches taller than his teacher. "I must be getting along now, Doug. You'll have me missing my next class, and after all, that's what we're here for."

"Yes, sir." Doug followed Preston into the corridor, where the sounds of voices flowed from the classrooms opening off the long hallway that ran the full length of the art building, from the gallery at one end to the student bookstore at the other. Chickie was gone and the other students had now mingled with the crowd in the corridor. Preston walked on to his office, leaving Doug to lope off on his own.

■ ■ ■

The sound of classes ending and students flowing, chattering and laughing, into the hall always reminded Betty Lane of a series of timed explosions from a war movie. She never tried working during the mid-morning change, and saved a few minor tasks to fill the fifteen minutes between classes. Although many of the college employees and teachers leaped at the chance for a quick coffee break, she preferred to drink her coffee or tea when it was quiet, without students dodging around each other and the desks to ask questions that any ten-year-old could answer.

This morning she had chosen the job of sending out announcements for the next exhibit, due to open in two weeks in a gallery that was nowhere near ready to receive a dozen canvases of varying size. Still, that wasn't her worry, she reminded herself as she applied stamps to the colored postcards. The two stacks gradually changed, the one on her left shrinking as the one on her right grew. As she stood at the L-shaped counter that kept students from flowing unchecked into the offices, she explained how to fill out a scholarship application ("The directions are on the form"), how to drop a course ("The directions are on the form"), and how to apply for a senior studio ("The directions are on the form"). When the last student had finally bolted for the corridor, late for class, after asking if the class had been canceled and countering Betty's reply with a wail in response ("But my roommate said . . ."), Betty savored the quiet and returned to her desk.

"They'll be settling down soon," the student affairs secretary commented. Not much older than those she advised, Karen Meghan always thought whatever was going to happen would happen soon. She was invariably wrong. At twenty-three Karen did not see the behavior of the students as distinct from her own, though she was convinced she was far more sophisticated than any of the adults around her. A talented photographer, she sometimes sold her photographs to the local newspapers, and she kept Betty informed of every step in her career. Betty listened, all the while smirking at Karen's hair, which was frizzy and dark brown, according to the new style, and her penchant for bright red lipstick. Karen noticed none of this, and went on insisting that as soon as another day passed, the students would turn into silent and serious workers, content to study without ever saying a word. Betty expected the students to grow silent at about the same time Karen did.

"You said that last week," Betty reminded her, sitting down at her desk and pulling open the bottom drawer. "Whose turn was it to bring the doughnuts?" she asked as she pulled out a plastic bag of individually wrapped tea bags. If she couldn't have tea served in a silver teapot, mused Karen, watching her, she would have a tea bag wrapped in silver foil.

"I don't know," Karen replied to Betty's question. "But I think it's the other office."

The administrative offices of the college were, in fact, no more than two large rooms connected by a small vestibule, which opened onto the main corridor of the building. Each of the two offices had been divided into smaller offices. The room given over to the president had been divided almost evenly into two spaces to accommodate the president and his secretary. The other office had been divided into three unequal spaces—the largest one accommodating Karen and Betty, the second one occupied by the dean of the college, and the third claimed by Preston Mattson. In the vestibule was a small desk and a couple of chairs where work-study students occasionally carried out their minor office duties. This morning two women students were chatting while they stuffed envelopes. Karen greeted them briefly and seconds later returned to her own office with two sugar doughnuts, handing one to Betty.

Well into her fifties, of solid, even girth from her shoulders to her knees in whatever she wore, either straight dark dresses or straight dark skirts with white or solid-colored blouses, Betty Lane was an anomaly. Making no claim to artistic talent, aesthetic sensibility, or creative ambitions of any sort, she unilaterally moved the artists around her through the chaos of their creative life toward what she considered of crucial importance: a tightly ordered professional future. This meant an office routine that ran like a nuclear submarine on a test mission, including her coffee break. Anyone working with her could even go so far as to recite the manner in which she cleared her desk every morning to make way for her cup and saucer of tea and her doughnut. All materials were placed into two or more stacks and moved to the side and edge of her desk, leaving her blotter clear. At the moment, a thick file stood on her left, and two stacks of completed student forms stood in front of her. Betty Lane sat slightly turned toward Karen, raising a tiny piece of sugar-shedding pastry to her mouth.

"Nothing for me?" a thick male voice said. The two women looked up to see Hank Vinnio leaning on the counter.

"Not a thing. Get your own," Karen shot back with a smile. Before she could pour her own cup of coffee, Hank was slipping under the flap in the counter. He pulled a small thermos from the long pocket on the leg of his green coveralls and poured coffee into a plastic cup. He then perched on Karen's desk and smiled over at Betty, who was giving as much attention to her second piece of doughnut as she might to the annual report.

"Aren't you here a little early today?" Betty asked after a few minutes. "I thought you were on the evening shift."

"I am," Hank replied, "four nights a week, Monday through Thursday. But one of the instructors wanted to talk about a lighting problem and getting things set up so the electrician can come in and work without any complications. So I said I'd come in early today." Getting no response from either woman, he swallowed a mouthful of coffee. "Hey, it's rough going to school and working at the same time. You girls oughta sympathize with me."

"You should stick to your janitorial duties for work-study students and let Buddy handle the rest," Betty said.

"Okay, okay," he said, laughing. "I admit it. I can use the extra money. What can I say? I'm always broke."

"Likely story. You just wanted to see the nude model in the painting class," Karen said with a grin. "I know you."

"Careful, honey," Hank said, taking up the game, "you'll give Betty ideas about us." He smiled at Betty, who didn't try to conceal her distaste for what she regarded as Karen's immature remarks. For all her years of experience, Betty still found it trying to train new employees to the rules of her office; she didn't like Karen giving Hank the idea he could drop in whenever he wanted and talk about anything that came to mind. She would have to talk to Karen directly before things got out of hand. Tall and slender with dark curly hair and graceful easy movements, Hank Vinnio could be a problem. He had already caught the eye of every young woman—and many not so young—at the college, but so far he had only used his charm to keep people at a distance. He had been careful not to get personally involved with students or teachers or other employees. But it was early days yet; they were only three weeks into the semester.

"Who exactly is making changes in lighting?" Betty asked. Such a major change should have passed over her desk at some point, but she didn't remember anything of the sort; she didn't like to think she had missed something important.

"The photography guy," Hank said. "Good idea, too. With all the chemicals those kids use, poor wiring could lead to a lot more than an overloaded circuit."

Betty nodded with her mouth full, and Hank, apparently taking this as a sign of encouragement, went on.

"The odds of having a fire start down there are pretty slim, but the potential damage—new buzzword, ladies," he said, leaning closer to Karen and winking at her. "The potential damage is enough to make us do something. So we're doing something."

"The whole place is concrete," Karen said with a look at the walls behind her. "What could burn?" She liked Hank, just as she liked almost everyone else she met, and was willing to adopt, if only briefly, his view because he was someone she liked.

"The books in the library," Betty replied thoughtfully.

"That's right," Hank agreed, glad to see he had convinced one member of his audience. "And once the fire got going, it could do a lot of harm—canvases, offices, the wiring. A fire is deadly." He grew serious. "I remember when I was a kid, there was a fire in my hometown in an old house. The place went up like a book of matches. Three apartments gone. A woman died. She was young, too." He looked from Karen to Betty. Noticing the gloom he had draped over both women, he said, "Hey, it was ages ago, when I was just a kid. Things are a lot safer now," he said to Betty, who was just then looking hard at the two large stacks of paper on her desk.

"I'm sure glad I don't work in an old wooden building," Karen said, shivering slightly. "I might be worrying about fire all the time."

"Me, too," Hank said. "So how about letting the sparks fly and modeling in the nude for me?" he asked with a practiced leer. He ducked out under the counter and through the door as a wad of paper missed him and hit the wall.

■ ■ ■

The still and perfect silence of a dozen students concentrating on the work in front of them was broken by a long bell signaling the noon hour. Trained and responsive, a few students leaned back on their stools; one dropped his arm to his side, dangling the brush to the ground; another put her hand on her hip and studied her canvas; two others stood up and turned away to their paint boxes. The community of spirit was gone and the studio now contained only a collection of young artists ready to move on to whatever the day held next for them.

The more committed students lovingly cleaned their brushes, working out the odd bits of paint as they assessed their work and let the fumes from the turpentine wreathe their heads and seep into their lungs. The room filled with murmurings and then the chatter of students eager to articulate whatever they had been feeling and thinking while working. A few stood apart, ruminating on brush strokes unsatisfactory to their critical eye but probably laudable to others.

Preston Mattson moved slowly from easel to easel, stopping to comment briefly, his voice modulated so that only the single student could hear him, then moving on to another, nodding and smiling. A girl in a denim shirt hanging out over black leggings whisked her hands against each other to dispel the dust of pastel crayons, then wiped her palms down the front of her shirt, leaving the residue on the puckered fabric. Preston's nose twitched, but not from the powdery colors turning into a pink aura around her. He glanced at the last painting and the last painter, nodded stiffly, and moved back toward the door.

"Surely this isn't by one of the students in this class?" Preston asked. He had stopped in his progress at a canvas that was propped against the wall near the door. His question was addressed to no one in particular, his comment cast into the silence around him. He moved closer and peered at the forest scene done in bright hues.

"Actually, it's Hank Vinnio's." Preston turned to the young man who had spoken. He was standing a few feet away with his paint box at his side, having stopped at the last minute to answer Preston's question. Seemingly perplexed, Preston repeated the name.

"He's a work-study student; he does maintenance work," the student explained. "He works in here sometimes on his days off."

"Ah, I see," Preston said. Behind him several other students listened, their cleaning-up duties in abeyance.

"He just sold it. I think he's keeping it here until the owner can come pick it up," the student explained.

"Is he?" Preston said with a strained smile. "Well, how convenient for him. Unfortunately, it's not convenient for us. I'm afraid he can't simply leave it here, to suit himself. It's in our way." He turned back to the painting, a look of distaste flickering across his face. "I'm sure we're very glad he's managed to make a sale, but this studio is for those who have classes in here. If you see him," Preston said, turning to address the room in general, "tell him to store his work elsewhere. We have other materials to worry about in here." Preston rearranged his shoulders beneath his jacket, and moved on to the nearest easel; he gave it his full attention before making a few encouraging remarks to the young woman hovering nearby. He walked past Hank's painting again, barely missing it with his left foot.

By now the members of the next class, another introductory studio for first-year students, were assembling, and their eager faces distracted Preston from his latest irritant. He watched the students set up their paintings and took another turn around the room. This was the part of teaching he liked best, seeing all those young and eager faces turned to him for approval, guidance, affirmation. He readied himself for the last painting class of the morning.

■ ■ ■

"The decision is yours," Larry Segal said to Chickie Morelli. "You can take any of my classes you want next term. Think it over." The instructor patted Chickie's shoulder as he stood up. Awkwardly, he put his hands in his pockets. "It's more than that, Chickie. The MFA program is young. If you graduated from here, you'd really set a high standard. What you have is more than just a nice talent." Perhaps feeling he had said too much, Larry Segal bolted for the door.

Chickie was alone in the print studio, his drawings spread out on the floor or leaning against the wall in front of him. Only Chickie's and Larry Segal's chairs were turned to face the back wall of the room, and Chickie felt cut off from all else but the figures pulsating on the paper. After some moments, he gathered up the charcoal drawings and neatly returned them to his black portfolio, taking care to settle them near the spine so they wouldn't slide and smear when he stood the case upright. One student entered as he left the room. It was just two o'clock when Chickie left the portfolio in a large closet by the furnace room.

In his late twenties, Chickie Morelli wore a thoughtful look on his face all day long, perhaps because of his tortoise-shell glasses or perhaps because he really was thoughtful. No one ever knew. During the hours required of him as a work-study student, he swept the floors, emptied the trash, painted walls, moved furniture, all with the same detached look on his face. Since he spent little time outside the school with other students, no one had the chance to probe his thoughts or feelings, and no one at the school was bold enough to pursue them during class time. But everyone noticed his aloofness, which to the younger students still in their teens suggested worldliness, intelligence, mystery. Chickie was thus deemed one of the most important students in the college. Because he was so quiet, he was also deemed one of the most mature, by teachers as well as students.

If he knew about these speculations, he gave no sign. Moreover, he gave little attention to the students who tried to befriend him. They were noticeably younger than he was, though not necessarily in years, and he had much on his mind, concerns of a sort that could not by their very nature occur to students so young, so idealistic, so callow. So at two o'clock in the afternoon, four days a week, Monday through Thursday, Chickie went to work as a part-time maintenance man, his mind far from the broom in his hands or the trash can hoisted on his back. His thick black hair fell over his brown eyes, but he barely noticed that his view was obscured, for his eyes were focused within. His hands swung full metal cans as easily as empty plastic ones, for his deep thought was the same as a practiced meditation in canceling the weight of the world around him. Only in one respect did it differ—it failed to quench the passions within.

■ ■ ■

The young man still had his left hand on his hip and his right leg bent, the cocky stance of the impatient and entitled. Buddy Lecroix had seen it a hundred times before; every year, for the last thirty years, at least one student felt entitled to enter the janitor's storeroom whenever he wanted, and every year Buddy politely sent him (it had never been a her) away. He had never given the keys to his storeroom to anyone, and at fifty-six he wasn't going to change. He didn't worry about it, either. In another hour the young man would be romping with his classmates, for that's how Buddy thought of them. They were pups, and life was still all play. That was how it should be.

Buddy reminded the student he had things to do, and politely bid him good afternoon, an expression he had learned from his grandfather and couldn't give up, though he never heard anyone else salute people with it. Still, he loved the expression. It had a leisurely air about it, suggesting the full day of a full life, not the harried and compacted hours of people today. Such a proper greeting measured out time as well as relationships, and he kept it alive in his life even if he was the only one.

The student screwed up his face, pursing his lips and squishing them from side to side, before turning away and heading up the stairs. Buddy shook his head and went back to his workroom. Each year they got younger and younger. His wife teased him, telling him that he was just getting older and older, but it wasn't so. Each year the incoming students knew less and less about getting along with people, being nice to the teachers and the staff just as a natural way of being. One of the teachers told him the students needed socializing, and Buddy said no, they didn't need lessons for parties. They needed to learn some manners like everyone else, and she agreed. Most of the teachers were like that, Buddy thought, and he was grateful to be where he was.

Buddy nodded to himself over his secret happiness, but anyone seeing him would not have suspected the feeling hidden below long loose jowls that made him look like a basset hound no matter how he felt. If anyone could see into the brown eyes he kept turned onto the floor, they would have seen a glimmer of humor and warmth, but the rest of his feelings he kept to himself. He never minded the students who tried to take over his storeroom or workroom. Their fathers were usually CEOs or doctors or lawyers, and the children of such parents seemed to learn at an early age to assert what they felt was an innate superiority. Buddy nudged them back into line and hoped they matured before they moved on in life. They usually did.

The door to the print studio stood ajar and Buddy poked his head in. When he saw Chickie Morelli in the far corner studying a row of drawings spread out on the floor, he withdrew. He liked Chickie, a hardworking older student who was easy to get along with. During the first weeks of the term, Buddy had come to accept the new arrangement of work-study students helping him with the maintenance; it wasn't a change he had sought. He had two part-time assistants who were old enough to be relied on; they knew how to carry a job and get their work done; and they didn't think they were too good to clean up after other people. But the best part was that they were students; they were moving on as soon as they finished their course work. In a small school, that was something Buddy had to think about no matter what anyone else might tell him. For years he had warded off the suggestion he hire a younger man to assist him, fearful of being pushed aside by a subordinate. But this year he didn't have to worry about that, he told himself; these assistants wouldn't want his job if it were offered to them. He repeated this to himself daily, his own prayer and chant.

Buddy stripped the gloves from his hands and turned to a broken lamp on the table. The bright red bulb used in darkrooms sat off to one side while Buddy unscrewed the base and inspected the cord. It was a few minutes after three o'clock when he reinserted the red bulb, the glass casting a pink shadow, lightening the red and purple patches on his hands and wrists.

■ ■ ■

At six-thirty in the evening Lisa Hunt slammed shut the car door and looked across the parking lot to the college building just beyond. After a glance at the other cars, which must have proved satisfactory in some way, Lisa took a long stride toward the main door, her short blond curls glinting in the setting sun and her long arms swinging free. She crossed the parking lot in a few quick strides, stopping at the foot of the stairs to study a young woman emerging from a red Alfa Romeo parked in a faculty parking space. Unabashed about her personal habits, Lisa studied people openly, but since she did so with a kind and curious expression on her face, her behavior was tolerated. And since her face was pretty, the objects of her curiosity were often flattered by her interest in them. Few recognized the intelligence and independence in the smiling eyes. Ellen Mattson, Preston Mattson's wife, certainly didn't.

It was just as well, for as Lisa waited for Ellen to reach her she wondered what was wrong with the other woman's appearance. Dressed in a light wool skirt and coordinating jacket, Ellen had pale green eyes and pale blond hair, a woman drained of color in such a way that Lisa at first thought there must be a physical or psychological reason for it. She had felt this way since first seeing her a few weeks earlier, but there was no sign that Ellen was sick or unhappy. It was as though Ellen were devoid of personality and had sought to camouflage it in expensive clothing, hairstyling, and makeup, which in turn only emphasized her physical qualities. For her part, Ellen took Lisa's scrutiny as merely her due.

"You're in my painting class, aren't you?" Ellen said to

Lisa after arriving at the steps. Lisa assented and introduced herself.

"Watch it!" a man's voice yelled behind them. Both women jumped to the side as a large handcart whisked by them on the sloping macadam, held back by a grinning Hank Vinnio. "Sorry, ladies," he said with a smile that suggested he wasn't very sorry at all. "Can't have the students run over by their own art materials," he called out as he let himself be pulled along by the cart.

"A regular cowboy," Lisa said as she regarded Hank's receding back. She turned her amiable smile to Ellen, but the other woman was trembling and stretching out her hand for the stair railing. Her face white and her eyes wide, Ellen pressed her other hand to her chest as she gulped air. Lisa was at first amused by the melodramatic pose Ellen immediately fell into, but thought it grossly overdone. The man with the cart was surely just showing off. Lisa reached out to steady the other woman, whose hands were cold and clammy. Lisa hadn't thought they were really in any danger, but obviously Ellen had.

"Hey, easy does it," Lisa said to Ellen.

"Sorry." Ellen took a deep breath.

"That really rattled you," Lisa said half to herself. "But you were closer to him."

"What?"

"The guy with the cart. That really rattled you."

Ellen took another deep breath. "Yes, I guess it did."

"Here, sit down." Lisa helped her to the lower step. "We have plenty of time."

"Thanks." Ellen sat and pressed her hands onto her knees, willing her body to relax. She took another deep breath and pulled herself up with her hand on the railing.

"He was pretty careless," Lisa said. "But no harm done." She ran through ideas to distract the other woman from her scare. "That's a nice car you drive."

"Thank you. It was my late husband's," Ellen replied as

she mounted the stairs. "He gave it to me for our first anniversary."

"Is it fun to drive?"

"I suppose so. I have nothing to compare it to. It's the only car I've ever owned really. When Joey died—that's my late husband—he had a Rover, but I never drove it. I gave it to Preston when we got married. It seemed a good idea."

"Lucky Preston."

Ellen smiled and said, "I never saw myself driving a Rover."

"I never saw myself driving an Alfa," Lisa commented.

"Well, no, you wouldn't, would you?" Ellen said sincerely as she passed through the door Lisa held open for them.

■ ■ ■

The loaded handcart rolled to the end of the white stone college building. Hank maneuvered it around a corner to a loading bay, cursing the cars filling the parking lot and blocking a direct route to the loading dock and the smaller parking lot behind the building. The bay was closed. Jumping up onto the ledge, he banged on the metal garage door, and waited. When no one came in the time it took him to pace the ledge, he pushed on the bell for deliveries. The door soon rose and Chickie Morelli looked out.

"A late delivery," Hank said, nodding to the handcart. "I forgot everything would be locked up."

"I was just leaving when I heard the buzzer. I go off duty at six o'clock," Chickie explained.

"You must be Morelli." Hank introduced himself. "I come on at six. How come we haven't met before?"

"I don't know. Bad timing, I guess. Need any help?" Chickie looked at the cart outside. "It's after six and everyone else has gone. Just the evening students are here."

"Thanks," Hank replied. The two men began unloading the cans of paint, crates of steel sheets, and cardboard boxes. They made quick work of it.

"Seems strange stuff for an art school," Hank said. "This is more like what I used to deliver to auto body shops."

"Sometimes there isn't much difference in what we do. Just where we do it and why."

"And how much we get for it," Hank added.

Chickie laughed and agreed. "I hear you just made a sale."

"Yeah." Hank stopped working long enough to put his hands on his hips and shake his head in disbelief. "That was the easiest three hundred bucks I ever made." The two men moved the larger items into the painting studio, trying not to disrupt the evening class in progress. Under the instructor's mildly disapproving gaze, they stacked cans and crates against the back wall, pushing aside student work in their hurry to be done.

"How late are you working tonight?" Chickie asked the other man as they grabbed the last two containers.

"Till ten o'clock. Everyone has to be gone by then."

"I admire what you're doing," Chickie said suddenly, stopping outside the studio door. "Working full-time and going to school is hard, particularly around here, where you have no family." He stepped back, embarrassed. "I mean, I heard that. The kids were talking, you know."

Hank laughed. "They got that part right, but don't worry about me. I'm not all alone in the world. I have a few people I can count on for help." Not for the first time, Chickie noticed that Hank said everything with a grin, a smile, a wink.

The two men deposited their loads and headed for the door. On his way out, Hank stopped to look over the shoulder of an older woman who was painting a bright acrylic picture of a vase of flowers. Unperturbed by Hank's bold gaze, the older woman went on painting until Hank finally said, "Not bad, honey. Make van Gogh jealous." From another corner of the studio a brush clattered to the floor and a student shifted the position of a stool. Hank's foray into the work of the class had broken the first spell of concentration of the evening.

■ ■ ■

Lisa Hunt wiped the paint from her brush with a rag and sat back on the stool, surveying the small canvas propped up on the easel in front of her. Her long legs stretched out, she sighed and shook her head.

"It's awful," she said. "Absolutely awful." She smiled. When her boss, Lee Handel, had told her a year ago that he was afraid that she was wasting her life at the Marine Press, she had set out to put his mind at rest. But no amount of reasoning could convince Lee that life should go on as usual, particularly after he had personally confronted and laid to rest his own demon, in the form of Miss Beth O'Donnell. Although not personally responsible for her death, Lee Handel found in the murder investigation and its aftermath a passage from anguish to peace. Now he saw life in a brighter light and pushed Lisa to do the same. Though insisting she already did, Lisa could not penetrate Lee's new armor of optimism. When humor, appeals to Mrs. Handel, and finally a threat to quit failed to deter Lee, Lisa signed up for an art course.

Temporarily abandoning her secretarial duties, she plunged into the world of graphic design, found herself more than a little talented at designing books, and went back to work for the Marine Press in another capacity. Unwilling to let her stop there, her boss urged her on to greater expressions of her artistic talent. Curious but not driven, Lisa settled on painting and signed up for the open painting course on Monday evenings at Massasoit.

The mixture of ages among the students made the prospect of the course in painting palatable to Lisa, and the presence of one or two other students as ill equipped as she thought herself to be made the course tolerable. Her own good sense made the class fun. She had accepted after the first two weeks that she probably wouldn't get the hang of it, as she told the instructor, but she would see it through. Besides, she was enjoying herself.

Ellen Mattson, however, was a different sort. Every week, the wife of the painting professor carefully opened up her paint box, taking out her brushes, paint tubes, and palette knife; then closing her paint box, she neatly draped a rag on top. She flicked a few specks of dirt from the easel and walked to the row of shelves along the back wall, where she stored her other materials. From the moment when Ellen first raised her brush to the canvas to the last stroke of the evening, she was a portrait of the artist, her every pose a picture of the creative imagination at work. She never slouched, slumped, or tapped her toe in exasperation. She leaned forward, back, dabbing, concentrating, shifting her stance this way or that, never breaking from the intimate dance with her easel. When she stepped back to appraise her work, it was a studious eye that looked down on the paint. She was nevertheless aware of those around her, and when she heard Lisa's comment, Ellen leaned back far enough to cast her eye at her neighbor's canvas.

"Awful," Lisa said again with a broad smile at Ellen. "I really don't know what I'm doing here."

"It's a seascape, isn't it?" Ellen moved her eye over the painting from top to bottom, then right to left, not pursuing the sight lines established by rocks and sand.

"Yes, at least it's supposed to be."

"Well, I recognize it."

"Thanks." Lisa turned her critical eye on Ellen before saying, "It looks so different in my head."

"I think it looks fine." Ellen presented Lisa with her most encouraging smile, the sort that mothers often display for young children who are struggling to make perfect cookies that are destined to emerge from the oven as ashes. Lisa added the smile to her mental file on Ellen.

"I'll never make a painter." She gave no sign that she felt any disappointment at this discovery.

"Why are you taking the class if you don't think you can paint?"

This was such a reasonable question that Lisa chuckled softly before she said to her classmate, "My boss." She sighed and sat back down on her stool, whether defeated by her boss or by the painting she did not reveal. "I work for the Marine Press, and my boss, Mr. Handel, wanted me to take an art course, so I signed up for this. I know I have no talent, but I didn't think it would be so obvious." She looked again at the painting before her. "It's just awful." She seemed so genuinely pleased with this conclusion that Ellen took another, closer look at the canvas.

"No, it's not. Not really," Ellen said, the encouraging tone in her voice even more obvious.

"Yes, it is." The low smooth voice came from behind them, and both women turned to see a tall man with curly red hair looking over their heads at Lisa's painting. Well into his forties with a deep tan despite his red hair and freckles, he nodded vigorously as he spoke. "Quite right." He managed to give the two short words a swing and a burr. "'Tis awful." He smiled as he shook his head and then turned his attention back to his own easel.

"You see, I told you so," Lisa said to her companion.

"Who is that man?" Ellen asked in a whisper. "He paints beautifully, well, realistically, anyway."

"That's Gregory Stewart," Lisa said, raising her brush to her canvas again. "He has a greenhouse in town." She studied her latest dab. "Pay no attention to him." She raised her voice so those around her could hear. "He takes art courses just for fun, so he can torment the rest of us struggling beginners." The last two words were tossed over her shoulder; a low laugh came back in reply.

Ellen wielded her brush again but leaned closer to Lisa. "He never speaks to anyone." She made a poor attempt to conceal her suspicions. "He just stands there painting. Don't you think he's a bit strange?"

"He probably thinks we're strange," Lisa said philosophically, her mind again on her work.

Ellen ignored this. "Well, if he has so much talent," she said, trying again to convert Lisa to her way of thinking, "why isn't he a successful artist?"

This comment finally caught Lisa's attention and she turned to the other woman. Surely Ellen didn't really mean that?

"I've had to work very hard to develop my talent," Ellen said, as though she were talking about customers for a store, "and I still have a long way to go." Lisa was more than a little discomfited by the other woman's apparent confidences, and looked around at the other students nearby to see who else was listening to this careening conversation. Though it was common among students and even adults today, Lisa wasn't one for instant friendship and unprompted confessions. After all, she was just here to have a little fun. Nevertheless, unwilling to seem rude, and not wanting to contradict Ellen and so find herself in a fruitless argument over whether or not Ellen had talent, Lisa leaned over to look at her canvas, and silently agreed with part of the other woman's self-evaluation. The human figures were awkwardly drawn and the design of the scene was far too ambitious for the artist. This could turn out to be a very difficult course, Lisa concluded.

"I have to be good because my husband teaches here, but I've taken painting classes for three years along with drawing, silk screening, engraving, and watercolors and I still have problems." Ellen did not try to conceal her resentment.

The number of logical potholes yawning in Ellen's statement surpassed Lisa's mathematical skills, and she said only, "You've taken just about everything offered here."

"I know, and I think now I just need to work on my technique." Ellen cast a critical eye on her current work.

"Why don't you try something else?" Lisa suggested. "If you're not satisfied with your progress, that is."

"I don't know. Preston says it's just a question of developing basic talent."

Lisa took another look at her friend's canvas and wondered if Preston were really so blinded by love for his wife that he thought she should be encouraged as an artist. "Well, I'm never going to take it again," Lisa said. "I'm an awful painter, and I hope after this semester I never have to look at another one of my paintings again." She tossed her brush into a jar of turpentine to punctuate her determination.

"What will your boss say?"

"He'll try to encourage me," Lisa replied with a wry smile, "but I'll just tell his wife the truth. Mrs. Handel understands these things."

Ellen took one more look at her companion and went back to work, but around her others were stopping and stepping back for a final appraisal.

"Well, I think I've had enough for one night," Lisa said.

"Me too," Ellen readily agreed.

"I need some more paper towels," Lisa said after inspecting her brushes. "Do you want some?"

"Thank you," Ellen said. "That's very thoughtful of you."

In a few minutes Lisa was back from the ladies' room with a handful of paper towels. She looked around for Ellen.

"She left," said a lilting soft voice behind her. Lisa looked at the easel where Ellen had been working, and the other woman's paint box was indeed gone, but the painting and a jar of turpentine were still there.

"She has to come back to put away her painting," Lisa said to Gregory Stewart.

"No, she doesn't, lass. She's left that job for you," Gregory Stewart said as he passed her, carrying his painting and paints as he headed for the door. "If you're foolish enough to do it," he said as he disappeared into the hallway.

2

WEDNESDAY

EACH SPOT on the surface of the earth undergoes a number of seasons changing its tone and feel, but only one season will tell the character of a place. For Mellingham, the season was autumn. With a winter too harsh, a summer too soft, and a spring too short, Mellingham most truly revealed itself in the fall.

Only the old-timers could date the arrival of the season to the day, hour, and minute by the shifting of the wind, as though the earth leaning so far on its axis finally tipped over into the next quadrant; for everyone else autumn came and went gradually. Like his father before him, however, Joe Silva knew when the change came, a legacy of his early years on his father's boat. Even if he was sitting at a desk, something made him raise his head, look around, as though he had felt the earth shift beneath him, dropping him into another time. He knew after this moment life had other ways to confirm the change, for autumn—the finest of seasons in Mellingham—also had its drawbacks.

The cooler air energized the summer's drowsy citizens, and what people had ignored at 92 degrees suddenly became urgent at 68 degrees. It was only a question of which town issue would attract their new energy. Silva waited, considering the debates that languished in May for want of local interest. He was ready to bet the issue this year would be Henry Muir's proposed gallery.

Prescient but modest about it, Silva pulled a folder from a desk drawer and flipped through his notes on Muir's plans. Still unmarried in his mid-fifties, Henry Muir cultivated a personality that Silva at first found hard to fathom. When Silva arrived in Mellingham in 1985 to take on the office of chief of police, he had made a point of learning about the town at different times of day and night, getting the feel of the town as it changed during its regular hours. He memorized the lunch crowds (such as they were), the evening walkers, the weekend cyclists, and the occasional home-grown *malandro*, the troublemaker inevitable in every community. They were all as he expected. Henry Muir had been one of the few surprises after midnight.

The sculptor worked late into the night and sometimes even until dawn. His barn, still standing after two hundred years and now filled with his stone and the artwork of others, glowed through the night. From under the door seeped light and inexplicable sounds with no rhythmic consistency to lull a listener nearby into tolerance. His neighbors complained regularly and Henry just as regularly replied. He grumbled about their Yankee ways—their hidebound habits, as he called them—and their love of the mundane. Roughing the blister into a callus, he bragged that one day he would expose every one of his neighbors to truly advanced art. Respected for his own work, he wanted nothing in his barn that might feel synthetic, the result of too great an influence of civilization.

Henry even walked as though he were inspecting the ground before him for signs of pollution or corruption. Hunched over, his eyes pushing up his thick black eyebrows as he peered at others strolling by, Henry made his way into town every morning, his hands still dirty from the work of the night just past. At the old drugstore he pulled a newspaper from the pile left for the store owner, dropped his change—the first of the early morning—and turned homeward. When he heard the slapping of sneakers on the pavement behind him, he leaned toward the building or fence and watched the runner pass by. Others might take his bent and glare as a sign of disapproval, and he was glad to let them, but Silva knew too that this was a mere projection of their own feelings. In truth, Henry had spent so many years bent over at work that his body had shaped itself to his task of life rather than to his feelings; in his heart he was straight like the posts and beams of his barn and open to the world. In his hands he had the strength of five men and fists like the granite he loved best, the golden veins of stone bleeding into his palms. Only the love of the figures waiting to be released from the material resting inert beneath his tools kept him from raising his head and changing his form. Whatever the villagers thought of him, his hard work alone guaranteed him the solitude he loved.

Silva saw the sculptor on most mornings when he made his way to work or just drove around town in the early hours. On those mornings a part of the chief returned to the person he had once been, when the early morning quiet was not pleasant or quaint, but eerie and cautionary. On such mornings Silva thought himself out of place in the small town, as though he had been planted there by a sardonic god to test Henry, or perhaps to test the town itself. Unable to hear the rain or see the weeds on the sidewalk, Silva stood outside himself, watching himself watching the world, and only Henry seemed to notice him in his distant orbit.

Only after several months did Silva realize that Henry Muir could cultivate his character as an iconoclast only because he was the fourth generation to live in the tiny clapboard house and work in the large barn. In his angry denunciation of the other local artists, he was merely carrying on the Muir family tradition. After learning this, Silva came to look forward to the annual zoning contest between Muir and his neighbors. And so, no doubt, did Mr. Muir. In his surly disdain for his neighbors' love of the pedestrian, every year he promised newer and more outrageous artists as his companions in the gallery in his barn, and then, as a salve, promised not to hire more than a dozen assistants to help him in his business. Henry's annual visits to the classrooms of the Massasoit College of Art in search of a worthy student to take on as an apprentice were famous, the stuff of legends. They were a predictable part of the early fall. Henry liked his autumn crisp.

■ ■ ■

A painter for all his adult life, Preston Mattson nevertheless wore to work neatly pressed slacks and a jacket and tie. He saw no reason for artists to be sloppy or present a poor appearance, even when they were working. When the new acrylic paints first became easily available to artists in the 1960s, he was quick to try them, finding the ease of cleaning up after working with them one of their chief attractions. He spent one of his happiest afternoons that year in the chemistry lab, breaking down the paint into its components. To his fellow students he expatiated on the acrylics' vivid colors, range of hues, and ease of application. In truth, after the ease of cleaning his brushes, he noticed and appreciated most the lightness of the paint on the brush, giving his hand the feeling of a long mushy pencil rather than pigment-laden brush. It was the closest he got to experiencing the sensuous side of making a painting.

In dress and environment, he was equally meticulous, finding orderly surroundings conducive to thought and planning. For many years while he was single, he found it easy to maintain complete control over his physical surroundings, unbothered by the amount of time it required. Since marrying Ellen, however, he'd had to expend more time on organization but had also found he had more time to do so. It was the expansion of his time and world that filled his imagination, and so he was even willing to let Ellen's problems intrude on his life. On this morning, for instance, he had, in fact, spent the first hour in his office just thinking about his wife's attitude. Ellen could be a trial sometimes, no matter how much he steered her in the right direction. She resisted so many of his efforts that he occasionally despaired of ever making her into what she should be. Last year he had tried instructing her in drawing and still winced as he recalled the disjointed figures she produced under his tutelage. They agreed then that husband should not teach wife, but the problem nagged at him.

Still turning over different possibilities in his mind, Preston stopped at the doorway to the main studio. Across the room Hank Vinnio was working at an easel on a charcoal drawing. Preston could feel an unusual bristling sensation in his stomach, a sign of how intensely he disliked Hank, but this was almost immediately blocked. Arriving out of nowhere almost the day before classes started, Hank had casually revealed a talent no one could ignore, and been taken up by two other teachers and admitted to the college. It's not what Preston would have done. He would never have admitted someone who showed so little awareness of (or interest in) the protocol of the school, who was so obviously not ready to join a community of artists, as Preston repeatedly put it to himself. But the man was here, and he seemed to dislike Preston as much as Preston disliked him, a situation the professor found almost intolerable. So unpleasant was this reality that Preston constructed various scenarios in which he overcame Vinnio's aversions to him by astute guidance and mentoring. Since Preston had almost no tolerance for an atmosphere of hostility, these imagined scenes had a persuasive power, altering his view of Vinnio, who became an inept beginner in need of nurturing instruction rather than an arrogant natural talent who felt free to say whatever came into his head.

The painting teacher grew more and more tolerant over time as he began to see Hank fitting into the college as Preston saw it, the small community that had been home to him for twenty years. He even began to see Hank as one of his own students, learning from him, thanking him for his guidance, complimenting him on his brilliant work. Now, on first seeing Hank in the studio, Preston felt a certain compassion for him. The image held as long as Preston didn't look into Hank's eyes. Smiling to himself, Preston strolled into the studio where students were waiting for the next class to begin. He busied himself among the canvases at the back of the room, having convinced himself that Vinnio would welcome his approach. Vinnio remained silently at work.

"I think that's coming along very nicely," Preston said after walking over to watch. The outline of a graceful figure emerged on the drawing paper. It would have been obvious to anyone that Hank Vinnio had talent, untrained perhaps, but talent nonetheless. The artist didn't reply but kept on working.

"It's good to have new talent here," Preston continued, "to broaden the experience of the more established students." Hank worked quietly still, not even turning around to acknowledge the compliment.

"I understand you're working with Larry Segal." Preston clasped his hands behind his back and rocked on his heels. "Good man, Larry. Very challenging for his students." Preston recalled a heated conversation with the drawing teacher during which the younger man had insisted he had the right to turn away untalented students. As head of the department, Preston had carried the debate, but Segal had not been a gracious loser.

"My wife finds Segal's course very challenging," Preston continued. "And your role as model certainly plays a part." He was pleased with how he had slipped in the compliment and repeated it to himself several times while staring up at the ceiling. When he looked down again at the easel, Hank was looking at him full in the face. Well, thought Preston, the man is not immune to flattery after all. How interesting, he mused. Satisfied, he wandered among the other students working nearby.

The Wednesday morning drawing class was a small group of advanced students who assigned themselves, with the approval of the instructor, specific problems. Preston could hear Larry Segal in the hallway scheduling private meetings with one group, then listening to the plans of another student. In another moment he would enter and draw the students together to discuss the work they had done on their own over the previous week. As the studio filled with students, Preston moved to the door. At the other end of the room, several young men and women were gathering to discuss their progress so far. They moved over to Hank's side of the room as Preston moved away, and drew the other student into their conversation.

"This one took longer than I thought it would," one student began.

"It's weak here. You sort of lose control along the edges," another commented. The critique continued with diverse opinions and suggestions, ranging from specific artists for the students to view as examples to a new brand of charcoal.

"I started this one three times before I finally began to feel some shape to it, something I intended," another student began.

Preston lingered at the back of the room, intrigued at the commitment of this group of students, many of whom he had had in his painting class. He hadn't been favorably impressed with any of them, but allowed as how oil might not have been their best medium. They certainly seemed willing to work now, so perhaps they had learned something from his class after all.

"I wouldn't mind more time for this if you could manage it," another student said, addressing Vinnio. Though ostensibly only serving as the model for the group, Hank had taken on the role of instructor as well, directing this group of students when he stepped down from the dais during his break, and they were eager now to ensure his comfort and convenience in their plans.

"What's good for you?" another asked.

"Today and tomorrow are bummers," Hank replied.

"You don't want to take Saturday, do you?"

"Not really, but I will. Afternoon is okay," Hank said with a slanting smile. "Besides, I can use the extra money." Preston was again reminded of how unattractive he had originally found the man. His face never relaxed in a natural way, as far as Preston could see. There always seemed to be another reason for the grin than the conversation he could hear.

"Do we have to get permission?" another asked.

"Will someone be here to let us in?"

"Don't worry about that," Hank broke in. "I have a key. I work here, remember?"

Several students replied in enthusiastic chorus.

"After lunch for a couple of hours?" another asked.

"Yeah, sure, okay. A couple of hours after lunch," Hank repeated.

Against his will, Preston was impressed with how much the students liked working with Hank. They were willing to come in on a Saturday and Hank was willing to come in and help them, although he did get paid for it. Preston tried to dismiss it as the typical enthusiasm in college students but found it difficult to override the resentment he felt for Vinnio. Then he thought of Ellen, and how much work it had taken her to learn as little as she had. Her drawings of Vinnio, done in an introductory drawing class, were particularly paltry—in spirit, in size, in skill. She never spoke about her work as the other students did, never even seemed to have the same enthusiasm, the same drive to get it right. Even as he thought this of her, he felt an uneasy stirring within him, a feeling more and more common in the last few weeks that he couldn't slough off. He turned around to look at the drawings tacked to the wall and came to a decision. This might be just the opportunity she needs, he thought. She needed a peer guide, and one was available right now. She could come in and work with the others.

Even as he grasped this idea, the impediments to its realization became evident. Most immediate was Ellen's unpredictable reaction to his suggestions. Still not certain after three years of marriage what was typical behavior for his wife—or any wife, for that matter—Preston found Ellen's behavior sometimes daunting, her self-absorption and stubbornness sometimes baffling, and her withdrawal in the midst of a domestic crisis always mystifying. Only in the area of her training in art did she seem willing to defer to his views, but lately she showed signs of resistance even there. It was perhaps best, therefore, that he exercise his influence in this instance as discreetly and as subtly as possible.

Preston considered his first step. He would see that Ellen worked here on Saturday, but he would let her discover for herself the greater opportunity that awaited her. He had other plans for that afternoon, so Ellen would have uninterrupted hours to improve her drawing. And the other students should be glad to add to their number, he decided, leaving the studio at last, to the relief of the drawing class.

■ ■ ■

Like an elephant slumbering in a gully on a moonless night, the old gray furnace waited for a change in temperature to signal the time for its awakening. Shiny despite its several months of rest, the gray steel furnace filled the small room in the college basement. Buddy Lecroix stood by the light switch while the dean, Evan Goldman, admired the condition of the furnace room. Usually silent and respectful, today Buddy was perplexed and uneasy as he followed the college dean from room to room. Evan had been heard to say more than once that Buddy came with the new building when the college first moved in thirty years ago, and a lucky thing it was too. A crinkle along the lower half of Buddy's face was suspected to be a smile when he first heard Evan's comment. There was no sign of crinkling this morning.

"Thanks, Buddy." Evan walked past him and into the hallway. In his early fifties, Dr. Evan Goldman was the only recognized scholar on the faculty, having published a biography of the painter John Sloan and several monographs on the other members of the Ash Can School. Known affectionately as Doc, he entered his classroom with his mind already enraptured by the topic of the day. With the slides handed to the projectionist, he began lecturing—though a more apt word might be *discovering*—until the bells clanged throughout the school. He talked without notes, without text, without a light in the room, about the art on the screen, sharing whatever rose from his heart and emerged from his vast library of stored knowledge. After the first week students understood that he would cover the period designated in the title of the course at his own pace and that the textbook could serve as no more than a guide. Evan Goldman expected his students to be resourceful. Despite his reputation as the toughest teacher on campus wherever he taught, his classes were filled every term. His students adored him.

Evan liked Buddy, recognizing in the janitor a man of dedication and decency. That was what made his visit to this part of the basement and Buddy's domain all the more distressing. So far the rooms were just as he had expected them to be—neat, orderly, spare, and locked. Evan wished he were anywhere but there. He stopped in front of a steel door and waited while Buddy unlocked it, then stepped into the storeroom. He glanced around the shelves, calculating in his head the stores in each category. His years in army ordnance had left him with a rare ability to estimate large quantities with accuracy. In seconds he was satisfied that Buddy had everything in storage he was supposed to have. Evan was deeply relieved.

"Thanks, Buddy," Evan said, turning to him and smiling. "I appreciate your giving me so much of your morning on such short notice." Buddy followed Evan out into the hall.

"You missed one room," Buddy said. "Right here." Buddy motioned to a long narrow closet with a window at one end. "My office, I guess you'd call it."

"I don't have to see that," Evan said. Buddy stood where he was in the hallway, and after another second Evan stepped into the room. Buddy followed him and closed the door.

"What're you looking for, Doc?" Buddy stood inside the door, his arms hanging at his sides. Evan leaned back onto a stool.

"Nothing." Evan scratched his head. It was a tic he had and he knew it. Scratching his head allowed him to hide his shame when he or the world had failed to be all he had expected. In this instance he was ashamed of himself and what he had just done, for it suggested complicity on Evan's part, and there was none, of that he was sure. In the brief reprieve he gave himself, he decided to tell Buddy the truth. "One of the students said he couldn't get any paper towels and other supplies because the storeroom was either locked or empty. At least that's what he was told. He was also told not to complain, just to keep quiet about it. Amazing, just amazing."

The dean told Buddy only what the janitor had already surmised; Buddy could even guess the name of the complaining student, but the rest of it, the added suspicion and ill will, were a shock. "Who told him that?" Buddy leaned forward as he spoke. "Who told him not to complain?"

"He was a little vague because he didn't want to get anyone into trouble." Evan started to look away, then turned to face Buddy. "I'm sorry but I had to check. The boy's complaint made it imperative. I didn't want the student to go off thinking his suspicions were justified. There was a sense that some of us

SUSAN OLEKSIW

weren't"—he paused to search for the right word—"weren't working for the school's best interests. Myself included."

Buddy's face twitched, his jowls hanging a bit lower, his hands stretching down to his knees. A cold fear seeped into his back, like the damp of a dark November day. He tried to push the feeling away and reason himself back to safety, but his thoughts betrayed him. He kept hearing the accusation against both himself and the dean. If Dean Goldman, a man who might teach an extra course if enough students requested it, could be accused of questionable behavior, what might students say about Buddy? He thought about the school he loved, and the charge didn't seem possible. He worked long hours; he treated the boys and girls right, digging their cars out of the snow in winter, giving them change for the telephone or the vending machine when they were desperate, helping them find a cheaper room to live in. But all of it added up to nothing if one student could poison his life and his reputation. All he had—and he knew it—was what the dean and the president thought of him. He had given them his best, but how was he to show that? Why was it so easy to destroy a name, yet so hard to build it up?

"Students aren't what they used to be," Evan said, unaware of the turmoil in Buddy tumbling behind his sad but placid exterior. "They work on everything but their courses."

"Who was it?" Buddy asked the question without moving, as though he hadn't heard the dean's comment.

"Who? Well, I'm not really sure who was behind it, but I have an idea. Don't you worry about it, Buddy. I'll talk to him," Evan said. "And I am sorry. I don't know what we'd do without you, Buddy. I hope you'll forgive me for having to do that inspection."

"One of the part-timers? One of those work-study guys?" Buddy kept his eyes on Evan, trying to catch any flicker of recognition, unwilling to let the dean move on. Evan said nothing. Buddy's jowls shook as he nodded his head slowly.

He knew now that he must have been deceiving himself into trusting the older students. He was still the same foolish man he'd been when he first started there, but this time he would learn from it. His fists sank deep into his pockets, keeping his shoulders from sagging any lower. Evan put his hand on Buddy's arm.

"I'll take care of it, Buddy. It won't happen again."

No, thought Buddy, it won't.

■ ■ ■

"Good luck." The proprietor of the student bookstore closed the door behind her, leaving Kathy Fazio alone. Originally intended as a place to make student and faculty work available for sale to the college community and others throughout the year, the room had gradually assumed the guise of a storeroom of hopes abandoned. Wide steel shelves ran along one side, and on the other was a sturdy railing below a bulletin board for the display of prints, paintings, or other artwork stored on the shelves or in the bins along the back wall.

It was Kathy's job to locate and assemble in one place the various drawings and paintings of Professor Mattson for the spring exhibit. Looking around at the rarely disturbed room, Kathy instinctively gathered up her white nylon slip, which fell to her knees over black leggings. The slip was topped by an oversized shirt in an orange print, but not even these ludicrous shades could diminish the beauty of her white velvet skin and coal-black hair. Only the slim ivory bone passing through the base of her nose could do that.

Kathy turned to the first bin, which held unmounted charcoal drawings, and carefully passed over each one, drawing out two that bore Mattson's signature in the bottom right corner. This early success excited her and she tacked the sheets to the wall above the railing. She began to hum, imagining drawings and paintings mounted in splendor in the gallery on a warm spring evening, guests holding champagne glasses (for all her modern attire, she had the same fantasies as her mother had had), she and her friends discoursing at length about foreground, background, chiaroscuro (a word she loved), technique, tools, even kinds of paper. All of a sudden Kathy was jolted to find herself at the end of a stack of artwork. She had been so engaged in her dreams that she had no idea what she had just examined. Dutifully, she went back to the beginning, and this time tried to pay attention to each work.

The drawings flapped in the light breeze after Kathy opened the small window in the far wall. So close was the room after almost an hour that she wondered if the locale itself weren't a deterrent to the sale of the artwork kept therein. Cramped, close, and ill lighted, the room smelled musty, like a burial vault or a dank cellar, and yet she knew it had been chosen because the climate inside could be controlled for the preservation of materials.

The drawings on the bulletin board overlapped, and a breeze flipped up the top ones to reveal the smaller ones underneath. The breeze gave them an animation, an energy and a fluidity that the individual pieces lacked intrinsically, and their flapping and crackling in the light cool air drew and held Kathy's eyes, though she was not yet certain what she was seeing. Her mind had that vacant feeling that comes when you try to remember something you know you have forgotten, almost ready to dismiss it as unimportant—but not quite. Kathy set aside the prickly feeling that she didn't quite recognize what she was looking at and turned to the shelves filled with canvases.

Eager yet timid, Kathy crawled into the first steel shelf, forgetting her initial worries about her white slip, and rummaged through the canvases. She found six, with dates on the back ranging from 1977 to 1989. These she arranged against the wall, setting them on the floor, and cleared a space for herself on the shelving. With her chin resting on her knees, her arms embracing her legs, Kathy surveyed the results of her mission.

After several minutes she checked the signatures on the abstract paintings to make sure she had the paintings standing properly, upside up and downside down. All was in order. She sat back down again, peering at each painting, cocking her head on one side, tipping back to the other. Then she checked the dates on the paintings, and then on the drawings, rearranging them until drawings on the wall and canvases on the floor were in chronological order.

The zest and raw energy that struggled to find expression in the earliest work seemed to disappear from the later work rather than emerge as a guiding strength. Kathy pondered this, unsure what it meant. Reluctantly, she saw in the later work a sameness to the pictures, a preference for fuliginous colors, the kind of smoky colors she wore in the winter when she was depressed; twisted lines broke rather than flowing into infinity. In the landscapes, there was an earthboundness that weighed down Kathy as she passed her eye from one part of the scene to another. She frowned and looked closer. Somehow, she hadn't expected them to be this way. But now she couldn't remember what she had expected. She shifted in her place on the shelving, took a deep breath, but nothing helped. She couldn't get it. The paintings eluded her. A modest girl, she decided that her judgment was unsound and she would simply have to remain alert to the wiser evaluations of other students. Comforted with this solution, Kathy rose to the task of transporting the canvases to the storeroom behind the gallery.

■ ■ ■

"Add it up again, Marilyn," the pimply-faced young man said. "I'm sure we must have done better than that." Doug pushed away the Harbor Light menu and leaned toward Marilyn, sitting opposite him in the booth.

Marilyn's long brown hair brushed against the Formica-topped table as she bent her head over the list of figures. She tapped the numbers into a pocket calculator, waited, then repeated the figure. "Sorry, Doug, that's what it is."

"It can't be." He took the calculator from her and replayed the exercise of adding up a short list of figures. When the total appeared, he shook the small machine as though to jog the numerals on to greater heights. Disgusted, he shoved the calculator back across the table. "You really aren't very good at sales, are you?" He shifted in his seat to conceal the tone of annoyance he knew must be creeping into his voice, but his companion must have been used to him for she simply ignored him. All around them people were eating lunch in the Harbor Light restaurant while the two students thrashed over their morning's work. No one minded except Steve Badger, whose ready intelligence had already calculated the fraction of tuna fish sandwiches not eaten and the loss thereby sustained by him. When Doug passed him on the way to the men's room, Badger estimated the cost of the water and sewer charges for one flush and added that to his loss. It was at moments like this that he longed for that old rolling towel in the rest rooms, the only thing he never had to replace during its lifetime. Clara might complain, but it sure beat buying paper towels every month. When Doug passed Badger on his way back to his seat, Badger glanced over his shoulder to make sure the student had turned off the light; he hadn't. Growling softly, the restaurateur vowed if students took to doing their homework in his booths, he'd reinstall the rolling towel no matter what the milk and food inspector said.

In an end booth, Marilyn frowned and studied the sheet of paper. A practical young woman with a flair for photography and drawing, she had come to the college in Mellingham after two years at a university in Boston. She had made this decision, reversing the usual pattern of New England migration, when she had found urban life less stimulating than intimidating. The atmosphere at the small school appealed to her and she at once found a place as one of the few students with a practical mind and skills to match. For the first time, however, she was encountering resistance to what her calculations told her, and it stalled her. Again she went down the list of names on the left and the two columns of figures on the right. The figures in the second column were much lower than those in the first. Some were zeros. On the second sheet, the second column was blank.

"So how's it going?" The salutation came from a young woman with a cheerful round face and frizzy blond hair spread out around her head like a shredded halo; she sat down beside Marilyn and grinned. A young man followed.

"Okay, Noel," Marilyn said. "How about you?"

"Awful," she said with relish. "The economy's playing havoc with everything." She slapped a large manila envelope onto the table and looked around at the lunch crowd.

"Did you have any luck?" Marilyn asked.

"Practically none," Noel said. "No one thinks they can afford anything right now. We must have hit twenty stores just this morning, and five in Mellingham alone when we first started out. Only two out of all of them were interested. Just interested." She clucked in disgust at the parsimonious habits of the local merchants. "Steven is disgusted." Steven nodded to confirm this, then turned his attention to the waitress, who was studiously avoiding him. Badger was keenly attuned to this interaction, savoring it for the opportunity it afforded him for firing Clara, one of his favorite duties as a restaurateur.

"So's Doug," Marilyn said. "But he thinks it's all my fault. It's killing him trying not to say so." She chuckled. Doug offered a tight smile to prove he had a sense of humor.

"Don't worry. We'll get the hang of it," Noel said. She looked from table to table to see what other people were eating.

"I hate to tell you this, Noel, but this may have been our best day," Marilyn said.

"What? Come on, Marilyn; it's not that bad. We're just having a bad day; besides, we're just getting started on this. We'll get the hang of it."

"Maybe. At least, I hope you're right," her friend said. "This isn't going at all as we'd planned."

"Stop worrying. Let's get something to eat." Noel smiled, knelt on the banquette, and waved her arms, which not even Clara could ignore.

■ ■ ■

"That's a very good idea, Betty," Preston said, nodding his head slowly as he looked off into the distance.

"Thank you, sir," Betty Lane said. "I wanted to tell you before you went off for lunch because there's just a chance I can get—"

"A very good idea," Preston repeated, interrupting her. He pursed his lips and nodded some more while Betty Lane stood silenced beside him. Professor Mattson had developed the habit of cutting off the ends of her sentences in order to hurry along the conversation, and each time it happened, Betty's neck sank lower into her shoulders until her large white lace-trimmed collar seemed to be pushed out straight from the downward pressure. In an effort to conceal her anger, she dusted off imaginary dirt from her hands and clasped them in front of her black skirt.

"I think I have just enough time to—"

"A very good idea." Preston cut her off again. Whatever she wanted to do before the afternoon advanced remained her secret. She had caught up with Preston at the end of his last class of the morning, presenting him with an idea she wanted to keep confidential until a suitable time. Standing beside him before he could disappear for what Betty knew would be a long lunch, she explained her idea, pausing when students passed too close to them, and continuing when Preston stopped to nod to his wife, who settled herself on a stool to wait for him. Now, having presented only half of her case, she waited, long accustomed to Professor Mattson's practice of drifting into meditations and ruminations.

"Definitely a good idea," Preston repeated. "And he certainly deserves it. Definitely a good idea." Betty relaxed slightly by raising her chin a fraction of an inch and leaning back on her heels, both motions imperceptible to the casual observer, but a sure sign of growing confidence. She was past the first obstacle, at least.

"Long overdue, certainly," Preston continued.

Betty nodded as she released a tiny sigh of relief, having negotiated the shoals of Preston's more unpredictable reactions more deftly than she had expected. This could turn out to be an unusual semester.

"But is it enough?" Preston turned to her with that boyish look of wonder and innocence that had so often and so predictably misled his companion of the moment. The question caught Betty off guard. She had expected resistance, not encouragement, which is what it now sounded like.

"Enough? How do you mean?" she asked.

"Enough. Just that. Is it enough? We are capable of so much more and certainly we owe so much more. I think everyone would agree with that. After all, the dean—" He left the sentence hanging.

"I don't mean to suggest that this is the only thing we'd do." Betty's mind pushed against the dark fog that had suddenly enveloped her lucid plans.

"I should hope not." Preston looked down his nose at the sturdy middle-aged woman who for twenty years had guided the college past the barriers and reefs that awaited the small art school. "I should think we'd want to do much better than a mere congratulations during an exhibit for someone else." He turned to her with his most forgiving smile.

For the first time, indecision showed in Betty's eyes. "I didn't think—"

"Of course not," Preston consoled her, looking away again and missing the anger that flashed across her face, leaving only a set look of resolution. "I don't expect you to think of everything. That's why I go over these things with you. Certainly the dean deserves far more after ten years of service than merely being mentioned at someone else's show. Of course, he's far too gracious, too modest, to say anything, but to make the man take second place—well, it hardly seems right." He turned to her again with another sympathetic smile.

"I didn't mean—"

"Of course you didn't," Preston interrupted her again, still smiling. "And I'm glad you thought you could ask me. I'm flattered that we work so well together. And it was a good idea. It would be a pleasure to share the spotlight with our dean. But somehow, well, I just hope we have enough time to plan something more meaningful for him."

Betty didn't smile or nod as Preston looked down at her. She predated him at the college by only a few months, and in all that time she had never learned to like him or respect him. But they had learned to tolerate each other, and sometimes she even found she had anticipated him correctly. Those were her best moments, and she thought today would be one of them. Her disappointment was bitter.

"I'm sure you can think of something more worthwhile, Betty," he said, patting her arm. "And I'm sure the dean deserves much more, from all of us. You've worked for him for how long now? Nine years, is it?" Betty clenched her teeth as she nodded. "Well, we certainly owe him something more." To indicate that he considered the conversation closed, he turned to his wife.

"How was your class this morning?"

"Fine." Ellen held her arms across her chest, her glance wandering from one object to another, her attention barely keeping up. She dipped her head to one side, then the other. If she were younger, she might appear to have been pouting. Betty glanced from one to the other, aware she had lost more than Preston's attention. Still smarting, she left the studio, her back rigid.

"You seem to have gotten more of your charcoal on you than on your drawing." Preston looked her up and down as he snapped at her. "Tidy yourself up a bit, dear."

Ellen glanced at him, startled by his tone of voice.

"I have to get back to my office for a minute, dear. Then we'll have lunch." He strolled out of the studio, nodding to the few other remaining students. Behind him Ellen inspected her pale cream silk blouse. Her hands and blouse were covered with flecks of black dust. She looked around for a rag; seeing none, she sighed in exasperation.

"I know just how you feel, Mrs. Mattson," a voice said from the other side of the room. Ellen jerked her head around to see Hank Vinnio. Too surprised to speak, she stared at him with her mouth open.

"There you are, working hard on your various art projects—is that what you call them? Projects? You work hard and the guy doesn't even notice. Doesn't even help you put away your stuff." Hank shook his head. "That's real hard." He smiled. "But if that's as hard as it gets, hey, you're one of the lucky ones. Right? I mean, like, what do you have to be afraid of out here? Everywhere you go, you've got friends. Yeah. People who know you, like seeing you. You know, just like seeing you around. Nice job too—taking art courses from your husband. Yeah, you're one of the lucky ones. Living out here in the country. Real nice out here. I never been in a place like this before. I like it. A lot. Easy, you know what I mean? Nice people. Pretty place." Like a snake moving to the motion of the flute, Ellen leaned forward as Hank circled around in front of her, his smile sending forth each word while his hands rested at his hips. "Pretty, pretty, pretty." He spoke softly so that only Ellen could hear, but even so, two students who walked into the studio, chatting and laughing, were too absorbed to notice the conversation they were interrupting.

■ ■ ■

"I'd rather not say anything directly," Doug said to Steven. "You know how sensitive Marilyn is."

"Sure," Steven agreed as he finished his lunch. Doug reverted to his one current interest as soon as their companions, Marilyn and Noel, excused themselves briefly. He might have been surprised to realize how little Steven shared his interests, but he didn't bother to look at him, so absorbed was he in what he imagined to be his own injuries from working with Marilyn. He slipped into his monologue on the loss occasioned by their inept partners.

"She'll never be any good at sales," Doug concluded. "Hasn't got the knack. She's always agreeing with the guy she's supposed to be selling. We've wasted the whole morning following those two around." He tore off a piece of his sandwich.

Doug had few close friends at the college, preferring to spend any spare time hanging out near the faculty offices near the bookstore and downstairs in the hope of improving his talent by proximity to successful artists, or at least those who made such judgments. As a result he alienated the other students, who preferred to spend their free time dangling their feet from the reception desk or contemplating the vagaries of the soda machine. Steven preferred a classroom in the basement, with its windows opening onto a gravel courtyard. He once drew a still life there that so surprised him by its excellence that he wondered if it were the room, the chalk, the paper, time of day, or any of a multitude of other factors. Superstitious but ashamed of it, he nevertheless did his best to reproduce the setting of the moment of his best work, and found his drawings steadily improving despite it. Discouraging moments took him back to that drawing, and the memory eased his path again. Right now he was thinking of a painting that was going well, which was how he spent most of his time in Doug's company.

With the exception of the student committee to present Preston Mattson's spring show, Steven had never had anything to do with Doug. And, he had decided while waiting for the girls to come back and listening to Doug's recital of events, he would never have anything to do with him again as soon as they got the preparations for Mattson's show under control. For now he would put up with Doug, so he nodded regularly, his mouth full, making no effort to reason with a person whose mind he considered not worth saving.

"I don't want to push them off the program, but, personally, I think they're more trouble than they're worth." Doug was too deeply absorbed in his own grievances to wonder about Steven's unresponsiveness.

Steven studied Doug briefly before saying, "Noel thinks it's the economy. She seems to think no one wants to advertise in a catalog for a local exhibit when they're not getting much business from their regular advertising."

"And you agree with that, I suppose?"

"No."

"Well, I'm glad to hear that. I was beginning to wonder." Doug leaned back in his seat, stretching his arms and shoulders. The patron in the booth behind him dodged to the side, then leaned forward to miss the flying limbs.

Steven smiled, judging the effect of his next comment. "I don't think it has anything to do with the economy. I think it has to do with the people involved."

"That's what I've been saying." Doug almost wailed his reply but contained himself. "Why didn't you say you agree with me?"

"Because I don't agree with you." He put down his sandwich, the better to watch Doug's expression. "I don't think Marilyn and Noel have all that much to do with it."

"Right, Steve," Doug said sarcastically. "You're making no sense at all."

Steven lost the opportunity to explain, if he had wanted to, as the two young women in question reappeared beside the table, talking animatedly to each other. Doug lapsed into silence and Steven went on eating.

■ ■ ■

Like any place of business, the college grew silent during the lunch hour, when most students drove into town or went home for lunch, or camped out in a classroom with a sandwich. The few café tables and chairs arranged in a snack area near the vending machines were, by some unspoken rule among the students, used only in the late afternoon or evening. Today was no exception. Only Hank Vinnio sat off in a corner, his sandwich sitting on the paper bag in which he had brought it that morning, and his thermos standing nearby. Rocking on the back legs of his chair, he didn't speak to the two students who approached the soda machine, and they seemed not to know he was there. Jim and Wally had their eyes on the change in Wally's hand.

"I told you. It's fifty-five cents. You're gonna have to break a bill," Jim said. Short with curly brown hair and blue eyes, Jim was a shorter version of his friend. Both wore dark blue T-shirts, jeans, and white sneakers. But Jim was always in a hurry and Wally was always methodical no matter how much time it might take. "Besides, I want something to eat too."

"Why don't you ever bring your own money?" Wally asked while he dug through his pockets for more change.

"I do." Jim lowered his head and glared at his friend. "But you keep borrowing it. You owe me lunch."

"I don't think I have enough change." Wally shifted the coins from his left hand to his right and proceeded to search his remaining pockets. "Besides, I didn't borrow any money from you yesterday."

"You owe me for last week. Come on, man. I wanna eat."
Impatient, Jim rested his hands on his hips and bounced from
foot to foot. "Break a bill, will ya?"

"I only have a five." Wally pulled out a nickel and added
it to his modest pile.

"That's enough. You get the sandwiches. A dollar each."
Jim nudged his friend aside as he looked at the sandwich offerings through the glass door. "The ham and cheese looks okay."

"You have to have exact change." Wally nodded to the
blinking red light that signaled the machine was out of one-
dollar bills for change.

"Use the change machine. Come on," Jim urged him.
"I'm hungry. I have to get to work pretty soon too."

Wally looked sadly at the collection of coins in his palm,
said okay as he put them in his pocket, and pulled out a five-
dollar bill. After he slipped the bill in, the machine whined in
protest, the bill finally disappeared, the machine keened, and
exactly one dollar in change fell into the change slot. Wally
lifted the flap for paper dollars but nothing emerged.

"My money! I lost my money!"

"Oh, shit." Jim hit the machine.

"I lost my money! That was my lunch money for the
week until Sunday. A buck a day." Wally pounded the
machine.

"Where's Karen? Let's get Karen. She's got the key.
She'll get our money back." Jim ran off down the hall. Wally
stepped back and gaped at the machine, waving his fist at it.
"My money! I don't believe it. My money!" He went toward
the machine, then back, dancing the two-step of anguish and
loss until Jim came running back.

"She's gone to lunch," Jim said.

"Lunch! I lost my money."

"I know. I know. I know. Calm down. I'm hungry too.
It's okay." He glared at the ham-and-cheese grinning back at
him, looked around for a solution. "Hey, I know." Jim was

suddenly excited. "My old man doesn't go to lunch until late. We can catch him. We can. If we hurry we can do it. We'll get him to take us to lunch."

"Yeah?" Wally's eyes dilated at the thought of a real meal. "Wow. Good idea," Wally said as Jim ran off. "God, I hope the car starts."

The snack area was quiet again. After a few minutes, Hank, still rocking on the back chair legs, closed up his thermos. He threw the paper bag into the trash, looked at his watch, and lit a cigarette. At exactly one o'clock he put out his cigarette and walked down to the administrative offices, where Betty Lane was just leaving for lunch and Karen Meghan was just returning.

■ ■ ■

"I wonder how Kathy's doing?" Noel finally asked after the four young people had finished their lunch. The restaurant was no longer crowded, and Badger was sitting at the counter while the waitresses replenished the napkin holders and cleaned the booths. When all four students ordered desserts, Badger's narrowed eyes widened and he even looked like he might smile. Instead, he dutifully sat down to test the carrot cake, a concession to new patrons who regularly asked for it. Badger considered carrots in a sweet akin to oatmeal before a steak dinner.

"Kathy has the easy job," Doug said. "All she has to do is find the artwork in the store."

"I meant her promotion idea," Noel said, breaking into Doug's lament. "She came up with a list of local people interested in the arts, you know, people the school didn't have on the mailing list. She's going to invite them all."

"Now that's a good idea!" Doug said. "She's finally on the ball."

Marilyn and Noel glanced at each other. Steven sat with his hands folded on the table, his handsome face giving no sign of his feelings. "You know," Steven began, speaking as though the idea had just come to him, "we might ask Mike Rabkin. He might have an idea about whether it's the economy or something else."

"And he's always interested in what we're doing at the school," Noel said, picking up on the idea. "Yeah, that's a great idea." She turned to Marilyn and Doug for confirmation. Marilyn nodded.

"He could give us some pointers," Marilyn concluded. "Yeah, Steve, good idea." She smiled at him. "Well, that's settled, then. He can tell us what we're doing wrong." She stood up. "Okay, I've got to get back to school. I've got a class this afternoon."

"Me too," Noel said. "I'll give you a lift. You two okay here?" She looked from one to the other. "Can you give Steve a lift, Doug?"

"Sure," Doug said in his least surly tone. He watched the two girls leave before turning to his companion. "Most of us will probably have to do double duty to make up for them, no matter what Rabkin comes up with." He got up from the table as he spoke. Fortunately, he didn't look back to see the expression on Steven's face.

3
SATURDAY

A WARM SUNNY SATURDAY in the fall always means one thing to a golfer, and Ed Correll was a golfer, passionate yet analytical as he made his rounds. In light cotton slacks and a jersey, Ed began every winter with the tanned face and forearms of the avid player, the softer pink of his upper arms, like the underbelly of a fish, coming into view only on the hottest days of the year, when he reluctantly wore short-sleeved cotton shirts. Since first discovering the game at the age of fourteen, Ed always found time to golf on weekends, ignoring snow in December and icy winds in January as long as the course was open. In fifteen years he had never missed more than a single open weekend each year.

Ed's brown hair bunched against his visor as he estimated the angle of his next shot. At such moments he could ignore even a carload of teenagers rumbling across the tee, a quality his friends and colleagues envied. His single-mindedness drove away many who might be friends, so he usually played either with a large group of men from the bank, alone, or with Preston Mattson in a lonesome twosome. Ed stood out as one of the few who could tolerate Preston's manner of play, which was not only bad but also interspersed with his own inane commentary. He seemed incapable of focusing on his game. It usually took silence from Ed during the first four or five holes to quiet Preston, who thereafter interjected jovial commentary only before his own shots. So on this balmy Saturday, in the mid-afternoon, the two men decorously enjoyed the autumn warmth that had driven Ed's kids to ride laughing and squealing to the park.

"Good drive, Preston," Ed said automatically as he checked his golf bag. This was just one of many comments Ed would deliver during the game without any regard to their suitability; it was his sole contribution to the social aspect of the afternoon.

"Thanks. That airplane didn't help," Preston said, looking up at a thin blue sky. His ball never went where he wanted it to and it irritated him more than usual today. Preston waited while Ed took his shot. When his drive failed to satisfy him, falling several feet short of what he had hoped for, Ed clenched his teeth, his hands around the club in a spasm of anger and frustration, then turned back to the electric cart. He didn't hear Preston's hearty compliment and wouldn't have welcomed it if he had.

"How's Ellen these days?" Ed asked as they drove on. In his late twenties and an officer at a local bank, Ed had developed the knack of asking all the right questions without ever caring about the answer. His apparent disinterest often served to entice his golfing partners to unusual confidences and confessions, for which Ed rarely felt any sympathy.

"She's fine," Preston answered. "Over at the school taking a few extra classes. Bring her drawing up to par." Even as we speak, Preston added to himself, recollecting the train of events he had brought on track for that afternoon.

Ed nodded as he inspected his clubs. "Didn't realize Ellen wanted to be an artist." Ed pulled out one club, considered it, then shoved it back into his bag. This part of the course often frustrated him and he was determined to break his record here. He felt the weight of the club as he walked back to the ball. "Never knew she had artistic ambitions."

"I'm afraid she doesn't have ambitions. She's very hard to motivate."

"Ellen?" Ed looked up at the sun and tugged at his visor. "Really? I always thought she was too easy to motivate. She always did just what Joey told her to do."

"Is that so?" Preston said. "I expect it was youth. They were young, after all." For the most part Preston thought Ellen's previous marriage to Ed's brother, Joey Correll, an asset, since the other man had been well liked, but that good-will did not extend to Joey himself. It did not please Preston to learn that someone else had been able to influence Ellen.

"Yes, they were." Ed stopped. "Well, maybe not that young. Joey was already a success and he was a only little younger than I am now." Ed studied his club. "Then again, he never told her to do much. She mostly spent her time shopping, and once in a while she had an idea for one of his developments."

"No doubt the latent artistic ability I'm trying to nurture now," Preston said. Talking about Ellen's first husband made him uneasy. Joey Correll had been only a developer, or at least that's how Preston thought of him, and yet when others spoke of him the dead man sounded dashing, almost charismatic. Preston chalked it up to the romanticization of memory.

"I don't remember Joey ever saying anything about Ellen having artistic ability," Ed said, looking skeptical, "but he did say she had a good idea where the money was. Who was going to move where to buy a big house, that kind of thing." He swung and watched the ball arc into the sky. At such moments he almost felt himself reach beyond who he was, and he watched the ball with his heart, soaring on and on, but then the ball fell to earth, once again small and hard and weighted. He was mortal again. The ball landed only a few feet from the cup but Ed was oddly saddened. In a rare moment of empathy, Preston thought his friend must be missing his older brother. Unaware of Preston's change in feeling at that moment, Ed went on speaking, as though no other thought had intervened in his mind or Preston's.

"Actually, Joey said he made one of his best deals based on one of her hunches. Well, a guess, actually."

"I don't recall her telling me she was involved in Joey's work." Preston was feeling unreasonably irritated by the direction of the conversation. The goodwill he had felt dried up like a puddle at midday; it rankled to think that Ed knew his wife better than he did.

"She wasn't involved," Ed said, moving to the side. "That was exactly what Joey always wanted, for her to be involved, but he said she just wasn't interested."

Preston prepared to follow Ed, now feeling larger as he approached his ball, for he had gained on Joey. "I'm concerned about precisely the same thing, her inner drive. She seems to lack goals." Ed looked over at Preston for only the second time that afternoon. "But I think I've overcome that problem. She has been following my instructions on her artistic career to the letter. Right this minute, in fact, she is working on her drawing at the college. I think we'll find she has ambition in her." He swung at the ball, the thickness of his torso hampering his movements.

The ball flew up, then arced to the left, landing in the low-lying shrubbery beneath some trees. It was well into the rough, almost out of bounds. Preston blinked in surprise at the complication. This sort of thing was always happening to him. "It's all that traffic. Every time they repair the roads around here, it gets worse." Grumbling, he walked into the shade, poking around in the undergrowth, then stooped. The ball flew onto the fairway where Ed was just passing with the cart. Preston kicked the ball up to where he thought it should be, not far behind Ed's ball.

Ed didn't notice; most of his mind was on the two strokes he had shaved off last Sunday's score. Preston's comments about Ellen barely interested him. He had inquired after her as a courtesy and then just followed along as Preston inflated the conversation, but now he was getting tired of it. He thought Ellen a passable sort, but he wasn't really interested in her. She only mattered because she had been married to Joey. His older brother had all the signs of major success coming his way when he first met Ellen, Ed recalled, and he had gone on to succeed after they were married, but somehow the direction had changed. Instead of the interesting cluster communities and special environments Joey had been interested in, he went to work for architects designing exclusive and expensive private homes. He was making more money, but it wasn't what Ed had expected of a brother so imaginative and creative.

Watching Joey take an ordinary job in construction and make it interesting and personally rewarding had made Ed feel that he too could transcend the mediocrity he knew defined him. It made him believe he could be more than what he was, ordinary, average, mundane. He longed for that moment of discovery, of sudden awareness of something greater in him, convinced that it would come, that it was within breathing distance. And then Joey had died, in a stupid, cruel car accident, and everything he was and everything he seemed to promise Ed he could be died with him. It was Ed's death as much as Joey's. Then Ellen had married Preston Mattson, almost ten years older and never married. Ed could not stop wondering what Ellen had seen in Preston, a man as unlike Joey as any could be. And now Ed was expected to listen to Preston's whining.

Ed's lack of interest in Preston's concerns often characterized their Saturday games, but this time they left the older man frustrated. More interested in the reputation of playing with a banker than with the experience itself, Preston had learned to overlook Ed's usual manner of disengagement, but today it irritated him. Even worse, he played badly, much worse than usual, which Ed ignored. By the time they left the course, the art teacher had no idea what his real score was, what it should have been, or what he might reasonably make it so that he could reply to the casual inquiries about his game.

The several searches through the rough along the fairway for his lost ball left scratches on his arms and ankles and grass stains on his slacks; the sand traps left sand in his shoes. By the end of the game, Preston was also tired and out of sorts.

On their way toward the clubhouse Preston tried one topic then another to restore his emotional stasis, but nothing worked. He was just settling for a day of crankiness when he spotted Gregory Stewart standing in a tight group of club officers. The Scotsman had what looked like plans rolled up under his arm. Preston turned away from the group and another member hailed him robustly and asked his score. Mumbling his reply, Preston filled out the charge slip with celerity. When he was pressed to stay and learn about the plans for the clubhouse grounds, he was glad he could claim another engagement. The plans would be approved, Preston was certain; the men on the committee seemed to think every idea Stewart had was brilliant, so there was little reason for him to look them over and offer advice. He slipped out while the others gathered around as Stewart spread out the sheets. It was just 3:35.

■ ■ ■

Perched on a granite foundation that was the pride of quarriers and builders for half a century, the three-storied Victorian clapboard house rose like a tower over the cluster of one-storied stucco buildings that was downtown Mellingham. Settled on the first floor, the Whimsy Gallery fronted on Lee Street, its large bow windows bathed in north light. In addition to its role as a gallery for local artists, the Whimsy sold art supplies, art books, and framing services, along with the remnants of its original incarnation as a stationery store.

The Whimsy was unique in Mellingham but a replica of a type of meeting place found by art students around the country; it was one of those places that year after year attracted students from the local art school, not because of its location, services, or goods (which were exceptional), but because of the personality of the owner, in this instance, Mike Rabkin. The pleasantly worn-down feel of the old house extended after more than twenty years to the owner. Mike's tall, stocky frame had fluid lines much like the old painted woodwork; his sneakers squeaked on the hardwood floors, which shone like his cheeks in winter. Over the years his thin wavy hair had taken on the color of the soft pine flooring. The house settled and his knees creaked. He was generous and easygoing, and counted the annual crop of new art students one of the assets of his life. He enjoyed seeing their work and listening to them plan their careers. When four painting students came to him with a problem they couldn't solve, Mike Rabkin was glad to listen, even on a Saturday afternoon.

"What do you think, Mike?" Noel asked, turning to face him directly. "Have we gone about it all wrong?" On her lap sat the remains of her lunch. She chewed on a carrot stick while she waited for a reply.

"It sounds like you've been pretty thorough," Mike said as he pulled a mat knife with a steady hand. The students watched him in silence until he reached the end of the cut and straightened up. He turned the piece of blue mat board.

"Thorough?" Marilyn repeated. "Maybe. But not successful. We're not getting anywhere." Stirring her coffee in a paper cup, she seemed more resigned than worried. In fact, the failure of their mission was more intriguing than distressing to Marilyn, prompting long silence and much frowning but no fretting as she tried to find a meaning for this unexpected turn of events. This limited degree of disengagement allowed her to let other interests claim her attention, so while the others thought only of Rabkin's reply, Marilyn was glancing through the stack of prints waiting to be framed. She was equally curious about the equipment on the broad table that almost filled the back room where Rabkin worked, and especially about the elbows of frame samples hung on the wall and stacked on another worktable. "We must be doing something wrong," Marilyn said after a silence.

"Of course you're doing something wrong," Doug said.

"Aw, come on, Doug," Steven broke in. "That's not fair. Don't push so hard. We're all using the same approach and it's just not working."

Doug glared back at Steven, who said, "And we all have to figure out a solution if we're going to have a catalog for Mattson's exhibit. We have to work together on this." The tone of warning directed to Doug in the last sentence was not lost on the two girls.

"How far have you gotten?" Rabkin asked as though there were no discord among them. He drew his knife carefully along another line drawn lightly in pencil.

"Not far at all," Noel said. "We have four small ads, a few maybes, and some donations—small ones—but we counted on having ten times that by now." She watched Rabkin. "It doesn't add up. No one seems interested in buying anything and we really were counting on them to make up the cost of the catalog."

The students' comments punctuated the long pauses given over to watching the knife cut through the mat board. Rabkin often applied the overlooked truth that a man or woman working devotedly at a craft can capture and hold the attention of the most disputatious, and so the gallery owner worked and questioned as Doug grew calm and Noel less intense.

"Spent any money yet?" Rabkin asked.

"No, but we already talked to people," Doug said. "We have most of the text ready to go. We want to get moving on this." Steven looked at Doug in surprise.

"What?" Both Noel and Marilyn were caught off guard by Doug's news.

"Estimates?" Rabkin asked. He positioned the board again.

"We know what it'll cost," Doug said.

"How much is that?" the two young women asked together. It was obvious that only Doug knew how much it would cost.

"I didn't know you'd gone that far," Steven said. "Who wrote the text? And the estimates? Who got those? I thought we were sort of working on the assumption that the kind of catalog we got depended on how much money we raised."

"Yeah. What about the rest of us?" Noel said. "Don't we have any say in this?"

"Sure, sure." Doug tried to dismiss them, then smiled to defuse the tension when Noel glared at him.

"We have to look at how much money we do have," Steven said. "We could still have just a two-page deal with the ads on one side and some text about Mattson on the other with a list of the works in the show."

"That's not a real catalog," Doug said. "Don't worry. I know what a real job will cost."

"How much?" Marilyn asked. "And what's a real job anyway?" Steven put his hands in his pockets and leaned back against the wall.

"Listen, the whole thing is under control," Doug said. He crossed his arms and stood against the counter. "More to the point is why no one has sold enough ads."

"Aw, come on—" The two women spoke at once.

"Fair question," Rabkin said, positioning his knife on another penciled line. All four young people looked at him in surprise. "Why is it no one wants to buy ads in a catalog for an exhibit of an artist they know well?" Rabkin drew his knife carefully down the line, and this time the students listened, not because they were mesmerized by the steady hand, but because as soon as he finished, he would answer his own question, they hoped.

"There must be a reason," Rabkin said, looking up at them. Four pairs of eyes moved from his hand to his face.

"We thought it might be the economy," Noel said, nodding at Marilyn to include her in the statement. Steven joined them in a friendly debate on whether or not the students were trying to raise money at the wrong time. Doug listened, though he was leaning away from the others, apparently uninterested. When the three felt they had exhausted every aspect of the idea at hand, Steven turned abruptly to Rabkin and said, "What do you think?"

"I think you have to be realistic." The easy acceptance of their plight fell on their debate like a spotlight, casting all else into darkness and illuminating only the present. Mike continued, "If you don't have enough money for a catalog, then you don't have a catalog."

"But we should," Doug said, speaking again with the intensity of their initial discussion.

"Well, we don't," Steven said. "And that's that." Both Marilyn and Noel murmured agreement, then reached for their knapsacks.

"You have to go with what you've got," said Rabkin as he cut the fourth and last line on the mat.

"That's another problem," Steven said, but no one heard him this time.

■ ■ ■

At a few minutes after three o'clock, Chickie Morelli put fifty-five cents into a vending machine and listened for the rough descent of his can of soda. He turned back to the long dark warehouse and walked the width of the building, peering down each aisle into darkness. The high wooden shelves of scaffolding were packed in some spots with gray and white ribbed containers.

When he first came to work at the warehouse at the end of the summer, Chickie thought the containers were pathetic, a sign of a meaningless life reduced to a box as a symbol of its vacuity. He almost sneered at people whose lives could be reduced to two or three boxes. Then he realized that his possessions wouldn't fill even one container, not even the smallest. That shook him, and thereafter he was ambivalent about the part-time job though it paid him well and gave him lots of free time. He thought at the outset he would feel rooted, substantial, and instead he felt minute, as though he were shrinking, a cast-off man in a warehouse packed with cast-off things.

In another part of the old factory a door slammed. A forklift started up. The weekends of silence had left him with a good ear for distant sounds, for few people came close enough to occupy him. He sipped his drink as he walked back and forth. In almost five weeks he had never been called on to lift a container for an owner, and sometimes he wondered if anyone came to this storeroom even during the week, when he was assigned to another area.

He looked at his watch; less than two hours to go, but those were long hours. Refusing to be bored, he had already swept the main aisles, checked the seals on all the ground-level containers, and cleaned the forklift. He pulled out a paperback novel and read a few pages, but he couldn't get into it. Unlike other students who had part-time jobs, Chickie never got used to writing papers or reading textbooks at work. The warehouse was to him a place apart from college, from the rest of his life, so he could never bring himself to study in the dead hours of work.

But he did draw. For Chickie, drawing was like breathing. His lungs filled with air and his fingers sought a crayon. He kept ends and bits in his pants' pockets so he would never be without. He finished his soda and left it in a paper bag for recycling, and pulled out a small pad of paper and a charcoal pencil. Perched on an old wooden crate near the entry, Chickie began drawing a section of the rough plank flooring, laboring over the cuts and grooves and knotholes. This is what he did wherever he went, and all places were the same to him when he was drawing. His soul was in his fingers.

■ ■ ■

Ellen listened to the large door wheeze shut behind her, the soft gasp filling the hall of the empty building. She stood and listened. Nothing is as empty as a school building on a weekend, for the spirit of teachers and students doesn't linger. An old house emits the feel of its owners, giving off a warmth or coldness according to the life lived therein. But a school absorbs nothing and radiates nothing; it is curiously neuter.

Ellen was glad to be alone. Persuaded by Preston to work on Saturday, she had agreed to spend the better part of the afternoon in the studio, but his insistence that she get to it soon after lunch discomfited her and so she stalled until after three o'clock. Now she was glad she had done so. The painting studio, lit only by the late afternoon sun, was dotted with empty paper cups, a remnant Ellen recognized. She decided to leave them for Buddy to find in the morning. She knew how he would react; she had seen him once when he discovered trash left from a student gathering on a Sunday afternoon. Angry at the mess and worried that the students had managed to get into the building at all, Buddy had cleared up the mess but kept it to himself. Timid, Ellen had concluded, feeling only contempt for anyone who might have a weakness she refused to recognize in herself.

Ellen's disdain for the slovenly habits of the students eased her thoughts past the awkward confrontation she had managed by luck to avoid earlier in the afternoon. Relieved, she crossed the room. Her reluctance to work with the younger students did not signal a gnawing doubt about her ability, quite the contrary. Despite Preston's assumption that he was shaping his wife and remolding her apparent disparagement of her own abilities, Ellen harbored the secret conviction of the mediocre; she alone could see the talent that rested in her eye and hand, but someday others of greater vision than those around her now would see and acknowledge her blossoming genius. She especially liked the phrase "blossoming genius." Until that time came, however, she saw no need to situate herself among the lesser talented, who had a tendency to talk critically of their own and others' work. She did not find this behavior motivating or edifying.

Going to her regular spot at the back of the studio, Ellen opened her drawing tablet and set it up on an easel. Uninspired but obedient, she began to work on her drawing. Whatever was awkward in it dissolved under her eye, if not her hand, and the graceful way she held the crayon. Uncertain how to change or improve the forms before her, she scratched and smudged here and there, subscribing to the theory that doing something is better than doing nothing. She finished the drawing to her satisfaction and began another.

"If you'd come earlier, you coulda had some company." The sentence was dropped into the quiet like a pebble in a pond, the volume magnified by the silence it punctured. The amiable tone was undone by the rasp in the man's voice. Ellen was startled, and tilted her head around the easel to see Hank Vinnio leaning against the doorjamb. "Ellen Mattson, isn't it? Have I got the name right?" He smiled, pushed himself off from the steel frame, and walked over to another easel nearby.

Ellen nodded, her hand poised in midair. Arm unmoving, her back rigid, she waited for Hank to speak.

"I don't have to introduce myself, do I?"

"No." She set down her charcoal on the lip of the easel.

"Surprised to see me?"

"Yes. No."

"Well, you weren't the only one." He laughed. "Honey, you are the last person I ever expected to find in a place like this. A pretty place and a real, honest-to-God student."

The implied insult pricked her to respond. "Yes, Hank, I'm a real student." She tried to muster disdain for his question.

"Married the head guy, too, I hear." His voice softened and Ellen looked at him keenly.

"He's head of the painting department. So what?"

"So nothing." He walked around the easel and inspected her drawing. "I'm glad you're doing well." He smiled.

Ellen's eyelashes fluttered as she avoided meeting his gaze. Instead, she began to put her charcoal away, her movements careful and slow, each of an equal measure.

"You are doing well, aren't you?" He waited for her to reply. "You can tell me."

"Preston has a very good job, but he's only a teacher, after all." She arranged the crayons in her box. "But we like a quiet life. That's what we have, a quiet life." She slid in an eraser. "And we do know a lot of people around here. Preston's been here for some time, after all." The tone was not thoroughly conversational, nor was it the haughty tone Ellen more often used.

"Oh yeah? I wasn't thinking of him. I was thinking of you." He took a few steps around the room. "That's a nice car you drive. I bet you get some kicks from that." He moved closer as he spoke. "Chickie tells me that Preston isn't your first husband. It was nice of Chickie to tell me that, to fill me in on all the people here, especially you and Preston. Nice guy, Chickie." Ellen finished putting away her charcoals, snapped the box shut, and closed up her tablet. She had managed to avoid his eye, keeping her own intent gaze on her task.

"He told me about this guy Joey Whatsisname."

Ellen didn't answer the implied question. Standing rigid in front of her easel while Hank moved a few inches closer, she drew her body back, her shoulders stiffening, her chest shrinking in at each sound of his voice.

"I hear he was very good to you."

Still she said nothing.

"I hear he left you more than a sports car." He moved a step closer, and she could feel his breath brushing beneath her ear.

"I hear it's real nice not to have to worry about money."

The odor of stale sweat and the musty smell of lust seeped from his clothing and hung around her like a wet blanket.

"You don't have to worry, do you, Ellen?"

Still she didn't answer.

"Do you, Ellen?" His hot breath curled around her throat.

"No," she finally said in a whisper, her body aching in the vise she could feel but not see. Now was the time to run, she knew, but instead her eyes held fast to his feet, to his brown sneakers with brown laces. There was a smear of red paint on the right toe and a smear of green paint on the left toe. It made her think of Christmas, and that was crazy. She should be thinking about running, running out of the studio and down the hall. The doors were unlocked, she could get out, but she had to move to do that. And she couldn't take her eyes off his shoes.

"Is that fair, Ellen?" He spoke again in the soft voice, smooth like paper that cut. "I ask you, is it fair?"

Still she was silent.

"Ellen, is it fair?"

Before she could force herself to answer, he lunged at her, grabbing her by the shoulders and yelling his question at her again. She pushed him away and fell back against the storage shelves. Rims of paint cans cut into her back and head and the arm she threw out to keep herself from falling. Hank toppled back onto a stool, his right arm swinging out for support and knocking down an easel. She saw his shoulders rise as he moved to spring at her. Her hand felt the side of a cardboard box and she pulled at it as he came toward her again. The box of jars fell on him, and she saw his arms reach out to steady himself. She grabbed her tablet and box of charcoals. She heard the crash of cans and boxes as she ran from the studio, out the door, down the hall to the main door and the parking lot beyond.

■ ■ ■

The cash register buzzed and pinged, and the customer smiled on receiving her change. She gathered up her purchases and walked out onto the street. Mike Rabkin watched her go, then walked over to the bin holding a dozen large lithographs. Preston Mattson flipped through the last of the prints in the bin and then pushed the lot of them back against the wall.

"Interesting," he commented.

"Yes," Mike agreed.

Preston couldn't bring himself to say any more though he knew that at another time he would have airily thrown out words like *underdeveloped, prosaic, promising*, without even looking up to see if Mike Rabkin was listening. It was a friendship he had taken for granted for years, until this week, when Mike's seemingly idle comment about Preston's canvases had signaled a change, one that Preston had feared for some time but had been unwilling to face. He had avoided the gallery owner's hints until he could do so no longer. Mike Rabkin's summons to the gallery on Saturday afternoon could not be ignored. Even so, the painting teacher could not bring the issue out into the open; Mike would have to do it if it was to be done at all.

Preston moved to another bin holding several posters of various sizes and flipped through these. He wanted to seem as though he were making a quick and sophisticated assessment of what he was seeing, but his mind registered only the artistic tradition—impressionism, abstract expressionism, realism— and he felt incapable of finding that part of himself that should make an aesthetic judgment. He felt nothing rise from his gut to tell him that this one was good, that one was bad. He waited and felt the sweat bead along his upper lip. When had he forgotten to feel what he knew in his head?

His fingers manipulated each mat board in a rhythm of their own while his thoughts struggled over each abyss looming before him. The many phrases and insights he had practiced over the last few days and recited during the drive over this afternoon dissolved into awkward stops and starts.

Whatever he said sounded stupid, then embarrassing, so he had said nothing after a while.

Mike walked back to the counter and began sorting through sales slips. When Preston finished with the second bin, he moved to another, this one of charcoal drawings, again striving to know what comment might be appropriate, even adequate. Then his eye caught a signature at the bottom of a drawing. Hank Vinnio, Preston discovered, had three original drawings in the bin, and the prices on them were higher than anything Preston had ever considered charging for any of his works until he had been long out of school. The remaining drawings rippled toward him as his fingers moved automatically and nimbly over the corners; he flipped the pile back and stood away. On the shelves above the bins were rows of stationery, paper tablets, and other office and party supplies. The supply of cards and office goods was dwindling, and a discerning eye would have noticed they were not being replaced; instead the remaining stock was being consolidated in a smaller area, nearer the door.

"Nice, aren't they?" Mike said after Preston had finished looking through a bin of photographs.

Preston flipped back through a number of them and abandoned his search for the right expression. A few years ago, perhaps even a few months ago, he would have slipped into an easy rapport with Mike, asking sincere questions and learning from Mike's replies. But now he couldn't find a question in his head, and he didn't even seem to be in his own body, so strange did he feel. Frustrated and confused, he felt rise in him the hearty manner that had become a second skin.

Preston turned to the other man with a pleasant smile, saying, "Very nice, indeed. I feel very comfortable here, Mike, very comfortable." He patted the stack of photographs. "We're all impressed at the college with how you've built up the gallery. And it's a natural association for us." Thinking of Vinnio's drawings as he said this cut into his gut.

"Kind words, Preston. Thank you."

"Don't mention it." Preston raised his hand. "Don't mention it. A natural association. I couldn't think of anyone I'd rather have handle my work. That's exactly what I told the gallery in California."

Mike's eyebrows rose and his neck stiffened. "How do you mean?"

"I told them I wanted my work right here, right here. They're very accommodating people." Preston nodded vigorously.

"When's it arriving?" Growing accustomed to Preston's increasingly bizarre machinations, Mike knew what the other man's circuitous comments meant.

"A few days or so." Preston was still avoiding Mike's direct gaze. "Yes, I feel very good here." He slapped the stack of photographs again.

The hearty persona lived on without him, it seemed to Preston, and it too was determined not to raise any uncomfortable issues with Mike, or even to let him raise them. When had Preston first adopted this bluff manner? Was it genuine now merely because he had used it so long? He could go on thinking these thoughts, evaluating the effectiveness of his performance even as he repeated fond enthusiasms to Mike.

The merest suggestion of a scowl spread over Mike's face, but he brought out a smile instead. "I'm hoping all of my customers will feel comfortable here."

"And your artists," Preston said. "Yes, Mike, you've done a very good job selecting original work. I can easily see why this side of your business is doing so well." Preston passed along the bins. "I think everything comes together very nicely," Preston said.

It was out—the unspeakable fear, the threat, and so far he was fine. Emboldened, Preston strolled the length of the bins. Surely his work, the work of a man as important to the local art world as he was, would always be sold here, always be part of the stock of the area's only genuine art gallery, the only gallery to eschew schlock and focus on authentic local work. Preston's reasoning seemed unassailable.

Mike clenched his teeth and broadened his smile, but what he had to say was sincere. "You know, Preston, it hasn't been easy building up the gallery side. Most people think they can't afford original art. They only hear about the millions spent on a van Gogh. They don't know you can get a good photograph for fifty dollars or a good litho for thirty-five. My job is reaching those people. And to do that, I've had to throw out the tried and true and take a risk. That's the way business is. If you want to get ahead someday, whatever you do, you have to take a risk. Well, for me this is it."

Mike looked along the wall at the bins holding prints and drawings. "I'm getting all new stock, Preston. All new." Perhaps aware of how harsh he must sound, he looked around as though to find a hint on how to soften his position. "It's sort of like some parts of town—all new people, all new streets, all new homes. Maybe I'm being foolish," he said as he came out from behind the counter, "but I've made up my mind. I'm making a change. It's time." He picked up a bundle of oil paintings tied together and handed them to Preston, who took them with a tight smile. The string holding the paintings was cheap, fraying hemp, he noticed, and the gallery was still organized as though it were a stationery store selling cheap reproductions.

"I'm sorry, Preston, but I have to do this. I know it's affecting a lot of people I like, artists I've had here for a long time, but it's time for me to try other things. I appreciate your offering me first crack at your other work, and I'll send on the crates just as soon as they get here."

Preston mumbled as much of a reply as he could manage, he no longer felt sympathetic toward his old friend. If Mike was having trouble making a go of it, well, it was to be expected that the artists had to pay for it.

"Have you looked at the Rockland Gallery in Boston?" Mike asked as he led Preston to the door.

"I have heard of it, of course," Preston said, trying to effect a disinterested look as he gripped his bundle. He couldn't even remember which paintings he had brought here.

"The owner does some painting himself. He's a natural for you. Give him a call." They reached the door. "Look, whatever happens, let me know what you do, okay? I mean it."

Preston dropped the bundle to his side as though it were a suitcase as he walked to his car. How did artists feel when they were dropped by a gallery? How did he feel? He wasn't even sure he knew how he felt, only that he desperately hadn't wanted to face Mike, but all his efforts to achieve that had failed.

When the art teacher was finally gone, Mike slipped his hands into his pockets and turned away from the door. This was the time for the pep talk he had scripted since deciding to change the artwork he sold. It was hard having to send away the artists he couldn't sell, but he knew he had to do it. Not until he realized that he had to do it or lose the whole business did he learn to say no, no matter what. Now, discovering he could do that smoothly bothered Mike Rabkin far more than the doubtful glances he used to get sometimes from customers and artists when they saw the lower end of the range of work his gallery offered.

Mike put away the sales slips from the morning, just as he had put away the old friendship that no longer allowed him and Preston to talk honestly to each other. Whatever had changed Preston into a painter who would never live on canvas no longer concerned Mike. He soothed himself with the philosophical thought that not all friendships are meant to last forever. But the worst part of it was that he had once liked Preston.

■ ■ ■

"Now straight," Betty Lane said to the driver from her place in the backseat. The woman driving the small foreign car crossed straight through the parking lot, past the main entrance of the art school, and around the building to the back, where two cars were parked in the small gravel lot between the building and the stone wall built years ago to hold back the hill. Farther away sat a navy blue Dumpster.

"My car's right there." Betty pointed to the small red car parked near some shrubbery. The driver drew up beside Betty's car and pushed the gearshift into park. Finally still, the four women were slow to move. Tired and hungry, one sighed, another rubbed her face, still another shifted in her seat. Into the stillness came a soft voice reciting rock-bottom prices for home linens, children's fall jackets, and fall bulbs.

"Oh, do shut that off," a woman said from the backseat. "I can't stand the thought of one more sale."

"Me neither," said the passenger in the front seat. She turned off the radio. The spell of weariness broken, the four women pushed open the car doors.

"We should have sorted everything earlier," said the driver. "Now be sure to check everything again when you get home. I'd hate to open this stuff at Christmas and find you ended up with my husband's shirts and I got Betty's sister's dress and lord knows what else."

"I don't have a sister, so you don't have to worry about that," Betty said with her usual practicality. The other women chuckled and all four climbed out to sort through the parcels filling the trunk. After several minutes all four agreed Betty probably had everything she had purchased during their trip to New Hampshire and the malls. Betty opened the trunk of her car and piled in the bags.

"Now, let's just settle the gas," another said, "so we don't get as confused as we did at lunch."

"We were not confused," another said.

"Oh, come on," Betty said. "Not confused?" All three

laughed at the fourth, who folded her arms across her chest and glared in mock seriousness at her friends.

"Okay, okay," she said. "I give in. You were confused." She winked. "All right, Betty, how much do we owe?"

When the figure was calculated and agreed on, all three pooled their money to the driver, who said, "So we go again in a month? Okay? Who's driving next time?"

"I'll drive, if you don't mind getting back early," the front-seat passenger offered. "Next month I have to do all the carpooling for the junior sports, which means I have to pick up my son by three, so we can't be as late as today. Is that all right with everyone?"

"We can manage that," Betty promised her. After several more reassurances about their schedule next time and mutual compliments on their day together, the three women settled back into the car and drove away. Betty Lane was left alone in the parking lot. She slammed shut the trunk of her car, and was momentarily startled by how loudly the sound reverberated in the small space between the building and the stone wall.

The Saturday afternoon stillness was almost as deep as that on Monday mornings, when she arrived at work right after Buddy Lecroix and before any of the teachers and students. For a few minutes the school was in order and the world of work at a staid pace, but it never lasted.

Betty walked around to the driver's side. From the corner of her eye she caught something flicker in the breeze. Near the fire door was a crumpled-up piece of paper, one of the few she had ever seen on the college grounds. Buddy never tolerated litter, and he gave his work-study students a special lecture just on that subject; at least once a day he walked the perimeter of the building looking for odd bits of litter others might have missed. With a comradely sigh, Betty went over to the paper.

■ ■ ■

At 4:30 Gregory Stewart sat in his van on Packard Street wondering how he was going to get into his own place of business. Three old greenhouses made a T shape, joining in the center in a nineteenth-century stone building that housed offices and an area for making floral arrangements. On Saturday afternoon, cars lined the roads in all directions while their owners sated themselves with the fragrances of the land. He settled back in his seat to listen to an American spiritual on the radio while he waited for a customer to leave. It was the end of a glorious fall day, and he stole the few moments to enjoy it without a qualm. In his view, New Englanders didn't appreciate the color and warmth of their own landscape.

In a few minutes a car backed out onto the road, bags of chips and mulch hanging out of its trunk. Gregory drove through the new opening onto a narrow dirt track that led to the back of the greenhouses. He parked his van and unloaded some loose clay pots through the side door, noticing as he did so a familiar figure waiting nearby while he finished his work.

"Hi," Lisa Hunt called out to him when he slammed shut the van door. Her blond curls gleamed in the late afternoon sun as she approached him. "Mrs. Handel wants to know why her chrysanthemums didn't come up this year."

"Maybe they're dead," he replied with a slight burr and a grin. "She waited long enough to ask about them."

"Thanks a lot." Lisa stuffed her hands into her jeans' pockets and laughed. "Maybe I'd better start again. Mrs. Handel's garden has a hole in it where her mums should be, so I said I'd come over to see what's wrong." To herself she added that she would never volunteer to do so again. "So what's wrong with them? Do you know?"

"Can't paint, can't garden. You are a wonder, lass."

"Mrs. Handel warned me," Lisa said with mock malice.

"Did she now?" He raised an eyebrow.

"Yes, she did. Now what about her mums?"

"Is there no one inside who knows? Not one among all the fine young people I employ?"

"Not according to Mrs. Handel."

"Ach," he commented, his accent growing thicker. "Too right, she is. Come along." For all his apparent wrath at his inept employees, he smiled his widest smile and headed for the greenhouse door. Lisa had no doubt that he would use Mrs. Handel's mums as an excuse to hire another teenager to work solely with that flower, for Gregory Stewart, unmarried and childless, collected the lost among the found. Every year he hired a new crop of surly, pimply-faced high school boys and girls, jollied them through the season until their better natures could no longer resist his goodwill, then promoted them into the real world, stronger, happier, savvier. He loved to complain about the turnover in his business, but any youngster who took him seriously and attempted to stay on was courteously corrected and retrained. Gregory Stewart's mission, however, was not to reform teenagers but to spread the love of plants. Teenagers were his pollinators.

Lisa followed him into the greenhouse, a lover of the product of gardening, if not the process. She especially loved the places of gardening for their warmth and smells. Walking among the raised steel beds filled with mums and asters and other plants of the season, Lisa could almost feel her body drawing in minerals and moisture through her pores. In here she lived her own photosynthesis. She tried to show none of this as Stewart walked on ahead of her, and she might have been surprised had she known that he had already guessed what she was thinking. Some people gardened only because of the sensuous experience.

"What color does she have?" he asked without looking around at her.

"Actually, I don't know." Lisa was embarrassed at her own ignorance. This was, after all, the whole point of her errand.

He raised an eyebrow. "The garden fronting the street?"

"Yes, that's the one."

"White." He pulled two pots from a bench. "Here, try

these. They're good for a few more weeks, and if she's polite to them, they might come back again next year."

"I'll tell her."

"You might pass it on to your friend," he said, nodding to the door into the shop. Lisa followed his gaze to where Ellen Mattson was giving lengthy instructions to a young man. "She buys new plants every year without waiting to find out if the old ones will bloom again. 'Tis a waste, that."

■ ■ ■

At 4:45 Buddy Lecroix settled himself into a chair on the screened-in back porch. It was late. It was cool. It was Saturday. He had nothing to worry about until Monday morning, when he went back to work. Vinnio had taken over the afternoon at the school, promising to get all the students out by four, and he'd kept his word. Buddy didn't like the idea of letting a student—especially Vinnio—take on such a responsibility, but Vinnio had been very persuasive. Then again, Dean Goldman had made a point of assuaging Buddy's fears, and so the janitor had relented. Besides, Buddy liked the idea of a free afternoon.

The brown bottle was cold in his hand, and the beer slid down his throat, cool and easy. He even felt the yeasty foam still working in his mouth. He let his head fall back and closed his eyes.

In a few minutes the noise of five o'clock would begin. His boy would be home after a long afternoon of football at the park, or wherever the boys played these days. His wife would be home and start pulling out pots and pans for dinner, ignoring the plastic trays that came with the microwave he gave her for Christmas last year. She'd used it for only two weeks, then got tired of it, claiming that the food didn't come out right. Buddy couldn't tell the difference for the most part, but he let it go. At this moment, nothing could upset him, annoy him, harm him. He was at one with the world, just as his body, lightly wrapped in an old hunting jacket, was just warm enough to let him feel at one with the air around him.

His wife's car drove into the driveway; he could hear the brakes squeaking as she pumped the car to a halt. He would have to do something about them—but not now, not for a while. Right now his life was perfect.

■ ■ ■

Sergeant Ken Dupoulis pulled his cruiser to the side of the road. Late Saturday afternoon was an easy time to patrol. It was a time of hiatus, between the busy hours of a weekend afternoon and the socializing hours of the evening. Between four and six o'clock people were more often at home, between events or winding down their day. Fewer cars were on the streets, fewer calls came to the station. On a nice day, it was a good time to be out on duty. Either side of those hours could be hectic and wearying, but that was then. Right now Dupoulis's biggest worry was closing a car door.

He strolled up the driveway toward a blue station wagon, its passenger-side rear door hanging open, and a towel, baseball bat, and seat belt tied in a tumbled mass hanging half in, half out of the door. He arranged the equipment on the backseat, tucked in the seat belt, and closed the door. Through the side window he could see a young woman settling three boys around a kitchen table. It was just five o'clock.

Ten minutes later, humming to himself, Dupoulis drove up to the Massasoit College of Art. This was the farthest out he drove from the town, the farthest out of any building still part of Mellingham, except for some hunting shacks back in the woods. Somehow it made sense that the art school should be on the fringes of the town, sort of the way it fit into his life. Dupoulis, for all his youth, wasn't sure what to make of the students he sometimes saw here. Some of them had orange hair, earrings in their noses, strange clothes, and they talked funny, about interior meanings and other phrases that made no sense to him. He couldn't figure out how they planned to make a living working with clay or paint. That was another reason he liked patrolling on Saturday afternoon—he was less likely to run into anyone who made him feel uncomfortable.

The accusation from his girlfriend a few weeks ago that he was becoming insensitive and reactionary still rankled. It all started because he laughed at the idea of going out to a gallery exhibit at the school. They'd argued about it, but she'd won the day by saying this wasn't something they could win by debate, but only by actions. He never knew what to say to her when they argued. He felt like he didn't have any tongue.

Dupoulis parked in front of the main door and went up the steps. He pulled on the door handle. It was locked. That was just what he'd expected. There were four more doors, all fire doors at other ends of the building. He was glad there was no one here to make him wonder if his girlfriend was right. Besides, it was still a bright afternoon, just the kind for a good ball game and a clambake on the beach. He began to think about his plans for the weekend. Whistling, he skipped down the stairs and around the building, heading off to his right, checking the first door, then moving to the door in the back parking lot. It was locked, as was the old rusted pickup truck by the Dumpster. He moved around the building, checking the last two doors, which brought him once again to the front parking lot. By then he was in good humor. By the time he was in his car and driving back to town, he'd decided that maybe the art kids weren't so bad after all. Behind him the white stone building sat solid and serene, covered with a sheet of gold sprinkled from the sun as it dipped down to meet the black outstretched arms of an oak tree.

4
SUNDAY

A THIN STREAM of red liquid, more sticky than damp, threaded its way along the edge of a patch of drying brown oil paint, then mingled with a darker puddle that lay under a box. The ribbon of red passed through blotches of green and orange. Hank Vinnio lay surrounded by color, bounded by red, and held in place by crates, boxes, jars, though he was past the point of noticing now.

Unable to absorb at once the meaning of the scene, Buddy Lecroix stood well away from the corpse that had once been his part-time assistant and the various objects that seemed to have killed him. His eyes moved from object to object, trying to understand consciously what he could not absorb emotionally. He backed toward the door, rigid and cold.

Outwardly calm, Buddy walked to the nearest telephone, the pay phone near the vending machines, and called the police at 5:27 on Sunday afternoon. When he looked back down the hall, it was empty. Larry Segal was gone. Fear made his neck swell and he pulled at his collar. The police would be here in minutes, and he would have to tell them about Larry.

Buddy walked back to the painting studio and Hank Vinnio, praying that Larry knew nothing about the corpse and was just hanging around until Buddy told him he could leave, and then praying Larry had gone and the police wouldn't ask why Buddy came over to the school at five o'clock on a Sunday afternoon. If only Larry had learned how to use the school alarm like anyone else, then Buddy wouldn't be here.

No, no, no. Buddy shook his head. He started to lumber back and forth at the far end of the studio. No. It was just an accident—anyone could see that—and it didn't matter who'd found him. Buddy stopped then and turned to look at Hank, whose face was blocked by the crate. The janitor didn't like Hank, but no one deserved to die unregretted. Devious and dangerous though he might have been, Hank deserved as much as anyone at that final moment.

Regret for his earlier feelings for Hank mingled with fear, fear that he, as janitor, would be held accountable for the manner in which Vinnio died. Though it had been Vinnio's job to stack the materials, he had done it carelessly, and checking up on that and ensuring safety of the students who used the room was Buddy's job—and he hadn't done it. Buddy could see Hank's face now, the face of the man who might be as much trouble in death as he had been in life.

Buddy stepped back a pace when he heard the police siren. He armed himself once again with the words of Dean Goldman about his reliability, generosity, importance to the college. The dean had all but promised him that none of the part-timers could take away Buddy's job, and Buddy had come to believe him. And now, he supposed, that was true for another reason.

■ ■ ■

Joe Silva dropped the receiver onto its hook on the wall and then wiped the receiver with a handkerchief from his back pocket. The last thing he had been expecting was a telephone call, and he looked it. The dirt on his bare feet was less than that on his hands, but the knees of his rolled-up gray cotton pants were encrusted with dry dirt and a damp gray grit; his arms and shoulders were covered with a gray dust. A few cobwebs were smeared across his black T-shirt. For once he couldn't just drop whatever he was doing and jump into his car after the summons over the telephone; no one would appreciate seeing the chief of police show up at a murder scene looking like a laborer lifted from a construction site. He would have to shower and change.

With the longing of a man who has drifted into a private world only to be wrenched from it abruptly, Silva thought of the cellar he had just left. After weeks of planning, arranging time and space and waiting for the right weather, he had awoken this morning to the perfect day for laying a cement floor in his cellar for a work area. He didn't mind the dirt floor, the outcropping of rock at one end, the river that rose with each hurricane in the center of the cellar. He didn't mind the musty smell from the laundry he hung every weekend or the brownness that met his eyes every time he descended into the earth. He didn't even mind digging out the ground to make a level surface for his cement flooring, a gray island in an ochre and beige and brown sea. He was actually glad of the excuse to dig, to feel his whole body moving against the earth, feeling the resistance and the giving way of the grainy floor. The sweat running down his arms and legs, like a stream curving around stone as it cut a path among his muscles, was his reward. The first square of cement, bounded by two-by-four inch soft-pine boards, lay soft and pregnant with heat, its surface releasing the energy within that it might be smooth and even in time, like the soul of a deeply peaceable man after an angry argument. In a large rusty wheelbarrow sat the beginning of the concrete floor for the second square. Joe had been cutting the gray powder with water, making the two into one with a shovel when the phone rang. Only the reminder of who he was, of his job, had made him leave the work. Pulled to the phone by duty, he was pulled back to his Sunday task by a love of the sensuous.

Reluctantly, Joe turned his mind to the news of a suspicious death at the Massasoit College of Art. The faculty and students were distinguished in his mind by their unsuburban-like appearance. They triggered yet undermined his long-shelved feelings of inferiority. Once before Joe had been uncertain what to expect when he first arrived on a campus, but that had been just about thirty years ago and he'd been only eighteen.

Some people keep memories at arm's length, standing apart from whatever they had lived through once though the feelings might be resting and waiting within. Joe was not one of those. Triggers brought back old and recent moments and all their patterned colors of emotions for him to know again, like a conductor instructing a pianist to perform the opening bars of a particular sonata or etude or mazurka. The phone call from the station awoke all the ambivalences of his arrival at Northeastern University in 1963, the lure of a new intellectual world that would efface the sensuous world of physical labor he had already accepted as a given of his life. The comfortable familiarity he might have been expected to feel for the art college in Mellingham was blocked by the differentness he sensed in the faculty and students. Now he would find out if that was his prejudice.

Joe tore off his T-shirt and slacks, amused that he could still feel such garb inappropriate for a college campus. He could not imagine dressing in the 1960s as students did today, and he smiled as he thought of the shirts that hung in his closet from his college days, neatly washed and ironed. He had worn a new shirt and tie to his first class, along with a sports jacket though it was a hot September day. For most of the rest of the term, however, he was careful to wear his older shirts with the neatly turned collars, his mother's tiny stitches matching the original machine stitching. His roommate had never understood how the underside of his collar could get so frayed and the inside stay so new. He'd asked Joe if he wore his shirts inside out when he was working to protect them. Joe was so amused by the idea that he almost told his mother, but decided not to; as soon as he settled into life on campus, he found he was losing his knack of knowing immediately how she would react to such alien ideas.

Joe tightened his tie and tugged at the aprons. His mother had never understood why he wanted to go to college if he was going to end up wearing a uniform; he didn't try to explain. She had kept track of everything he had earned and saved for his tuition and his uniform had hardly seemed worth it. He aligned his belt buckle, fitting himself behind the badge and the gun and the dark, navy fabric. It felt almost the same as the day he had put on a uniform for the first time, for ROTC, during his freshman year, discovering in the stiff fabric and sharp creases a sureness that was his but had never before been externalized. He doubted they had ROTC at the art school.

■ ■ ■

Sergeant Ken Dupoulis never analyzed how he felt about his life as a policeman. He had never wanted to be anything else or live anywhere else, and only in recent months did he realize that he wanted to feel rooted in other ways. His girlfriend, Lynnette Hall, brought it about when she admitted she was thinking of breaking up with him because they weren't the same sort of people. Ken argued that they were, pointed out how similar their backgrounds were, and challenged her to refute him. She said that proved her point and he was lost, confused as well as unhappy.

That argument stayed with him and he finally invited Lynnette, with flowers and a bottle of red wine (which he bought after ten minutes of great uncertainty), to make lunch with him in his apartment on Sunday afternoon. She agreed. He relaxed, then warned himself not to get overconfident, and set about arranging the afternoon. Life was pushing him toward a crossroads and he wanted to make sure he didn't stumble onto the wrong path.

For four hours on Sunday afternoon, Ken practiced the fine art of not arguing with his girlfriend, listening as well as he could to ideas he thought deep down were a lot of nonsense, though he did have to admit that Lynnette seemed to have an awful lot of fun in life. He supposed that was why he liked her so much. As the afternoon wore on, he thought life was just about perfect—he and Lynnette were back on track and he might soon get another promotion. He had the two things he really wanted in life. He was lucky and he knew it. Then he heard the sound of police cars swerving and blaring down the streets of Mellingham. Life had indeed given him both at once—and now it was giving him the chance to choose between them. His eyes puckered at the sound of the sirens. His eardrums twisted at the words he knew Lynnette was speaking as she sat across from him at the kitchen table. She was here, in front of him, in his own home, telling him things he had never known about her in a voice intimate and confident at the same time. He could feel spaces opening up inside him he didn't know he had, all because another part of him, something outside his policeman's brain, told him she meant to fill those spaces. He would have sat through burning walls falling on him, poison wending its way down his gullet, a hammer beating on his toes. But a police siren was a different matter. He bolted for the telephone.

"Frankel?" Dupoulis yelled into the telephone as soon as someone lifted the receiver at the other end. He didn't have to wait for the officer to identify himself; he knew the roster at work as well as he knew his own name. "What's happened?"

"Hello, Ken. I thought you were off duty." The other man was unruffled.

"I am, but I heard the cars. What's happened?" Frankel was not a man to be hurried, and Dupoulis had to wait while he finished whatever it was he was doing. Dupoulis tapped his foot.

"Buddy Lecroix found a body at the college. The chief went out." The last sentence was added as an afterthought. "He'll probably be there for a while. I'll tell him you called. No need to come in." He hung up and left Ken standing with the receiver in his hand. When he put it back in its cradle, there were creases in his palm where he had gripped the black plastic casing. Still rigid, he turned back to Lynnette, who looked stunned. In a split second he knew he had more to account for than mere rudeness.

"The siren." He knew even as he said it that it was not a good reason for breaking into what she had been saying. "The siren." He repeated it, trying to push other words out afterward. For two seconds he'd had the two things in life most dear to him—Lynnette and his career—then had passed to having neither. Frankel hadn't called him in, and the look in Lynnette's eyes was more than he knew how to cope with. The doubt in her eyes changed to hurt, then anger. Maybe she was right; maybe he was growing insensitive.

"I'm sorry." He sat down again but Lynnette leaned back in her chair as though she were pulling away from him. When he opened his mouth to go on, she raised her hand to stop him. The disdain in her eyes would have been enough, and he looked desperately around the room for some sign of how to undo the damage. When Lynnette rose to leave, he said, to his everlasting good fortune, "I'm not going. It doesn't mean that much to me." And he meant it.

He said no more. Instead, he settled in his chair, blushed, and held his tongue. He no longer wanted to chase the police car, and he no longer tried to hold on to Lynnette. If he had lost both, then he had lost both. Lynnette studied him in silence.

■ ■ ■

With his feet planted firmly apart and his hands in his pockets, Joe Silva, the chief of police of Mellingham, watched the other men and women move swiftly around the painting studio as they recorded every aspect of the scene before them. The body of Hank Vinnio had lain in wait for the police in a pool of paint and turpentine and cold coffee. The scene hadn't improved significantly with the removal of the body. The stains, cans, and crates remained; only their focal point was gone. With the departure of the EMT crew and police investigators, and now with the departure of his own crew, Silva began to imagine more clearly what could have happened. Buddy Lecroix stood by the door, still and unnoticed like a half-empty carton of juice in the refrigerator.

Hank Vinnio had bled to death, of that Silva was certain on the basis of what he had seen when he arrived. It might be unprofessional of him to say as much to anyone else, but in his own mind he was certain. Unless the man had ingested something that killed him simultaneously with the crash, Vinnio was an obvious victim of loss of blood. A huge gash across his forehead and over to his temple was the ugliest cut but not the deadliest. Silva stepped over the dark red pool of blood that spread like an undulating wave onto a beach of green paint, the bottle that had contained the paint smashed by the back wall. He had spent some time with one of the lab men learning to recognize the different paints that swirled over the floor, the slow seeping oil, the splattering but quickly drying acrylic, and the watercolors that left almost a dust when dry. It was like learning to recognize different kinds of sand in the desert.

Except for the gash on his neck and across his forehead, Hank Vinnio had looked almost asleep lying on the studio floor. On his chest rested a crate, against which one of his hands pressed, as though he had tried to ward it off before it fell on him, knocking him down. His right arm was raised and thrown out to his side. The police had had no trouble finding the shard of glass that had gashed his throat; then they had found a bloodstained paper towel in the trash bin near the back wall.

Silva stepped away from the colorful chaos, its former

focus now indicated by a zigzagging stretch of white tape. As much as he steeled himself every day for the maltreatment of one person by another, he was still discomfited by violence. But unlike some officers, he was not surprised to find it anywhere, including in the idyllic small town that was now his home. Small towns were peaceful only on the sidewalks; their homes and shops were greenhouses for violence. The chief turned around to face Buddy.

"Did you call any of the officers of the college?"

Buddy nodded, his entire head moving up and down on his shoulders; he looked like a doll on a stick.

"The president wasn't home. I tried at the number he left for emergencies, but he wasn't there either. I tried a few other places, but I couldn't get him. Then your men arrived."

Silva had guessed something of the sort would be Buddy's answer. When he had first come to Mellingham as chief of police in 1985, he had made a point of meeting the old hands in the local institutions, the janitors, the garagemen, the delivery men and women, the ones who kept the institutions going—or brought them to a halt. Buddy looked much the same then as now—in his green khaki coveralls, his thinning hair turning gray, his brown eyes sad but smiling while his mouth drooped. Then as now, his hands hung down to his knees.

"Sorry you had to stay so long," Silva said as he neared him. "I'm leaving an officer here for the rest of the night. I may want to get another look and I don't want anyone blundering in." He looked back at the pool of color.

"Hank Vinnio, I think you said his name was." Silva looked at him for a reply. He pulled out his notebook and said, "What can you tell me about him? How long did you know him?"

Buddy wilted under the question. Ordinary conversation could be a burden to Buddy, not because he lacked words or understanding or thoughts that sought expression but because so many thoughts crowded his head that choosing which one to send forth was difficult and slow work. He hoped the chief would keep his questions simple, and Buddy vowed to keep his interpretation of them simple. He had known Hank Vinnio in one form or another all his life, but this one, the one lying on the floor only a short time, and the person hidden inside the body, concealed in sinew and silence, shorter still. But that's not what Buddy said. He said, "Not long at all. Not long."

"Who were his friends? Do you know? Anyone who might help us?"

Buddy looked solemnly at the chief. "I don't think Hank Vinnio ever made friends, not the way you mean it, not even if he lived in the same place for all his life. He wasn't the type." Buddy sighed from the effort of saying so much. A simple no would have sufficed, but it seemed almost an untruth to Buddy.

"That sounds like you didn't like him very much."

"Yeah," Buddy said, nodding his head. His arms seemed to get longer.

"Care to tell me why?"

Buddy opened a stick of gum and folded it into his mouth while he thought over Silva's question. "Just general principles." This was as simple as Buddy could manage. It was late and he was tired.

"That doesn't sound like you, Buddy."

Buddy considered this observation. "Sometimes I just don't like someone." He moved over to the window and stared out at the few official cars remaining. As several drove out, one drove in. He watched it draw up to a police officer near the door. Silva was willing to wait while Buddy chose what he was going to say, for unless he turned out to be implicated in Vinnio's death, the janitor's views would contain the first true estimate of the dead man's character.

"He was a work-study student. You know what that is?" Buddy turned around to face the chief. He put his hands in his pockets one by one.

"Someone who works for the school part-time in exchange for some tuition money," Silva said.

"Yeah, that's it. Vinnio worked for me four nights a week, from six to ten at night. He worked some other hours if we needed him. He locked up four nights a week."

"So he had a key," Silva said. "We found several in his pocket. I'll have someone bring them around so you can identify the school key."

"He had a key, but he wasn't supposed to use it like this was his home, coming in whenever he wanted, weekends, nights, whenever." Buddy looked over at the pool of color.

"Did you know he was here this afternoon?"

"Not today. Yesterday I knew he was going to be here, with some of the other students. I called to check they were gone in the afternoon."

"What time?" Silva asked.

"Just before five. No one answered, so I figured he'd done what he said he was gonna do."

"What was that?"

"Get the kids out by three or four. He told me some of the kids wanted to do some extra work with him. Since he had a key, I decided to let him. I didn't like him much, but he wasn't stupid where his job was concerned. So I called to see if everything went okay. When he didn't answer, I figured everyone had gone home and that was that."

Silva liked Buddy, his open ways and easy honesty, but something about him now wasn't part of the Buddy he knew. "What kind of worker was he?"

"He used to work in a warehouse," Buddy said. "He looked it." Silva avoided looking directly at Buddy's creased khakis and well-ironed shirt. When Silva had first met him, Buddy had still been showing up at work in a tie even though that made him almost the best-dressed man in the building. "A warehouse," Buddy repeated. "That's where he belonged."

"How so?" The casual nature of his question belied

Silva's deep curiosity. It was rare to hear Buddy speak so harshly of anyone.

"He wasn't like most people who wanted to go back to school after being out working. The older ones do their work and go home. They don't hang around like the kids, talking about the careers they're going to have and how important this artist was or that one. They're serious, but they have other responsibilities." Buddy's mouth shifted into a circle as his gum passed from one side to the other.

"Why do you think he was here?"

"I dunno. I dunno." His hands sank deeper into his pockets, his fists clenched, and his neck sank down into his shoulders, as though his body were shrinking away from a contaminated atmosphere closing in around him.

"Where was he from?"

Buddy shook his head. "Never said. He liked to hint, Vinnio did, about what a hard life he'd had." Buddy paused and turned back to the chief. "That doesn't cut any ice with me. He had everything anyone needs—he was young, strong, had a decent job."

"He wasn't that young." The temptation to commiserate with Buddy over the attitudes of a younger generation was strong, and that irritated Silva. He liked to think he was objective about everyone, and hated to be reminded of his own biases. "How old was he? I couldn't tell from looking at him."

"Thirties," Buddy said. "He was a whiner. Thought he should have everything coming his way. At least that's how he talked when he first got here."

"And then he changed?"

"Yeah. Then he started saying he had something coming to him—soon." He paused. "He joked about how college was giving him opportunities, just like people said it would."

■ ■ ■

Silva leaned back in the swivel desk chair and surveyed the office. Betty Lane's desk was neat and clean, just what he had expected when Buddy had told him where the nearest private telephone was, leading him to the administrative offices and unlocking the door. Silva picked up the receiver and dialed. It was well after ten o'clock, late enough for people to have picked up on the death and started talking about it. He would soon know if someone else had already reached the dean.

Someone else hadn't. Silva reached the dean while he was still sitting in front of the television set, drowsing his way through the latest murder mystery. Much as he loved them, Dean Goldman could no longer stay alert much past nine o'clock, an embarrassment if a school meeting went late, and a social liability if he was a guest at a party. When he was a host, the problem didn't arise; he just remained on his feet as long as he had to. Chief Silva's call brought him to his feet and full wakefulness in seconds.

The chief quickly relayed where he was and why he was calling, and Goldman received the news in the same outwardly calm manner. When Silva paused to give the dean a chance to interject a question or comment, there was only silence. Silva went on, telling him what he wanted—in a word, access. Access to the building, to the students, to the faculty, to the records.

The chief didn't need to ask for this, and Goldman knew it, but Silva wanted something more—cooperation on a level that ensured that no matter how difficult or unpleasant the investigation might become, the college would support the police and save Silva the trouble of official action to pry information from those concerned.

Dean Goldman was the right man to call. Buddy Lecroix, as an employee, might naturally think of the president first, but not Silva. The president of the college was a man of the community, raising money, visiting other institutions, expanding the realm of the school. He was conservative in public and sometimes mystified by his own charges on campus. He was not an artist. Dean Goldman, on the other hand, had a scholar's love of the truth, even when it went against the academy. This much everyone knew. He was glad to give Chief Silva carte blanche.

■ ■ ■

Only three lights blazed in the modern home of the Mattsons. On a winding road that led to the next town, the redwood house with the cantilevered roof sat well back from the road, approached by a circular gravel driveway that looped around a bed of purple irises long past their flowering. At night the street-lights faded away by the edge of the drive, letting the house stand discreetly beyond the unseemly attention of the material world. In the back, the neat yard lined with rose beds gave onto wild growth thickening as it climbed the rocky hills. Lights from the neighbors' equally important houses glimmered through the shrubbery in the early evening, but now all was dark, except at the Mattson home.

One light shone in the kitchen, where Ellen sat in night-gown, bathrobe, and slippers at the kitchen table. She slipped the toast back into the toaster a second time, after deciding that a light golden crust wasn't exactly what she wanted. As soon as anyone got to know her at all, he—or more likely she—invariably remarked on how young she was, though she was clearly in her mid-thirties. The comment referred not to her youthful appearance but to her outlook on life, and it was not always complimentary. The comment was sometimes the only way the speaker could express what was otherwise inex-pressible. Ellen Mattson, for all her sophisticated fashion and arrogance of manner, was at heart a child. She still enjoyed—and looked forward to—the thrill of staying up late at night with toast and milk, or a large bowl of popcorn. At the moment, all her attention was on her toast, on getting it just right, and she conversed with Preston only out of habit.

"Who was that?" She kept her eyes on the toaster even as she spoke, taking note of the time as well as her husband's departure and return from answering the telephone in the front hall, the site of the nearest phone. This arrangement brought comments of disbelief from anyone who visited her. But so little time did she spend in the kitchen that she had never felt the need for a telephone in that otherwise practical room, and so the telephone with its answering machine sat in the front hall, assisted by another in Preston's den, as he called it, and a third upstairs in the bedroom. Ellen waited for an answer.

"That was the dean." Preston stared at a spot between his nose and the table. The tone of his voice broke her concentration on her toast and she looked up.

"At eleven o'clock at night?"

Preston rested his palms on the table and eased himself into a chair. He wore a shirt open at the neck, slacks, and slippers, not yet ready to end the day. "He wanted to make sure I was coming in tomorrow."

"The dean called for that?" Ellen made no effort to conceal her contempt at the dean's behavior. She went back to her toast. At any other time, Preston might have noticed his wife's increasingly disturbing habit of sneering at others behind their backs, particularly those who held a respected place in the community, but right now his mind was engaged by far more important things.

"Well, maybe not only that," he said, still going over his conversation with the dean.

"Well, what then?"

"He wanted to tell me—" He paused, then met her eyes. "Hank Vinnio was found dead at the school tonight." For a few seconds, each looked into the other's eyes, beyond the mask, the pose, the emotional clothing they wore to shield them from the world. Both glanced away at the same time.

"What?" Ellen said. Her hand was poised in the air, a squib of butter sliding off the tip of the knife and plopping onto the plate below. "It can't be. It's not possible." The color in her face seeped away, and slowly her hand came down to the table, seemingly of its own volition.

"Buddy Lecroix found him when he went over to check the alarm system." Preston spoke each word as though in an effort to hear each one clearly and thereby convince himself of their meaning. "He bled to death."

Ellen gasped. "But, but—" She rested her arms on the table.

"That must be a terrible way to die," he went on, ignoring Ellen's interjections.

"Yes, terrible." She put down her knife.

"He had his throat cut."

"Preston, please." She dropped her head and the toast was only inches away from her mouth.

"I'm sorry. How else can I put it? That's what happened. That's what the dean said." The first shock began to dissolve then, and Preston retreated into his bluff persona. "Of course, it sounds terrible. I'm sorry, my dear. You must be shocked." His voice sank an octave. His normal tenor became a baritone when he was trying to impress others.

"He had his throat cut." Ellen repeated his words, not yet fully believing the news and trying to make it real by repetition.

"That's what I said. Are you all right?" Preston suddenly seemed to notice her and her unexpected reaction. He might have expected shock, then morbid curiosity, if he'd had the presence of mind to look ahead. Instead, she seemed thrown off balance, as though she had expected something else and couldn't accept what he had told her. "Are you all right? You seem so, so, so different." It disturbed Preston that Ellen failed to react in a way he could understand, particularly when she failed to need the kind of charity he was willing to extend. At the moment she should have been seeking his comfort; instead, however, she was coldly reviewing what he had just told her, inspecting each word. "Ellen, are you all right?"

"I'm fine, dear, just fine." She smiled, then tried to hide it. "I just never expected such news. I mean, we're sitting here having a snack at almost midnight and the dean calls to tell you someone died at the school. You're right, dear. It is shocking, but we mustn't let it upset us. After all, you barely knew him and he wasn't one of your favorite students, was he?"

"Well, no."

"What did you say the dean wanted?"

Preston grew more uncomfortable in the wooden chair. "He wanted to make sure that I'm going in tomorrow. The police will want to know everything they can about Vinnio." He paused. "I suppose they'll want to know about all of us."

"All of us?" Ellen put down her toast.

"Of course. He was murdered."

"But surely he had a fight with someone, someone they can find out about. He must have had a fight with someone. Maybe he was into drugs, or he stole something. Someone must know about it. Why would it have anything to do with us at the school?"

Preston listened to this garbled analysis of the crime. When she stopped, he thought for a moment before speaking. "The police don't seem to have any idea who did it, and so they're going to be investigating everyone at the school who knew him. I suppose they have to." He slipped back into his earlier honesty. "I guess they think someone at the school did it. At least for now. But Chief Silva will get it sorted out, don't you worry." His bluff confidence restored, he suddenly felt hungry and looked over the offerings of the kitchen table.

"Yes, of course," Ellen said. She picked up her knife again and swiped a piece of toast with it, smearing her thumb with butter. "Does the school keep extensive files on its employees?"

"Just the usual," Preston said. "Background information. Work history, place of birth. That sort of thing. Is there anything to eat besides toast?"

■ ■ ■

Once again alone in the studio, Silva pulled a stool over to the row of tall, narrow windows and sat down, looking over at the back wall and visualizing the stacks of crates, jars, and other paraphernalia of the painting life as they might have been originally. He pondered the laws of physics that might allow a stack of crates and boxes to tip over onto the unsuspecting. There was also the matter of the gash in Vinnio's throat.

The rest of the room looked much the same as it always did, or so he had been told. Silva had never been in an artist's studio before and he wondered what the fire chief would say. The room was probably safer than it looked, but it was dangerous to his eye. Still, that wasn't his problem. His problem was Hank Vinnio.

Silva settled onto a stool to take advantage of the late night quiet to think through what he had learned so far. It was probably the only chance he would have, he reminded himself, to study the space without interruption—or might have had. Even as he settled to his task, a knock on the studio door interrupted him.

A tall and thin young man, his thick brown hair falling over his wide brown eyes, poked his head into the studio, jerked his head one way and then another, until his eyes fastened on Silva. "May I come in?" He stepped through the studio door. His tweed jacket was flecked with brown the same color as his hair, and his hands rested in the pockets of his khaki slacks. Larry Segal was not casual or unconcerned, but could think of nothing else to do with his hands. It seemed more polite than crossing his arms over his chest and tucking his hands under his arms, but if he became confused, he would do that too. Seemingly shy but in fact in awe of the world, Larry Segal stood willingly on the sidelines and watched. Anything closer to the center of activity made him wretchedly nervous.

"Who are you?" Chief Silva asked. Larry introduced himself.

"The officer said you might want to talk to me." He

waited for Silva to reply, but the chief wanted to know what this denizen of the art world might offer on his own. Larry Segal cleared his throat. "If you do—want to talk to me, that is—I was wondering if you could do it now, or maybe I could come in to the station tomorrow? Or the next day? Or whenever you think is a good time." Larry leaned forward as he spoke, then back again. Silva meditated on the effects of deference on a police officer. The first time a recruit puts on a uniform, the world changes for him. If he had wanted respect, he got it—and a lot more besides. Strangers feel compelled to say hello on the sidewalk, bullies feel threatened waiting to cross the street, and shy people sidle their way through a parade to stand behind him. The man before him might be an extreme version of the last.

"You're the teacher who called Buddy about the alarm not being set. Is that right?"

"Yessir."

"Why don't you show me?" Silva decided to keep Segal there long enough to find out what he was like. The two men walked to the front door, where an officer paced. Silva nodded to him and he left the building, an exchange Segal noticed, letting his mind scoot into byways of body language so long that Silva finally had to call his name to get his attention again. "You were saying?" Silva prompted.

"I was? Oh, yes, I was." Segal stepped up to the door and a small square of plastic with numbers and lights. The plaque looked like the push-button inset from a telephone with lights ready to flash on the top and right-hand side.

"This is the alarm," Segal said. "Yes, okay." He looked at the blinking lights. "I don't know how it works. I just know what I'm supposed to do when I come in on the weekends and what it should look like when I leave. This afternoon when I came in it didn't look like that, how it was supposed to look, so I figured someone else was here."

"You have a key?"

"Right. A lot of the teachers do, and some of the part-time janitors, too." Segal looked uncomfortable. "I suppose that seems lax to you."

"Was anyone here? Did you hear anyone, see anyone?" Silva asked, not wanting to admit just how lax this key business seemed to him.

"No, no one. But I wasn't looking at first. I just went down to my studio to get what I wanted and do some work."

"Can anyone come in and out with a key without setting off the alarm?"

"Oh, sure." Segal beamed at the chief. "It's a very simple system. The alarm is just for nights and weekends."

"So if the building is locked but the alarm's not set and you unlock the door, nothing happens. Right?" Segal nodded, delighted that he had finally given the chief what seemed to be useful information. Silva thought of the thousands of dollars wasted on a security system never used because it was never understood. "You said you went down to your studio to work. About what time was that?"

"Maybe four o'clock."

"Go on. You were downstairs working."

"Yes. So I was ready to leave by five and I went upstairs. I knew no one was downstairs, but I didn't know if someone had left while I was down there, so I called out as I went down the hall but there didn't seem to be anyone around. I looked around some more and I knew I couldn't set the alarm, so I called Buddy. I thought maybe he could tell me over the phone how to do it, set the alarm, I mean, but he seemed to think it was better for him to come over and do it himself. So he did. He's very conscientious."

Silva took note of the vote of confidence and studied the alarm.

"He found Hank." Larry offered this in the nature of a prompting.

This wasn't the first time Silva had heard something so

obvious as to be inane from a witness. It was this kind of comment year in and year out that drove some of his comrades
into cynicism and contempt for the civilian, no longer able to
sympathize with, or even recognize, the ordinary person's way
of coping with shock. In his early years, Silva reminded himself of this every time he felt rise in him an urge to reply with
sarcasm, and now he felt only sympathy and kindness in
answer to the voice of confusion and dismay in those he was
duty-bound to aid in distress. He thought it sometimes the
greatest challenge he had ever met.

"Yes, I know." Silva smiled. "But you didn't. How is
that?"

"You're right, I didn't." Segal pondered this point, wondering what it meant.

"When you were looking for someone else in the building, you didn't look into the painting studio? Just poke your
head into the doorway?"

"No, I didn't think anyone was in there."

"I see." It was a reasonable reply. Silva looked back down
the hall, which turned to the right, toward the stairs, just
opposite the doorway into the studio. "What sort of student
was Hank Vinnio? Was he one of yours?"

"No, but he probably would have been." This was familiar ground, and Larry relaxed, his mind shifting to the area he
loved best. To Silva's eye and ear, the shift was a transforma-
tion. Larry loved his work and felt at ease in it with every part
of his body. Silva waited for the pedantic tone that usually
erupted at this point in the voice of a professional kept waiting
like an inferior, but it never came. Larry was genuine and sincere. "Anyone who majors in painting," Segal explained, "is
expected to take some drawing courses. All I know about
Hank was what I heard from others and what I saw of his canvases. He was pretty good."

"Better than average?"

"Much better. Definitely."

"So he was pretty serious as a student."

"No, I wouldn't say that." Larry Segal stepped back a pace and gave Chief Silva a skeptical look.

"Why not?"

The simplicity of the question stumped Larry. He tried to think of a simple reply, to match the simplicity of the chief's question, but all he could think of to say was, "I don't know. I just don't know. I never thought of him as a serious student." Logic was not one of Larry's talents.

"How did you think of him?"

Larry gripped one idea after another, but nothing felt right. "He was mismatched. He had what could have been a great talent and he barely hid a contempt for intellectuals and artists. He had no idea what his gift meant. It was just a way to make some easy money. I think that's why he went back to school, too. There was money in it."

■ ■ ■

The building shuddered as Larry Segal pushed the door shut behind him, leaving Silva to assimilate the work of the evening. Segal's description of Hank Vinnio placed him squarely in the center of the school, a man whose anger was guaranteed to alienate everyone he met, which meant everyone at the school. And this, though Segal had been unwilling to say so, is exactly what had happened, Segal being the one exception. The students envied Vinnio and learned from him, but they cringed at his barbs no matter where they landed; the faculty felt uneasy with his unshaped talent and unshackled personality. Segal said nothing about the staff, but he didn't have to. Silva already knew how Buddy felt and that was enough.

Chief Silva snapped shut his notebook, closing for now the list of names of those who had the most to do with the victim while at the school. It was a long list. For the moment Silva savored the emptiness of the building, listening for the sounds unheard during the busy day, the secret language of the night. After his first week of college classes, long ago in 1963, he had returned to one of the classroom buildings and stayed, just sitting in an empty room until the janitor threw him out. Those hours, impossible to explain to others, helped him see himself in another world.

The classrooms he had seen so far at Massasoit were different from those of his youth; here were large open spaces almost as large as an airplane hangar, and looking like one too. The solitude of such spaces had always held a special attraction. He understood the lure of a retreat, the religious life that promised dissolving boundaries within and infinite dimensions beyond.

Silva laughed at himself. He knew what was happening now, the desire for a respite, a time to order his thoughts before plunging into the investigation full time. He loved the sensual side of life too much to abandon the real world: the golden autumn, a good meal, the trash, the smog. He loved it all. His worn soles scraped along the concrete floor, grinding down a chip from a charcoal crayon and a filament from a cigarette filter. He was tired; it was time to leave, to go home and think about the pieces of violent death left behind. Steps coming up the wooden stairs to the front door called him back, and that made him angry, a sign that he was more than a little tired.

"Sir?"

Silva turned around at the sound of the familiar voice.

"I thought you were off duty this weekend, Ken."

"I am, sir," Ken Dupoulis said. "But I thought I'd just see if you were still out here."

"We're just about to leave." He motioned to Dupoulis to follow him. "We found Hank Vinnio right in there."

"Frankel said his throat was cut." Dupoulis repeated the information the other officer had given him half an hour ago after he walked Lynnette home, all the way to her apartment

two houses down the street from his own. Dupoulis later marveled at his calm and disengagement as he listened to Frankel's description of the murder scene. When he suggested Dupoulis drive out if he still wanted to, Ken actually had to think twice about it. When had he found in himself this new detachment? He felt like he was inside someone else's skin, hearing a stranger talk. He heard a voice say, "Frankel said a teacher found him."

"Not exactly. Larry Segal found the alarm not working and called Buddy Lecroix, the janitor, and he found the body."

"Who was he? The victim," Ken corrected himself.

"Hank Vinnio. Part-time student and part-time janitor. Mid-thirties. Up to a month ago, he was just a drifting laborer, at least as far as I know. He was new. New to the school. New to the area."

"Vinnio," Dupoulis repeated. "It sounds familiar." He tried to bring the memory into focus but his thoughts blurred. "I can't get it," he finally said. "But I keep thinking I've heard his name before. Are you sure he's new around here? Maybe he was in trouble in the area some time back."

"Maybe," Silva agreed. "We have a lot of checking to do. If he's been in trouble, we'll know soon. From what I've heard so far, he didn't seem quite the straight student type." A *malandro*, from the sound of things, Silva thought. He was long past the time when he muttered his personal reactions in Portuguese, but he still heard them in his head.

"What do you have so far? Time of death? Weapon? What?" Dupoulis asked.

"Time of death seems to be some time yesterday. Probably by five o'clock. Buddy called the school to see if Vinnio had sent the students home and locked up. Since no one answered, he assumed the place was locked up safe and everyone gone. You were on duty yesterday afternoon, weren't you?" Silva asked.

"Yessir. I checked the college at the usual time, about five o'clock, and everything was locked up tight. No cars in the parking lot, just a pickup out back, also locked."

"The truck seems to be Vinnio's, but we didn't find anything in it. Segal, the teacher who called Buddy, had to use a key to get into the building. It seems a lot of the teachers do, and they may all be like Segal. Good on unlocking doors and not so good on the alarm." Silva shook his head. "We'll have to work according to the time frame we have, but it could change. So many people had access that we're going to have to locate in time a lot of people. Anyway, he died pretty soon after he was hit, but there are some problems with how he died." Silva looked over at the white outline on the floor.

"Such as?"

"Well, first of all, someone or something knocked him out, and then someone slashed his throat. But whoever it was seems to have waited between knocking him out and cutting his throat." Silva turned to face Dupoulis. "That's a guess, an assumption I'm going on, but it seems to be a valid one. We'll have to wait for confirmation, though, but keep it in mind." He turned back to the studio. "The lapse in time raises some interesting questions. Like why. We looked to see if anything else might have gone down while Vinnio was lying here, but we haven't found anything."

"So there's no chance of it being an accident," Dupoulis said. "A bottle didn't crash down on him and break against him. He didn't fall on the crates and bottles, for instance."

"No, his throat was cut deliberately," Silva said. "It was pretty obvious."

Dupoulis considered this. "That's a risky way to kill someone, to use a crate to knock him out and then find a murder weapon at the site, like a broken bottle. Risky."

"Risky, or just an accident someone made use of," Silva said.

"It sure doesn't sound planned."

"Agreed," Silva said. "But he's dead just the same.

Someone hated him enough to kill him in a way that took nerve."

"Bold and opportunistic," Dupoulis said. "Does that sound like the kind of people you'd expect to find at an art school?"

5
MONDAY

LIKE THE VAST MAJORITY of his comrades in uniform, Joe Silva had joined the police force to help people. It was a simple idea, so simple as to seem contrived, and yet it was true. Moreover, it was so much a part of his identity that he never thought twice about acknowledging his motivation whenever the question came up—always from someone outside the force. It never seemed the least bit sentimental to him either, only sound, elemental, honest. And on some days it was good to remember that for the most part his career had lived up to his hopes. For the most part.

Today could well be a different matter, Silva thought as he rummaged through a stack of folders on his desk. For the last fifteen hours his mind, when awake, had been on one problem only—the death of Hank Vinnio—and making as much sense out of it as soon as he could. That seemed a sensible reaction to a bloody crime, and one that any normal citizen of the quiet town of Mellingham might be expected to harbor, and certainly it was the reaction of his own officers, as was evident in the already voluminous pile of paper teetering on his desk. And yet it was not the only possible reaction he could expect from the citizens of the town. The voice on the telephone was telling him that. Chief Silva listened to the thinning silence.

"Murder?" the elderly man's voice said. "Anyone I know?" Silva named the victim and the location, wishing he didn't have to. The silence grew thinner.

The caller stopped to find out exactly who had died before offering the required words of shock and sympathy and turning again to the matter that concerned him: Henry Muir and this year's plans for the gallery in his barn. "Anyway," the man concluded, "you know why I called." The last was delivered as a statement, and Silva did indeed know. The other man went on to detail his objections, mostly concerning parking, to Mr. Muir's current proposal. "Shall I let you get back to me on that?" Silva agreed he would, and said good-bye. Why, he wondered, did police work always come down to cars and traffic? If there were no cars, would there be no need for police? For a brief moment, Silva envisioned robbers fleeing on foot only to be captured by citizens walking to work, people out jogging, and others idling on a bench in the sun. Corrupt men and women of business, no longer able to conceal their arrivals and departures by black-windowed limousines, would be easy and fair prey for the press corps. The fantasy amused him, so that when he looked down again at his desk, and the diagram of a traffic pattern lying there, he was smiling.

"It is better, isn't it?" Sergeant Dupoulis spoke from the doorway before Silva knew he was there. "But I didn't think you'd want to take the time for it now."

"What?" Silva blinked and realized his sergeant thought he was smiling at the diagram, and the chief, to hide his surprise, concurred. "It won't take me too long. I'll just go over it now," he said. "If I don't deal with it, someone will point out that Vinnio was an outsider and already dead, but Oxbow Lane is here and its residents are very much alive." Dupoulis nodded and disappeared into the outer office.

The four-page traffic report and diagrams detailed the current traffic usage on Oxbow Lane, a small residential street running off the old colonial highway that passed through the town now as a sedate scenic route. Henry Muir had long operated a small gallery in his barn, and every year submitted a request to the planning board to expand the gallery into a full-time business, and the board just as regularly turned him down. But this time something was different. In the first week of September, Mr. Muir hired an attorney and told one of the selectmen that he meant to win. He had the law on his side, as he put it. Worried about the change in Henry, the selectman reported the conversation to a member of the planning board, who was rattled enough to ask the police for a traffic report, seeking in advance a shield against Mr. Muir's impending attack.

The report was excellent, in Silva's view, a fair and accurate assessment of the number of cars that might be expected to visit Oxbow Lane each week. The range in the figures reflected Dupoulis's interviews with the traffic officers in other towns and his own shrewd knowledge of just who might be expected to visit an obscure avant-garde gallery in a tiny village far from any urban center.

The first time Silva had seen the report, he endorsed it unreservedly and sent it on to the board. But they disagreed and sent it back. They sent no cover letter to explain their reservations, objections, or questions, either. They didn't have to. The telephone calls Silva was getting told him everything he needed to know.

Silva looked over Dupoulis's neatly drawn traffic pattern, newly revised, and wondered if the equivalent experience for a neurosurgeon was threading his own needle. Undoubtedly, surgeons of any category did not thread their own needles or clean their own tools. Silva reread the traffic evaluation, noted the minor revisions Dupoulis had made, and wondered how this small controversy would be settled. Dupoulis had done a good job—every time—but no one but Mr. Muir was going to be satisfied with a report from the

Police Department that said Oxbow Lane could easily handle three to five more cars per day, an estimate wildly beyond the range of any known experience in the area but one that Henry Muir loved to quote to his neighbors. Even though most of the merchants in town hoped Henry would attract some generous patrons, none of them expected him to be so fortunate as to get more than two or three visitors a week. After all, he was planning on selling modern art, his own and that of some of his peers in the area, none of it the kind of thing tourists might buy to hang on their walls to remind them of their visit to a quaint New England village.

Mellingham merchants were a reasonable lot, but Henry's neighbors were not—and Henry knew that. His annual bragging about what he intended to do to put Mellingham on the map as a center for modern art successfully alienated all who lived in Oxbow Lane. But no one admitted it was this attitude that repelled them. On the contrary, residents of the narrow road claimed the area to be a center of community responsibility, and in their digressions to prove their point, artists somehow turned out to be disreputable— they weren't quite sure why it was so, but artists were definitely not the sort one wanted to have around. Mr. Muir, despite his reputation, was himself an argument against his own business, since, at the very least, he was planning on bringing in outsiders. Silva had already listened to enough mental contortions to make him wonder at the fear the creative spirit inspired in otherwise seemingly sane people and at Henry Muir's cranky devotion to riling his neighbors.

Silva put away the report for the time being. The members of the zoning board wanted answers to a long list of questions, and the residents wanted answers to another list of questions— and not necessarily the same answers, either. But this time they would have to wait—at least until he got the murder investigation under way, or until the Muir issue grew so hot that it landed in the lap of the selectmen.

He pulled out another folder and called for Dupoulis to join him. The sergeant stood in the doorway while Silva scanned the reports. "That's it?"

"So far," Dupoulis replied. "Frankel spent a lot of time last night on it. If Vinnio ever got in trouble, it wasn't under that name. We're still waiting for some more replies to come in, but Hank Vinnio was straight and clean as far as we can tell. There's nothing in his apartment to make me think he was up to anything we might be interested in."

Silva shook his head. A murder victim innocent in every way made no sense unless it was a random act of violence, and that was something Silva doubted very much. Besides, everything he'd been told about the victim so far led him to expect something dark in his past.

"Sir?" Dupoulis queried, still in the doorway. "There was one thing."

"Go ahead," Silva said.

"An old man up the coast saw the report of Vinnio's death in the paper this morning," Dupoulis said, naming a small town not far from Mellingham. "He remembers a Vinnio family from about twenty years ago."

"What does he remember about them?" Silva asked.

"Not much," Dupoulis said. "They had a boy. He said he was a punk; that's what he remembers. He said Vinnio was always on the verge of trouble but always managed to slip away at the last minute. He didn't sound like he liked the kid at all."

Hank Vinnio was turning out to be just what Silva had been led to expect from Buddy's description of him. He was *malcriado*, badly raised, and ended up a *malandro*, a troublemaker and who knew what else. "What happened to the rest of the family?" Silva asked.

"He doesn't remember for sure, but he thinks Vinnio got too close to serious trouble and the family moved. He thinks the parents are probably dead by now, but he's not sure. No siblings."

"Well, you'd better start checking it out," Silva said. "Anything else?"

"Just that he wasn't surprised Vinnio ended up dead."

■ ■ ■

Betty Lane reached for the cup of tea sitting on her desk, remembered it was cold, and withdrew her hand to her lap. Her fingers flexed and stopped in the clawlike shape of a bird falling onto a tree limb. She knew her reaction to the morning's unexpected chaos was unreasonable but she couldn't help herself. Arriving at work at her usual time, she had found long plastic ribbons laced around parts of the building like an artwork by Cristo, students milling about and then lurching at her, shouting questions, wailing and pleading to get into the painting studio, and police officers passing along the hallway, ignoring her along with the students. It was an unwelcomed and almost shattering feeling to be suddenly unworthy of notice. Her first, almost instinctive, reaction was to assert herself, to brush them out of the halls, away from the doors with a sweep of orders practiced over the years, but when she pushed in the always open door to her office, such imperious and commanding visions popped like a balloon, pricked by the greater pain before her. Karen Meghan held a sheet of paper in one hand while she rifled, with her other hand, through the drawers holding the personnel files.

"What are you doing?" Betty said with all the outrage and uncertainty she had not been able to release since entering the building. Karen looked up, her red eyes welling with tears, and replied that she was only gathering material the police had asked her to put together. This was so reasonable that Betty was hard put to justify her anger. She would have been even angrier if she had known that Karen, young enough to still have the benefit of the uncanny perceptiveness of the adolescent, had interpreted the older woman's anger as her only permissible expression of fear, and therefore was not in the least offended by her boss's otherwise inexplicable treatment of her that morning.

Instead of complimenting Karen on her presence of mind, however, Betty said, "Why wasn't I called? I'm the one who knows all the employees and their records." To this Karen made no reply, only offering a confused look, and Betty grumbled, her low complaints filling the air like the pungent smell of vitamin pills escaping from a bottle kept in a warm cupboard. As she felt herself sinking into a long symphony of untuned instruments playing in her head, she shook her hair away from her face and, once again in command, told Karen to render the police all the assistance they needed and consult her whenever she encountered a gap or other problem in the records. Relieved to see Betty once again in her usual frame of mind, Karen promised she would and smiled a genuine smile of relief, glad not to be the one responsible in this crisis.

That, unfortunately, was the only moment when everything seemed in order, at least as Betty regarded order. When she went out to question a young police officer about the locked studio, she received polite but meaningless replies, which so frustrated her that she wondered if it would be grossly impolitic to complain. At first she was undecided, but pressed by the crowd of fused bodies squished against the counter in her office, Betty dialed the police station. Unable to get through to Chief Silva, she had to settle for the officer on the desk, and his practical but unsatisfactory advice. Pulling out a red Magic Marker, then changing her mind and choosing a green one, Betty printed a notice in large letters that the painting studio would be closed until further notice. Finally, the weight of the weekend's events hardened around her and she drew out another sheet of paper and made up an announcement that students would be expected to give a short statement to the police and be available for questions. As she heard these words in her head, the noise of the building died away so that when she looked up, the door to the office was filled with the nine heads of a Hydra, each one different. Before her was what seemed to be a single body with curly brown hair, braids, a short orange flattop, and more; patches of colored eyes swirled from face to face, and lips were stunning in their apparent silence. The whole body looked like a monster on a television with the sound turned off. The vision lasted only for a second, until she pulled the signs from her desk and headed for the studio door.

"You'll have to let me through if you want to know anything," Betty said to the questions that crackled around her. As she moved into the hallway, the students sensed a change and information now coming to them, and swallowed their cries. They were subdued until she reached the locked door of the studio, where she taped up her signs.

"That's all I know," Betty said, turning back to the crowd. The questions began again, but the woman moved away, knowing that the single moment of silence for the day had just passed without her even having had a chance to enjoy it.

She put down the flap in the counter, once again in her office, and the telephone gave its fourth ring. Karen made no effort to answer it. She too had tuned out the rest of the school while she coped as best she could. That bothered Betty less, however, than the strange young man sitting beside her desk with a notebook open on his knee. When she looked over at Karen for an explanation, the younger woman looked away. The cup of tea she had been till then determined to enjoy, as a measure of her resistance to chaos, no longer sent off a shimmer of steam. Betty sat down and for the first time in her career said, "Who are you?"

"Mickey Concini," the young man said. "I'm a reporter for the *Traveler*." He smiled the winsome smile of the young, the eager, the neophyte, and Betty wondered if that was the only reason he looked familiar, or if he had been a student at the college in the last few years. It didn't matter, she decided, because he didn't matter. Nothing mattered but bringing order to this chaos and getting her life back to normal. Here it was, barely eleven o'clock in the morning, and she was already exhausted, and now this youngster wanted her thoughts, the insides of her head. Even worse, her tea, a special blend of ginger and other spices she had purchased in Chinatown only a few weeks earlier, was wasted, its soothing qualities having seeped into the mug, or the air, or, worst of all, the plastic spoon. It wasn't fair, thought Betty; it just wasn't fair.

"That's all I can tell you," she finally said to Mickey Concini's third question on the same point. For the next few minutes she watched the young man scribble in his notebook. She recognized the style of shorthand and was momentarily disoriented to think of men learning shorthand or typing. Dressed in jeans, a striped shirt, and denim jacket, the young man went on asking questions for the local newspaper. He was so obviously a beginner, or at least at the bottom of the heap at the paper, that Betty was led to conclude that Hank Vinnio wasn't important in the area, his death ranked no higher than a minor accident, and life would soon be back to normal, perhaps even by lunchtime. This was an entirely new prospect and cheered her up enormously. She was wrong, of course, but it would be a few days before she realized just how wrong. Emboldened by the prospect of calm and a return to normality, she said, "Why are you so interested in this?"

"I'm not," he said, letting his pen rest in his hand. "It seems to me, and my boss, just a run-of-the-mill murder, but I missed the cues on another death a little while ago. Maybe you heard about it? The woman from New York? Beth O'Donnell? No?"

Betty's features automatically took on a disapproving look, as though Mickey Concini were suddenly engaging her in salacious gossip. In fact, she was stuck on the idea of a run-of-the-mill murder, a concept she found hard to file anywhere in her capacious mind.

"Well," the reporter continued, wondering what he had said wrong, "I missed it and my boss sent me over to make sure I don't miss anything this time." Betty managed a smile and swallowed her ambivalent feelings.

"Is there anyone who could talk about him as an artist? Someone on remembering his work?"

Betty decided this probably wouldn't do any harm and tried to think of someone. "Well, he wasn't here very long."

"Did he sell anything?"

"I don't know. Professor Mattson doesn't encourage that in the beginning. He thinks students should concentrate on developing themselves into artists." She was suddenly aware of how strange this sounded and might have continued to explain but for the look in the reporter's eye.

"Mr. Mattson sells some of his stuff in town, doesn't he?"

"Yes."

"In a frame shop?"

"Did you have any other questions about Mr. Vinnio?" Betty's return to her office persona was instantaneous. The last thing she wanted was a reporter doing a story on other people at the college, at least not now. Mickey knew when to withdraw, and did.

Mickey Concini looked up and down the long hallway, taking in the clusters of students and how differently they looked from his classmates of less than four years ago. Then, anyone who went around with any kind of books, even art books, was more than a little strange. Here, everyone had books in hand. But other than that, he decided, they looked okay. It might be fun to interview one or two. His eye swept from one to another until he spotted an older student who had just stopped to read the signs taped to the studio door. Hurrying toward him, Mickey introduced himself.

"Chickie?" the reporter repeated aloud. "Short for?"

"Just Chickie."

"You know him? The guy who got killed?"

"Slightly."

"Can you tell me something about him? I mean, he was an older student like you—" Mickey paused when he saw an expression he couldn't read flicker in the other man's eyes. He seemed to be punching a lot of buttons today he didn't even know existed. "Was he a good friend?"

"No, I barely knew him. We just ran into each other once in a while. We had the same classes and we had the same work-study job."

"Part-time maintenance, right?"

"Yeah. Right. Look, why don't you talk to Buddy Lecroix, our maintenance head? He saw him all the time."

"Good idea. Where would I find Lecroix?"

"Downstairs, probably."

"Thanks. Anyone else I should talk to?"

"You might try Larry Segal. Over there," Chickie said, nodding to a man talking to a group of students nearby. "He teaches life drawing." When he noticed Mickey's blank look, Chickie explained the term. Mickey wrote it down.

"Was Vinnio any good as an artist?"

Chickie studied the reporter as though the answer to this question were as important as the identity of the murderer. "So-so. He had talent."

"But he wasn't great," Mickey was quick to conclude. "I was wondering if there was an angle about how the art world and the school lost one of its brightest lights. You know the kind of thing. Professor Mattson mourns the loss of a protégé, a new star, something like that." He stopped. "Isn't Mattson the chief artist around here?" Once again, Mickey waited for Chickie to answer; he was beginning to find the older student irritating.

"Not exactly," Chickie finally said. "He's head of the painting department, but there are a lot of good people here. Even if he were, I don't think Mattson would have picked Hank as his protégé."

"Not enough talent?" the reported probed, convinced he was onto something.

"Not enough talent. In Mattson," Chickie said as he turned to walk away.

Nasty, thought the young reporter as he scribbled a few notes, and interesting.

■ ■ ■

Karen sniffed, dabbed her eyes with a tissue, and flipped through three more files. She sighed and sobbed and slammed shut the file drawer. Called to the office early in the morning—at seven o'clock, to be exact—by the dean of the college, Karen had spent the early hours trying to absorb the shock but being thwarted by the necessity of finding files for the police, answering the telephone, and explaining the workings of the college to the dean, who suddenly had more questions than her mother on Saturday night. This wasn't at all how she had imagined a major crisis would be; she barely had a moment to get the details straight; and certainly no time at all just to think about it and swap ideas with her friends or the students. Betty Lane was no help either; the woman was working like a zealot who sniffed victory. And now Chief Silva himself was standing behind her waiting for the files. She wasn't getting to enjoy the excitement of it at all. Instead she was being pushed and pounded. At this rate the murder would be old news to students and faculty alike before she even got a chance to get her share of a gossip.

"I know it's here," she said to Silva, who stood patiently by her desk as she searched the next file drawer. "I remember him saying he didn't have any close relatives. He was quite clear about that. I asked him. His parents are dead." She sniffled.

Silva could well imagine the young woman before him pursuing her curiosity into whatever byways it led her. What piqued his curiosity, however, was that Vinnio had apparently been unperturbed by such questions, at least when they came from Karen.

"He was telling me once how hard it was because he was just a kid when they died, a teenager," Karen went on, pushing her head into the cabinet to get a look at the back of the drawer. "He said that's why he remembered them and everything about them so well, because it was all he had of them." Thus bringing herself to a new valley of sadness, Karen stopped her search to sob.

Vinnio was taking on an unexpectedly sympathetic coloring in Karen's narration, but also a greater clarity. There might be reasons he was *malcriado,* but he was so just the same. "Just how old was he when his parents died?" Silva asked.

"I think he was in high school." Karen's face suddenly assumed the look of one considering nothing more serious than the list of ingredients in a recipe. "I know he said he had an aunt still living."

"That's what I'm looking for. The name and address of the next of kin."

"It seems so little. Just an aunt." She rifled through another group of files. It was hard for her to think of Hank as dead. More real to her was the paucity of family, and she wondered if her sadness might be more a response to the turmoil around her than to the sudden loss of a man who worked in the college and occasionally pestered her for a free tea bag. In that he was different from almost everyone else on campus. Other people wanted something from the office, but few pushed until they got it.

Karen's mind drifted into a reverie of Hank's character while her hands went on searching. What struck her first was that he was most aggressive about the vending machines. Sometimes he lost money in the change machine and jollied her into unlocking the door so he could reclaim his money right away, but sometimes his five-dollar bill wasn't on top and he had to rifle through the stack of bills to get his, a five below a number of one-dollar bills. She'd never stopped to think about this before. It seemed unlikely, though, the more she thought about it now, that quite so many students had used the machine in the interval between his encounter and her rescue mission. And yet Hank was so open about everything that it never seemed before more than bad luck when he lost his money. Still, the memory nagged at her and she considered telling Chief Silva, just to get it off her mind.

Unaware that her face betrayed her pattern of thought, Karen went on searching and Silva went on watching, intrigued by the changes in her expression. By the time she came to the file with Hank's name on it, she was thinking hard about his problems with the vending machines.

"Here it is," she said, handing a manila folder to the chief. "He told me he had just one close relative. I said that was so sad, but he said I didn't have to worry, not about him. He had a few people he could count on for help if he needed it. That made me feel better but it really was so little." She began to sniffle again.

Silva read through the file, taking down the name of Vinnio's aunt and hometown. Karen no longer pretended to be talking to Silva; she was too concerned now with her own thoughts about the dead man. The oddities of his life had moved her to contemplate the oddity of his death.

"It's ironical when you think about it," Karen said philosophically. "I mean Hank dying that way."

"Really?" Silva's attention was captured by her new tone. "Why do you say that?"

"Well, we'd just been talking about dying, but I think he was afraid of dying in a fire."

"Did he tell you that?" The least expected idea now floated before Silva, that Vinnio's death was the result of a long campaign, one that the victim was aware of and helpless to stop. "Had he had any accidents lately? Any trouble outside work, at home?"

"No, I don't think so. I don't think it was anything that had happened to him. It was just something that came up a few days ago. He was in here the other day, during our coffee break—he always dropped by if he was here—anyway, he was telling us about a huge fire in his hometown when he was a kid." Karen recalled the scene, her glance moving to the corner of the desk where Hank had perched. "I don't think he ever expected to die from a crate falling on him."

Silva waited, then put his notebook away and returned the file. It wasn't odd at all to him that Vinnio might have had death on his mind, not if he was playing the game he sounded like he was playing. Silva glanced at Karen, who was frowning and thinking as she stared at her desk; she didn't seem to have picked up on the implications of what she had passed on to Silva. He rose to leave, but before he could turn away from her desk, Karen looked up at him.

"Chief Silva," she said, "there's something else I think I should tell you." Silva sat down again to listen to Karen's version of Hank's woes with the vending machine.

■ ■ ■

"They don't seem to know very much," Preston said to Betty Lane as he swung back and forth in his chair in his office. "Even though it seems a fairly simple matter."

"Yes," Betty agreed. When Professor Mattson called Betty Lane into his office a few minutes after one o'clock, just as she was about to escape for lunch in the town, she complied with ambivalence. The ongoing crisis that had made her office almost unbearable had been shut out by Preston by the simple act of closing his door to his office and staying inside. Entering his cubicle, therefore, meant at least a respite from the racket that still echoed up and down the corridor, but it also meant, Betty knew from experience, some inane task calculated to make the chairman of the painting department feel he was the center of attention once again. Unable to slip away unseen or claim a prior call from the dean or president, Betty complied, answering Preston's questions with her back to his closed office door, admiring the efficient soundproofing of the tiny office.

"And they don't need anything more of the school?"

"What? No, no," she said. "I don't think so, but with the police one never knows. I suppose Chief Silva still has to question a number of people. Apparently he's planning on doing that today. Another officer has been questioning the students who usually have class in there, anyone who knew," she paused, "the deceased slightly, but not well." If she noticed the tautology in her reply, she left it uncorrected, for once, but Preston didn't notice. Nor did he ever.

"I wonder what sort of investigator Chief Silva is," Mattson said, looking up at the ceiling.

"I'm sure I couldn't say." Betty snapped shut her mouth in her obvious reluctance to say anything against the chief of police, but her distaste for the man was obvious. Her shoulders straight and stiff, she stood even straighter when she mentioned his name.

"He is, after all, not local." She said this deferentially, knowing that Preston would take this as she meant it, a complimentary reference to their long association with the area. They might not be natives, but they were almost as good as.

"An awful thing to have happen," Preston said, thereby revealing that he was beginning to brood on the death. "To lie there all those hours."

"Quite," Betty said, watching him suspiciously.

"He must have lain there for several hours before he died. At least, that's what the police think."

"Yes," Betty said. "It's better not to think about it, Professor. After all, it's not really our business, is it?"

"No, I suppose it isn't. Still," he said, swinging back and forth in his chair, "I think we have to take command of the situation."

Betty Lane was nonplussed. This was not at all what she had expected. She was ready for extra work, time-wasting work, but not a foray into the purview of the police. She tried to deter him and salvage her quiet lunch. "Ah, sir, I think the police—"

"Forget the police," Preston said with a languid wave of his hand. Betty groaned. "This is an opportunity to instruct the students in the artists' health hazards." He banged his hand on his desk. "Don't we have some sort of booklet about this? The dangers of various chemical substances for artists?"

"Well, yes," Betty said, "but—"

"No buts. This is just the time for it." Preston ignored Betty as the idea sprouted and bloomed before him. "A careless death in the studio. What better time to drive home the message." His voice grew fervent, like a minister warming to the sins of his congregation.

Betty barely had time to agree before he sent her off in search of various publications on health hazards for artists in the studio. At first she was angry that he had outmaneuvered her, for she had over the years sketched a number of responses to Preston's more common but oblique tangents, but as she returned to her desk, she reconsidered. If this temporary obsession kept him occupied and relieved the tension in the office, she would gladly go along with it. Anything might be better than riding the free-falling car of his emotions. Nevertheless, she wondered how the students might regard this plunge into safety precautions.

Betty pulled out a large manila folder from her right-hand drawer and fingered the sheets and brochures, wondering how long Preston would stay with this issue. If it kept him occupied for a week, she would be satisfied, for she realized at 8:30 that morning that the police would be in and out quietly but relentlessly until they were satisfied. The more occupied the faculty and staff were with their work—or anything else, for that matter—the easier it would be for her to cope with the police and the inevitable turmoil.

After she finished checking the files, Betty closed the drawer with the toe of her black patent-leather shoe, straightened out her neat woolen skirt and white silk blouse, and collected the pile of pamphlets. She made no effort to read them, and had no curiosity about their contents or usefulness. It wasn't necessary for her job, she reasoned. In fact, she was persuaded that such enthusiasms might interfere with her efficiency as a secretary. And so she remained the highly efficient business secretary who would have been equally well suited to the small businesses that prospered in the town.

"This should be everything." She deposited the pile on Preston's desk and was glad to see that it was more than he had expected.

"Ah, excellent," he said with a tight smile. "That will do admirably. Thank you, Betty." He dismissed her with a wave of his hand. It was just after 1:40, too late to meet her friends for lunch.

■ ■ ■

Chickie Morelli made no objections to stopping his work to speak with Chief Silva, which alone told Silva something he wanted to know. Scheduled to begin work at two o'clock for Buddy Lecroix, Chickie had only an hour to himself Monday through Thursday, and he willingly gave it up today for the chief, or at least he appeared to do so. Turning his back to Silva, the student put away his work and settled himself on a stool, ready for Silva to begin, all without a question, a challenge, a comment of any kind.

When Silva told him that he planned to talk to Buddy's other work-study students, Chickie still said nothing, only waited. It was as though he had something important to say to Silva but only the perfect question, planed smooth like a ship's keel, could bring about the conversation the chief wanted. Silva probed with the ordinary questions, tacking closer to the other man's life.

"I need to know where you were on Saturday," Silva said.

"Mostly at work. I was at home and then I went in to work." He outlined his work schedule at the warehouse, making sure Silva had time to get it all down.

"I'll have someone check the times; we'll be doing this with everyone." Chickie nodded. "You work with a crew? People who were with you all afternoon?" Silva asked. Chickie shook his head.

"I was alone most of the afternoon. I always am. The super'll tell you that." He offered no more, and Silva asked him a few questions about his job before changing the topic.

"Why this school? And why now?"

"I wanted to come back East, and I spent time here with an aunt and uncle when I was younger. It seemed the logical place."

Silva made a note but forbore from commenting that it didn't seem much of an answer. He knew a lot about Chickie from the personnel files before he arrived and for most people that was enough; the personal interview brought him specifics about the events surrounding the crime and told him what the other person was like. But that wasn't happening in this interview. Chickie was honest if somewhat laconic, but he was also much more complex than Silva had anticipated. The chief was beginning to feel that his questions penetrated no deeper than a mosquito bite, and were being taken just as seriously. He felt frustrated. "You worked closely with Hank Vinnio."

"No, not at all." Chickie answered quickly, and Silva thought he heard in the other man an eagerness to distance himself from the murder victim.

"You were both working for Buddy, weren't you?"

"Yes, but we had different shifts. I get off at six and Hank came on at six."

"Still, you would have met four days a week when the shifts changed." Silva watched to see how Chickie handled this persistence, for he was certain the relationship of the two men as workers had something to tell him.

"Maybe."

"What does 'maybe' mean, Mr. Morelli? Did you meet Mr. Vinnio when the shift changed or didn't you?"

Chickie rearranged his feet on the dowels of the stool. When he looked up Silva was staring hard at him. "He wasn't usually here when I left work."

"You left early?" Silva hadn't expected Chickie to turn out to be an ordinary chiseler; his instincts told him something completely different about the student.

"No. I left on time, or later." Chickie paused. "I didn't even realize who he was until two weeks into the term because he was late to work so consistently. I said hello to him in classes as though he were just another student, but I didn't realize he also worked here. I think someone must have spoken to him about it, his coming in late so often, because he started to show up on time this past week. As it was, he was still late more often than not. But he had talent, real talent." The last sentence rushed out of him like a flame from a newly lit gas jet. And yet it seemed to Silva far too mild a reason for Chickie's earlier manner, laconic to a point verging on sullenness. There had to be more.

"I didn't realize he was one of the serious ones," Silva commented.

"He wasn't. I don't think he really understood the extent of his talent. I don't know. Maybe he did and just didn't care." He shrugged, perhaps defeated by the inexplicability of Hank's attitude.

"What makes you think someone spoke to him about his tardiness at work?" Silva asked, shifting course.

"It was just a feeling I got. He came in mad one day, complaining about Professor Mattson and Buddy Lecroix. I figured Buddy had complained to the dean and the dean had told Mattson to have a talk with Hank."

"So Hank was Professor Mattson's student."

"No," Chickie said, starting to laugh. He waved his hand and shook his head to erase Silva's misunderstanding. "Professor Mattson was in general responsible for all of the painting students, but Hank was definitely not one of his students. They didn't get along."

"How do you know that? Did they have a run-in?"

"Sort of. When Hank first arrived he didn't know anyone here. Well, the first day of day classes was a Tuesday, but the first evening classes were on Monday. Hank apparently passed Mattson in the hall; Mattson was carrying a finished canvas, I guess. Anyway, Hank took one look at his canvas and figured he was looking for the Monday evening class, and gave him directions for it. Mattson did not like that at all."

"So?" Silva said. "Mattson must be pretty thin-skinned."

"The Monday evening class is open enrollment. If you can find the building, you can take the class. It's designed for anyone who wants to try their hand at painting. Sometimes someone with talent wanders in, but mostly it's for adults who want to do something artsy for a few weeks." Chickie indicted the entire membership of the Monday class without any sign that he knew this might be unfair or unjustified; nor did he seem to be trying to provoke Silva to challenge him. Silva made a note to find out just how good an artist Chickie Morelli was supposed to be.

"So Hank in effect insulted Professor Mattson," Silva said.

"Yup. And after Mattson introduced himself, with all the dignity of his position, Hank just shrugged and walked away." Chickie laughed to himself.

"This is what Hank told you."

"Right. So you see, if Mattson had told Hank to toe the line, he would not have been very happy about it."

Silva could imagine the pleasure a *malandro* like Vinnio might gain from telling this story to anyone who would listen; it made the head of a department look bad in a number of ways that would appeal to Vinnio and others like him—vain, insecure, angry, dishonest. Silva wondered if the older student had any like-minded friends here. Vinnio might have had talent, but apparently not the temperament for art school or an art career.

Chickie's story added another layer to the armature on which Silva had been creating his portrait of the victim. The figure was thick and round now, and his features were still uncertain, but they were gaining shape with each interview. And so were Mattson's.

"Did he ever say anything else about Professor Mattson, or anyone else he might have had a run-in with?"

Chickie shook his head. "He just said a few times that Mattson was a lucky man, that he got a lot of breaks."

"What did he mean by that, 'a lot of breaks'?"

"I have no idea. I just thought he meant in general that Mattson was lucky to have done so well." Chickie's eyes slid away like a marble missing its mark in a pinball machine. Whatever he had just told Silva had made him exceedingly uncomfortable.

"Just how intense was his resentment of Mattson?"

"Not very. It was just that one run-in. They stayed out of each other's way after that." Chickie was trying to soften whatever expression he had painted on the dead man's face. Silva wasn't surprised when Chickie looked at his watch, feigned surprise at the time, and sought an end to the interview so he could get to work on time. Silva let him go, wondering just how sensitive a middle-aged painter might be if he were insulted by a brash but talented laborer.

■ ■ ■

Preston Mattson's character was not the product of chance, the effect of a capricious will upon clay. Quite the contrary. Preston gave much thought to his behavior, holding himself responsible for even the smallest nuances in his life. In his earliest years this trait meant an authenticity in his relationships, but as he responded to the new demands of administrative positions, the trait produced almost the opposite effect. By the time he reached forty, his self-consciousness was a habit without depth.

A man conscious of his public image, Preston never moved hastily, no matter what the provocation. He moved at a self-aware pace everywhere, a pace designed to reveal casualness and easy control. The provocations of the day tested the limits of his patience and self-discipline, and he was not found wanting. In retrospect, he was actually pleased with how he had conducted himself, and his failure to find Ellen at the door when he arrived home had irritated him. For the first time that day he didn't have an audience.

The customary sounds of his home in the early evening also did not greet him. Monday evenings required a light and simple repast, since Ellen left immediately thereafter for her painting class, and Preston had come to enjoy the muted sounds of the preparations. But tonight he heard the drawers slamming and cutlery crashing into the sink in a syncopation distinct from the usual soft, rhythmic sounds of the housekeeper. Recognizing the rare but distinctive cacophony of his wife at work, Preston moved toward the kitchen, where he now expected to find her, and this irritated him even more. It did not agree with his image of himself to have a wife who preferred the confines of the kitchen to the pleasures of greeting her husband at the door.

"Ah, there you are," he said to her back. Ellen was standing at the sink tearing apart a head of lettuce as he spoke; she did not turn around or acknowledge his entrance in any way. This irritated him further. It probably would not have mollified him to know that the effect of her behavior was unintentional, a measure of how little her husband's arrival could grip her mind, for her thoughts were just then on one of the few philosophical questions ever to enter her head. So unexpected was this radical view of past and present connected in one life that she could barely contemplate the salad before her with any equanimity. Each choice, even to something so minor as cutting next a tomato or a green pepper, filled her until she felt no larger than the discarded pulp of the fruit before her. All else was crowded out of her consciousness, even—or perhaps especially—Preston.

"You've stopped attending classes, have you?" Preston asked in a flippant tone. The irrelevance of the query penetrated the miasma surrounding Ellen and she turned to her husband. She gave the only reply she could think of.

"I didn't feel well. And Mrs. D. had to leave early, so I had to get back."

This was not what Preston had expected, and he was momentarily stalled as he tried to find another failing to charge her with. The less comprehensible her behavior was, the more aggrieved Preston became, and the more he tried to reach her through accusation. He held in the back of his mind that by luck or by insight, one of his accusations would hit a target and Ellen would respond in a manner that would relieve him of his ill will. He had no idea what that reply might be, but he was certain it existed and he only had to knock it loose, like a clay pigeon fired in a skeet shoot.

"The police were questioning people all day today, anyone who knew the victim, other students, faculty, staff. The janitor too, I suppose, since he found the body." He waited for Ellen to turn around. "I expect they'll be coming back tomorrow." Ellen wrung the head of lettuce in half.

"I see no reason for you to be fussing over dinner quite this early," he said to her back.

"I don't feel well. I just want to get it over with."

"I see. Well, I'm sorry you're unwell." He watched her work for a few moments. "From what the police say, Hank Vinnio died Saturday in the painting studio. They seem to think he fell unconscious sometime earlier, in the evening or perhaps in the afternoon. They're not sure." He waited, but still Ellen made no comment.

"I don't recall if you mentioned seeing him on Saturday when you went over to the school." Irritation and frustration alone had brought him to this question, and now he wished he hadn't asked it; but he felt compelled to go on. "Did you?" He tried to make the question sound jovial, a mere filler of the silence.

"I really want to get this done, Preston." Ellen spoke in the tone of exasperation reserved for those times when she found herself alone and responsible in the kitchen. Foolishly, Preston felt warmly toward his wife for the first time that evening.

"Of course, dear. I just thought perhaps you had seen Mr. Vinnio on Saturday and could perhaps tell the police that he was fine in the afternoon. They might find that useful." He had faced the undulating black doubt in his heart squarely, in his view, and felt strengthened by the encounter and his handling of it. He need have no worry of any unseemly involvement in Vinnio's death. Moreover, Ellen might even have useful information for the police. It pleased him to think his wife might help them in an important case. Satisfied, he let his mind drift again to the immediate problem. "I'm sorry you're not well. Don't overdo it, now. It's much more important that you not overtax yourself. Let's see how quickly we can manage dinner." He went to the dining table, checking the preparations and fussing over a fork here and a spoon there. Satisfied with these arrangements, he moved into the living room and settled down with his newspaper.

■ ■ ■

Brushes dabbed on canvases and students pondered their work during the regular Monday evening painting class. Chief Silva had finally decided he'd had enough of the studio and released it for regular use. The students had all but lunged through the door to set up their canvases, then discreetly, shyly, awkwardly, avoided the large stained area near the back. At first they worked in an uneasy silence, then a soft buzz rose as students began to talk among themselves on ostentatiously irrelevant and unimportant topics—the weather, the latest campaign news, the rotting apple in the still life. The red-haired man dabbed, scraped, studied, and dabbed again.

Lisa Hunt cocked her head to one side, then the other, and was generally displeased at what she saw from both angles. She looked over to her right, but Ellen Mattson wasn't there, so she looked to her left. She knew she was being nosy, but ever since she had watched Joe Silva investigate the murder of Beth O'Donnell, she had a free-running curiosity about murder. She wanted to know whatever there was to know, and who knew it and what they thought about it. She leaned forward to listen, her paintbrush waving aimlessly in the air. After a while, her attentiveness paid off. Though later than she had expected, the students began to talk among themselves, in twos and threes, about Hank Vinnio's death.

"Right there." The man nodded to the stained floor.

"I can't believe it." His companion glanced skeptically at the stain. The older the age of the student, the less interest he or she evinced, and the less time spent on it. As a result, Lisa found herself edging closer to her left, where two young women were painting less and less and talking more and more.

"Aren't you surprised there are so many people here tonight?" the first one asked. "When I heard about what happened"—she paused to look around in case anyone was listening—"you know, I almost didn't come." She glanced at her friend. "I thought more people would object to having a class in a room where there was a murder."

"Shshshshsh." Shocked, her friend tried to quiet her.

"Well, it was—a murder, I mean."

"Shshshshsh." Her friend looked around again. "Who was he? Did you know him?"

"You know who he was. He used to come in here sometimes. He used to watch one of the other women. She wasn't very good, so I think he was just hitting on her, you know, kind of interested. You remember." She tried urgently to get her friend to understand.

"Who? Who was he after?"

The other woman looked around, then shook her head. "She's not here tonight." Lisa ran her eyes over the other students, making a mental note of those who were missing, or at least as many of them as she could remember. She wasn't aware of Vinnio's having been interested in anyone in particular.

"What did he look like?" the second one asked.

"He was dark. Don't you remember him?"

"Sort of. What was he like?"

"I don't know. I never really talked to him, just said hello once in a while."

"Wait a minute. Didn't you have coffee with him one time?"

"Yup. You know what he told me? He said—"

Lisa leancd forward to hear, grasping her easel to steady herself. "Ow!" She fell back onto her stool and quickly stuck her fingers in her mouth. A few seconds later she extended her hand to study the damage: blood from a small cut stained the jagged edge of a broken purple-painted fingernail.

"Oh, look at that," she moaned.

"Life chipping away at your disguise?" a soft Scottish voice said.

6
TUESDAY

POISED on the threshold of maturity, the art students had listened intently during the last day and a half to the news about Hank Vinnio, maintaining an uneasy silence in the presence of faculty members passing on information about the death and the police investigation. Once satisfied that Hank's death did not entail an inordinate change in their daily life, the majority of students exhaled in relief. They were not callous or unfeeling, or even uninterested; they were merely their age. Self-absorbed and easily pricked to sympathize, they just as easily returned to their usual thoughts, their glimpse of the real world disappearing like sunspots at dusk. They focused once again on their own pressing problems; for some this meant studying for a test or writing a paper, for others it meant mastering the art of developing color film, and for a smaller group it meant managing the details of Professor Mattson's exhibit.

Doug, Steven, and Noel studied the figures Marilyn had printed on a large pad of tracing paper and set up on an easel in the corner of an unused painting studio. A few other students, at first curious about the trio watching Marilyn and then interested in their project, had drifted over to them, pondered the figures, and settled down to learn more about this unusual form of expression.

"Orange for the right column," one newcomer said, thinking only of design and shape, not content.

"Awesome," another commented, equally uninterested in the significance of the chart. "And shades of rust red on the other column."

"That's not what it's for," Noel told them. Her glance at the pad of paper, however, suggested she too was straying from Marilyn's intent. The grumbles and mumbles, like pebbles rolling down a slope, prodded others to speak up until comments and questions bounced like boulders tumbling down a hill. Then, just as suddenly, the students fell silent.

Chickie Morelli sat apart from them and listened. Abjuring any interest in the exhibition or the gallery, he nevertheless managed to appear at every meeting, unnoticed until silence fell, which sucked him into the circle, like matter into a vacuum. And yet he drew away every time. Now the other students, perhaps unconsciously, skipped a beat in their debates, halting just long enough for Chickie to interject a comment, but so far he hadn't.

"I don't think it's made any difference," Noel said, referring to Hank Vinnio's death.

"Of course it has," Doug said. He sat up straight to emphasize his view.

"No, I don't think so," Noel repeated, gaining confidence after she reconsidered her opinion and again found it valid. "No one was very interested in the show before Vinnio's death, and no one's very interested now. His death hasn't made any difference at all." When her efforts to qualify for a grant from the local arts council failed, after spending most of Monday morning talking informally with the council secretary about the Byzantine rules, Noel had given up and gone to visit Marilyn and complain about her bad luck. She was not yet ready to admit defeat, fortunately, for Marilyn too had ended the day with her own flock of failures, but her reaction was different. Friend and friend had settled down to take a hard look at their progress so far. The result had been

Marilyn's chart of figures. For Marilyn, seeing was believing. Noel was her first convert.

"Noel's right," another young man broke in before Doug could insist that Noel was wrong. "I was out most of last week. No one was interested then. We might as well face it. We thought we had a really hot idea for a show, but we have nowhere near the money we need to pay for it."

"Yeah. We still need money for framing, publicity, a brochure of some sort."

"And food." Lots of murmurs accompanied this announcement.

"Let's face it. No one cares about the exhibit—at least no one outside the school." Again, a chorus of voices concurred.

"Have you raised any money at all?" Chickie asked. Less surprised by the question than who it came from, the students stumbled in their acknowledgment before thinking of an answer.

"We sold just four ads and got a few donations. Small ones," Noel replied first. "And if we don't have a catalog or some kind of program for the exhibit, we'll have to give the money back." This prospect seemed more real and more depressing than the failure to raise the rest of the money, and Noel lapsed into a brooding silence as she contemplated returning the funds so laboriously and embarrassingly solicited.

"That's really nowhere near enough," Chickie commented as though to himself but loud enough so that everyone else could hear him. "And your chart represents, left, what you've done so far with Mattson and, right, what you think now you could do with this new idea." The others nodded, murmured, and turned their eyes to the chart. For long seconds they contemplated its symmetry as much as the information it was meant to convey.

Only Doug looked on, grim and dissatisfied. He leaned back in the metal folding chair, tilting up his chin and locking his arms across his chest. Every rippling of his body announced his opinion and no one there was inclined to challenge him on it. "I shouldn't have left it to you guys. It's too big a job for beginners. You have to be able to—" A rush of sound, cries of anger and protest, groans of annoyance, arose from the others.

"Look, it's done," Steven said. "Marilyn's come up with a really good idea; it'll get us out of the hole. No one loses face and we get the money we need. Tomorrow, if it's all right with you, Noel, we can tell the people who bought ads what we want to do. If they like it, they'll probably let us keep their money and use it. If not, we'll just have to give it back."

This declaration prompted another wave of sound, but this time of enthusiasm. A few called out suggestions for improvement, advice on how to approach the store owners and other donors. Steven nodded at the most ingenious ones and found himself anticipating conversations he might have tomorrow.

"Thanks," Steven said. "I'll try that. Look, guys, I have to get downtown now. I can't give my life to this exhibit. We'll let you know what happens." He got up, folded his chair, and leaned it against the wall as he spoke. Not wanting to be left with Doug, Noel followed Steven's lead. The departure of two of the principals of the project signaled an end for the other students as well, and slowly, almost uncertainly, they left the group and wandered out of the studio. Doug remained in his chair, making notes on a small pocket calendar. Chickie watched him.

"Well, that's the end of that." Doug tossed the notebook into his black leather portfolio case, which stood open against the wall. "Unless you've got any ideas."

"Nope." Chickie hadn't so much as uncrossed his legs while the other students departed.

"This is really going to look bad." Doug grimaced at the floor. "Really bad."

"Why?"

"Why? Are you crazy?" Doug, startled, jerked his head up to look at Chickie. "The guy's the head of the place. Mattson is the man around here. How's it going to look if we can't even manage a decent show for the chairman of the department?" He spoke passionately, then leaned forward, resting his forearms on his legs. "The guy won't want anything to do with us."

Chickie sat, thinking this over. "Is that bad?"

Doug gawked at him, indignation growing in his face. "Is that—" He stopped as he caught Chickie's firm, direct gaze. Doug's look of indignation changed to confusion, then thoughtfulness. Chickie stood up, folded his chair, and leaned it against the wall.

■ ■ ■

Lisa's eyes locked with those of Steve Badger, owner of the Harbor Light restaurant, who stood at his usual spot at the end of the counter near the kitchen door. Without sending so much as a ripple across the starched white apron that draped him from chest to knee, he moved his eye down the row of booths along the wall until he came to one with an empty banquette. Lisa slid into the booth and settled down on the sturdy red leather seat. Ed Correll nodded to her and went on with his lunch. His ready acquiescence made Lisa wonder if anyone ever thought about challenging Badger's practice of assigning seats. It might be churlish, even rude, for a diner seated at a booth to refuse to share with a newcomer, but was that also true of someone standing at the door who was willing to wait until a booth was empty? Lisa didn't know anyone who had chosen to defy Badger, who was reluctant to let anyone linger unattended for entirely avaricious reasons.

When Steve saw Lisa settling in, he left his post in a stately manner befitting his size and good opinion of himself and his customers and made his way to her booth. The only

thing Badger enjoyed more in life than firing his chief waitress, Clara, on alternate Mondays was complimenting his customers, and he was glad of the opportunity presented by Lisa
Hunt. When he was finally willing to let her choose a meal, he
passed her order to a waitress.

Lisa expected her partner to look up, but her lunch
arrived before any sign of acknowledgment came from Ed.
Clara plunked down a plate in front of Lisa, announcing the
order in a voice anticipatory of complaints, questions, and
grumblings. To Ed, however, she gave a quizzical look and
carefully placed a bill near his plate. This occurrence Lisa considered as strange as if Badger had not spoken to her. Ed
turned over his bill and counted out a modest tip. Still curious, Lisa said, "This must be the only place that still serves
tuna fish on plain white bread and canned tomato soup." Ed
smiled but said nothing. Lisa tried again. "No one will ever
accuse Badger of being pretentious, at least."

Ed gave an obligatory smile of appreciation, seemed to
accept that something in the nature of a conversational comment was expected of him, and said, "You're a friend of Ellen
Mattson's, aren't you?"

"Yes, I suppose I am." This was not at all what Lisa had
expected, and she thought she might regret her overtures.
After all, she only wanted to pass the time without having to
think. "How did you know?"

"I saw you two together a few days ago. At the college."

"We take a painting class together. I'm terrible, but she's
only awful."

"Oh, I see," Ed said.

Well, I don't, thought Lisa.

"I don't see much of Ellen anymore," Ed said. When Lisa
looked blank, he explained. "She used to be my sister-in-law.
She was married to my older brother, Joey. Joey Correll?" he
said. "He died a few years ago in a car accident."

"Yes, now I remember. I'm sorry. Ellen told me she'd

been married before." She tried to recall exactly what Ellen had told her. She had a vague recollection that cars had been part of the man's life as well as his death. "It must have been tragic, especially since he was so young. They couldn't have been married very long."

"A while. They were very young when they got married. She was just twenty, and Joey was a few years older, but he was already out of school and started in his construction business."

"I don't remember him at all." In truth, Lisa didn't even recognize the name.

"He did most of his business north of here." Ed waved his check and a ten-dollar bill at Badger, who swooped down on the outstretched hand in a matter of seconds, a mass of white filling the narrow aisle. Service at the Harbor Light was at certain moments startlingly swift.

"How long ago did he die?" Lisa asked.

"Just a few years ago," Ed replied, obviously surprised by Badger's sudden appearance. It dawned on Lisa that Ed seemed a stranger because he was; she never saw him in places like the Harbor Light, where she expected to see everyone she knew at least once in a while. From Clara's treatment of him, he might be a tourist, even an enemy. "Joey died just when things were really starting to go his way. They'd been married ten years, and things were really looking good for him."

"That's too bad." Even as she said this, she wanted to know why this younger brother still seemed to feel so strongly about it.

"Yeah. He'd already done in a few years what most of us take a lifetime to do, or at least our entire careers."

The tone of jealous resentment was not lost on Lisa, who leaned back in the booth, replying only with an "Ahh, I see." Lisa knew where Ellen and Preston lived, and as nice as the house was, she thought Ed had an exaggerated view of his brother's success, at least based on what she had seen of Ellen's lifestyle. But that was none of her business, she reminded herself. Let this be a lesson, she thought, to avoid a companion for lunch just for the purpose of conversation.

"He was right in the middle of cutting this big deal and he showed up one day with this teenager almost, Ellen. He'd married her over the weekend. And we'd never even heard of her, let alone met the girl." Ed continued to shake his head, then gave a short nervous laugh when he caught Lisa's eye. She smiled. "I guess it didn't really slow him down, though; he made a lot of other deals after that. So there was no harm done." When he went on, he seemed bent on recasting his earlier views. "We were all really fond of Joey and we hated to see him grow up, I guess." Ed might have been satisfied with his effort to soften his comments, but Lisa could still hear an undercurrent. "And then he died," he said, forgetting his brother's ten years of marriage and career as a developer.

Ed disengaged himself with a skill Lisa admired, but not enough to forget his words: "no harm done." That was certainly one of the most peculiar ways in which anyone had referred to a relative's marriage. The jealousy was still evident after all these years, and Lisa wondered if it was the loss of Joey or the acquisition of Ellen as a sister-in-law that lay behind it. Ellen was, even to Lisa, a trifle unsettling. In little time Lisa had learned to tolerate the other woman's personality, mainly because she had no intention of getting any closer to her. Ellen had little to say about herself and her life, yet she always seemed to draw the spotlight to her. If she put Lisa off, what must she have been like as a new member of a family? These qualities in the newcomer to a close-knit family could easily produce resentment, Lisa reasoned. She thought back to the day they had met in the painting class. Ellen was a terrible artist, even Lisa knew that. No. They'd met before class, in the parking lot, near the steps. Lisa's sandwich sat uneaten long enough to raise concern in Badger, who 364 days out of 365 only cared if a customer paid the bill.

■ ■ ■

In twenty years as an artist, Preston Mattson had rarely found himself staring down (or up) at his canvases with an objective eye. Granted, he had never had much opportunity since taking on administrative work, but the few experiences from his earlier years remained foremost in his memory. The worst part of these had nothing to do with art. He had never lost the small knot in his stomach that came when he was looking at his artwork. He had overheard an early painting instructor tell another student in a college class that she could consider herself professional, or at least mature, when she no longer winced whenever she looked at her work. Such an experience in the artist's early years was partly the embarrassment of the young, the kind of immaturity and self-consciousness that brought giggles from boys and girls when they heard words like *frigate* in a poem read aloud in class. Preston knew this; he even lectured himself, but to no avail. Over the years he had persuaded himself that this was just the result of his shyness, a trait he had found useful to invoke at several points in his career.

On this day, however, the practical demands facing him crowded out any finer feelings, as he now described his discomfort. He forgot his awkwardness as he looked at the dozen or so canvases scattered around his living room, propped on the sofa, leaning against the fireplace, sitting on chairs. He might never stop wincing, but over the years he'd learned to speak quite eloquently about his work, about the patterns that had reappeared over twenty years, the colors that darkened or lightened but never changed dramatically. Preston prided himself on his consistency. He knew that Albert P. Ryder had spent years reworking one figure in an effort to resolve a particular aesthetic problem. Preston couldn't recall what that problem was, but he liked to point out to friends and colleagues how he too had concentrated on resolving one particular aesthetic problem. He was, of course, careful who he said this to.

He counted fourteen paintings, and there were supposed to be fifteen. He looked around him, then in the kitchen near the cellar stairs, where he found a small unframed canvas, and returned to the living room. When he placed the canvas on the floor and let it lean against the sofa, he was momentarily taken aback by the sameness of the paintings in the room. For all his talk on why he did this or did that, he sometimes wondered why, in fact, he did. He set that question aside for another time, as he always had before.

Preston was expecting three crates from California, where he had sent, more hopefully than realistically, a number of paintings to be shown by a gallery that had expressed interest after his success with a poster design. Unfortunately, nothing had come of his hopes, and the crates were on their way back. They would make his task easier, but not much more so. He still had most of his best work right in front of him.

Taking a deep breath, he stepped back for a good look. He had set out his paintings to make it easier for him to pick a certain number, a select few, for his exhibit. He should have made the choices long before this, he knew; but he'd had other things on his mind. Only now did he feel ready, even eager, to choose and arrange. That was a side of the gallery duties recently assigned to him that he had unexpectedly found he enjoyed. It was gratifying to think he had a natural ability for administration. Perhaps his natural abilities better suited him to the dean's position, or even the president's, than to teaching. His mind lingered on this, but he admitted that the prospect was not in the immediate future. Once again, he turned his mind reluctantly to the task at hand.

Most of the canvases were 16 by 20 or less, a fact that had slipped his notice until now. That meant, he calculated, that he could show more than he had originally intended. Granted, he'd always known it would be an intimate show, since the gallery was small, but the realization that he could include more paintings warmed him.

Pondering the display, he recalled another set of canvases stored in the basement. An excellent idea, he thought. He could hang canvases from every period of his career, showing the many different ways he had approached his art. A retrospective, he said to himself, mulling over in his imagination the vision of a show of the work produced during the last twenty or more years.

And yet, somehow the idea didn't seem quite right. Preston shifted a few paintings around on the sofa, trying different arrangements by size, color, date. Since they were all abstracts of the same pattern, he had fewer options when it came to subject matter, so to speak. He had stopped doing landscapes several years ago, finding them increasingly unsatisfying. But even the few realistic paintings and drawings Kathy Fazio had recovered from the college store and moved to the gallery wouldn't noticeably alter the overall feeling of the collection now before him. Perhaps he was going about it wrong. He considered arrangements by title, by shape, by medium (oil, acrylic, watercolors). More than an hour passed while he carried canvases first here, then there.

After a while Preston felt tired and even a little unsteady on his feet. He cleared off a chair and sat down, facing at eye level the paintings on the sofa. Some of these he had tried to sell through the galleries in the surrounding area when they had first opened. The various owners over the years had been interested, even occasionally enthusiastic, but nothing had ever come of his many meetings with them. The only instance when he had achieved anything resembling commercial success was when he had submitted a design for a festival poster at Ellen's insistence, and with some pointers on what to include; the print had sold but not well enough to justify a second run.

Those had been heady days for Preston. An agent had gone over the original painting for the design with a care and intent the professor rarely witnessed. Perhaps he should include that one in the show. There were a few other instances when someone had looked closely at one of his paintings, and he remembered each one. Preston meditated on those moments, the individual canvases rising in his mind like skyscrapers in a desert, sunlight turning them into jewels. More enthusiastic than he had been since he started, he turned back to the canvases scattered around the room. He would select those canvases that had produced the most intense responses in the viewer. So thinking, Preston drew from the scattered paintings the select few that had made viewers pause, if not purchase. He arrayed these along one wall of the living room; there were five.

Well, at least that's a start, Preston thought with a sigh.

■ ■ ■

Lisa Hunt watched the officer slip out of the police station, the grim look on his face reflecting the equally grim look she caught on Chief Silva's face as he moved around his office. If this is what the investigation is producing, she thought, maybe things are worse than I thought. She was drawing away from the front desk when Officer Maxwell nodded to her from Chief Silva's doorway.

"You look like you were going to change your mind," Silva said to her as she settled into a chair and tried to rearrange her legs. She had long, graceful, athletic limbs, he saw, but she never seemed to be doing anything athletic. She must have been born with them. When he looked up, he was glad she was still glancing at the notices and awards on the walls. He wished he didn't feel so uncomfortable. He would gladly talk to her about any subject, at any time, but he wanted it to be outside his office; anywhere would do. Here, he felt defined by his job, his person erased by his title. And with Lisa he wanted it to be the other way around, his title erased by his person.

Chief Silva was locked inside his own thoughts, so he did

not notice how curious Lisa was about his office. Subscribing to the theory that our homes and work places reveal more about our character than our words, she was eager to have a legitimate reason, short of an arrest, to get a look at his place of work. But now that she saw it, she was disappointed. Either Joe Silva had no personal identity or the office was far too small for him to express himself. She was about to choose the latter interpretation when she caught sight of a grouping of small framed photographs hung low on the inner wall. They hung below a group of framed awards, but she wasn't close enough to them to see what they were.

Turning to face him, she let her eyes run over his desk, but the only personal item there was a cube of Plexiglas that displayed small squares of lace, each face of those she could see showing a different pattern. This too was unexpected, almost inexplicable. She thought of the hours they had spent together after the murder of Beth O'Donnell, getting to know each other again. Those had been weeks of personal discovery too, and Lisa now realized she must have ignored the signs of someone else in Joe Silva's life.

Lisa immediately set about speculating who might have given him the Plexiglas cube. She dismissed Mrs. Alesander, his landlady, at once, and fixed her sinking heart on an unknown lady friend. Well, she thought philosophically, the man has a right to keep his private life private. But what really rankled Lisa was her complete ignorance of this woman. Chief Silva had managed, in a town the size of Mellingham, to actually have a private life, a life unknown to the rest of the town. It was hardly credible. An unfamiliar feeling, one she refused to name, churned slowly in her stomach, gathering force, and even as Lisa was relating calmly to Chief Silva her first meeting with Ellen Mattson—and Hank Vinnio—she was coming to know a part of her she did not know existed.

■ ■ ■

Buddy leaned into the classroom, glanced over it, and turned off the lights. He continued his walk down the hall, his eyes sliding to left or right as he passed a dark doorway. He stopped at the entrance to the school offices. Light seeped out below the door. Art students might be dedicated enough to spend long hours at work in the evening, but the staff was not; school offices were locked by five o'clock. When Buddy heard a drawer close, he rapped lightly on the door and leaned in.

"Now what?" a voice grumbled from within. Buddy waited until Betty Lane appeared from the dean's office.

"Good evening, Miss Lane. What are you doing here at this hour?" Since the discovery of Hank Vinnio's body, Buddy's manner had been more subdued than usual, but this was nothing to remark upon in the eyes of his fellow workers.

"I'm still working, would you believe. Honestly! Chief Silva has been asking questions about everyone." She didn't try to hide her irritation.

"Silva?"

"Silva. And I've been racking my brain for answers. That man wants to know everything, but he doesn't come right out and ask. He asks about one thing," she said, waving her right hand, "and to answer that you have to figure out something else." She waved her left hand. "And then something else after that. Honestly!" She waved her hands back and forth like a metronome, then stopped the rush of words suddenly with an exasperated sigh.

"He's very thorough."

"I'll say." She smiled at him. "But it meant I didn't get any work done all day. I thought I could get something done as soon as everyone left and the place was quiet." She looked up at him, suddenly aware that seeing him here was as unlikely as her being here.

"What about you, Buddy? What are you doing here?"

"Since we're down one part-time position," Buddy said, managing to make it sound as ordinary as November gray, "I thought I should be here in case anyone wants to work late. No one seems to, though, and the Tuesday night classes have been canceled. Someone thought having classes last night was in bad taste. I guess the dean didn't realize they were having them. He thought the room was still closed."

"I heard." Anyone who saw her might interpret her expression as a sign of grief for the dead man, but those who knew her might guess she was concerned with the loss of revenue for the school and the scheduling mess she would have to clean up at the end of the term when all the teachers tried to make up the missed classes during exam week.

"Anything I can do for you while I'm here?" Buddy offered.

"I wish you could. The police are going to need all the help they can get if they think they're going to find a murderer in this place." She slammed shut a drawer in disgust. Buddy's hands sank into his pockets.

"He's asking about everyone," she said. "How long they've been here, where they come from, what they did before. Who liked him, who didn't. All that sort of thing."

"You are the logical one to ask," he said.

Betty laughed at the compliment, but she did not protest.

"I suppose he has to be thorough," she went on. "But I can't see why he has to waste so much time on Ellen Mattson. And Professor—Well, that's a waste of time, too. But I suppose he has to consider everyone who was at all connected with Vinnio."

"A lot of it's just routine. That's all," he said, remembering Chief Silva's comment to him. "Mrs. Mattson, for example, is just another student to him, someone who would have seen Vinnio around and probably talked to him once in a while."

"Oh, no, Buddy. Not Mrs. Ellen Mattson. Some of the others, maybe, but not her. He wasn't anyone she'd want to know."

"Oh." Unable to think of a good reply to any discussion threaded with innuendo, Buddy held up his end of the conversation by listening with his entire body. The more vehement Betty became, the more Buddy leaned in her direction.

"Why, even Professor Mattson is a step down for her, so to speak."

"Oh."

"Her late husband was quite the young man—handsome, rich, charming," Betty said with a sly smile.

"Oh."

"He was a developer." She nodded to emphasize her point. "Made quite a lot of money as a young man, right away."

"Oh."

"He died when he was quite young, in his thirties, I think. About the age Ellen is now. Left her quite well off." She sent a knowing look to Buddy while she put away another file.

"Oh. Who was he, her late husband?" Buddy was still wondering why he had never heard that she had been married before, but then he took little interest in most of the professors. His life was elsewhere.

"Joey Correll. Ed Correll's brother. Now that's someone you should know. He'll be showing up regularly, getting to know the place. He's just getting involved with the school now, a new supporter. He's on some new committee. We'll have to be extra nice to him."

"Well, that's good for the college. And at least she wasn't a widow for very long." Buddy's heart was never very far from a charitable feeling.

"Less than two years," Betty said. "I think." She pondered this for a moment. "Actually, it must have been less than that," she said slowly. "She said just a few months ago she'd been married almost fifteen years altogether. So that would mean she must have married right after Joey died." She paused, frowning. "Odd, I don't remember it happening so fast."

■ ■ ■

For the first time in years Joe Silva let his office grow dark while he sat at his desk, digesting the facts accumulating about the death of Hank Vinnio and listening to the sounds of the shift changing. At least that's what he told himself he was doing. In truth, he was staring at a now-empty parking space where Lisa Hunt had disappeared into a white compact car just after turning back to wave at him watching her from his window. It might have disconcerted him if he hadn't been so pleased. He flicked on the desk lamp and buzzed for Ken Dupoulis.

"You said you had some ideas?" the chief said to the sergeant when he arrived in his office.

"Yessir. Nothing major, but I think we have enough to narrow our sights a bit." Chief Silva settled down to listen and observe. In the last forty-eight hours he had noticed in Ken a flash of something different; unwilling to probe, the chief had left it to the younger man to accept or reject an offer to work on the murder investigation. Silva was glad to have him on board and was amused by the occasional sign of a new maturity he saw in him. It reminded him of his youngest sister's child, whose admittedly brilliant insights never overcame the disadvantage of the speaker's age and rank in the family. He wondered what it must be like to be the smartest one in any group and never be taken seriously because of age or size, or any other characteristic. How frustrating it must be to listen to the less intelligent because they will not hear.

"Well, let's take a look at what we've got." Silva turned to the desk and picked up a sheaf of papers. "The pathologist called in this afternoon with his best estimate of time of death—Saturday from noon to around five in the evening—on the basis of his stomach contents. We know that Vinnio was working with a group of students till around three o'clock, when they left him alone—or so they thought—in the building. Buddy called at maybe ten or fifteen minutes before five and no one answered. You found the place locked and dark at five o'clock. It looks to me like we've got a time frame," Silva said.

"Did the lab find anything else? Drugs? Health?"

"Health was average for a man of his age who lived alone. His diet wasn't all it could have been." Silva suddenly realized, to his discomfort, that he shared something with the deceased. "But no drugs. Not on him and not in him."

"And not in his apartment," Dupoulis added. "We certainly don't know much about him."

"We know enough." Silva turned over another sheet of paper. "Let's see. Hank Vinnio. Age thirty-five. No steady employment; he signed on at the college as a work-study student working for Buddy, who, I might add, didn't care for him. Before that he seems to have bummed around, with an occasional odd job. What else have you got?"

"He had a brief stint with a delivery company before joining the college, very brief and just before. He was with the company about three full days." Dupoulis looked through his notes.

"Doesn't sound like a steady worker. And before that delivery job?"

"At a warehouse. Then, before that, just bumming around," Dupoulis said.

"Well, at least there's one interesting thing about him so far."

"What's that?"

"Where he comes from." Silva named a small town on the northern border of the state.

"Why is that so interesting?"

"That's the same town Betty Lane is from," Silva said. "And Ellen Mattson."

"Both of them?" Dupoulis was incredulous.

"Both of them."

Dupoulis took out a roll of mints and loosened one with the tip of his thumb. He stared at the floor while he thought this over. "Those aren't the names I would have expected you to come up with. Did the information come from the school files?"

"I got it this morning from the office. But you're right. The focus is not where I expected it might be." Silva could still recall his surprise when he'd caught the name of the town the second and third times. An entire frame for the murder shifted in his gut, and people he had barely noticed before that moment came into sharp relief.

"So there's a likelihood that both Mrs. Mattson and Miss Lane knew Vinnio before he came here, but neither one has said anything to us," Dupoulis said. The implications of this information were obvious to the sergeant too, and he shook his head while taking them in.

"I want the number of the police department up there; the chief might remember something about them, one or all three of them," Silva said. Dupoulis made a note. "Now tell me what you picked up."

"Nothing about the three of them knowing each other, that's for sure." Dupoulis flipped back through his notes. "Betty Lane has been here for about twenty years. She's efficient, reliable, and admired, if not liked. The dean thinks she could run the place without either him or the president." Dupoulis crossed his legs and tried to recall the impressions he'd received from the students, staff, and faculty as he asked them about the school and each other. "I got the impression that Vinnio was just another student, and not a particularly important one."

"Me, too. Most of the students and staff seemed to think he was okay, but one of them had some experiences she couldn't square with his role as the sensitive young artist." Silva passed on Karen Meghan's story of the vending machine.

"Do you think she realized it was a scam?"

"I'm not sure," Silva said, "but I think she was beginning to."

"What about Buddy? What did he think of him? His opinion should be worth something, since Vinnio worked for him."

"Buddy didn't care for the guy. He made that absolutely clear, no regret at his death at all."

Dupoulis exhaled loudly. "That could be something. Do you think there could be some reason behind that? Some kind of grudge he has against Vinnio? The murder wasn't premeditated, at least from the looks of it. Suppose he finds Vinnio conked out in an accident, he takes a chance and cuts him. His problems are solved, whatever they are." Both men thought about this scenario. "It doesn't sound like Buddy," Dupoulis finally said.

"It's still possible, though. He called Vinnio at the school just before five, but he said he was at home for the rest of the afternoon, doing nothing, just enjoying the weekend off."

"No alibi?"

"Nothing. We'll have to keep an eye on him anyway. He found the body and he could get into the school at any time." Silva gave the order in his usual manner, calm and professional, with no sign of how deeply it disturbed him to turn Buddy Lecroix into a suspect. He added, more softly, "All those teachers with keys make me nervous." Eager to move on, the chief said, "There were a couple of other people who bothered me. Chickie Morelli, for one."

Dupoulis shook his head to indicate that he hadn't met this one.

"He's got something on his mind, something that seems to have to do with Vinnio, but I can't rattle it loose."

"Alibi?" Dupoulis asked.

"He seems to be covered for the entire time, but I want to keep an eye on him anyway. He says he was at work and I have the name of his supervisor at the warehouse, but I think he can tell us something. It may take a while to get it out of him, but I have the feeling he's holding something back. Anyway, he can wait. How about the rest of the students?"

"Most of them seem pretty straight. A group of them met with Vinnio at the college on Saturday to get some extra help. He seems to have been willing to do that, come in on the weekends, but I guess he charged the school for it, sort of like overtime. Anyway, they met on Saturday afternoon, then the kids left. They all left together in two cars, so no one stayed behind. And they insist there was no one else in the building when they left, except Hank Vinnio." Dupoulis stopped to read off the names of the students. "It'd be hard to crack their alibis."

"It's unlikely they were all in it together, so if they say they left together, then we have to accept that until we learn differently. But at least it tells us that it was someone who came to the school later. That might help us narrow it down. What else? Did any of them say anything about the school that might help?"

"There's a bunch trying to do something for Mattson and it's not working out and they're feeling kind of disillusioned." Dupoulis briefly recalled a moment after two very long and frustrating interviews when the confusion surrounding the preparations for Mattson's exhibit had almost gotten to him, but mindful of Lynnette's accusation of his increasing insensitivity, he held his tongue and was rewarded with the realization that the students were mystified by the situation they found themselves in. A more objective student later confirmed this.

"Was Vinnio part of that?" Silva asked.

"Not that I can see."

"What about teachers?"

"That's the funny part," Dupoulis said. "Most of them talk about their teachers like any students do," Dupoulis said, missing Silva's bemused expression. "But two of the teachers really stand out. The kids rave about Larry Segal; they have nothing but praise for him. But Mattson is a different story. They're very careful about what they say about him."

"I thought you said they were trying to do something for him," Silva said.

"They are; that's what doesn't make sense. Some of the first-year students think he's wonderful, but they're not in this group working on the exhibit."

"What about Mrs. Mattson?"

"She was a tough one to interview, and no one seems to know much about her because no one mentioned her. She's sort of on the edge of the school. No one seems to like her very much. She used to be Ellen Correll."

"She's an artist, too, isn't she?" Silva asked.

"I guess so. She takes classes. She's in the Monday evening painting class this term. I got very little out of her today, and my general conclusion from the way she's regarded by everyone else is that she probably is more faculty wife than artist in her own right."

Silva nodded agreement, thinking once again of Chickie's comment about the Monday evening class. He resisted understanding Chickie automatically because a part of him wanted to defend the Monday evening students, to see them as the geniuses marginalized for the threat they posed to the college faculty. It was a romantic notion, conveniently disguising the lingering feelings of inferiority from his own college days. Getting the story about Vinnio's clash with Professor Mattson from Chickie Morelli only complicated matters; Chickie hardly seemed like an insider and yet he was obviously on the inside by merit. Silva wondered what people like Chickie thought of people like Ellen Mattson. "Correll," Silva murmured. "I remember the name. The guy died in a car accident a few years back."

"That's him. Ed Correll's brother."

"Okay, I got it. Well, I still want to know if she remembers Vinnio from her early years." Silva made a note to himself. "She seems to have acted as though she didn't know him at all and he did the same, but I'm beginning to wonder. I want to be sure about this." Dupoulis leaned forward as Silva repeated what Lisa Hunt had told him earlier in the afternoon about her first meeting with Ellen Mattson and Hank Vinnio.

The sergeant thought about it, then said, "It almost sounds like he was trying to get her." Silva nodded in agreement. "Are you thinking Saturday was some kind of self-defense gone bad?"

"I don't know what I think about it yet, but she and Vinnio grew up in one small town and ended up in another small town," Silva said. The twenty-odd years he had spent watching people destroy their lives and then try to salvage what was left had convinced him that there was a pattern to our lives, a pattern we could either drift with or shape, either submit to or transform, and both choices seemed predetermined, despite the role we thought we were playing. Whichever part of ourselves we chose, fate supplied the matching pattern; one was positive, the other was not. Police work had made Joe an optimistic fatalist. If it turned out that Ellen Mattson and Hank Vinnio had a connection reaching back in time, Silva would not be surprised.

"Those are the two people I would be least likely to connect," the sergeant said. "Do you think we could be making too much of what Lisa saw?"

"I don't know. When you look at it closely, it sounds like nothing." But it feels like something, Silva thought.

7

WEDNESDAY

THE TORREYS were a typical family of Mellingham. Over the generations they had dabbled in many occupations, lobstering, fishing, clam digging, greengrocery, gardening, and dairy farming, not from any love of the outdoors, of nature and its many challenges, but from something far more basic—a love of food. Finally, the younger members of the preceding generation (who are even now rapidly becoming the older generation) suggested a shortcut to their goal—a restaurant. Let others produce, the Torreys would consume. They did not expect, from any misplaced modesty, to succeed beyond the point of breaking even; financial success was not a goal but a by-product of keeping the restaurant open and the food cooking. To ensure even that much, however, each member of the family repeatedly reminded friends and more distant relatives to support the Torreys' family café. So modest were they, in fact, about their future prospects that for several years they did not have a sign until a younger member of the family produced one in shop class in high school. It was this young fellow who actually named the restaurant the Family Cafe, since he couldn't think of anything else anyone had ever called it.

Located in what had once been a bank, the restaurant made full use of the premises, storing canned goods in the dis-

used vault and tucking the chef (a title held by various relatives, who learned to take turns over the years) behind a
grilled window originally meant for a teller. A coat of paint
transformed a counter along the wall from a built-in check-
writing desk to a luncheonette counter.

The menu was simple: if the Torreys ate it at home, the
patrons ate it at the restaurant. That meant meat loaf, spaghetti, steak (rarely), chicken casserole, turkey loaf, and scrod.
Always scrod. When it came time for a new recipe, for family
and restaurant, Mrs. Torrey went back to the first cookbook
her mother ever gave her: *Casserole Cooking: One-Dish Meals for
the Busy Gourmet*, by Marian and Nino Tracy (The Viking
Press, 1943). This had remained a favorite, for Mrs. Torrey
understood the measurements (in cans) and the ingredients (in
English). It was plain fare, for the most part. The Torreys
never served snails, for instance, or those strange furry fruits
from Australia. Mrs. Torrey was firmly of the opinion that
animals had fur, fruit did not.

The Torrey restaurant was the obvious choice for anyone
who needed food for the soul as well as for the body, and it
was an unexpected, and unarguable, success. Never one to
face good fortune squarely, however, the senior Mrs. Torrey of
the second café generation insisted on maintaining a polite
pessimism. There would be no expansion, no increase in
prices, and no change in the menu. Why go to all that trouble
in a business bound to go under? Business only got better, and
the Torreys finally capitulated to success by opening a
branch—in the cellar—catering to young people (the next generation had a surprisingly large number of children) and hir-
ing the cousins, one of whom was also an art student.

When Marilyn Torrey Hayes asked her instructor Larry
Segal for an advisory meeting, he was more than willing to
meet her wherever she suggested. Knowing that she was a
Torrey on her mother's side, he suggested the one day when
he could only meet for lunch, then waited for her reply. Larry

agreed with alacrity to meet Marilyn at the Family Cafe, a man with an appetite headed for a restaurant with food. Unfortunately, he was bringing his bad habits with him.

Larry Segal held the small file of drawings and photographs in his lap, leaning the folder against the edge of the table as he flipped through the individual pieces. The Torreys, used to such strange guests who let their minds stray from the food beneath their noses, had arranged a few tables along the front wall with extra elbow room to accommodate the readers and crossword puzzle fanatics. Mrs. Torrey kept her eye on them, nevertheless, and people like Larry Segal were never far from furry fruit in her mind. Only her niece Marilyn's insistence on Larry's good character had warmed Mrs. Torrey's opinion of him—that and his good sense on his first visit to the restaurant in ordering two servings of meat loaf. It was a meal he remembered fondly.

At that moment Larry was analyzing the shading on an arm. Across from him, Marilyn was eating a salad between peeks at Larry. Mrs. Torrey also had her eye on him, for in front of the drawing instructor, at the small Formica-topped table, was a plate of her son's best spaghetti fast going cold. Tall and thin with thick brown hair, Larry was perpetually hungry because he had not learned how to do two things simultaneously, or rather how to divide his attention between food and something else, anything else. Consequently, the something else held his mind while his meal waited, usually going cold or getting warm, either way becoming inedible. At the moment he was absorbed in Marilyn's drawings and had forgotten about his lunch, having blocked it partially from his view.

"Are you sure that's what he said?" Larry asked Marilyn without taking his eyes off the drawings.

"Yes. Unformed. That's what he said."

"Hmm." He turned over two more sheets. "Did he say anything else?"

"Immature. The portraits especially. He said they were immature." She rested her fork while she took up a knife to butter a roll. Her aunt, strolling among the tables, tried to justify in her own mind Larry's absorption in the folder of drawings; she failed.

"Young man," she said, no longer able to restrain herself, "you haven't eaten a bit of your lunch. Are you sick?" She glared down at him, and Larry had an odd sensation of being suspended in time and space, of being lifted from the present and sent drifting. He looked up at this short sturdy woman looming over him, her untidy gray hair flying out in wisps like electrical charges, her brown eyes snapping.

"It's all right, Aunt," Marilyn said. "This is—"

"I know who it is," Mrs. Torrey interrupted. "It's Mr. Segal who hasn't eaten a bit. Are you all right? You want meat loaf?" She studied the spaghetti, now made with new onions from the South, wondering if her perpetual fear of exotic foods would prove to be prophetic.

Larry shook his head and hastily took a bite, all the while keeping his eyes on her.

"That's better." Mollified, she wandered off in search of other neglectful patrons, seeking proof for her pessimistic predictions to give her husband later that evening.

"I'm sorry," Marilyn said.

Larry didn't hear her. "What a lovely woman."

Marilyn blushed. "You're very kind. I know she can be intimidating, but she means well."

"An uncanny resemblance to my mother." Larry spoke as though he hadn't heard Marilyn, then returned to the folder in his lap. He flipped forward to the face of an old woman, wrinkled and smiling, done in charcoal. He studied it in silence, imagining the person, the dreams and feelings of another life, before turning to the next drawing.

"I don't really understand how to respond to the criticism," Marilyn said.

Larry nodded, still silent. He turned to the figure of a young man sitting hunched over on a bench. The drawing, again in charcoal, reproduced the flexed muscles, the bones in the hand beneath firm flesh. Every inch was part of the body of an athlete waiting, leaning forward ready to jump into a basketball game that the viewer could imagine being played just outside the picture. Marilyn finished her salad. The restaurant was like home to her, and she could sit alone any time and not feel uncomfortable.

"How long was the critique?" Larry asked.

"About five or ten minutes. He wanted to spend more time with a man in the evening class who was there to get something from the bookstore. I guess he had to get back to work—the man in the evening class, I mean."

"God, I'm hungry," Larry said suddenly. The sudden shift in his attention might have disconcerted another, but not Marilyn or any other students who had worked with Larry, for his hunger always, eventually, inevitably got the better of him. It was just a matter of time. He rushed to his eight o'clock class three times a week and suddenly remembered as he wielded crayon over paper that he had left coffee and a bagel sitting on the hood of his car—outside the coffee shop. Afternoon classes rumbled with Larry's futile search for the sandwich he had left on his chair an hour before. The students often speculated, in a kindly fashion, how long it took him to actually eat dinner. Larry noticed none of this. Each discovery of a meal missed was a revelation. Marilyn knew what was coming. He closed the folder and tucked it back into the black portfolio leaning against a leg of the table. Satisfied that all was safe, he turned to his spaghetti, eagerly took a large bite, and slowly chewed while his face registered surprise, under-standing, and disappointment. He stared at his plate before pushing it away. The spaghetti was as cold as a drab day in March. He looked around the room, then turned to Marilyn.

"I'm sorry, Marilyn. I thought it would be helpful to you

to have another point of view on your work. Mattson used to be good at helping students see their strong points." He shook his head and looked around for the waitress. "I don't know what's wrong with Mattson." He waved at the waitress. "Your work is good, solid." He repeated the last word several times. "No, it's better than that. You're one of my best students. You have talent and a future in this." There was no doubting his sincerity. Then, softly to himself, "God, I'm hungry."

"What do you think I should do?"

"Is there a menu here somewhere?" He probed beneath his plate. "About Professor Mattson, you mean? Well, if you can, you should stick it out. He won't like it if you drop out of his class right now."

"Is there any way I can switch to another section?"

"I doubt it. Preston notices that sort of thing," he said as much to himself as to Marilyn. "You're better off just putting up with it. Don't worry, Marilyn." He smiled and patted her hand, eager to comfort her. "The rest of the faculty knows your work. You'll come through this one class with Mattson all right." Marilyn smiled back. Satisfied with his counseling session, he said, "God, I'm hungry. Let me buy you lunch."

■ ■ ■

Jonathan Abbott had the serious look of a young man mature beyond his years, and Chief Silva regretted that he might grow even more serious before the case of Hank Vinnio's death was solved. The chief offered the art student a cup of coffee, and was glad when he declined; it meant he had something to say and wanted to get down to business. Perhaps, Silva hoped, he might not be the first casualty of the murder investigation after all.

With his green eyes and sandy hair, Jonathan looked at first sight as though he should be a shallow, fun-loving student, but even the briefest second glance pierced the veil of his good looks to reveal the harder lines of character. Silva was relieved that Jonathan had come of his own volition rather than finding himself shocked and disillusioned during a routine questioning into giving information he would rather withhold, for the first and sometimes greatest pain was in watching decent people grope for their accustomed reality as they came to see friends and acquaintances in a different way. Jonathan Abbott, however, had spoken little to the officer who originally interviewed him, impressing the policeman with his circumspect and precise speech.

"I had this in the back of my mind," Jonathan said as he crossed his legs. His khaki slacks were ironed with a sharp crease, but he lived alone, the chief knew. "It didn't really connect and then when it did, I wished it hadn't." His face became the color of his slacks and Silva feared he might be sick. He was gaunt from his high cheekbones to his thin ankles in well-worn moccasins. He raised his eyes to Silva's, the sign that he was past the preamble and into the main text.

"I work most of the time in the print studio."

Silva raised an eyebrow.

"I do engravings mostly, some silk screens. Anyway, the print studio is downstairs, near the furnace room and the storerooms. You can see the windows from the parking lot. It's quieter down there than in the rest of the building." Silva nodded, patient. He was not one to be short with any member of the public who came to the station to offer information. Any officer soon learned how much of police work depended on a tip from a citizen, the passing of what seemed ordinary at the time to the only person who witnessed it. Without people like Jonathan Abbott, Silva knew he'd have a file of unsolved cases—and a slew of angry residents. Jonathan could take as long as he liked.

"I don't work at the school as a work-study student," the young man said. "I have a job in Boston, but I know what the setup is here." He looked down again, and Silva knew the young man had met another obstacle. "I know all the guys who are on work-study—Chickie, Wally, Jim."

"Do you know Buddy Lecroix?" Silva didn't need an

answer. The distress in Jonathan's eyes told him what this interview was about, and he moved to nudge the student over the hurdle of acknowledgment. "Whatever you have to say may seem loaded to you, but it may only be a small piece of the puzzle and not as serious as you think."

Jonathan was relieved, though somewhat skeptical, and continued his story. Once he had made the decision to speak to the police, he had steeled himself against doubts, regrets, and biases, so much so that by the time he got there his information seemed ominous and his guilt in ruining another man's life almost unbearable. This was partly the result of his age and partly of his conscience. If he hadn't made the decision first, before considering his feelings, he very well might not now be telling Silva about his work at the college. "The print room is quiet and sometimes I'm in there for hours without anyone coming in. People go by in the hall but no one ever comes in."

Silva nodded, aware of what was coming next, and he was willing to give Jonathan the benefit of the doubt, even more. Silva believed the student was genuinely uncomfortable in finding himself privy to a private conversation.

"I overheard Hank." He sighed. The worst part was over, the decision to tell what he knew. "Hank had keys," Jonathan said, now looking straight at the chief, "to everything but one or two storerooms. One day in the beginning of the term, he ran into a student looking for Buddy. The guy needed paper towels or something. Hank told him not to bother. He said he'd already tried to get a key to that room from Buddy and the janitor was adamant about not giving him one. Hank said he had a feeling that Buddy kept the only key to the storeroom for a reason and if the guy wanted something from there he might just as well forget it."

Now it was Jonathan's turn to wait and think. And the more he did so, the more the information sounded to him unimportant, silly. He began to wonder if coming to the police with a story of an overheard conversation was foolish, petty, even neurotic. If he hadn't been pushed, he might not have. The murder had seemed surreal to Jonathan, something staged that could be critiqued and corrected. But Hank never got up and the correction was never made. Now absurd comments half heard while his mind was straining for something else took on an importance he didn't want them to have. Like decent men and women everywhere, he recoiled from violence and its celebration.

"You're suggesting that Hank was accusing Buddy of pilfering, and the other student understood that," Silva said.

"Yes." Having made his choice, Jonathan stood firm.

"Do you think Buddy knew?"

"I think so. The kid—whoever he was—sounded very indignant and said he was going to talk to the dean about it."

Silva considered this. It was entirely possible that Hank had set in motion a sequence of events that could only move in a tight circle, one that began and ended with him. Hank accused Buddy of stealing indirectly; but the unknown student became the public accuser. The dean or president might investigate, and Buddy might be suspended—or even fired—if something were wrong, whether he had any responsibility for it or not. That could mean hardship for Buddy, maybe worse. If he left his job under duress or suspicion, Silva speculated, he might never get another one. That might be the kind of fear to drive some men to act, but, Silva had to admit, it was hard to imagine Buddy acting with that kind of passion. And yet, Silva knew, that didn't mean Buddy was without feeling or incapable of acting on his feelings. As Buddy had readily admitted to the chief, he didn't like Hank Vinnio, and didn't mind saying so. Worse, he had spent Saturday afternoon at home, alone, right up until the time he said he called the school just before five o'clock and got no answer. If Buddy was threatened by Vinnio, how far would he go?

"What did Hank say? Did he urge the student on? Try to pacify him? What?"

"He seemed to agree that it was a good idea." Jonathan paused. "The kid said it was too bad Hank wasn't the regular janitor. He said Hank made more sense. He was there all the time and he knew what the students needed." The words came out awkwardly, with the boy gulping in air as he spoke.

"What did Hank say?"

"I couldn't hear."

"Has anyone else ever made such a suggestion about Buddy, to your knowledge? Any hints? Any complaints about anything?"

"No. I never heard anything like it before." Jonathan looked at the floor, and Silva guessed there was more. He was certain the boy had said what he came to say and yet he wasn't relaxed, relieved that the hard part was over.

"Something else?"

"No, no, not really." Jonathan tried to smile but turned his head away instead. He couldn't dissemble over this. "Yes, there is." He took a deep breath.

"Go ahead," Silva said.

"My dad was the maintenance man in my high school." He pushed himself up in his seat and Silva saw defiance, pride, confidence. "Buddy's a lot like him. When I told my dad what had happened, I told him I wasn't sure I wanted to come down here and let Buddy in for all kinds of suspicion, but my old man—Wow!" Jonathan opened his eyes wide, then smiled, first to himself, then at Silva. "He told me if I didn't get down here, he'd come out to the school and drag me down here." Jonathan Abbott leaned back in his chair, a study in pride and joy.

■ ■ ■

"And where were you on Saturday afternoon?" The young man who said this slid into the chair beside Betty Lane's desk, his thoughts on the delightful image of police questioning faculty and students alike, and he failed to notice the reaction of his chosen audience. Betty Lane blanched. The envelopes in her hand jerked free and landed on the desk blotter, and the student automatically said he was sorry, unaware of how shocking his unthinking behavior was. Betty gathered up her envelopes, tapped them into a neat pile, and wrapped an elastic around them as though waiting for the young man to announce himself properly.

"Haven't you heard?" he said. He dropped his backpack on the floor beside him, planted his feet on the chair rung, and unbuttoned his denim jacket. "It's been wild." His eyes bulged in enthusiasm. "The police have been asking everyone where they were on Saturday afternoon. For real!"

"Haven't you got a class?" Betty asked.

"It's just like you see on television. They really do ask all those things. Who did you see? Where were they going? I mean, wow. Huh? Class?" he said, finally catching up with Betty's question. "No," he said, still smiling at his joke. "Not right now. I thought I'd put in some office time. I need the hours if my paycheck—"

"Go study in the library, then." Betty stopped him in mid-sentence, and he slowly deflated, his eyes settling on her, his smile waning. During those seconds, he flushed, then rose to leave, embarrassed by her anger with him and uncertain about what he had done to deserve it. Betty glared at his back as he disappeared through the door.

With the departure of the student, Betty was left alone in the office. Resting her elbows on the desk, she dropped her head into her hands. In the days since the discovery of Hank's body, the regular routine that was her pride and, she liked to think, the school's backbone, had cracked and creaked and finally broken under the unbearable strain of murder in their midst. Students unable to understand the intrusion of so ugly a reality into their lives turned it into a television show, watching the real police and comparing them to their favorite fictional ones, while the faculty, hanging on waving limbs, sought safety on the unfamiliar terrain of office work, leaving Betty at her desk to cope alone. The moment of solitude and quiet came at a time of desperation, and she moved to close the main door between the corridor and the cluster of school and faculty offices. Once again at her desk, she pulled toward her a list of things to do, checked off two items, and picked up the telephone.

"Hello, Pam," she finally said into the receiver. The voice on the other end said hello, and for several minutes carried the conversation, to which Betty assented with a soft hum.

"Yes, that is making everything more difficult," Betty said, sagging in her chair. "The police are here all the time. Then they leave and come right back again. I've barely kept up with what I absolutely have to get done so people can get paid." Her eyes strayed to a nearby stack of envelopes. The phone rustled soothingly in Betty's ear and she relaxed against the back of the chair, shaking her head.

"That's exactly the problem," she said. "No one's getting anything done, but I'm the one who's supposed to keep everything going while everyone else falls apart."

Again the voice commiserated, and again Betty nodded.

"Well, actually, I practically had to throw one of the students out of here in order to get any work done. Really, I can barely finish a thought half the time. Everyone's lost; no one knows what to do. And do you know what I had to do for the chairman of the painting department in the middle of all this? Artists' health hazards. I ask you. Now, in all this mess. And on top of that, I'm here all the time looking for things for the police."

The voice buzzed and Betty nodded, then listed some of the files she had been called upon to produce in the last few days.

"They must think the school knows everything just

because the murder happened here." The resentment in her voice grew. "Oh, absolutely. They should. You're absolutely right. They should be paying me for all the extra work I'm doing for them. Oh, I agree. But you know they won't."

The voice hummed and Betty nodded.

"Never. They'd never give me any more for this. I'm sure of it."

The voice murmured and Betty nodded.

"Oh, no, a raise is out of the question. Especially now." Betty's glance moved to the door of the dean's office. She listened to the soothing noises from the other end of the telephone. "Do you really think I should?" she asked. "I don't know, Pam. Things are tough all over. Sometimes I wonder why we even bother driving up to New Hampshire to the outlets. The prices aren't much better up there, either."

Pam's response seemed to change her mind, for Betty started to nod; then she stopped, as though thinking. She said, "Don't you remember Guido the Greengrocer on the radio with the price for Granny Smiths this year? And the eggplant?" Betty listened. "It's everything. Everything's gone up. Since when is fifty percent off so great at an outlet?" Again, Betty considered Pam's reply. "Well, you were driving. But it does depress me. Anyway, I called to tell you that Catherine said she'd drive next time for sure. She wants to leave early and get back early because her daughter's in a soccer game or something like that. Or maybe it's her son." Betty stretched out one leg and wiggled her ankle, then did the same with the other leg.

"You are an optimist, Pam. No matter how early we leave, we'll never cover that many stores. Well, it doesn't matter to me. I just need to get away this weekend, to recover." Betty stretched her toes again. "They're not going to give me a raise while all this is going on, and it's going to take them at least a year to recover from the bad publicity." She pushed the stack of envelopes farther away from her just as the office door opened.

"Oh, you're absolutely right. Absolutely," she said. "Just lock the door, turn out the lights, and put my feet up. Let them do without me. You're right, I should," Betty said with great satisfaction. "We know what would happen then, don't we?" she said darkly.

■ ■ ■

"Bumpy," Dupoulis said, poking his head into the doorway to Silva's office. The chief swung around in his chair to look at his sergeant and hear him explain his strange announcement.

"His first name," Dupoulis said. "You wanted to talk to the chief of police in that town up north, and the woman on the phone kept saying Bumpy. Right?"

"Right," Silva said, recalling the earlier conversation that had left him almost defeated, but not for the first time. He had left a message and promised to call back, capitulating gracefully to the person who sounded like a true Yankee at the other end of the phone line. For all his years in a New England town, he had never met a character who seemed to stand behind the cliché of the old Yankee—until that phone call. Only his curiosity about the woman kept his frustration in check.

"Bumpy is the guy's name," Dupoulis said. "Bumpy Philips. And his office is in his car."

"That must be a very small town." Silva had not thought anything could make him feel less cramped in his own office, but now he pondered his good fortune; he had never had to make do with a car for an office.

"He's also mayor, fire chief, and the town's only plumber. Plumbing comes first. It pays. At least that's what his wife says," Dupoulis explained.

"Was that his wife who answered the phone?"

"No, that was the postmistress, who is also the town's only electrician and schoolteacher. All three jobs she took over from her father."

"She told you all that?" Silva sometimes wondered if small-town folk recognized each other through a secret code. Dupoulis, for all his extended Greek family, could call any other town in New England and learn all he wanted over the telephone, as long as the person answering the phone was also a townie. "What people tell you," he mumbled half to himself.

"Yes sir. She seemed to want to talk, said she hadn't had any customers for two days." He relayed this with a certain note of wonder in his voice. Dupoulis joined the police force with an eagerness for work that was a temptation no small-town force could pass up, and had learned during his first few weeks that there were no slow days, only periods of calm during which wise men and women rested for the onslaught to come, when they would be roundly harangued at three o'clock in the morning for not being around when people needed them. Sometimes Dupoulis wondered how he had ever managed to miss the parallel world that existed in the nighttime until he joined the police force.

"Well, in all that news, Sergeant, did she say how I could get Bumpy on the telephone?" Silva grew serious, his mind again on the murder.

"You can call him tonight at this number at seven-thirty." Dupoulis handed over a slip of paper. "He'll be expecting your call."

Silva took the paper as though it evoked a memory he was reluctant to let slip away. In seconds he had passed into a place Dupoulis had learned to recognize. Silva's tendency to drift within himself when a thought embraced him or a mood swirled him away had unsteadied others, left them uneasy, particularly those used to only the concrete of the here and now, those who imagined no other reality but the physical world around them. Dupoulis was the exception; he only waited for a sign of his chief's return, ready to listen to whatever was on his mind. When Silva spoke, it was with a tone that made Dupoulis alert.

"This case," Silva began, "has an elusiveness like Bumpy. It's here, all right, but it's all over the place, too. It's just like Bumpy. More like a case for a sleepy town in the dog days of July." He paused and turned the slip of paper over in his fingers, as though looking for an explanation on the other side.

"A man is knocked out and left for a while, then his throat is cut. And then he took some time to bleed to death." Dupoulis recalled the reports he had read earlier in the day.

"Sort of like the murderer had all day and wasn't worried about anyone turning up to interrupt him—or her," Silva said. "That was taking quite a risk, especially considering the number of people who have reason to be over at the college on Saturday."

"I think of schools as pretty empty places on the weekend," Dupoulis said. "The murderer may be someone who doesn't know how much goes on over there on Saturdays and Sundays."

"Or someone who knows precisely what goes on and what doesn't go on, and how to avoid being seen by anyone else," Silva speculated.

"And that description fits just about everyone who admits to being over there."

"That's right. Buddy Lecroix found him," Silva said. "And he makes no secret of not liking the guy. And after what we heard this morning from Jonathan Abbott, Buddy could have a strong motive for wanting Vinnio dead, at least in his own mind. That school is a pretty small place. I don't think the dean would want any acrimony or suspicion if he couldn't fix it fast. And no school, no matter how much they might like an employee, can afford to keep on someone they no longer trust or someone the students don't trust. Buddy was vulnerable, no matter what he or the dean tries to tell me. And if Buddy thought there was a chance he might lose his job because of the machinations of a newcomer like Vinnio, he just might do it. He just might kill him."

"What about the students? We know a bunch of them were over there working just before Vinnio got hit by all those crates. Did any of them sound like they had anything against Vinnio?"

"No, none of them seems to have disliked the guy, or even felt strongly about him one way or the other. They admired him as a talented student, but no one seemed to like him a lot personally. Of course, that might just be the result of his being murdered. The students may be backing off because they're frightened. Either way, we haven't gotten much out of the students so far."

"The statements from the teachers and the women in the office didn't have much in them either," Dupoulis said. "They thought he was good, but he wasn't like them. At least, that's what they tried to get across to us. I still think he was a bum and the teachers knew it."

"Maybe, but what bothers me is they don't seem to have had much to do with him," Silva said. "They all encouraged him, but they kept him at arm's length, from what they say."

"Does that mean you're eliminating Professor Mattson, Larry Segal, and the other instructors?"

"No, not at all," Silva said. "Mattson is still very much in the running. But Segal is out; he spent the afternoon having lunch at the Harbor Light."

"The whole afternoon?"

"Wait till you read Badger's statement." Silva laughed to himself.

"How about the office staff?" Dupoulis continued. "Betty Lane and Karen Meghan and the work-study students?"

"Betty's definitely still with us," Silva replied. "Karen is out. She was with two friends shopping the entire afternoon. I want to question her some more because I think she knows a lot about how the school operates. I also think she's told us something, something important about the victim, somewhere in all she's said to us in the last several days. You know something else? I think she's the only one out there who actually liked him, at least for a while."

Dupoulis watched his chief. "What're you making of that?"

"Nothing for sure," Silva said. "It's just that she's the youngest, she has the least invested in the school, even though she was a student there. And she's the one who thought he was okay. No, this murder has to do with the school and the staff and the faculty. It has to do with what they know about each other, maybe something so ordinary that they think it isn't worth repeating."

"Aren't you assuming a lot?" Dupoulis said.

"I don't think so. From the way people have been talking, Lane, Mrs. Mattson, and Vinnio knew each other only through the business of the school, never talked to each other more than was necessary, and got along just fine. But Betty Lane, Ellen Mattson, and Hank Vinnio are all from the same town," Silva said. "I know that now. And you know that now. The question is, who else knows that?"

■ ■ ■

The college art gallery was empty except for four students sitting on the floor in a corner and a young man in a chair. The most recent show had been removed, and the paintings for the next show had not yet arrived. They were originally due later in the day, but the young gallery director, so absorbed in the real-life drama happening right in front of him, had forgotten to call the temporary storage facility in Boston to deliver the four crates. The order had finally been given, but not soon enough to ensure the student assistants had work throughout the week. Now, despite their promises to help on the weekend, the young artists sat in the gallery at the end of a free afternoon, and the young director could only look on, worrying about how much he could get done—alone—on the weekend and who he could call in desperation on Sunday morning to help him finish the preparations for the opening on Sunday night. By the time the students had settled into their discussion, the director had sunk to worrying how much this snafu might affect his annual evaluation.

Marilyn waved away a bag of potato chips, her lunch and discussion with Larry Segal still undigested. Doug and Steven also waved the bag away when Noel offered it to them.

"Well, at least it hasn't been a total waste," Marilyn said. Her cheerful attitude when she arrived back on campus that afternoon perplexed her friends. In response to their queries, she insisted all was well, as always. It was the last part that perplexed them.

"How do you figure that?" Doug asked.

"I learned how to ask for ads, how to sell the idea of an ad book, how to estimate what I needed. All that kind of stuff." Marilyn beamed at the three around her.

"Ever the optimist," Steven said. His easy move into a position of leadership in the group seemed natural and right, and only Doug was irked by it. He opened his mouth to speak, but Steven cut him off.

"Let's get on with what we have to do. Okay?" He looked around at the others. Marilyn and Noel quickly assented and pulled out their notebooks. Steven motioned to three other students who had appeared in the doorway to join them.

The gallery director, hearing the call to action, looked around, expecting for a brief, exhilarating second to see the longed-for crates, but nothing had changed. He lapsed into a grim silence, arranging the paintings on his clipboard, trying to come to know them by title and dimensions so well that he could get them in place and up in record time. He barely heard the project under discussion around him. He longed for and dreaded five o'clock. He had lost—wasted, would be the accusation—an entire afternoon; the students were learning nothing from him.

Steven moved down the list of questions on his pad of paper and the students debated each point readily. The students were a different sort now. No longer frustrated by the failure to sell ads, no longer worried that they knew nothing about mounting an exhibit, and no longer unsure of every decision they made; they were ready to grapple with the reality of their experience and learn from it whatever they could. Willing to confront their original goals, face their failures, and scale back their plans, trusting to their intentions to bring them out all right in the end, the students settled down to enjoy the process of planning all over again. Doug listened from the edge of the group and said nothing. Since he was no longer the center of the action, he no longer even felt a part of the group.

■ ■ ■

Mike Rabkin motioned to a student waiter and the young man changed directions, turning on his heel to slip between two guests standing back to back. The steel tray was rested on the edge of the white tablecloth and Mike helped the boy unload the platters of food. Mike patted him on the back when they were finished but his mind was already on the small clusters of guests at the door. Judging them happy with the wine and conversation they already had, Mike moved his eye to Henry Muir, who was leaning toward a regular customer and a student Mike knew only as Chickie. The three seemed intent on a photograph Chickie had pulled from one of the bins, or at least Chickie and the customer were intent. Henry seemed to be a remote third, studying the other two men as much as the photograph. Mike hoped they didn't spill food on the artwork.

A few guests poking among the hors d'oeuvres, holding royal blue cocktail napkins beneath either ginger ale or wine in small plastic glasses, reminded Mike of more immediate concerns. He again moved among his guests. It would be some time yet before he could relax with them; for the present he listened to the conversations around him. The sound of voices engaged in intense discussion at the very beginning of the evening had reassured Rabkin that his party would survive the tragedy of the weekend, but his discovery of the topic of murder in almost every small group eventually bothered him enough to wish he had canceled the party, for his guests seemed to have chosen this event as the best opportunity to analyze the police investigation thus far. He took time to down half a glass of wine as he checked on the food in a back room.

While Rabkin was struggling to catch up with the pragmatic approach of his guests to murder, they and the rest of Mellingham were doing their best to explain the murder in the most agreeable (to them) manner. Long past the period of self-consciousness, the fear of putting a foot wrong with an insensitive question or of seeming ghoulish with inquiries, Mellingham's best had already developed a large number of theories about Hank Vinnio and his death. Rabkin learned of these and their jumbled details, and of which emotions weighed heaviest in them: curiosity, compassion, fear, fastidiousness, revulsion. As he went down the list he found himself feeling fear. He was a businessman and wanted nothing to do with a crime that might leave a stain for any reason, even one so innocent as having sold art supplies to the victim. This discovery surprised and shamed him, a startling contrast to the ordinary, daily friendship he felt for the school and its students and teachers. He decided against expressing his feelings after listening to the elderly Mrs. Marks's opinion of the murder.

"You see, he's shocked," she said to Rabkin after she had delivered her opinion. "You think old ladies should be sweet and modest. Well, I say, blow it." It was well known that Mrs. Marks liked to adopt her grandson's vocabulary—to the best of her ability—just so there would be no misunderstanding in her audience. "He sounds like the kind of person who deserved to be murdered. Some people do, you know. And age has nothing to do with it, so forget this nonsense about being cut down in the prime of life." Her last comment elicited a few unguarded comments of agreement from some young people standing nearby, and Rabkin wondered if he was the only one surprised at the turn of the conversation.

"I can't imagine anything more crippling than not being allowed to speak freely about it either. I don't want to be someone's stereotypical image of the grandmother."

"Don't worry, Gran," her grandson suddenly said from behind her. "That won't ever happen to you."

"Ruffian," she said affectionately to the teenager, lapsing into her own vocabulary.

"People get what they have coming to them," another guest said.

"I agree," Mrs. Marks said. "If that young man—what was his name? Vinnio?—got himself murdered, he was probably asking for it. It doesn't have anything to do with me. It doesn't mean I have to get new locks on my doors." The old woman's stoutheartedness had a bracing effect on the younger men and women nearby, whose furrowed brows grew less solemn and whose strained eyes widened and smiled. The unsentimental attitude beneath her words was less important than her apparent determined independence in the face of a malignant fate lingering nearby. Even Rabkin admitted to feeling a certain pull in her words.

"The police seem to think it was someone at the college." The simple observation from a young woman Rabkin didn't know once again drew the crime into their personal world, into the college many had known and supported for years.

"It can't really not be," another guest said. "After all, how likely is it that someone would wander in on a Saturday afternoon and kill the janitor?" No one could bring himself or herself to consider it an ordinary likelihood.

"It could have been someone he knew from Boston, someone who had a grudge against him and found out where he was and came out here and—" the woman halted when her feelings caught up with her imagination.

"The police seem to be questioning only people around here," a teenager said. For him the murder was no different in emotional content from a television show; it was something to watch and stay up with but nothing more.

"It's just an excuse," Ed Correll said. He had stood on the edge of the group for minutes, rotating the plastic cup in his right hand while his left hand jangled keys and loose change in his pocket. At each remark from another guest, he turned his head and waited, then turned to the next speaker. His unexpected comment seemed an intrusion, a challenge, a jolt from outside. "They're just asking anything they think they can get away with." The tone with which this puzzling accusation was delivered brought the conversation to a halt as everyone looked over at him, trying to assess the speaker as well as his views. Ed didn't notice; he was too concerned with his own view of the investigation. "They're asking everybody just anything that comes to mind."

"Maybe they need to see that it's not important." This came from a young woman in her twenties. She turned to Rabkin and said, "I'm probably the only one here who hasn't been interviewed."

"Be glad," Ed continued. He went on speaking without any regard for the expressions on the faces of those around him. Had he looked, he might have felt embarrassed; as it was, he felt only inchoate churnings within him that pushed him to speak. "I need some more wine," he said suddenly. That was the last thing he needed, thought Rabkin as he struggled through the crowd to intercept him. In his hurry to get by, he jostled Chickie, who by then had moved to a row of paintings. Rabkin's customer was still listening, and Henry Muir was still hovering nearby.

■ ■ ■

The voice on the other end of the telephone had gone from jovial to questioning to thoughtful to professional as the speaker realized that Joe Silva from Mellingham did not need a plumber, was not standing in a burning building, had no complaint to make about town services, and only wanted information from the chief of police. Bumpy Philips was glad to give out information.

"Hank Vinnio?" Bumpy repeated. He worked hard on remembering, not because he was slow or stupid, but because a disembodied question had no reality for him. Important as the telephones were to rural areas, Bumpy settled his business face to face; being required now to produce thoughts normally shaped through a handshake and rising and lowering eyebrows momentarily threw him off his stride. But only momentarily. "The family moved away some time ago, maybe almost twenty years ago, when Hank was still a teenager. That's about all what I recall." Bumpy went back to thinking, and Silva explained that he had found the name of Bumpy's town listed as Vinnio's hometown on his personnel file.

"Well, well, well," said Bumpy. "People do tend to remember this place fondly." He seemed pleased with Silva's news, which raised Vinnio several notches in his estimation. He didn't hold with all that civic promotion that seemed to dominate holidays down south of the border of his town, but he was open to a little old-fashioned loyalty. "Of course, it's easy to like if you don't have to live with the disadvantages. And the Vinnios have been long gone."

"Do you have any idea where the family moved to?" Silva knew it was unlikely that anyone would remember after so many years, but he had to ask.

"None," Bumpy said. Silva could hear the genuine regret in his voice, or perhaps it was sympathy, being able to guess how important the information must be to a fellow police officer. Silva wondered if Vinnio had kept an affection for the town because he'd been happy there, or if he and his family had moved around so much over the years that that was the only place he could think of as home or even as a last long-term residence.

"What exactly happened to him?" Bumpy finally asked. Silva explained. "Gee, that's too bad." The genuine feeling in his voice reminded Silva once again of the different kinds of worlds police inhabited. Bumpy could still recognize the loss in the death of one human being, but he was now the rare breed of officer; most of the rest of us, thought Silva, see far too many to keep alive on the surface the feelings of regret and sadness called forth by each death. Silva imagined he would like Bumpy if they ever met.

"We only have the information Vinnio left in his personnel file. He wasn't here very long, so no one knows much about him. I was hoping you could help us there."

"I wish I could. I can't even tell you anything about the family." Bumpy sounded regretful.

"That's all right. I appreciate the effort. I'll send out a notice to the departments in the areas where he's worked. That may get us somewhere," Silva said.

"Well, maybe I can help with that," Bumpy said. Silva had to smile at Bumpy's eagerness to help. "Do you want his wife's name?"

The words stung the air. Silva was uncertain he had heard the other man correctly. "His wife?"

"Yeah," Bumpy said. "She might be able to help. I think she lives down in your neck of the woods."

8
THURSDAY

HIS NOTEBOOK RESTING unopened on his knees, Silva tried to remember how Ellen Mattson had first appeared to him. Some people saw the world as an unchanging vision from first day to last. Silva was not one of them. He had long ago become aware of how people and places and things changed according to how his feelings for them changed as he came to know them more intimately. Ellen Mattson had changed dramatically in the last few days, but he could no longer remember how she had looked before Saturday.

Ellen was shrewd, that he knew, but he was still undecided about whether or not her shrewdness was conscious calculation or the natural instinct of a woman determined to survive. As he waited for her replies to his questions, he supposed it didn't, in fact, matter because the result was the same: she had moved through life in a way that ultimately benefited her regardless of what happened to others. Silva didn't like her, but he knew that that too didn't matter.

He had decided to question her in her own home, partly because he wasn't sure where she stood in the investigation and he didn't want to frighten her into calling for an attorney, and partly to see what her home would tell him about her. It told him nothing. Never in his life had he found himself in a room with such expensive objects, and yet there was no sense of coherence, no sense that a person with an identity was behind the choices and arrangements. Nothing matched or clashed; nothing blended or fought. It was a room of random choices and none of them worth looking at twice, just expensive. After his first good look at the living room, he regretted his decision to question her here; his regret only deepened as she dodged and modified his questions to suit herself. He missed the sobering atmosphere of the police station.

"I just want to go back once more to your earlier marriage," he said after following her on a circuitous raid into neighborhood politics. Her digressions were long, disjointed, and increasingly snide. Her first one had ended on a noticeably spiteful note. This was a side of her he had not anticipated, but so far her smaller emotions did not appear when he asked her about anything connected with Vinnio's death. She smiled graciously at him and waited for his question.

"You said you were twenty years old when you married Joey Correll. Is that right?" She nodded silently, still smiling.

"According to our information, you married Joey in . . ." He flipped through his notes, named the town, and looked at her for confirmation. She nodded. "That's right next to your hometown, isn't it?" Again she nodded. Silva wanted her to volunteer the information he already had gained, or react when he led her to it. Perhaps that was what he wanted most of all—a reaction from her, any reaction, something to tell him how she felt about Hank Vinnio now—but she was obviously going to make him work for it. "The man who died, Hank Vinnio, also came from your hometown. Did you know that?" Again she nodded. I might be offering her the weather report for the week, he thought.

"You did?" His hope for some sort of sign from her grew weaker.

"Isn't that why you're here?"

"Yes," he said. The woman made no sense to him. He

decided once again to let her lead the way, risky though it might be. "Why don't you just tell me about it?"

"Do I have to?" She spoke like a child ordered to a particularly boring task.

"Yes." He prepared himself to speak gently. "This is a murder investigation."

She sighed and patted her skirt in place. "I was very young and my mother said it really wasn't my fault. It didn't matter. Not really. I mean, not in the long run." She lapsed into silence. Sensing that this might be the prelude to what he wanted her to talk about, Silva struggled to find the right words to nudge her into a full explanation of her early years.

"How exactly did she come to think so?" Silva thought this was as vague as he dared get.

"Well, I was only fifteen," she said. Silva felt his hand tense on the notebook; this was what he wanted, and he dared not let even a sigh distract her. He nodded encouragement; she smiled in response, then added. "Of course, so was Hank."

"You were both pretty young," Silva agreed. Now he had her; it was only a matter of getting her to spell it out. There could be no going back now. Still, he had to get the information from her, and that meant keeping her calm. He didn't care about her marriage, but if it got her talking, he would let her talk. Silva stifled every sign of a reaction to her words.

"So neither one of us was really to blame," she said. "Don't you agree?" She truly seemed to expect an answer, and Silva felt himself slipping on soft ground into a world of no rules, no boundaries, no consequences—except for him.

"You trust your mother's opinion," he said.

"Oh, yes. She said to just forget about it, so I did."

Silva wondered at the havoc a casual word could bring to the world. "And Hank? What about him?"

"My mother said he probably forgot about it too. After all, he ran away, didn't he?" It was too late in her recital to deny the worst, her marriage to Hank, but Silva still didn't dare let her know how little he had known until just this minute. She could easily withdraw into a sulk and refuse to give anything but the tersest replies to his other questions, and he still had a lot more to get out of her.

"Certainly looks that way," Silva agreed. He held his notebook very still as he decided to put his guesses into words. "And you never thought about getting a divorce?"

"No, not really," she said with a shake of her head. "It didn't seem necessary. I never heard from Hank again, so I knew the marriage was over. And by the time I met Preston, well, it was like something that had happened to another person, if you know what I mean. It wasn't me anymore, so I didn't even tell him. You can understand that, I'm sure." But the chief of police was sure he couldn't, and her open, winsome look didn't change his mind.

"I really couldn't say, Mrs. Mattson, but he'll find out one way or another now."

"Really?" The prospect seemed to unsettle her. She recrossed her legs. "Well, I don't suppose it really matters," she said, dismissing the feelings of two dead men and one still alive.

"You might want to check with an attorney about that," Silva said before asking her about Vinnio. The more she spoke about the past, relinquishing a truth long forgotten or denied, the more her eyes wandered, rolling upward and across, but never resting on Silva. He was just as glad.

"When did you realize who he was?"

"Well, I don't know. I guess one day he just started talking to me and I knew it was him. I mean, I'm not really going to notice a janitor, now, am I?"

"Did you discuss divorce with Mr. Vinnio when you realized who he was?"

"Oh, no," she said, staring straight at him. "I didn't want to talk to him at all."

"Did he bring it up?"

Ellen looked past Silva to the front hall beyond. "Did you hear anything? Preston isn't due back so early in the day, but you never know." She started to get up, but Silva's voice held her.

"I'm just about at the end of my questions." He was relieved to see her relax. "How often did you talk to him?"

"He sometimes modeled for a drawing class, so I saw him in class." Her eyes again moved to the front hallway behind Silva. "But that's all. We didn't take any of the same courses. And I only saw him a couple of times in the studio." She addressed the last to Silva, as if this were the most important information she had to offer.

"Did you ever see him outside? Downtown anywhere?"

"No, never." She closed her eyes and shook her head.

"Well, I appreciate your information." Silva rose. "I may have more questions later, if you don't mind."

"Fine." She rose with alacrity to show him to the door, once again in command.

"I assume you will want to be the one to tell your husband about your marriage to Hank Vinnio." Ellen was startled by the chief's words behind her and turned around.

"Me?"

"Yes. He will have to know at some point." Despite her offhanded admission of bigamy, Ellen was shocked at Silva's advice. Her face turned white and she clasped her hands. Silva was surprised by her reaction. He had expected embarrassment, awkwardness, even severe anxiety, but this was far more extreme. Even though she had just minutes ago finished narrating with occasional awkwardness a secret she had held for twenty years, Ellen only now looked scared. Could she have thought that by telling Silva she was absolved of all further obligation and responsibility? Did the prospect of facing the truth openly scare her that much? She might be frightened because she was still basically a child, Silva allowed, a woman who had never had to face an unpleasant moment with herself. Or she might be frightened by the prospect of facing Preston.

Silva slammed the door to his cruiser. He couldn't imagine Preston Mattson in the role that Ellen's reaction suggested for him, but her fear was real. Silva had accepted Mattson's personality at face value, seeing nothing beyond the man's egotism and vanity. Was there more? Was Preston a man of suppressed anger, a man who concealed a cruel nature or a violent one, making him dangerous enough to frighten his wife? The chief turned the key in the ignition. Ellen's fear suggested other possibilities. If Preston were indeed capable of violence, how would he have reacted if he had learned, perhaps by accident from the personnel files kept right outside his office, that Ellen and Hank Vinnio came from the same town? More important, how did Vinnio react when he came upon Ellen and Preston, happily married and well off? Vinnio might have hinted to Mattson that Ellen was more to him than a fellow student. However intended, such a sly hint could be expected to upset any husband.

Mattson, for all his foppishness, was a wild card. Silva just couldn't imagine what the painting teacher might do if he figured out that Hank and Ellen were married once—and were so still. Other men had killed for less.

■ ■ ■

The door clicked shut and Buddy polished the doorknob before moving on to the next room in the basement. He pushed open the double doors into a dark musty-smelling storage and work room. It always bothered him that the room should smell so stale and dank when he regularly opened the back door to the outside, even in winter. It was the easiest way to dispose of the trash.

With a grace and an economy of movement more often associated with athletes and dancers, Buddy lifted and arranged recently emptied trash baskets, moved cartons stored by professors, and cleaned and locked away the tools. No one who had employed Buddy had ever complained about the care he took of his equipment, for he was a man who wanted only a few things but he wanted those well cared for. Quantity of gadgets did not interest him. He stood quietly at the long worktable built into the wall, rubbing an oily rag over a vise, his fingers caressed by the cloth and gently kneaded by the rounded edges of the vise below. At times he forgot who he was and where he was, letting himself drift into the perfect intelligence that created tools, cutting and melding their pieces to work together like the bones of a human arm. At times he imagined that he might even return to his regular duties on the floor above him and find the rest of the world gone, for that is how it felt when he stood alone watching his hands work, as apart from him as—what? He couldn't think of a comparison. His mind seemed slow and only came alive as he worked at the bench.

Perhaps it was not his mind, though. Perhaps his hands and fingers had their own intelligence; that would explain the devices he made for his wife's kitchen—the cupboards that swung out and around, and the recessed lights that wiggled with a switch. He could not explain how they worked, not even to the electrician who came to the school once or twice a year to rig up gadgets for the teachers.

The electrician put him in mind of his tools again. Now it would be his job to call the electrician, work with him on the changes the photography teacher wanted. The brief period when a work-study student had taken over that task came to an end on Saturday. Or was it Sunday, the day he called the police? Buddy always tried to be accurate, even when it was only his own ruminations he was considering. It was Saturday when Vinnio died and therefore Saturday when everything changed, Buddy concluded. He folded the rag and placed it on the end of the bench.

Like everyone else at the college, Buddy began the week with a determination to carry on in every way possible, to keep his part of the school business in order. But by the middle of the week, by yesterday, Wednesday, he realized how futile his efforts had been. He had gone through the motions of his job and for the most part kept the school cleaned, secure, and safe, and yet little things didn't get done, he criticized a student, and he'd had nothing to say to Mrs. Lecroix last evening. The death of Hank Vinnio was getting to him.

Buddy let his hands fall down to his knees as his eyes moved around the room. This was his place. He supposed it was a poor thing to be proud of, to covet, but he was and he did. This was what Vinnio was threatening in his first weeks on the job and now there was no threat, no danger, no dissension. The relief he felt mingled with an unexpected feeling of sadness for the death of another human being, and Buddy wondered if that would be as much as he would ever let himself feel for the death of Hank Vinnio. At least it was more than he had let himself feel so far.

This discovery buoyed and cheered Buddy, so he blinked and looked quickly around him. Perhaps he wasn't doomed to be forever contained beneath a lowered sky, unable to think upwardly like others. He moved over to finish putting away the tools left out since Saturday. Vinnio rarely put things away but Buddy could not be angry about that now. He even allowed as how he himself had done the same thing on his first job, but only once.

The room was almost in its usual order when Buddy spotted two large black wastebaskets. Standing clear by the door, the two baskets might have been invisible until that moment—left there for days. Buddy tried to remember when he had brought them down, frowning, tilting his head one way and then another. It was Monday, he realized. On Monday he insisted on sticking to his regular schedule and this was what he did; only he tripped up in the end, forgetting about the baskets until now. It startled him to realize he had walked by them day after day since Monday, not even noticing them.

He pulled them to him and headed for the Dumpster, emptying one, then the other. He glanced inside the second one to make sure it was empty and noticed a cotton tissue stained red stuck to the bottom. He shook the basket. Still holding it aloft, he stopped and looked again, first inside the basket, then in the Dumpster. He turned the baskets around and read the office numbers painted on the sides—Ad 1—for the administrative offices on the first floor. He wasn't so slow that he didn't immediately know what to do about it.

■ ■ ■

At the sound of Preston Mattson's voice coming down the hallway, Betty Lane leaned over a pad of paper, giving the appearance of intense concentration. When Preston came through the door, all he saw of her was the top of her head and her shoulders as she brought to bear her body as well as her mind on her work. He had caught her like this several times in the last few days but dismissed it then as he did now. Betty was probably just losing her eyesight, to be expected at her age.

Both Betty and Preston might have been surprised, even flabbergasted, to discover their minds had been on the same topic, but that was the only similarity in their thoughts. Betty was disagreeably aware that she was now most definitely middle-aged. It wasn't a matter of a few gray hairs, which she had. It wasn't a matter of declining eyesight, though she had that too. It wasn't a matter of twinges in her hinges, as an athletic friend said. It wasn't even a matter of no longer dreaming of things she might do sometime in the future, for the future was either past or with her now. She knew that, and she could live with it.

Her fear now went deeper. She feared the newspaper and

its unrelenting reports on ageism. She never gave aging any thought except when she read about it. Even if she had wanted to be optimistic, cavalier about not climbing stepladders, shunning warnings on calcium and iron, the reporters would have beaten it out of her, so she capitulated. And she did so thoroughly. She let every article scare her unreasonably. She memorized the innocuous-seeming theme of every report: a woman in her fifties had few prospects, or none. Thwarted at every turn, she thus found herself concentrating hard on a job she'd had for years and could do most of the time with her eyes closed.

Betty Lane knew the college better than the president, had more accurate estimates of enrollment, tuition costs, town fees, and the staying power of teachers and courses than the dean, and handled the students better than the most popular teachers. But now it seemed to count for nothing. She was a secretary, with no credentials to speak of, growing old, her years of adherence and dedication falling away to reveal only an illusion of who she was. She resented the truth.

Preston raised the wooden counter, unaware of Betty's feelings, and went on talking as he slipped through. The students remained outside the counter, listening. Eventually Betty raised her head to listen also to Preston's present discourse, for he was standing in the center of the office expatiating on the artist's commitment to his work. Professor Mattson always needed an audience, it was true, but his need had never gone as far as this before. For all their talk of the artist's life, few teachers dared lecture students on anything as personal, as intimate, as private, as the manner by which they might prove a love of their work. That would be like staring at the sun during an eclipse.

"For some, it's a very easy choice," Preston said to the students. "It's like breathing. One doesn't choose to breathe; one simply does." Betty winced.

"Are we going to have some sort of career day to help us

get started?" one young man asked. Now this was the kind of student Betty understood—and appreciated.

"All the help in the world won't mean a thing if you lack the basic commitment," Preston replied. "Your integrity as an artist is all that matters."

The students were silent, and Preston accepted this as an invitation to continue; he obliged and went on in this vein for several more minutes before dismissing the students and their mundane concerns of earning a living. He closed the door to his office before he could hear the rumblings among the three students about ivory towers and other expressions not dear to the heart of a painting teacher. Betty heard it all but had no idea how this new attitude among the students might play itself out. To Betty's mind, Preston's behavior was becoming almost as good as a television show, and it might even turn out to be as amusing. She was careful not to smile, however, when she saw Preston's door open and the painting instructor approach her desk.

He began without preamble. "I think, Betty, that there must be a hundred details to tend to for the—ah—upcoming exhibit," he said, referring obliquely to his own show. "I'd be glad to tend to them now, at least some of them. It's important that we stay on schedule."

Betty permitted herself the sweetest of smiles. "The students are handling everything."

"Really?" Preston looked dismayed. "Everything? I'm sure there's something I can help with."

"Nothing whatsoever," Betty said, still smiling.

"I see. How commendable."

Betty wished he would look her in the eye so she could enjoy his discomfort. "They're conducting themselves very maturely." She broadened her smile ever so slightly. "When they realized they'd taken on more than they could handle, they just scaled back their plans. I call that terribly mature, don't you?"

"Terribly." He spun around on his heel and marched back into his office.

■ ■ ■

Frustrated in his efforts to gain control of the exhibit, Preston returned to his desk, a queasy feeling in his chest growing into a waving anxiety. His thoughts might have turned immediately to Betty Lane and her obstructionist techniques, but he did not at that moment feel secure enough to lash out at her. For years he had cruised by her, pleased with how adroitly he handled her questions, problems, complaints, but in the last few days the balance between them had shifted in a way he did not understand and could not explain. She wasn't quite the same now.

Well, no one was quite the same, not after the murder, he realized. Though the memory of the dead man in the studio was always an uncomfortable thought, this day Preston used it to explain the change in Betty—and in some of the students too, for that matter. In this way Preston comforted himself enough to turn his thoughts from the anger taking root within him to a task that might occupy his free hour. The problem was that he couldn't think of anything he wanted to do.

Being a methodical man, Preston began a search for a task by looking through his bottom left-hand drawer, working his way up to the top drawer, then moving across the top of his spare neat desk to the top right-hand drawer, where he found the packet of materials on artists' health hazards. His eyes widened and he grasped the packet eagerly.

The manila envelope held twenty-eight items on health hazards for the visual artist, ranging from one page to twenty-four pages photocopied on both sides. He organized the material into piles by medium (painting, theater, silk screening, and so on), setting aside four on painting and paints, and settled back in his chair to read. The idea suddenly occurred to him that this must be what it's like to work in a business office. He felt comfortable and warm and secure and important at that moment, raising his head to listen to the familiar sounds of the students changing classes and office doors opening and closing as professors and instructors drew back from their solitary work and readied themselves to join with others. He was glad to be there.

The first article was "Art Painting" by Monona Rossol, printed on stationery with the heading "Center for Safety in the Arts," with an address in New York City. He glanced at the table listing pigments and the hazards associated with them. Some of the hazardous elements seemed vaguely familiar, and he frowned while he tried to remember what *phthalo* meant. He began reading and was pleased to discover a fact in the first paragraph he could use in his class discussion. This, he concluded, could be a pleasant addition to the introductory talk he gave to his studio classes.

As Preston moved through the first page he was congratulating himself on his early decision to switch to acrylic paints, but by the second page he had lost his smugness and was using a dictionary. At several points he wanted to put down the reports, but he read on, looking in each one for the final word that these warnings were now passé, erased by the manufacturers' changes in production methods and materials, but the reassurances never came and he turned eagerly to the longest report, "Certified Art Materials Are Safe," by Deborah M. Fanning, and the long list of products rated therein. Preston studied the three seals reproduced on the first page and willed his memory to recognize them, but nothing came.

The head of the painting department was not a coward, nor was he a brave man, a man able to confront any challenge directly and confidently. He needed time to digest the information before him, and then more time to open his painting box and look at each tube of paint. His hand curled into a fist as he thought of grasping tubes that might well have been poisoning him year after year, and he pushed himself up in his seat, as befitted the chairman of the department, but that just let the fear sink lower in his chest.

After another hour of reading he put the report on solvents used in the theater arts into the pile, no longer eager to learn, knowing how Pandora must have felt. For a second a feeling of resentment and anger thrust upward and then stalled, for the information he had gained that morning was almost overwhelming—almost. And it wasn't just the information that his paints might be dangerous to him; it was something deeper. It was betrayal. Yes, that was it. He felt betrayed—by his work, by the art stores, even by himself. It was a feeling he hardly knew how to name, let alone assimilate, but it was there.

Once again that week, Preston stepped forward on familiar ground and found it wasn't there. It was like the times when he was a child coming down the stairs with his eyes shut tight and miscalculating the last step. Sometimes his knee was jolted by finding the floor beneath his foot; sometimes he pitched forward on a collapsing leg when the floor turned out to be a step lower than he had reckoned. The old feeling of finding the ground not below him came back to him. Nothing was where it was supposed to be this week. Preston was scared.

■ ■ ■

At five minutes before two o'clock Chickie leaned his drawing tablet against the wall in Buddy's work closet and dropped a black canvas bag containing art materials beside it.

"It's a good offer," Larry Segal said to him as he leaned through the doorway. "I won't kid you about that. But it's up to you." Chickie nodded and Larry loped off to his next class. The student was left feeling even more confused and indecisive than when he first walked into the building an hour earlier and picked up his mail.

This wasn't what he had planned for, worked for,

dreamed about, but then, when he stopped flailing in his heart he could admit, and hear himself clearly doing so, that he had not planned at all. Older and wiser, in ways not sought, than the other students, Chickie had left California to fulfill a dream, and yet he was even now hampering himself, finding roadblocks—and when necessary creating them—while he worked responsibly through his classes. What was the need that was dogging him, rushing up behind him and startling him with a yap, a nip, a brush, pushing him to the side and leaving him off balance?

He had tried to see in Hank Vinnio a comrade, a compatriot, perhaps even a role model, someone who understood the challenges and problems facing a talented artist returning to school long after he should have graduated, but the more he saw of Hank and the more he was around him when their schedules overlapped, the less he saw of what he was looking for. That was the hard part. The illusion Hank Vinnio's presence at the college had allowed Chickie to foster in himself was sullied first along the edges, and then blackened throughout during the last two weeks. When he feared he was introjecting this image, he knew he had to stop—and he did. But where did that leave him? And with what?

When Chickie first felt what was happening to him, he made up his mind to continue on the path he had set for himself at least for the rest of the term, at least until he could calculate the cost to himself of what he had done. He was pretty sure that no one else could discern a change in him and he was careful to treat the college community as he always had, but he knew a change was coming within him, and this one he wasn't sure how to handle.

Sometimes, when he was working the charcoal on paper, watching shapes emerge from the few lines that fell almost haphazardly across the white ground, he persuaded himself it was years earlier and he felt differently. This moment of imagining opened up spaces inside him and gave him room in which to work, freeing him from a present that had come to be oppressive rather than liberating. But the moment only lasted while he was working in a solitary place, and was lost when he saw the drawing nearing completion or heard someone approaching.

He knew these feelings too well now and his heart sought another image to symbolize his promise. He wanted to think Larry Segal was right, that he had let himself be unreasonably affected by Hank's death, but it was impossible for him not to be, for he was equally affected by his life. And now, now, he had reached the point of making a decision because he had to, one more decision that might, like the others before it, large and small, lead to even greater unexpected results.

The buzzer sounded, announcing the hour; Chickie felt a surge of delight, and this too surprised him. During the weeks he had worked for Buddy he had adopted a routine, and he enjoyed this type of balance in his life, periods of ordinary work whose ordinariness was its greatest pleasure, not the result or location or associations of the work. He wanted to put the feeling into color and lines. Maybe he would, later that evening.

■ ■ ■

Lisa Hunt pulled the form closer to her. At any other time she would be relieved to be handed a one-page form to fill out, but today the brevity of the task before her was itself a problem. Unlike the other students old and young, Lisa had a curiosity that could not be satisfied by a desultory chat during painting class or an intense discussion by the candy machine. She wanted information.

Her first idea had been to plant herself in the path of Chief Silva, but so far she had not been able to divine his current path. She had hung around students who had taken classes with Hank, only to be shooed away by Officer Maxwell or

Officer Frankel. Chief Silva never appeared at these interviews, and she couldn't find out who he was talking to. She had managed to meet Vinnio's landlady, but after Dupoulis's visit no one else came to question her, a fact that disappointed both women. Lisa even went so far as to spend a couple of hours with Henry Muir, but no one from the police came anywhere near him. Mike Rabkin had been easy to find, and even easier to engage in conversation, but his mind was on faculty exhibits, not student corpses. It cost her thirty-four dollars to disengage herself. By now she felt she had a special talent for discovering the innocent in the case, and that was exactly what she did not want to know.

Lisa had a curiosity pulsating within her, a second heartbeat long dormant and only now animating her. She tapped her forefinger on the form, hoping she had at last chosen wisely. Betty Lane walked back to her desk, confident she had solved another problem for a student. When the secretary settled herself again in her chair, Lisa was certain she had made the right choice. After twelve years working in offices, she knew what the coffee break could reveal.

Lisa spent several minutes looking for her pen in her purse, gathering odds and ends to one side, then shaking the bag so everything fell to the other side, the jangling needing only a drummer to give it musical shape. Betty and Karen made tea at their desks. Lisa pulled out a black fountain pen, unscrewed the top, and placed the top on the other end of the pen, aligning the clip with the nib. She weighed it in her hand; it felt right. The two other women discussed Karen's sister's behavior over the weekend as Lisa pondered the first question on the form: "Please type or print neatly your full name." She read the question twice, just to be sure.

"I told her it would backfire," Karen said. "I told her."

With the speed of a four-year-old learning to write, Lisa printed each letter of her first name and last name, and considered making up a middle name, something very long. Never before had she regretted the omission of a middle name; it had given her an advantage in grade school, ensuring that she, with one of the shortest names in the class, could finish and turn in her papers first, but now the lack loomed large, like a great failing that only wisdom outlines late in life, and she resolved to raise the matter with her mother next time she saw her—if she could remember. She crossed the *t* with a firm line running equidistant on either side of the ascender.

"You never know," Betty Lane commiserated.

The second question requested her address. Again with deliberation, Lisa began printing her address, street, and town. By the time she reached the state, Betty and Karen had finished with the misguided sister and moved through the polite preliminaries to a detailed look at the manner of Hank Vinnio's death. For this Lisa would be willing to write all fifty states with her left hand. She began the zip code with a perfect circle.

"Now, if he had died in a fire, that would have been poetic, even," Karen said. Lisa raised her pen like a dog's ear straightening at the smell of a raccoon, but Betty's head moved too. Betty's tightening face seemed to warn Karen of danger, but the other woman was young, untuned to her colleague's nonverbal messages, and wanted to make her point. "I just meant that he'd been talking about that awful fire in which his mother's friend died and then next thing you know, he's dead."

"Good heavens, you're becoming superstitious about it," Betty said. "The poor man couldn't have known, and besides, it's too ghoulish to think about," she said with a ladylike shudder.

Lisa kept her eyes on the form and the next question: "Circle the program in which you are currently enrolled." Once again she made a perfect circle, then crossed it out and consulted the list of programs on the back of the form. The general air of disdain that pervaded the office whenever Karen and Betty were required to attend to students wrapped Lisa in invisibility. She read the list through, wondering how two seemingly intelligent women could come to regard as normal an employed adult taking up to twenty minutes to fill out a one-page form.

"Chickie's the one that surprises me," Karen said after a thoughtful silence while she chewed a cookie.

"Why?" Betty asked. "He seems perfectly normal, just as he always has."

"That's what surprises me," Karen said, bouncing forward in her chair. "Hank's always sounded like Chickie was his closest friend out here but Chickie doesn't seem upset at all by Hank's death." Karen shook her head in disapproval.

"Hmm," said Betty, thinking this one over. "Well, maybe they weren't as close as he made you think. He was something of an opportunist, after all. He just might have wanted to make himself look good by saying he was close friends with Chickie. After all, Chickie is the most talented student here."

Lisa sucked the end of her pen as she contemplated Betty's comment, keeping her finger on the next question: "Do you have a local bank account?" Karen gave equal attention to Betty, who was just then dusting crumbs off her skirt into a paper bag with rolled edges.

"Maybe Hank just meant they had a lot in common," Betty said when she looked up and saw Karen staring at her. "That they were in the same boat, so to speak, not that they were really good friends, the way you took it."

"I didn't think about it like that," Karen admitted.

"Well, if you look at it closely, Chickie isn't really one of us, is he?"

"How do you mean? He seems okay."

"I'm sure he is. I just mean that he's always on the outside. He never really joins in, gets involved with the other students, you know, in school projects and things."

"No, I guess not," Karen said. "Maybe that has something to do with his age. Maybe he thinks all the other students are kids in comparison."

"They are," Betty said.

The image of Chickie and his dark hair falling over his eyes filled Lisa's imagination. Whatever memory she called forth, he stood on the edge of the group, in the doorway, at the back of the class, like a summer squall sitting offshore waiting for the afternoon sailboat races to start and send onto the sea fragments of a sturdy land. Chickie Morelli—a name to conjure with. Lisa gladly turned her thoughts to the paper in front of her and the last question: "Do you intend to sell your artwork through the college store?"

■ ■ ■

The sobering end to a lush season was nowhere more apparent in Mellingham than in the outlying parts of Gregory Stewart's greenhouse. The cold frames were open and empty, the plastic tarps that helped to gradually harden young plants in the spring rolled up, torn and frayed and dirty, all of a gray piece with the rough-cut wood of the frames and ground within. Chief Silva stood by stacks of empty wooden flats waiting for the owner to finish giving directions to his young assistant. A large man with the slow graceful movements of the farmer, Gregory Stewart slipped down from the back of the truck, wiped his hands on a rag he pulled from his back pocket, and extended a hand to Chief Silva.

"Your visit must mean you have something serious on your mind," Stewart said in his soft rhythmic voice. "Inside?" he asked, looking quickly at the young man working by the truck. Silva nodded his assent. Stewart's office was no more than an unfinished hut at the end of the main greenhouse with barely enough room for a desk and two chairs; at least Silva assumed there was a desk of some sort beneath the precariously piled stacks of catalogs, plastic bags, and potting trays. And a radio, he realized, as a cheerful announcer described a new load of lowest-ever-priced washing machines, just two hours away by car. Stewart snapped the radio off without even having to search for it in the clutter.

Silva kept the preliminaries short, explaining where he was in his investigation. "I still have to place a few people on Saturday afternoon, just to get it all clear in my own mind." Though he barely knew Stewart, Silva sensed that whatever niceties he might produce to deflect suspicion from any particular person would not deceive Stewart, but he also sensed that the other was a man of sound judgment and discretion. "Several people reported being here in the late afternoon, and I thought I'd see if you could help me there. Maybe you or one of your employees remembers seeing them. One of my officers may have already been over some of this with your people, but I'd like to go over a few names again." Silva opened his notebook to a list of names and read them aloud.

Stewart thought for a while. "Lisa Hunt was here." He paused. "Mrs. Mattson was here too, but I don't think they came together. It was late when I saw them. I'd been out most of the day. Only got back 'round about half past four o'clock. Or thereabouts."

"You know them both?"

"Sort of," Stewart answered. "Miss Hunt is a regular customer in a minor way. Mrs. Mattson prefers to order by the telephone and we deliver. She's not one for browsing as far as I know."

"Was she browsing on Saturday, or did she buy something?"

"She picked out a few things, but not what I would have expected her to get. She spent a lot of time going on about what she wanted with one of the boys. Both women are in that open painting class I take on Monday evening, and they talk to each other a bit."

"I didn't know Lisa painted," Silva said absently.

"I can't say she does in the traditional sense. The class is for fun, for trying out the idea of painting. Most of the people are there because they want to enjoy themselves, do something that's a little different," Stewart said with an easy smile. "Most of them have good sense about their abilities."

"Does that include Mrs. Mattson?"

"Well, now, it's hard to say." Stewart chuckled. "She surely looks down on most of the others in the class, though she hasn't enough talent to do so. She does harbor just a wee bit of pride in her work, fancies herself an artist who only needs to be discovered. Can't understand why no one discovers her." The twinkle had gone out of his eyes, and Silva wondered if he ever gave away any more of his feelings than that. "She takes the course because her husband tells her to, but she harbors just a wee bit of doubt about him too." Stewart spoke with the unsentimental intelligence of the person who relied on unreliable nature for a living; his quick astute judgments of plants kept him in business, whereas the same judgments of people kept fools and similar sorts out of his life. Such bluntness without spite or envy was a rarity in Silva's work, and his admiration for Stewart grew.

"How does Mrs. Mattson get along with the others at the school?" Silva asked.

"She gets along with them if she wants something from them, but I don't see more than that. Of course, I'm only there one night a week." It was plain from his voice that Gregory Stewart was one man who didn't feel any inclination to aid Mrs. Mattson.

"Did you ever see her with Hank Vinnio?"

"No, I can't say I have," Stewart replied. "But then he wasn't around all that much in the evening, just once in a while, and I never saw him anywhere else."

"No one else seems to have seen him around either—not at the school and not in town. That's the problem with Vinnio. He was new around here and kept pretty much to himself, yet he was dangerous enough to get himself murdered."

"Ah, well," Stewart said with a soft sigh, "if it's any comfort to you, Vinnio would have brought on his own death wherever he went, whatever he did. He was that sort."

■ ■ ■

Silva pulled the crushed gold leaf from the instep of his black shoe with his left hand as he held the telephone receiver in his right, resting his elbow on the arm of his office chair as he listened to Mrs. Rogers, punctuating her monologue with an occasional yes ma'am, no ma'am.

Mrs. Rogers always had a lot to say, especially on the topic of Henry Muir, and Silva at first had tried to redirect her to one of his officers, but she would not be put off. Convinced that whatever she had to say was important, she waited until Silva was due in the office before she called, and if he wasn't there, she insisted on being told when he would return. Silva had come to expect her calls in the late afternoon, and he steeled himself for her importunities, but her new complaint caught him off guard.

"A what?" Silva asked, wondering if he had misunderstood her. "Ma'am, he has to be a wanted person to be arrested, not just look like one. Lots of people wear overalls, especially artists when they're working. Mr. Muir is allowed to invite anyone he wants to visit him at his home."

Silva listened before adding, "And at his gallery." He swiveled in his chair.

"I see," he said, though he wasn't sure he did. Mrs. Rogers elaborated on her next point. She must have a list of lines of attack in front of her, thought Silva, as he followed her to her next argument. He had learned to cope with the first Mrs. Rogers he had ever known (and subsequent ones) by identifying the fallacies in their arguments (memorized in Philosophy 203, Introduction to Logic). Instead of growing heated, bored, or irritable, as many of his colleagues did, therefore, Silva at least entertained himself. Today Mrs.

Rogers was thrice guilty of *petitio principii*, or begging the question.

"It's really up to the town to do that, Mrs. Rogers," Silva explained in his most neutral voice. He listened to another disjointed complaint. "I can't order my men to inspect a house just because there's activity late at night."

Mrs. Rogers made full reply to this rebuff, and Silva pulled a twig from the heel of his shoe.

"I didn't realize you'd lived so close to Mr. Muir for so long," Silva said, feeling a growing sympathy for both parties, "but he hasn't broken any laws as far as I know." Silva paused. "The building inspector grants permits for any major work." This piece of minor information inspired Mrs. Rogers to describe to Silva a complete overview of the puzzle that was do-it-yourself home renovation in Mellingham, replete with dire warnings of the ill-renovated homes lurking on the market for unsuspecting buyers, who would be overwhelmed by amateur work in the electrical box and gerrymandering under the kitchen sink. Silva pulled a small stone from the cuff of his pants leg and dropped it on his desk next to the twig and the leaf and a small plastic bag.

"Yes, ma'am, I will do whatever they direct," Silva assured Mrs. Rogers as she hung up the telephone.

"Ken?" Silva called out as he put the receiver down. "Look out the back window and see if someone in the building inspector's office is answering the phone." Silva waited while Dupoulis left the room.

"Is that fair?" the sergeant asked with a laugh when he came back to report that the phone had indeed rung in the office in question in the other building on the green and someone could be seen nodding into the receiver.

"Yes," said Silva. "It is. She's sure Henry Muir is up to something. She didn't go so far as to ask us to raid the place, but close. She wants the police to make a surprise inspection and catch him in the act."

"Of what?" Dupoulis asked.

"I have no idea. But she's sure he's guilty of something."

"Too bad he's not part of the murder investigation," Dupoulis countered. "So far everybody involved in that crime seems to be innocent."

"Maybe not too much longer," Silva said, picking up the plastic bag. "This is a red-stained piece of tissue, something Buddy Lecroix found when he was emptying the trash can this morning. That particular trash can is from the school's administrative offices. Send it over to be analyzed, would you?"

"Sure thing," Dupoulis said, picking up the bag gingerly.

"Oh, and one last thing. Have you heard anything about Lisa Hunt lately?" Silva asked. Dupoulis shook his head.

"You don't think she's involved in the murder, do you?" the sergeant asked.

"I don't know," Silva said, looking perplexed. "Frankel and some others report running into her in the oddest places."

■ ■ ■

While Chief Silva was learning something about the nighttime activities on Oxbow Lane and the last worker in Town Hall was wishing he had gone home early instead of trying to finish one last budget calculation, Ellen Mattson was wondering how she could make Preston understand just how profoundly her mother had failed her—in giving guidance, in giving support, in giving her a way out.

"No, no, no," she muttered angrily after trying out several opening sentences. "I don't see why I have to pretend I did anything wrong. It makes things awkward, perhaps, but it certainly isn't wrong. I was married, he ran off, and so I was unmarried." This characterization of her situation cheered her and boosted her courage. She decided to simply tell Preston flat out when he got home and insist that he understand the predicament and be done with it. After all, these events were in the past and no longer had any bearing on her life. Her confidence grew. It was more than an hour, however, before Ellen heard her husband's car in the driveway, the sound of the tires crunching on the crushed red-and-gray stone grinding into her nerves. Wishing she had something to occupy her, she jumped when Preston walked through the front door.

"Ellen?" he called. He walked into the living room. "Hello, my dear. Why are you sitting in here?"

"Hello, Preston," she said. "I was talking to Chief Silva."

Preston strolled around him and raised an eyebrow. "And where is Chief Silva now?"

"He left," Ellen replied. "Shall we have dinner?"

"What did he want?" Preston felt compelled to question his wife, to maintain his presence as a figure of order and integrity, but at the same time he was reluctant to push too hard, for surely a chief of police didn't question people on idle matters in their own home. Ellen sensed this, for she was sympathetic in a way only capable of like-minded people. And so, both Ellen and Preston in their efforts to avoid an authentic conversation set out to collide in painful honesty.

"Well," Ellen began. "Well, he wanted some information to help him in his investigations." She resented Preston's failure to make this easy for her.

"I don't suppose there's very much you could help him with, but you should try," he said, turning away from her. "And I hope you did." He wanted his dinner, something restorative and satisfying.

"Of course I did. And he was absolutely charming." Composing herself, she folded her hands in her lap. There was no reason for her to let Preston make her angry. If he was insensitive to her plight, she would point that out to him at a propitious moment.

"Good." He looked down at her, less anxious now that he was confident the conversation was well in hand. "Well? What did he want to know?"

"Not very much."

"Now, now, come along." Preston smiled as he chided her. The more confident he became, the more paternally he treated her. Ellen bristled.

"Well, there was one thing you might want to know about." The irritation in her voice was obvious, a tone Preston especially disliked. He was always brought up short by her spitefulness, sometimes even scared of it.

"Really?" he said, trying to control his irritation. "And what might that be? I hardly think Chief Silva meant to leave important information to be disseminated as gossip. But do tell me." Preston did not try to conceal his disdain for the chief.

Ellen sniffed once and told him.

9
FRIDAY

PRESTON MATTSON occupied his desk on Friday morning like a general entering occupied territory, confident, even a little audacious. Still bringing him pleasure and pride was his discovery the night before that all his acrylic paints had seals of approval on them, declaring them safe from dangerous chemicals in manufacture or use. He dwelt on this discovery to the exclusion of all else, especially all else, not seeing his wife's face when he told her curtly, late in the evening, that he had to check his paints. He was an artist after all; he had no need to explain his every action to his wife.

With the same relief coursing through him, he straightened the pile of papers on his desk. The last few days might have rattled his easy sense of security, driving him to seek desperately though sporadically for an earlier normality. But now he did indeed feel better—and once again in control. Fortune was on his side. Without even knowing it, he had chosen materials wisely, and his wife might have made an error in judgment, like any young girl infatuated without proper parental guidance, but fate again had sorted that out for them. Preston had every reason to feel relieved, and he did. Things were indeed getting better. Even the unexpected ringing of the telephone now, at a few minutes before nine o'clock, did not irritate him as it might have the day before.

Upon learning in his early twenties that the proper time to call was between 9:00 A.M. and 9:00 P.M., he liked even now to speculate on the obvious lack of savoir faire of people who called outside those parameters. His customary greeting was all the sweeter knowing that he was tempting the unknown party to reveal far more than a name. He was both surprised and gratified to recognize Ed Correll on the line.

Preston recalled all the times when Ed had rebuffed his overtures to extend their friendship past the last tee on the golf course, and now the professor preened himself as he contemplated what he might say to the banker. The unexpected call gave Preston a welcomed opportunity to try a different tack. He opened his mouth to remind the caller of his current overwhelmingly complicated day and suggest a better time for a talk, but Ed forestalled him.

"I'll be brief, Preston," Ed said.

"Perhaps another—"

"Preston," Ed cut in again, "you know I was very close to my brother Joey, Ellen's, ah, previous husband. That's why I'm calling."

Ed's tone of voice and manner of presenting himself nettled Preston, and he wanted to reply in an equally assertive, even aggressive way, but somehow, his manner in such guise only seemed pugnacious, and if challenged afterward, he had a tendency to be waspish. He longed to be able to carry off such a style as Ed was now inflicting on him. He gritted his teeth and listened.

"I've just learned that Ellen was still married to Hank Vinnio when she married Joey." Ed paused. Preston was surprised that Ed knew what he had only learned last night. Ellen, foolish woman that she was, had committed bigamy, but both previous husbands were dead and he for one was willing to forgive and forget, though he supposed something more might be required officially, another wedding perhaps.

"It's like this, Preston," Ed said, pulling the other man back from his speculations. "Ellen knew she was married to

Vinnio when she married my brother—and when he died, she took property that should have gone to Joey's family, to our parents, and then to me. I'm getting a lawyer, Preston, for the return of my brother's property." Ed waited for Preston's reply, but poor Preston's mind was reeling. All he could see in his head was an anarchy of color and flashing and a separation within himself, head rising above body, and then only his eyes had feeling. Had anyone asked him at that second how he felt, he would not have known he had a body. He gulped. From a memory long forgotten came his mother's voice telling him to take a deep breath. He'd had to do that every time he confronted the neighborhood bully during the year they lived in Milwaukee. He gulped, then more evenly he gasped in, then out.

"Well." Preston managed to croak out a single word, determined now to maintain a semblance of his hearty manner. "It seems to me—" He never had the chance to tell Ed how it seemed.

"I suggest you get an attorney, Preston, though officially this is just between me and Ellen. I will, of course, look forward to seeing you again socially after all this is settled."

Preston was nonplussed as Ed moved nimbly from legal adversary to social ally. "I'm sure, Ed—" Preston began, eager to recapture even a modicum of their earlier relationship, but Ed stopped him.

"It's not something we can discuss, Preston." Ed cut the connection.

Preston held the receiver to his ear until a dial tone alerted him to what had happened, and even then he wasn't sure of it. He had learned to accept the hand of fate when he couldn't guide it, and over the years had managed to avoid calamitous accidents, the life-changing events that turned a man who might have been an avid gardener into a destitute farmer. He prided himself on the orderly manner in which he had arrived with security and sanity in middle age, and now both were being wrenched from him. The feeling of not being in control of his life made him feel he was hanging upside down, the bile from his stomach sliding down his gullet. He braced his feet on the floor and his chair jolted into the wall behind him. He was in control, he declared. He was still in control and would remain so: he would keep on top of this every step of the way. The law moved slowly, and the suit might even fizzle and die once Ed Correll got over the shock of Ellen's behavior. Ignorant of the law and easily tormented by his own imagination, Preston turned his mind to what he could do now. First, he would hire an attorney for Ellen, of course.

Shuffling Ellen onto an attorney lifted Preston out of the maelstrom, and he was able to meditate on Ed's intimations, trying to discern clearly what was behind his words. Ed Correll wanted to recover his brother's property. That seemed clear enough, but it wasn't clear what he might consider Joey's property. That could mean the cars, Preston's Rover and Ellen's Alfa Romeo. Both were nice, but they hardly seemed worth the effort. More likely, Ed was after their house, especially since it was mostly Ellen's house. Uncomfortable as that might be, losing house and car, Preston didn't see how it could go beyond that. Joey's money, according to Ellen, had been all tied up in a new venture whose complexity only grew with every retelling. The money went when he died—everything fell apart and the money just disappeared. At least that's what Ellen had always told him.

Preston tapped the letter opener on his desk, wishing he'd taken some business courses in college. He had avoided them with disdain, only fleetingly admitting that he found them intimidating. Though he had once questioned Ellen about Joey's business, it was clear even to Preston that she had no idea how Joey managed money. The letter opener tapped faster as Preston's annoyance increased and his fear burrowed below his defenses.

Energized by a growing sense of injustice, he pondered

his options as he saw them, and chose one—a new attorney for himself and another one, preferably in the same office, for Ellen, just in case the lawsuit became complicated. He wanted his interests as well as Ellen's concerns looked after, he told himself. Obviously, therefore, they needed two attorneys. Pleased with his prompt and temperate response to a looming crisis, Preston pulled out the telephone book and turned to the first name that came to mind.

■ ■ ■

The light breeze slid in through the opened window like a piece of paper under a door, ruffling the sheets Silva held in his hand. The fluttering distracted his eye, catching him unmindful of time and place. So deep was he in his notes that he did not stop to savor the moment of summer renewed that floated past him. A pleasure lost.

There was good reason for Silva to be so absorbed: he was at that moment reading a description of the murder weapon, whose survival was the result entirely of Buddy Lecroix's exemplary conduct on finding Hank Vinnio in the studio. Someone else might have left only mounds of crystals, like sparkling orbs circling around the sun.

His pencil moved on and doodled by Buddy's name, which headed a list of names reaching into a parallel world of hatred or revenge or some other motive unknown to those moving around the criminal. Buddy's name had to be listed, for he had found the body—Silva often wondered at the honesty in reporting such a crime that required others to assume a deception—and he had admittedly not liked the dead man. But there was more to it than that; Buddy had no alibi and admitted to calling the school just before five. To think of Buddy disliking someone enough to commit murder transformed him in the chief's mind, and Silva let his imagination range over a life simple and transparent like spring water, seeking a motive in his love for his wife and son. It was easy to imagine Buddy fighting for his job, and Silva tried to imagine him going as far as murder.

Silva's speculations did not improve with the next name on the list—Larry Segal, the drawing instructor. He too seemed to be listed for no other reason than he was there in the building when Vinnio's body was found and he had a key to the building. When it came to his whereabouts on Saturday, he was even less likely a candidate, for as absentminded as he might be about other parts of his life, he had almost a policeman's eye for the details of a lunch, a very long one he had shared with a friend at the Harbor Light diner, whose menu would not have inspired anyone else Silva knew to such accurate memorization.

The students who had met Hank on Saturday afternoon were also eager to help, but from different motives. As one student baldly put it, they expected to infer what the chief thought by the questions he asked. Even now Silva could see the young men and women ranged expectantly in front of him, ready to pounce on his first question. They went away mystified at police procedure in general and Chief Silva's reasoning in particular. At first they were impatient when the chief only asked what they ate, what Vinnio ate, when they finished eating. Then Silva wanted to know what they cleaned up and what they left behind. They too had been eager to please at the outset and frustrated at the end. They were more disappointed than Silva, for he had other names on his list, names that would have shocked the students had they known.

Ellen Mattson—a murderer? Silva let his imagination play with the possibility. Of all the people he had looked at closely—and the chief was confident he had examined every possible suspect—Ellen had the most obvious and most pressing need to put Hank out of her life. And even after he was dead, she was still guilty of bigamy. From that perspective, she had the most to lose in material terms, and had she been a different sort of woman, Silva might have extended that to include social terms, but Ellen was definitely not a different sort of woman. The strongest emotions he had sensed in her during his interviews were fear and spite, a meanness that he found himself discounting because it seemed like the spitefulness of a child. But she was no child, and at times she was even to him offensively amoral. Silva contemplated the nature of a woman who could discuss the act of bigamy twice undertaken as merely an oversight. Her insistence that she thought the marriage was legally over simply because Vinnio had disappeared from her life for at least a year left Silva shaking his head. He found her naïveté hard to swallow, but she wasn't the only one who had ever made such an assumption.

Unfortunately, Silva acknowledged, he had motive and opportunity for Ellen but he needed something more to tie her to murder. Given weeks to plan and unlimited opportunities, would she listlessly wait for a chance to murder a threatening ex-husband with a can of paint and a broken bottle? The circumstances might implicate Ellen, but circumstances weren't enough. Vinnio might threaten Ellen with exposure, even try to blackmail her, but exposure couldn't do her any real damage. Joey Correll had been dead too long for Vinnio's reappearance to change anything. She could remarry Mattson and argue she had never intended to defraud anyone when she married him and earlier, Correll. Exposure of her teenage mistake might embarrass her, but it couldn't harm her. No, if Silva wanted to charge Ellen with murder, he had to have more than that.

He needed to tie Ellen to the crime on Saturday afternoon or set her aside, and when he did so, when he let her drive off, leaving Hank alone in the studio, one more person came to mind—Preston Mattson. The door that let in Ellen, at least until five o'clock, when Sergeant Dupoulis found it locked, could also let in Preston, and any time after that, for he had a key to the building too. He had opportunity, in Silva's view, if he went directly from the golf course to the school or from Rabkin's gallery to the school, but once again he would

SUSAN OLEKSIW

need motive for an opportunistic and brutal crime as well as for a trip to the school that afternoon, and so far Silva could find neither.

Karen Meghan's words came back to him. The only one who had liked the dead man also contributed the most damaging information against him—his pilfering and insinuating. Hank Vinnio hinted he had two people he could call on if he needed help, and if Karen's recitation of Hank's complaints— about the vending machines and Buddy and others—were accurate, then he sounded like he fell into the category of extortionist and blackmailer. The question at the back of Silva's mind was whether or not Hank had ever approached Professor Mattson for money or favors. The word seemed strange, suggesting a kindness he was sure did not exist in the painting teacher. Silva couldn't see Mattson doing favors of any sort.

Silva was getting frustrated. There wasn't enough to tie Mattson to the crime; it would be stretching the time available to him from three-thirty to five o'clock, and although the murder could have been committed in a matter of seconds, it called for quick thinking and quick action—if Silva was judging it correctly—that depended on a number of intersecting coincidences. If Preston—Silva began and stopped himself. There were too many ifs in this case.

The sight of the next name didn't make Silva feel any more sanguine. Betty Lane was the standard anomaly of the art school, the chief had by now learned. Uninterested in fine art, uninterested in students and any other youth, Miss Lane was an executive secretary who kept the school moving. She had no close friends at the college, never took art classes, and only in the severest emergency did she work past her quitting time. But her name was on the list for two reasons: she grew up in the same town as Hank and Ellen, though she was a good twenty years older, and she picked up her car in the parking lot late on Saturday afternoon.

So far, none of this helped Silva in the least. No one saw her car going in or out, and no one saw Betty at the school or anywhere else after her friends left her off in the parking lot behind the school. She reported being there only long enough to transfer her purchases from her friend's car to her own trunk and to drop a few pieces of trash into the Dumpster. She took time to do this, Silva recalled, hearing her acerbic voice once again, because Buddy hadn't, much as she liked him, she was quick to remind the chief, and because Hank Vinnio, using his full name, wouldn't. He wasn't the sort to look around the grounds for the trash the newer students left behind. Years of listening to criminals of all sorts told Silva that Betty Lane at that moment was dangerously close to making herself into a caricature and an effort of will pulled her back into herself just far enough to convince Silva that she knew what she was saying, speaking against a murdered man, and didn't care.

But she too came back too late. Her friends, as curious as the students, begged to consult with each other before they settled on a final statement, like a team in charades, but they were agreed that they had arrived back close to five o'clock. The manner by which they arrived at this estimate, a method they shared with each interrogating officer, scrambled a few heads for the remaining hours of the shift. As near as Silva could figure, their timing revolved around prices quoted in late afternoon to entice serious shoppers to the malls in New Hampshire and Maine the following day. These weren't merely advertisements; these were prices chosen after mall employees had comparison shopped in malls in various parts of Massachusetts and points south. What surprised Silva even more was the apparent accuracy with which the women remembered the prices. The chief never realized until then how much he was missing on the radio.

It was Chickie who bothered Silva the most, however. Something about the student's relationship to the dead man was unsettling. Accustomed to finding extra work at the school some weekends, Chickie had instead reported for work at his part-time job in Boston, where, his boss reported, he worked the entire afternoon. Upon further questioning, the boss indicated that Chickie was so highly regarded as an employee that he was among those expected to work largely unsupervised on the weekends, the measure of their reliability being whether or not the work was done by the start of the next shift.

It was possible, Silva worked out, for Chickie to have returned to the school in time to murder Hank before five o'clock. He might have encountered Ellen or Betty but didn't. Once again, the problem was motive. Chickie's was weak, though there were signs that he no longer admired Hank and his achievements as an older student. There was even a suggestion that Chickie had caught on to Hank's tactic: attack when in the wrong; accuse the other first. Without saying so, Chickie had seemed uncomfortable that, in his weeks at the school working the shift from two to six, he had never met Hank coming on at six for the six-to-ten shift. This too fit in with Karen Meghan's statement about Hank.

There was still no motive in what he had about Chickie so far, and Silva reluctantly let the student slip to the bottom of his suspicions, as well as the list. And yet somewhere among the names was a murderer, of that he was certain. And equally certain was he that someone on the list was also withholding one piece of information that would help him sort it all out.

■ ■ ■

At one minute before nine o'clock, Henry Muir emerged from his green front door, his final slam sending a few more flakes of green paint to the doorstep, and glared up and down the street. Like a man many years older, he practiced breathing on the step before starting down the path and turning left onto the sidewalk. His eyes fixed on the ground, he raised and lowered his bushy black eyebrows at the single car that drove by, then slowed to get a closer look. Henry shifted the burden he carried in the crook of his right arm into the crook in his left. The car sped up and moved on. Still scowling, Henry turned up the neat path to his neighbor's house and knocked on the door. He waited. A vacuum whirred and he knocked louder.

Over the next few minutes Henry's head sank lower into his shoulders and his eyes burned more fiercely, but he made no move to go back to his own house. Instead, he scowled at the clean khaki pants that showed no sign of granite dust or solder or any other material normally found there. When the house eventually was quiet within, the sculptor banged on the door and stepped back. He thought this time he had been heard.

He was right. The front door with its cluster of Indian corn tied with a yellow ribbon was opened by Henry's neighbor, Mrs. Rogers, a woman in her forties who had alternately quarreled with and ignored Henry for the last fifteen years, but had never greeted him on her doorstep. She gaped at the hoary head and melanous brows and stepped back. Mr. Muir faced and overcame one of the greatest challenges of his life: he smiled at her.

"Your daughter's birthday," he said, extending the bowl of yellow roses he held in his arms. Too stunned to reply, the woman grasped the bowl automatically as Henry shoved it at her, then turned and walked back down the path and to his own home. She did not close her door until long after Henry had disappeared behind his.

For the rest of the day, and indeed for the rest of her life, whenever she narrated this event, two facts were always prominent, the core of the experience for her and her interlocutors: Henry Muir smiled and he was clean. No one took this news nonchalantly, casually, or even easily. At first it provoked shock, disbelief, silence. The only person not completely disarmed, or immobilized in some other way, was the intended recipient of the roses, the woman's fourteen-year-old daughter, who had recently discovered her reflection in a mirror and considered any such recognition of her beauty a sweet and suitable response. She wrote Mr. Muir a charming thank-you note and recited his act of sweetness to everyone she knew and a few she didn't. Henry Muir was a shrewd man.

■ ■ ■

Officer Frankel turned the pages in his notebook and then went on recording Ellen Mattson's monologue. Anxious to have her speak freely but afraid to push her lest she demand the presence of an attorney, Silva hoped to draw the woman into supplying the missing threads he had concluded she held in her hands. He had been listening to her for almost half an hour as she again narrated her activities on the Saturday of Hank Vinnio's death. So far Silva hadn't been able to get her any closer to the details of the afternoon. Everything she said made her sound scatterbrained and helpless, but, he noticed, she never put herself in any danger. His only hope was to ease her past her own defenses. He began to repeat his questions.

"And how long did you talk to him?" Silva asked.

"Not long. Just a few minutes." She answered as she had before, her eyes drawn to Silva's shoes. He had not thought her shy, and found this mannerism an irritant.

"Let's go over the conversation," he said gently. "What did he say to you?"

"He wanted to know if I remembered him."

"And did you?"

"Oh, yes," she said, looking up at his face. "I was so surprised to see him there at the school, but it seemed almost—unreal, I guess. I just couldn't believe he was there."

"Did you speak to him before Saturday?"

"No. There just never seemed to be the right opportunity, not that I wanted to. I saw no reason to initiate a relationship with him, if you know what I mean. Besides, I never ran into him alone before Saturday. Not really."

"Not really?" Silva echoed. Ellen shifted in her seat.

"No," she insisted, and Silva decided to leave that for now. "Did he try to contact you in any way outside school?"

"No, never," she said, her eyes again drawn to his shoes.

"No telephone call? No letter? Nothing?"

"Nothing," she repeated.

"When you first saw him at the school," he said, "did you think about seeking a divorce from him so you could remarry and regularize your current situation with Mr. Mattson?" As lucky as Mrs. Mattson seemed to be, Silva found it hard to believe that Hank Vinnio had not seen the possibilities inherent in his teenage bride's current circumstances. Silva's only question was, What had Hank decided to do about it?

"Divorce?" she said, starting to pout. "I told you. He left me. I never saw him again. He never called. He never wrote. It was years. I figured we were divorced it went on so long. I mean, how can you be married if you haven't seen or heard from someone for all those years? And I went right back to using my own name. I got my driver's license in my own name. I opened my checking account. I did everything in my own name. That's how everyone knew me. The marriage was over. That's all there was to it." That seemed to settle the matter in Ellen's view. "I mean, if he'd gotten married again, I wouldn't have minded."

"I see." Silva modulated his voice; wondered at her naïveté or daring, he wasn't sure which. In part, her willingness to be questioned a second time in the police station nudged him toward a belief in her innocence, but he still held firmly that she did know something that could help him and only her fear of getting involved in a murder charge seemed to be keeping her from speaking freely. "Mrs. Mattson, a man you married twenty years ago, when you were a girl of fifteen, reappears but never tries to speak to you. And you never try to speak to him. But on the afternoon when you're finally alone together for the first time and can speak openly to each other, you say you just talked about trivialities and then left."

"He was just standing there, right there," she said, her eyes focusing on a spot in front of her. "But I got scared and I ran. I just ran." Her voice rose as she recalled the moment, and Silva thought she was telling the truth, unlikely as the story seemed.

"Why did you run?"

"Why?" She looked at him sharply. "I don't know; I just did."

"How long were you there on Saturday?"

"I'm not sure," she said, to Silva's growing despair, "maybe an hour."

"Do you remember when you left?"

"Well, I know it was just after four, because the jazz program was starting on the car radio and that starts at four o'clock."

"So you were there from, say, three o'clock to just after four o'clock," he hypothesized.

"I guess so."

"Did you see anyone else while you were there?"

"No one," she said, surprising Silva with her definiteness.

"Did you see anyone in the parking lot when you arrived or left?"

"No. The parking lot was empty. Sometimes students leave their cars there and go off with someone else, but there were no cars there." Now that she was comfortable with the area of questioning, she answered easily and readily.

"So you saw no one coming in or going out."

"Oh." She stared back at Silva, who waited, hoping this was the moment of recollection. "Well, I did see someone driving out just as I came out of the building, before I got to my car." The chief waited while Ellen repeated this, reassuring herself of the accuracy of the memory. The slip of a shattered afternoon could be the piece he was looking for.

"What kind of car was it?"

She shook her head. "I have no idea; a car's just a car to me."

Silva sighed for the red Alfa Romeo parked down the street.

"Was it new?" Silva began. He led her through a list of questions designed to elicit details and ended up with a description of a car that was bright though not very, and new though not very, perhaps just recent and clean. It was not large, perhaps a coupe, if that was smaller than the average car, and it might have had passengers. And the driver? Oh, yes. It definitely had a driver; Ellen was sure of that.

■ ■ ■

Three large crates sat against the wall of the corridor, their wrapping a testimony to the ingenuity and lack of trust of the sender. Like any large parcels left unattended and in full view of passersby, they had begun to attract attention at once. A young woman with orange hair and high-top Day-Glo green sneakers stopped to look over one of the parcels, twisting herself over the top, bending down one side, leaning back to study the front.

"Awesome," she said after reading the return address in California. She walked on and minutes later her curiosity was mimicked by another student. During the morning break students clustered in front of the crates, debating what the contents might be but coming to no agreement.

A pair of faculty members stopped in front of the crates and agreed—on what no one nearby could discern—nodding their heads, stroking their chins, and walking on. Once the dean walked by, stopped only long enough to check the addresses on the parcels. By the middle of the lunch hour, the problem of the crates in the hall seemed to have been settled, for two work-study students showed up with a large folder of manifests and stood in front of the parcels. Wally and Jim studied the crates from a distance before walking purposefully up to them.

"We have to check off each one by matching the shipping numbers," Wally said.

"I sure hope this isn't going to take long. I want to get some lunch. I'm supposed to quit at noon. Buddy said we could. He said we could be strict about our hours." Jim, as usual, was in a hurry, patting the top of the first crate and bouncing from foot to foot.

"You didn't show up until eight-thirty this morning, so quit whining. Let's just get it over with." Wally slapped the crate and said, "So, what have we got first?" Jim leaned over the first parcel and read off the number, then moved on to the next one.

"They're all correct," Wally said. "That was easy." He smiled at his friend.

"Is that it?" Jim said.

"Yeah. Wait. No." Wally looked at his notes. "We're supposed to open them and make sure they have the correct contents. I think that's right." He reread his notes.

"What?"

"That's what it says."

"What's in this stuff?" Jim asked.

Wally read over the shipping invoices. "I think some of them are posters that Professor Mattson designed. Some are paintings." He paused again. "Okay, Jim, just open that one and take out one of the posters."

"Righto." Jim saluted and took up his hammer, pulling, prying, levering, until a piece of soft yellow pine cracked free of the larger frame. He looked inside as Wally stood back with pen poised. "There aren't any posters in here, Wally."

"No? Are you sure?" He peered into the crate. "Maybe in

one of the other boxes." Wally pulled out a pair of steel-cutting shears and turned to the next crate. Jim applied his hammer.

"See them?" Jim asked as Wally lifted off the top.

"Nope. Just paintings. Maybe in the next one." The two students opened the last crate.

"That must be them," Jim replied, pointing to a tightly wrapped poster-sized parcel within the crate. Wally looked in, agreed with his friend, and studied his clipboard, making checks on various sheets of paper. When his partner asked several times if he was done, Wally snorted.

"I have to get this right, Jim. Don't rush me."

"I don't see why we're doing this. I mean, they're not going back if they forgot to send something."

"That's not the point."

"What is? What are they doing here anyway? The gallery sells his stuff, we don't."

"Some mistake, I guess," Wally said. Conscientious, he wanted to do every job well, and sometimes he had trouble convincing his friend to go along with him.

"Here it is," Jim said, pointing to the address on the crate. "They should have gone to the gallery downtown. Should we send them on?"

"I don't know. He just called to make sure they got here okay. Buddy said to check."

"Who called?" Jim asked.

Wally flipped through the sheets on his clipboard, then looked at the address on the crate nearest him. "Him. That guy. Mr. Rabkin."

"Well, I don't get it," Jim said.

"Look, I don't know any more than you do. The gallery will call when they want them. Maybe Rabkin couldn't take them 'cuz of the stuff he's showing right now."

"So what do we do? We just can't leave them out here in the hallway," Jim said.

Wally looked around, for once in agreement with his

partner. It would be wrong, somehow, to store their art teacher's property in the corridor. Eager to do his best even under such confusing circumstances, Wally persuaded Jim to haul the crates into Preston's office.

■ ■ ■

Time is a state of mind and at noon most people in Mellingham had sloughed off the attitude of grief for a waning season and slipped back to their summer personae. A young mother lolled on the grass in front of Town Hall while her baby slept in its stroller, two retired men in jackets and ties sat on a bench in the park, high school students sat on the hoods of their cars while eating lunch, and office workers ate sandwiches outside their offices.

The students at the Massasoit College of Art set up their easels in the parking lot, turning to face the trees nearby. Instructors were glad to send students outside, whether they worked or not. Some of those who couldn't bring themselves to strive—for anything—on such a day gravitated to the lawn at the side of the building, where they ate lunch or napped in the sun. A few, however, were not permeated with the sun's warmth.

"What does it matter?" Marilyn said, staring up at the sky as she lay on her back, her legs drawn up. Marilyn was annoyed at having her fall interlude chilled by thoughts of the troublesome exhibit. She was eager to work on a show from beginning to end; but the deadline that had once seemed so far off, despite the gallery director's warnings, now seemed to promise endless months of worry instead of regular spots of pleasure and achievement.

"Doug seemed to think it mattered a lot," Noel said, pushing her hair away from her face.

"Has anyone seen him lately?" Marilyn asked.

The students looked at one another, each waiting for someone else to answer, but no one did. Marilyn sat up and rifled through her knapsack for her lunch. Finally, Steven, who had been sitting on the edge of the circle, said, "I think he's dropped the whole thing."

"What?" Several spoke at once, some shocked and surprised, and others uncertain of who they were talking about.

"Doug told me this morning that he expects to be very much unavailable," Steven said, trying to imitate Doug in his pompous moments. He spoke again in his normal voice, saying, "But Marilyn's right. It doesn't matter. We can do the show, get the experience, and then go on to something else."

There were several groans of skepticism and some of outright resistance. "But did you hear what Marilyn said?" another student said. "The reason that guy didn't want to get involved? I mean, he tried to be nice about it, but he made it sound like Mattson was a, a . . ." The student groped unsuccessfully for a word to finish his sentence.

"Schlock artist," Marilyn said. Kathy gasped. "Schlock," Marilyn repeated. She spoke the word as though she were trying it out, testing it for sound or meaning, for aptness.

"Yup. That was what it sounded like," Steven agreed.

"This thing only gets worse." Noel drew up her knees and rested her chin on them, wrapping her arms around her legs. Marilyn lay down on her back and ate her sandwich, examining it above her before taking each bite. She was the only one in the group apparently unconcerned. The others struggled privately with the word and what it implied. A cloud swept around the sun. Paul winced when Steven bumped into him reaching for his books; the two nodded curtly and averted their eyes. Others looked off toward the trees, admiring the view or the half-finished canvases, or nothing at all. No one spoke.

"Well, so what?" Marilyn finally said. "It's got nothing to do with us."

"What?" Noel burst out. "How can you say that? He's our teacher. He's the one who's supposed to train us and get us started and everything." The more upset she became, the more her manner of speech reverted to that of her earlier years. Her voice rose and fell, and her face was screwed up into a mask of outrage and distress.

"Yeah," said another, responding as much to Noel's emotions as to her views.

"What does that mean for our—"

"Nothing," Chickie broke in. He had been standing nearby, leaning against the wall of the building, paying close attention to their conversation.

"Nothing?" repeated one incredulously. Even the quieter ones seemed to think Chickie's comment called for a response and joined in the crush of opinions.

"There's no reason it should have any effect on you at all," Chickie continued. "When you show your work, people judge you on what they see, on what you've done, not on who you know or where you went to school."

"There's more to it than that," Steven said.

"Not much," Chickie replied. "Artists are lucky. We have a better chance of being judged for our work than anyone else."

"But people will want to know who we studied with," Noel said.

"What people?" Chickie countered. The students looked back and forth at each other, the net of future probabilities woven by Professor Mattson drying into dust in the sunshine.

"The only thing anyone can teach is technique, skill, the tricks of the trade. What I do with them, how I put it all together, depends on me, on my talent and who I am." He went on in this vein. The message was thoroughly reasonable, guaranteed to appeal to students who felt vulnerable, sometimes even victimized, by the vagaries of an art world they could only imagine but where they hoped for acceptance and, someday, recognition, but the passion with which Chickie delivered his pronouncement was the more gripping. Marilyn peered at him; others fell silent and listened; Steven cocked his head and watched. They were right to do so, for Chickie was unconsciously talking to himself, verbalizing one side of a conflict he had felt, but barely understood, since his arrival weeks earlier to begin his studies. For the younger students, the debate was little more than a recitation of phrases they had heard over the last few years, in high school and at summer art classes. They could have no idea of the depth of meaning and consequence Chickie imputed to each word.

"In other words," Marilyn said, watching Chickie as she tested her interpretation, "you think it doesn't matter who teaches."

"I don't mean that exactly," Chickie said, feeling he might have gone too far. "I only meant that finding out now that Mattson is out of touch with real art really doesn't mean anything good or bad for you. You can move on to other teachers."

"He's right," Steven said. He was eager to put the debate behind him. "It's not that bad, I guess. We're probably overreacting."

"I think it's awful," Kathy said. Hardest hit emotionally by the discovery that Professor Mattson was not greater than the life he lived, Kathy had the longest road to travel to restored equanimity. Whatever Chickie might be able to promise from the vantage point of greater wisdom and experience could not eliminate the disillusionment of a young woman who had come to college prepared to revere her teachers, matching every word of instruction with an act of study. To alleviate her turmoil, she jumped up, gathered up her drawing pad, and stumbled away.

■ ■ ■

Kathy lurched through the main door of the college, a rumbling of emotions in her breast too entangled for her to identify and therefore tame. On one level she felt betrayed but why or by

whom she could not have said. The most she might have per-
ceived was a failure of others to be what they wanted her to
think they were, and she knew it was not truly "they" but "he."

Kathy was one of those students who came with her own
feelings and identity already corralled by parents and sundry
relatives, having been judged to be safe from infection of feeling by a family determined to keep her as they felt she should
be. As a result, she had few defenses of her own, and therefore
none against a shock to a deeply held illusion—in this
instance, that professors, like parents, were what they said
they were. Unfamiliar with the reality of adults, Kathy was
also not yet able to dissemble for social purposes. The flush on
her face grew and stayed even when she found herself in a
near-empty hallway. Her abrupt departure from her companions left her with time before her next class. With nowhere to
go and nothing else to do, she turned in to the studio and
leaned on a stool. Relieved to be alone, she absently looked
around the room until she saw Professor Mattson. He looked
up from a canvas he had been studying. Their eyes met. The
color drained from Kathy's face and her eyes flashed with an
explosion of emotions he couldn't immediately recognize. To
control herself, she looked away, then stood, gathered up her
belongings, and made a second abrupt departure.

On leaving the group of students, Kathy had no intent of
conveying any of her feelings or reasons for them to Professor
Mattson or anyone else, and Preston expected nothing more
from Kathy, one of his favorite students, than a sweet smile in
greeting. What he saw in her eyes chilled him, threw him back
on himself in ways he had never experienced before. The only
time he had seen anything like it had been in the eyes of a
gallery owner in New York City to whom he had sent slides of
his work when he had first begun teaching and thought a one-
man show would help his career. He had forgotten the experience, letting it die in the overlapping needs of his life until it
lay buried so deeply that only an innocent like Kathy could

slip past his formal persona and find it. He had not named the look then and he could not do so now.

The expression on Preston's face was unchanged, but his hands trembled. He mumbled that a class was due shortly in the studio and he should therefore be on his way. His words fell unheard in the room. He carefully replaced the canvas he had been examining, putting it back in the stack along the wall, and walked from the room, down the corridor, and into his office. His eyebrows were raised and his eyes looked down as much as forward.

Inside his office, the desk chair rolled out smoothly and he sat down, remarking to himself that the annoying squeak seemed to be gone. That pleased him. He turned to straightening up his desk, tossing away the odd scraps of paper that reported earlier calls from Ed Correll (received), his wife (returned), the dean (delayed), and Mike Rabkin (received). Really, he thought to himself, being the head of a department was tedious, demanding work. Already he had attended to numerous administrative tasks, for which he congratulated himself. He should make a point of this to the dean and the president, he thought, drawing their attention to the amount of work he did around here. And he should give himself more credit for it, too. To this end, he decided that perhaps, just this once, he might take the afternoon off. Yes, this was indeed a good idea, he reassured himself as he finished tidying his desk. He would take the afternoon to restore his creative spirit, as it were. And with only the slightest of nods to Betty Lane, Preston Mattson left the school, prompting the dean, when he later learned of Preston's early departure, to speculate on his increasingly idiosyncratic behavior.

■ ■ ■

The most surprising aspect of a police investigation to Chief Silva was the adaptability of the suspects and those around them. Parents learned to greet police officers at the door as though they were no different from the gas meter reader. Office managers routinely rescheduled meetings, lunches, or days off to answer questions. Once again Joe Silva felt himself becoming part of the scenery: he knew where Karen Meghan kept her mini–candy bars (next to the bright blue-and-brown packets of diet food), how many pencils she sharpened every morning whether she used them or not (eleven), and her favorite brand of tea (Irish Breakfast). As an acknowledgment of the new intimacy between the police and the college, Karen sent every member of the police department, and their families, an invitation to the next art exhibit at the school. Most of the officers were amused, but Frankel asked for the evening off so he could attend.

Though more distant, the students were also friendly. Those who came into the office no longer looked intimidated or worried to see him there; some even greeted him with a smile, a nod, a wave. He was just Joe Silva, chief of police and an okay guy. He was glad of this, counting on it to induce unguarded and therefore useful comments among the students and faculty, revealing important undercurrents. Unfortunately, that didn't happen, and Silva had the uncomfortable sensation that he had taken on the role of the friendly fuzz.

Betty Lane, however, was a different matter. In the small office, Silva represented to Miss Lane one more layer of demands, interruptions, illogical questions, and random appearances. If she ever recalled exactly why the police were there, she hid it well. At some moments she actually managed to make Silva feel he was intruding, but he had it on reliable authority (Karen) that Betty made everyone feel this way at least sometimes, even the president of the college.

"I have the files ready for you," Betty said to him when he arrived at her desk at 1:30 that afternoon. "They're right here." She handed him a stack of folders.

Silva set the pile on the counter and fingered each one. "I

think I'll just look through them over here." He nodded to Karen's empty desk. Betty hesitated but Silva was already under the flap in the counter and moving toward the desk before she could say yes or no. Resigned, she returned to her sandwich and the notes she had been reading when Silva first arrived. No one wanted to remain at school on such a beautiful Friday afternoon (or any other one, either), so they rushed through their work in the morning, producing enough odds and ends of office work to ensure that at least Betty would have to stay. That might not have been their intent, but it was the result, which meant that lunch for Betty on Friday was usually a sandwich eaten at her desk, enjoyed over time if not over conversation. She nibbled at her lettuce.

"Hmmm," Silva murmured, nodding his head. He raised his eyebrows and nodded again, slowly turning a page. Betty watched him discreetly, chewing more slowly as her attention fastened on the chief, who kept his eyes on the file. Whatever it was he was reading, he was impressed. Betty sat up straight in her chair and strained herself a bit more, but she still couldn't see what it was.

"Your students are a dedicated bunch." Silva spoke with only a suggestion of a smile on his face. Betty leaned forward to hear his first words, curious beyond reason to know which file he had been reading, but his observation only brought confusion. She had not given him any student files, she thought, and then she remembered the one exception.

"Chickie? Do you mean Chickie?" she asked. Nothing in that student's manner had ever impressed Betty, and she was stumped now, trying to guess what Silva found so interesting.

"He put in a lot of time here," Silva went on, half to himself. "Nights. Weekends."

Betty listened and her mind drifted off to what she knew about Chickie. It wasn't much. Now that she thought about it, she had never really liked him. He was so, so—she searched in vain for an apt expression.

"Must have been quite a hard worker," Silva said as he flipped back to the beginning of the folder. Despite his tendency to take up her time, these brief, allusive, even cryptic conversations with Silva infused Betty with a sense of importance and complicity in his investigation. She alluded to them when with her friends but always shied away from revealing anything specific. It was clear to her friends that the chief of police was relying on Betty for her years of experience and her discretion. "Quite a worker," Silva repeated.

"All the students put in a lot of time," she said, feigning indifference.

"It seems like it must be more than that. He must have been a busy young man—putting himself through school, working here and in Boston."

He must be talking about Hank Vinnio, Betty decided. Well, she could agree with that. "Yes, he certainly made a point of working all the time," she said. "He was always here after the morning classes and he stayed until after everyone left in the evening." She crushed into a ball the wax paper in which she had wrapped her sandwich and dropped it into the wastebasket by her desk. "Just like Chickie." They were two of a kind, now that she thought about it. They were almost the same age, older students going back to school, working crummy jobs to get by, no family in the area, coming out of nowhere. "They were both always here sometime during the weekend. Chickie and Hank. Actually, I'm surprised Chickie didn't see something." With her right hand she swept the top of her desk, brushing the crumbs into her left hand. "Or hear something." She inspected the clean surface of her desk. "Think of the racket from those cans. But he must have talked to you already."

"We try to be thorough," Silva said, making a note.

"I suppose it's hard for Chickie," she said, suddenly feeling sympathetic, "since they were so close, I mean."

"Hmmm."

"I thought it was nice that the two had someone else here like themselves. It must have been tiresome for them to be surrounded with college kids all the time."

"So he and Hank hit it off," Silva said, looking up.

"Well, they had a lot in common, didn't they?"

10

SATURDAY

IT WAS NOT WHERE they were sitting—at the far end of
the design studio downstairs, which gave them a clear view
of the parking lot and the approach to the main door—that
gave the group an air of secretiveness, or even the lowered
voices as each one spoke quickly, decisively, as if they had
that moment and that moment only to speak their minds and
make their points. It was not the serious, intent looks on their
faces as each student listened to the words of the speaker
before adding anything. It was not even the unusual timing of
the meeting—8:30 on a Saturday morning—which might have
raised an eyebrow from even Buddy Lecroix, if he had known.
It was none of these that gave the group a furtive air, though
any one might have been enough by itself among other people.
It was, in contrast, the way one of the young men, sitting at
the edge of the circle of students, leaned forward to listen to
every word while holding his head tilted sideways so that his
eye could catch any movement at the door behind him. And
he did this, not because no one sitting across from him was
watching the door (several were), but because he could not
relax. Neither could any of the others. Despite a shared confidence that they had chosen a time and place when they would
not be driven out by teachers seeking an extra room, or intrud-

234

ed on by curious students, none in the room could relax entirely, so vivid was their confrontation with the deeper problem underlying their project. And so each one spoke in short but modulated bursts of passion, urging one course of action or another, finding flaws in one plan, this suggestion, that idea, an example. But they were intent on their goal, willing to grapple with their disagreements until they found a solution, so around the circle they went again.

A door slammed shut on the floor above them and the students fell silent, their eyes rising in unison to the ceiling, the young man with his head turned to the door slowly swinging his body to face the opening, all of them listening for footsteps coming closer. But none came.

"That's the door to the painting studio, I think," Noel said. Another nodded. They listened. Another door sounded, closing softly.

"That must be Buddy," Steven said.

A third door sounded, even more softly, and the young man closest to the door turned back to the group, saying, "He must be checking the studios. He's going toward the gallery."

A few of them sighed in relief; one man stretched his legs and leaned back in the metal folding chair, stretching his arms above him.

"All right," Steven said. "Let's go over it again. Buddy won't mind our being here but any teachers coming today might ask questions and I don't want to get Chickie into trouble." The others nodded, murmured, and some drew their chairs closer to the center of the circle. When they began again, the students were less urgent in their views but more certain of their direction. A suggestion was made, modified, accepted. Marilyn pulled out a small pocket notebook and began making notes, adding the comments and suggestions as they fell softly into the center of the room. After a while, the comments came less frequently, like the last few kernels of popcorn, the early popping frenzy making the final explosions sound muted by comparison. When the comments stopped altogether, and the students looked to each other in silence and agreement, Marilyn began to read her notes. Heads nodded when she was finished and no one spoke for a few minutes.

"I suppose we didn't have any choice." The resolve that had fired the others for over an hour was just now creeping into Noel's face, mixed with a sadness the others for the most part had put to rest. Her words broke the spell and the young man on Noel's left offered his reassurance, but only perfunctorily. The unpleasantness was over and he was glad, and now he just wanted to be away and on to work that had no awkwardness for him. The other students also turned their minds to other things, chattering in their ordinary voices as they stood up, collected backpacks and straw bags, and folded up their chairs. Their decisions having been made, the students let all self-consciousness fall away, and they became again the college students who knew no obstacles, imagined no restrictions, considered no consequences.

They were still talking loudly as they climbed the stairs to the main floor above, each one now deeply absorbed in the details of the coming day. Buddy, who was just then musing on the joys of a quiet school building, stopped in his chores at the sound of the students moving up the stairs. He reached the door of the gallery as the group moved down the hall to the main door, oblivious to the look of surprise and concern on the janitor's face.

■ ■ ■

At 8:35 Joe Silva watched a tall lean figure meander from station to station across the village green, stopping first at a wooden bench occupied by three old men, who took their places on the bench six mornings a week. The man remained long enough for all four to participate in the conversation before moving on to the next bench, this one occupied by a young mother with a baby carriage and a little boy stretching out his limbs to youth and maturity. The lean man had a few kind words for the boy too before he stopped at the water fountain for a drink. He had to lean in among a gaggle of boys straddling their bicycles, most of whom he knew and questioned on their plans for the day. Silva grew impatient, and he studied the building set back from the green.

He had seen hundreds of town halls, and most of them, at least most of the ones he recalled, were large Victorian buildings, built when towns and America first seemed to become conscious of a sense of grandeur in their soul. Now the buildings boasted the tallest ceilings, steepest roofs, and an infinite variety in design and decoration, most of it painted over so many times that sharp edges were now smooth. But all these buildings shared the same spot in the landscape.

In almost every town in America, the town hall sits in the center—on the green, at the one streetlight, near the crossroads, next to the church, across from the main store, or amid the only clustered buildings for miles—the rising cupola or arched roof reaching to the sky, mimicking the aspirations of the town residents, just as Gothic church spires were designed long ago to carry aloft the spiritual longings of the parishioners. People walk by, drive by, sit in front, and think of their town hall as a known place, the place to go for solutions to problems, an answer to knotty questions, help with awkward, unexpected dilemmas. Many can even recite all the offices therein and who occupies them, giving detailed lists from what seems to outsiders an easy familiarity. But, as Silva knew, all this was illusion.

The town hall, like the police station, is one side of an invisible line, as hard to see but as definite as the Tropic of Cancer. Inside the venerable old buildings are people employed by the town, which means by no one person but answerable to every person who comes through the door. This fact alone might explain why town employees, throughout the decades, have hunkered down behind their desks, braced themselves, putting their feet on the floor and hunching their shoulders, when a local resident walked though the doors. And yet they seem perfectly normal among themselves, laughing at the same jokes as those in the grocery store around the corner, or worried about the same changes in regulations as the insurance agent across town.

Town government is too often a world apart. A few notice after they have crossed the border, but most merely find themselves looking out at a town that now seems strange. It is not. They are different, and only a few are aware of the passage from one side of the line to the other even while making the journey. These were the fortunate few who embraced all sides and none, held the world in their dreams, and lived only in reality and this moment. They were rare. Joe Silva was one, and the man he watched crossing the green was another. When the chief of police saw Gordon Davis enter Town Hall, he rose and left his office.

"Looking a little fretful today," Gordon Davis said as Silva turned into the town clerk's office. "Got that murder on your mind?"

"Not at the moment," Silva said. "I've come about something else."

Gordon turned a penetrating eye on the chief. Mr. Davis was little more than sixty, but when the department hired four young men a few years ago for summer work, Gordon took on the task of supervising them. It was his job only *extra officium*, he kept telling people, and the young ones nodded vigorously, eagerly reassuring him that they too had heard of that. No one challenged him, so he added impromptu lectures on the virtues of seniority to the young men's routine. In return they dubbed him Old Gordon. Tall, lean, tanned, with rust-colored hair, Gordon didn't seem to mind the nickname, perhaps because it gave him an age his appearance denied him.

"Well, just tell me what I can do for you. It must be very important to take you away from a murder," Gordon said with a sly smile. "Mrs. Rogers called this week—twice. Thursday and Friday. I wasn't here, but I heard about yesterday's call."

"Mr. Muir seems to be a changed man," Silva said. "Is that just part of his nature, this changeability, or is there a reason for it?"

"Henry Muir?" Gordon shook his head. "Henry's a good man, for all his cold ways; good winner, too."

"You think he's won his case, then?" Silva asked. "Just with a bouquet of roses?"

Gordon threw back his head and laughed. "Those were the consolation prize," he said.

"You're going to have to explain that." Silva leaned on the counter, ready to admit he was out of his depth.

"Henry was in here most of last week." He glanced at Silva as he went to an old filing cabinet in the corner, pulled open a middle drawer, and flipped one by one through the manila files. "Pretty soon we're going to put all this old stuff on microfilm and put the film in the basement." Gordon sighed. "Right now we have boxes and boxes of old records all piled together down there. A fire hazard, if you ask me." Gordon looked square at Silva. "Tons of stuff." He shook his head. "The only way to find anything is to go through each box and hope you get lucky. Now if we put that stuff on microfilm, we'd have to go through each roll to find one document. Hard going, doing it that way. No one would be able to find anything," Gordon said. "Then, if we get computers for current stuff along with microfilm and microfilm readers for the old stuff, and both of them breaking down the way these new machines do, well, I figure we can hold out against anyone looking for information indefinitely."

Silva watched him flip through a file. "You're not sounding very public-spirited today, Gordon."

"No? Perhaps not. But without old records people sort of have to go along with the general consensus. Now, coming to consensus takes time. First you have to explain to people what's possible and what isn't. That takes a while. People take time to let go of their own ideas and catch up with the new ones. Then I have to remind them that the files, even if we do have them from way back, can go either way. They can support what you want them to support, or they can bury it." He paused to read a single sheet of paper. "They can go either way," he repeated. "Now that sort of scares people," he added while he read. "First each side thinks it will win if it can just get some old records to back them up, but then I tell them what they really might find and then, well, they start thinking they could be wrong, they could lose. And if they don't start thinking that on their own, I point that out very clearly," he said, looking over at Silva. "Now, that's when we start to get consensus."

"I see," Silva said. "What exactly did Henry Muir find here in the files?"

"Records, Chief, records. Zoning came to the town of Mellingham in 1942; it was the war that did it."

"I sure hope you're going to explain all this," Silva said. The arcana of small-town life, particularly in Mellingham, still threatened, after all his years here, to overwhelm him. "What did he find?"

"What he found was zoning records from 1942. February, to be exact. Henry Muir's father, Henry Senior, volunteered for the army, as did just about everyone else in town, but he wasn't going to go anywhere without a fight. There wasn't much he cared about back then, so he settled on his property to fight about. Farseeing sort of fellow, he was. He'd heard about these changes that came in with zoning laws and he wanted to make sure that if anything happened to him his boy, Henry Junior, just pink blubber back then, could carry on the family business."

"What was the family business?"

"Tool sharpening." Gordon chuckled. "'Course, that's not what he did for a living; that's just what he had for a business in the old barn. It was just the old man's way of giving the town a hard time. But he got what he wanted."

Silva laughed. "So the old business was grandfathered. But what about now? You're not telling me that Henry Muir wants to open a tool-sharpening business, are you?"

"Oh, no, not on your life. This is the Muirs we're talking about." Gordon glared at Silva, then his eyes grew wide with glee. "He got the new board of appeals, men who in 1942 had to look up the word *zoning* when they first agreed to take on the job, he got them to grant him and his heirs—this was wartime, you know—the right to operate any business on his property in perpetuity, regardless of lapses in use. They were thinking about the war. Not Henry Senior. He was just being as twisted difficult as he could think to be."

Silva shook his head, and Gordon said, "Folks didn't know too much about zoning back then. Those Muirs were always shrewd."

"So he knew he could do what he wanted all the time. Do you think Mrs. Rogers knows?" Silva asked, thinking of the neighbor who had long worked with her friends and neighbors to hold Mr. Muir in harness.

"Maybe. But I don't think so." Gordon wasn't sure about that, and thought for a bit. "I don't suppose it matters," he finally said. "The flowers put an end to it anyway. I guess that was the point of them, too." He chuckled.

"I can't believe it. Henry Muir has been going on about a zoning variance all these years as though it were the fight of his life, and now you're suggesting he probably knew all along he didn't need one in the first place. Why would he bother?"

Gordon turned a shocked eye on Joe Silva. "You've been here how many years and you still don't understand us?" He shook his head in despair.

"For fun?" Joe said. "You mean this is his idea of getting along with his neighbors? This is his idea of being a neighbor?"

"There's worse ways," Gordon said. "And no one told Mrs. Rogers to fight him."

"You're right about that." Silva agreed, but the force of Gordon's argument was not obvious to him. "So why the flowers? Why did he suddenly quit?" Silva asked. "What does he mean to do with the barn now that he's through teasing his neighbors about it?" This was what Silva really wanted to know. "The man has had a studio there for years and he's been trying to get permission to expand it for just as long. You're not telling me he went through all this trouble with his neighbors year after year never meaning to do anything different. And you're not telling me he quit just because he got bored. So what happened? Why quit now?"

"That is a poser," Gordon said, struck by Silva's question. "He's been bothering folks with his plans for years, pestering the zoning board, getting people upset, just for the fun of it. But this year it was different. First there was that lawyer. Then he came in here and found those old records. That's a feat all by itself. And now he's quit."

"So what's he really up to?" Silva asked, perplexed.

"That's a poser, all right," Gordon said. "It sure is."

■ ■ ■

The floor beyond the movable walls glistened beneath Buddy's mop as he worked his way toward the door. Already he had reached the center of the gallery, twice its normal size now that the folding walls had been pushed into a storage hallway to make room for the new exhibit. He would have to clean most of it again, after the paintings were hung, to get the place looking good for the opening tomorrow night, but he didn't mind. The white walls rose to steel beams and strobe lights and ropes and pulleys, up in the darkness like the hidden reaches of a theater. More and more Buddy thought of the art school, its faculty and students and staff, as players on a stage; only he didn't know who had taken the role of the audience.

He swung out the gray ropes of the mop tangled like worms struggling over each other in a bait bucket, and moved along the wall. The building felt abandoned, as it always did during the early hours of the day and on the weekend. At 8:35 on Saturday morning, it felt doubly so, and Buddy breathed in the loneliness of his work like a rare fragrance. His wife thought he was crazy to be going to work on such a Saturday, to be doing anything extra for the college after the dean had had the effrontery to inspect his storerooms, and even check his private work closet. Mrs. Lecroix was insulted and, if Buddy was any judge of his wife's reaction to danger and the fear it stirred up in her, she was likely to remain so. It didn't matter that Buddy knew the dean was following up a rumor and had to do what he did. It didn't matter that Buddy had been there longer than anyone else with never a complaint against him until now. It didn't matter that the dean had in the end apologized for the implications of his search. No, none of that mattered, as Buddy kept telling his wife. None of it. What did matter was the danger that lurked in the hallways and studios and classrooms day after day after day.

In his fifty-six years Buddy had never faced such a threat. He had faced everything else imaginable—except this. Buddy pushed the mop and as he did so he caught sight of his hands, and once again knew that he had mastered the skill of avoiding the immediately obvious. His hands with their red and purple scars slid the pole forward and back again. He had learned not to see them when he first understood as an adolescent that they were ugly. His wife instinctively understood and tucked work gloves into the car, in his lunch pail, in the garage, on his work desk in the cellar, but she never asked him to wear them. She said she liked his hands, but he would have gloves whenever he wanted them. Over the years he wore them less and less.

He even understood when the students laughed at him behind his back the first—and last—time he complimented one of them on her work. Back then no one wanted to be friends with the young man who was the janitor—it was too frightening, too threatening, too dangerous. Remembering the experience so long ago made him wonder about the person he had been, so proud of his new job, so curious about the school and what they did there, so eager to belong. It all turned out in ways he hadn't expected. He grew and the students didn't; each year they were more of the same, for the most part.

When the students became suddenly democratic in the 1960s and 1970s, they wanted him to stand with them while they protested—what he wasn't sure—but when they learned he had served in the U.S. Army, they challenged him, calling him a dupe. Even that was more confusing than upsetting, and he let it pass; after all, he had liked the army, but he knew others didn't. Instead, he grew more and more like his beloved building, abandoned to the solitude that consoles and renews.

Only one person had ever penetrated the world he had constructed, the safety that came from being the only one the college president and dean and faculty could always rely on— only one. Even now the terror that vibrated through his body when he first realized what Hank Vinnio had in mind lingered, ready to roll through his limbs. He had been here too long to start over again anywhere else. His job now was part of him; he had molded himself to it; he wouldn't fit anywhere else. He'd be all rough edges, sharp corners, bulges where he should be flat. This was the only place he fit. It was his.

When he thought of his son, the child that never came when he and his wife were young and still hoping and planning, the child that came after husband and wife had learned to accept a neglectful fate and make themselves into another kind of couple, when he thought of the child and himself without a job, he felt a cold sweat on his forehead spreading down to his jaw and then along his shoulders. He shivered, shook his head, hunched over his mop.

These fears were past, he reminded himself. They were

past. This became a chant, smoothing the push and pull of the mop into a dance along the gallery floor, calming him, reassuring him, blotting out the other thoughts that might tumble in on him in such moments of privacy. He finished one side and moved to the other, the frown on his forehead swinging down into a smile. He hummed a tune he didn't recognize.

The sweeps of the mop got wider as Buddy's heart returned to its normal size, for no matter how the outside world regarded him, he felt only goodwill to others. The mop brushed by a chair and Buddy heard scraping and other noise. Startled, he poked the chair, but decided he couldn't have made all that racket. The mop moved back and forth in a short arc while Buddy listened as the sounds grew louder and came closer. In less than a minute a crowd of almost a dozen students walked down the hall, chatting and joking and planning with each other—so many students and he hadn't even known they were there. It was just like a week ago, a quiet Saturday unexpectedly filled with students. How did they get in? And how did Buddy miss knowing they were there? The mop stood still in his fists.

■ ■ ■

The gray Rover lumbered slowly down the road, its stately progression unmatched by the feelings of its passengers. When Ellen had first given him the car, Preston had studied it distantly, unsure of what to make of it yet eager to make it his own. He had never thought of himself as a Rover driver, but after a while the gathering of images of the kinds of people who drove such a car embraced him entirely, and he grew to love his new possession. Whenever he drove anywhere now, his mind was often in England, moving over moors (as he imagined them) or up rocky slopes in Scotland. Nothing bothered him when he drove, not even the imminent destination, which on this morning was his office and an interview with Chief Silva.

In part Preston Mattson didn't mind an early Saturday meeting with Silva because he had slipped the stultifying noose around Ellen as soon as he hung up the telephone. Unfazed by the short passage of time since Hank Vinnio's death, Preston insisted that Ellen accompany him to the college, where she could get in a few hours of work before they went out to lunch. Cranky and distracted, Ellen agreed, and so she sat next to her husband, each oblivious of the other.

Dressed in a pale linen skirt, green blouse, and green suede jacket, Ellen Mattson sat with her small feet close together and her lips pursed. She was the only student in the history of the art school who dressed better than the trustees. Her hands rested on the painting smock folded neatly in her lap, her fingers pulling at a button, twisting it one way and then back again. Her meditations were not as pleasant as her husband's.

"You're making far too much of this, Ellen," Preston said after she repeated her complaint about Chief Silva.

"The police have on their hands the death of a young man no one knew." He paused to rethink this. "Well, at least that's the way it seemed." He ran his hands along the broad steering wheel, then continued robustly. "The police only want to get their facts straight. I see no reason to be concerned." He swerved sharply to avoid colliding with a young jogger weaving into the center of the narrow road. "I for one do not intend to let this investigation distract me from my work. I have, for far too long, let secondary matters like administration take precedence. My art, as a result, has suffered. I do not intend to be distracted anymore."

"But Preston—" Ellen began.

"Stop worrying, my dear," he interrupted her. "Didn't your attorney tell you everything was fine?"

"Yes, but—"

"Then stop worrying. There are people in this world who really have something to worry about, but fortunately you're not one of them." He turned to smile at her briefly, but his smile was little more than a flexing of his labial muscles, for his mind was still focused on a wild Yorkshire moor. The expression lingered as he rolled down the road well over the speed limit.

"Suppose they arrest me for bigamy? People keep talking as though Hank and I were still married." Ellen's meditations tended to the melodramatic; at each scene she grew in innocence while the antagonist sank in malignity. She had the imagination of a frightened child.

"Good God, Ellen. You make it sound like the police are harassing you." Preston also wanted to avoid the issue of their marital status, at least for the moment. "They only want to know what you can tell them about Vinnio. Whatever you know after all these years. Which is nothing. They're not going to bother you." Preston had heard the confidence and worldliness in his voice for so many years that he barely questioned the tone that escaped automatically. It never altered. His voice never grew intimate, doubtful, wondering, casual, except in the rarest of circumstances. Fortunately, he had never met anyone who might challenge his assumptions and attitude, or at least not yet, which was why he was mildly uncomfortable at the prospect of another meeting with Chief Silva. The man was polite but there was a certain quality in his manner—Preston couldn't quite put his finger on it—that bothered him.

"Just tell the truth and you'll be fine," he said, not bothering to look at his wife. The steering wheel played free for a few seconds beneath his fingers. His expression turned into a genuine smile as he felt the car respond to his hand, and he began to hum quietly as they neared the college. The first thing he would do on Monday, he promised himself, would be to talk to the dean of the faculty, to arrange a reduced teaching load and more time for himself. Yes, indeed, things were looking up.

■ ■ ■

By late Saturday morning the school had settled into its usual weekend routine, which meant that the few who were driven to work out problems on canvas or paper or in wood or steel were hard at it, benefiting from the deep silence though barely conscious of it.

Chief Silva, however, was, and therefore careful not to break it. Silva was not like other police officers who like to make a noisy entrance to see what it provokes and to ensure that all attention is drawn to the officer. He preferred to enter a silence, for it was the only time he got to see into other people's lives, to see them as themselves, unself-conscious. He caught the main door as it wheezed closed behind him, let it fall to softly, and moved quietly down the hall.

When he first revealed his intent to join the police force, when he was still a teenager, an older cousin took him aside and urged him to join the army or navy or air force, anything but the police. This surprised the young Joe and he listened to her as she told him he would become a stranger to his friends just as she had as a nun lost her identity as a girl of the neighborhood. Even after she left the order, she admitted to him, she was careful whom she told about her former life. Joe wondered about a vocation that brought out the same circumspection in a woman as life as a prostitute might. He thought then she was troubled; he understood later she was warning him.

Silva looked into the first painting studio, still dark in the gray morning light, and heard nothing. The rooms felt more like garages or machine shops than classrooms and he was glad for the opportunity to inspect at least one. In questioning students and faculty and reading statements taken by his officers, Silva had grown fond of the separate world that was the art school, warmed by the camaraderie the students shared, their innate curiosity about what the police were doing and how they were going about it, and their unusual perspectives on the world and their places in it. They were a happy breed.

He moved along to the next studio, just as large a room, but in this one the overhead lights shone from one end of the ceiling to the other. In the near corner, across from the main door, stood a young woman working at a painting set on an easel. Silva moved toward the center of the room rather than directly toward her, not wanting to distract her. He had received conflicting reports about the activity in the building on a weekend and had come to see for himself, making allowances for the effects of a recent death there. But it was much as he had expected. Only a few cars sat in the parking lot, their spacing indicating regulars who chose parking spots for the full day, under trees for shade and protection, close to a building to avoid careless drivers and the bumps and scratches for which Massachusetts parking lots were justifiably famous.

This particular student was new to him but then the serious ones generally held back and watched. He was aware that she had noticed him standing in the center of the room watching her; she turned her head quickly to look at him and then returned to her work.

"Am I bothering you?" Chief Silva finally asked when he was confident that he wasn't.

"No," she replied after a few moments, not looking up at him.

"I thought I might find a few of the students here." He watched her work from where he stood.

"It's Saturday." She smeared a swath of black paint in the center of the canvas, then tried a swirl of blacks and dark blues.

"I thought there might be a few around," he said. She went on painting, ignoring his comment.

"Hi, Buddy," she called out as she continued studying her canvas. Silva heard rubber-soled shoes moving down the hall.

"You must spend a lot of Saturdays here if you're so sure of Buddy's footsteps."

"I do." She stepped back from the canvas and turned her dark brown eyes on him. "What do you think?"

"Very striking," Silva said. "It could have been someone else," he said, returning to his earlier comment. "Another student, a teacher."

"No, it couldn't."

"Why not?"

"Because no one came through the front door."

"How about one of the other doors?" Silva probed.

"The other doors are locked. On the alarm, except the back," she said between daubs. "Do you think that's too dark?"

"No." He had no idea what she was doing or if she was doing it well, but he did recognize the importance of her observations. "How can you be sure of that?"

"Easy." She daubed at the black. "Hank always came in the back and then opened up the front. He might leave the back door into the back parking lot unlocked, but he wouldn't open any of the other doors. You can hear anyone coming in or moving around from either door on Saturdays because it's so quiet."

Unless, of course, they don't want to be heard, Silva thought. Aloud, he said, "Well, that takes care of Hank."

"Chickie, too."

"Chickie Morelli?" Silva recited the name to be sure. The girl nodded.

"They both did exactly the same thing, unlocking the back and then the front. We used to laugh about it, about how janitors do everything exactly the same way. 'Course, Chickie and Hank weren't real janitors, just part time, for school."

"Is that what Buddy does?"

"I guess."

"Didn't you come in the front door?"

"Oh, sure, but Chickie let us in early, for a meeting." She smiled at Chief Silva and suddenly seemed to realize who he was. Silva wondered what Buddy thought of this practice.

"So it's like this all day? Quiet? Only two doors open?"

"That's about it. We're very careful," she said, trying to redeem herself.

"What about the day Hank Vinnio died?"

"The same. Right up until I left."

"When was that?" He already knew the answer from the pages of interviews he had read, but today he was learning more than had made it onto the typed page.

"The usual. 'Bout three." She lost herself in her painting again. "I never know what to call my work. What do you think?"

"It's a real dilemma," Silva said.

"Oh yeah?" She paused. "What do you really think it is?" she asked, intrigued with his response.

"An enigma," he said jocularly, not wanting to offend her or sink in any deeper.

"That's right. That's what it is. I couldn't think of the word. Enigma," she said, rolling the word back and forth in her mouth and onto her lips. "That's what comes out of volcanoes." She pulled a scrap of paper and a short stub of a pencil from her paint box and made a note. Silva opened his mouth to correct her but decided not to. When she was through writing, she turned to him with a smile that bespoke the joy of accomplishment. "I never know what to call something when I'm through except what it looks like or how it makes me feel. And to me it started to look like that stuff that comes out of a volcano. You know, that stuff that comes out and becomes lava when it rolls down a mountain. I took geology."

"Oh," said Chief Silva.

"I knew it was related to *great*, or sounded like it, or something like that," she said. "I also took Latin," she said with pride.

"Ah," said Silva, once again wordless in the face of the creative mind.

■ ■ ■

The sense of competence and satisfaction Preston gained from his morning drive to the college carried him into his office and through the first few minutes of looking through his desk drawers. His gait and expression were not lost on Chief Silva, who recorded his wife's turn into the last studio after her husband entered the administrative offices. Despite the presence of the few other students scattered throughout the building, Ellen and Preston seemed to accentuate a loneliness. Silva didn't alter this view when he saw the chairman of the painting department happily shuffling papers at his desk.

Preston greeted the chief with a firm handshake, eager to set the tone if not the direction of the conversation. "What can I do to help you?" he asked with a generous stretch of his mouth.

"How did you come to send your wife to the school on Saturday afternoon, the day Hank Vinnio died?" Silva asked his question without preamble, studying the other man's reaction.

Mattson shifted in his chair, his eyes flitting from lamp to chair to door. "Ah, well," he said. He laughed and gripped the arms of his chair.

"As I recall," he began again, "she was having some technical trouble—with drawing, or something like that—and I thought, well, she should give some extra time to it. You know, extra work to catch up to the rest of the class. Saturday afternoon seemed to be a good time." Preston smiled, eager to end the matter. It seemed to him a meager question for a Saturday morning interview. He discarded his answer as soon as it was out. More confident in the face of Silva's protracted silence, Preston leaned forward to gather up a pile of papers on his desk.

"Did Mrs. Mattson normally work in the studio on Saturday afternoon?"

"Well, no, not normally." Preston was irritated. Silva seemed to be here for idle chat. "Sometimes she did."

"And you?" Silva was growing tired with the effort to be courteous to the professor, a man he considered as blind to reality as his wife was naive, but just as he felt himself ready to give in to impatience, he felt an inkling of pity.

"Me?" Preston seemed genuinely surprised at the question.

"Yes. Do you normally work here on Saturday?"

"Well, actually, no. No, I never do."

"But you're here today," Silva pointed out. "You suggested your office for our meeting." At first Silva had thought the location was meant to impress him with Mattson's position at the college but he was beginning to change his mind. The office might be the only place Mattson felt safe.

"Yes. We, well, the thing is, all this excitement over a murder," he began. "What I mean is, it's gotten us all a little off schedule. I was just trying to get back on schedule with my work."

"I understand you had no idea that Mrs. Mattson had been married twice before?" Silva said, changing the subject.

"No. No idea." His mouth was tight; the distress that passed over his face was quickly gone. "A childish failure to tell all, but harmless."

"You might want to consult a lawyer on that point," Silva said. Even now, given every chance, Mattson didn't say what Silva was waiting for, that he and Ellen had remarried quietly as soon as they understood the implications of her earliest marriage. Their silence on this added a cautionary sadness to the murder investigation. Silva was not a man who looked on the death of a marriage with indifference; each one pained him, perhaps because it reminded him of his own estate.

"You might have to defend your wife's claim to the Correll property in court."

"Ellen said—" He stared at Silva, wondering how the chief knew what had been bothering him since he first learned how Vinnio figured in Ellen's life. Until this moment, he had been certain that Ellen, though sometimes foolish and careless, wouldn't share everything with the police, yet Chief Silva's questions were coming closer and closer to conversations that had been among the most intimate he and Ellen had ever had. "Ellen said her lawyer told her that everything was all right. Everything was put in her name by Joey and there was no"— he paused to make sure he had the lawyer's words as clearly as he could remember them—"attempt to defraud. She honestly thought the marriage to Hank was dissolved and she married Joey in good faith. I think that's how he put it, in good faith. Nothing to worry about." He almost managed to sound jovial.

"I'm glad to hear that. Such a huge lawsuit could be very disruptive for you." There were times when Silva was deeply grateful for the gossip that swirled in Mellingham.

"Quite so." Preston kept his eye on Silva, watching for the next question.

"I'm surprised that Vinnio never tried to contact your wife directly. He had enough time after he arrived here, plenty of opportunities to talk to her alone in the building. Your wife never mentioned his bothering her?"

"No, she didn't. He might not even have recognized her." Preston thought this reply was a stroke of genius, putting Ellen and Hank almost in the category of strangers. His chest expanded by at least two inches.

"It seems from what we know that he recognized her all right."

"Ah." Preston's crisp striped shirt crumpled. His breath was short.

"But I'm interested that she never complained about him to you." Silva was more than interested. He couldn't conceive of a marriage in which two people wouldn't share something so basic as a surprise encounter with an ex-spouse. The Mattsons' marriage seemed a dismal affair to Joe. "Are you sure she never said anything?"

"Never," Preston said, suddenly convinced that truth and falsehood were equally dangerous.

■ ■ ■

The last classroom in the basement of the college building had been Chickie's favorite from the start. At the end of the long hall that wended past the boiler room, past the sculpting studio and the storage rooms, and around the maintenance workroom, the last classroom was for overflow—of students, classes, equipment, artwork. Here Chickie always found solitude, for the college was small and rarely had need of this space. Here he came to think through the few important challenges and changes to his life in recent weeks. The room was an after-thought, in design and appearance, and Chickie felt comfort-able here. When he walked through the door he tossed his head, throwing his dark shaggy hair to the side, releasing his sight to roam the world in front of him, confined though it might be.

He was hungry, since it was almost lunchtime, and this was his first chance to repair to his chosen place in several days. He pulled three chairs together near the full-length win-dows, arranged his sandwich and thermos on one, and settled himself on the other two. The day was normal upstairs: a few students were working privately, Buddy was finding extra work to do, and the building was mostly silent. The early morning meeting of students was over, much to Chickie's relief. At first he hadn't wanted to let them in, feeling himself disloyal to Buddy and pushed into the role Hank had taken, but he sympathized with them and finally relented. Most had left as soon as the meeting was over. Relieved, Chickie had seen the last student-filled car drive away only to see a police car drive in. It sobered him and he returned to work, but Chief Silva never sought him out, and when Chickie looked again, the police car was gone.

Only then did he realize that that wasn't what he had expected. He had returned to his work, subdued and expec-tant, and nothing had happened. Only when he realized Silva was gone did the solace of his room at the end of the hall draw him, only then did he let himself be drawn away. The shock of seeing his own feelings played out so clearly pushed him to face himself right then, and what he had made of his life. He didn't like it.

For a few brief weeks Chickie had seen in Hank a promise that what he, Chickie, was doing made sense, that it was possible to go back to something that was important to him instead of hunkering down at a crummy job for the rest of his life. But then he got to know Hank better, or know about him, Chickie corrected himself. Everyone talked about him, pointed him out, and Chickie overlooked the discrepancies in what he saw—Hank's late arrival at work, his repeated problems with the vending machines, his sly comments about teachers and students, his talk about a security as good as cash in the bank. But ignoring the truth only worked for a while.

Chickie finished his salami sandwich, the same kind he had made for himself every day that week, and wondered if his dissatisfaction with life stemmed from something as simple as boredom with his lunch. If his meals were less monotonous, would he be happy? He discarded the question in favor of a potato chip. If he spent his time on such questions he might never make a decision, and he had to make one. He knew that.

Hank Vinnio was a bum and worse. Chickie's father was right. Bitter as his words were, Chickie's father had been right all along. His son was turning into a bum, a drifter, a young boy with talent who became a flashy newcomer, an old man with a shtick, talent, always starting, never finishing. It would go on until he was a caricature of himself—fifty years old and just going back to something that had mattered to him as a kid, like painting, or writing, it didn't matter what, because it hid the truth that he'd never had a real life with a real job. The promise of Hank, someone who could use innate talent to change himself and the direction of his adult life, turned into a threat of what Chickie would become. Part of his mind said he was overreacting, that no two people had identical lives, but the pull had been so strong that the truth had been doubly painful. Hank was a fraud, a cheat, and a bum. Chickie was afraid of becoming just like him.

■ ■ ■

"That could be dangerous," Dupoulis said to his chief. The two men were sitting in the tiny room that served as Silva's office, Dupoulis on the chair wedged between the desk and the wall and Silva leaning back in his chair.

"Suppose she freezes," Dupoulis went on. "She might, you know."

"Yes," the chief agreed, letting his eyes rise to the cross-piece of the door frame. Every time he went to the town selectmen with a request for a new building, an addition, even a paint job on some of the rooms, they pleaded poverty and insisted that as long as the stationhouse was safe, neat, and clean, no one could ask for more. Literally. Silva toyed with the idea of letting the building decline. He calculated the normal maintenance after a mild winter and added a few calamities of neglect: water stains below windows left open by a harried officer, three-legged chairs propped up with out-of-date phone books, aluminum mesh flapping on screen doors. How long would it take for the stationhouse to become so disreputable that the town residents would demand a new building? The image of a battery of town residents besieging the board of selectmen for a new building delighted him.

He liked to think he knew who would lead the charge. The war could be protracted, considering the determination of the board to hold down costs and the residents to get what they wanted. Who would give in first? Who would force a decision? The police sergeant who was afraid of taking home on his uniform bits of old lead paint that might be examined— and swallowed—by his toddler? The town fathers, who would no longer be able to boast of their town's unmatched picturesqueness? The local business men and women who would fear the loss of income if the town center began to look run-down? Silva had just about chosen one group over the others when he realized Dupoulis was talking to him.

"Then we'd have worse than nothing," the sergeant said.

"How do you mean?" Silva asked, ashamed of himself for daydreaming. The chief liked to let his mind wander when he had a tough decision to make, regarding it as one way of finding the right decision. But he wasn't sure he wanted to explain that to anyone—or even if he wanted to try. He set aside the scenario that had so entertained him and turned his mind to practical matters.

"If she freezes after we suggest we can charge her with murder, we have nothing. And we have to have a confession of exactly what she did before we can be sure about the murderer. If we push it and charge her, we might have a case against someone you think is innocent, which is what I meant by worse than nothing," Dupoulis said.

"You're right," Silva said, sitting up and looking at him. "I'd have a charge against someone I don't want to see prosecuted. And dropping the charge later would make our case against the real murderer look weak and us incompetent."

"Maybe there's something we've missed," the sergeant said.

Silva swung his chair so he faced his desk and placed a sheet of paper on the left, then another next to it, and a third next to that. He studied them, then shook his head. Dupoulis picked up the first one and read it over carefully before placing it back on the desk. This case was easy now except for one frost heave on their road—and that from someone for whom the truth could be a release in more ways than one.

"He received a massive blow to the head," Silva summarized the sheet in front of him, "from a large can of paint, which probably fell on him. He was knocked unconscious. He was hit by other objects falling on him. His throat was then cut by a piece of glass, probably broken at the same time the paint cans fell." He put the sheet down and continued, repeating information he had gone over a hundred times in his head. Somewhere in all of this was a way to show the truth to the ones who needed to be motivated by it to speak. "One glass shard had paint on it but no fingerprints, and was found lying a few feet from the body. A scrap of paper towel from a trash barrel in the studio had blood on it that matched the victim's. Another scrap found in the trash can at the back of the building also had blood on it that matched the victim's. A third piece was found in a trash can from the administrative offices. The blood also matched the victim's. That can was collected on Monday and never emptied because Buddy was so distracted from his work."

"You know," Dupoulis said, "it'd be so much easier if people would use regular weapons."

"And leave declarations and confessions for us," Silva said. Both men laughed. Closing in on a murderer was both exhilarating and daunting, and both men knew the cost of a minor slip, an apparently meaningless detail.

"At least it's a simple murder. We know how it was done—nothing technical about it," Dupoulis said.

"And the time is clear, late afternoon. The evidence from his wounds, stomach contents, and Buddy's phone call all land at the same time—between three and five o'clock on Saturday afternoon."

"Just about now," Dupoulis said as he glanced up at the large clock on the bookshelf over the chief's desk. The time was 3:59.

"That's right," Silva said, looking up at the clock. "That's right. I wonder how much is the same today," he said half to himself. Before Dupoulis could reply, however, Silva went into the office next door, where he pulled a small radio from the bottom desk drawer. He had strictly forbidden any music in the office but he knew about (and winked at) the occasional use of a radio late at night. His men understood the exception and honored it. Now the forbidden sounds of rock, then rap, then jazz, roared and whispered into the room as Silva pushed the tab along the dial. When he stopped, everyone within hearing recognized the local radio station, which served northeastern Massachusetts and southern New Hampshire.

The announcer's voice gave the time and then segued into a list of prices for Golden Delicious apples, brand-name sneakers, and European-designed blenders. The prices were noticeably low, even to a man like Joe Silva, who bought his last pair of sneakers two years out of college and was still wearing them on weekends. The announcer concluded with a seductive promise of more to come at five o'clock and a reminder that all these goodies were available at the mall just over the border. His last words promised, in a voice that stimulated any fantasy a glamorous woman on television might inspire, a full list of the best farm and store prices for the following day, Sunday, up at the mall and surrounding markets. The promise of erotic experience in the voice guaranteed that most of his listeners at four o'clock would be back at five.

"That's it," Silva said, turning off the radio. "Go over to the station and get a statement about their program last weekend," he ordered Dupoulis. "Get a tape of the entire afternoon if they have it. And I want a car on Mrs. Mattson. I want to know where she is every single minute." Dupoulis's confidence that he had already identified the murderer was gone in a second.

■ ■ ■

Preston pushed aside the remains of the apple-and-onion casserole, a new recipe he hoped not to see again. It didn't help to remind him that the housekeeper's choice of menu usually reflected her conversation with Ellen the day before. Preston had once tried to impress this on Ellen, but her eyes had glazed over and the conversation had veered off in another direction. He thought then of all the times he had lost control of a discussion and vowed it would not happen again, particularly that evening. Since right after Chief Silva had left his office, Preston had been brooding on his situation, dissecting the chief's comments, and finding in them none of the reassurances his lawyer had so off-handedly given him. It was beginning to make him ill.

"I can see this situation has upset you." He was pleased with how he referred delicately to Vinnio's death and repeated the line to himself. Still, it was true that Ellen had been acting strangely during the last few days. Even now she wasn't responding as he had expected her to. "We're all upset by the way things are going, dear."

Ellen looked up at her husband, then lowered her head as she returned to her own thoughts. She mumbled an agreement several times. Only after several seconds did she realize she was sending her assent into silence. She looked up. "Didn't you say something, dear?"

"No, I didn't, Ellen." Preston pursed his lips and looked annoyed. "You're very distracted these days, Ellen. I'm worried about you." This was the truth. Whatever had happened over the last few weeks at the college between Hank and Ellen was still unclear to Preston, but Ellen's behavior over the last few days convinced him that something indeed had happened. He was worried. He didn't like not knowing. It made him feel vulnerable.

"Are you really?" Ellen seemed to find this cheering news. "How sweet of you, Preston." She smiled at him. "I thought you might be upset because of Ed Correll's threat. He seems awfully angry." This thought sent her off into another period of intense frowning.

"Yes, he does," he agreed. It was uncanny how she could go straight to the one point that was pricking him. Correll's threat of a lawsuit, for some reason, had not receded in significance. After the initial shock, Preston had expected the lawsuit and its implications to die down to the level of a personal squabble between friends, something easily settled during a friendly get-together, but that hadn't happened. Instead, for some reason, Preston seemed to feel more vulnerable to the law (as he envisioned it) and Ellen less so. This, of course, made no sense, and Preston explored various theories to explain it. He concluded finally, reluctantly, that it must be because they still held everything in common and remained living together even though they weren't legally married. He was still fully and equally involved in Ellen's problems, which seemed especially unfair for a man who always tried to do everything right.

"Ellen, dear, you really do seem agitated," he said as he shifted in his chair.

"I'm much better." Her replies came automatically; they would have suited any conversation.

"I think some time alone is what you need." The solution had come to him that afternoon, and he had spent almost two hours constructing a dialogue that might allow him to advance it. "Perhaps a visit with some friends is what you need. After all, someone you once knew, ah, quite well," Preston faltered, then continued, "someone has died. And death—of anyone— always requires some period of grieving." Preston was glad to be able to make use of this bit of popular lore, and smiled. "And you might feel more comfortable among your women friends." He wondered if this was going too far, taking too much of a risk in suggesting the intimate nature of her rela- tionship with Hank, but he decided he was brave to face it and gave himself a metaphorical pat on the back. "Yes, I think that would be just right."

"That's a nice idea, Preston, but I don't know if I feel like a visit right now." She was still deep in her own thoughts.

"Of course, you do." He pushed his plate farther away, forcing himself to go on smiling. None of his students gave him so much difficulty when he hinted at what they should do. He tried again. "You're always glad to see your friends. Besides—"

"Yes?"

"Well, I could use the time for my work and you wouldn't have to worry about me being here alone with nothing to do." This seemed such an eminently sensible argument that he wondered why he hadn't thought of it first.

"Your work?"

"Yes." She was starting to annoy him; he hadn't worked her recalcitrance into his script. "My art, remember?" He stopped himself before he could give in to the temptation to snap at her, composed himself, and said, "My art, my work, dear. I have a show coming up in a few months. I want to concentrate on producing new work for my show. I'm sure you can understand that."

Ellen's head nodded up and down, her face cleared of all emotion, her eyes fixed on her husband.

"Good. Then tomorrow will be exciting for both of us," he said in a tone that most adults reserve for talking to a child. "You'll enjoy the hustle and bustle of getting off to a visit with your friends and I'll get back to my work. It's all settled, then. Excellent." He left the table and resettled himself in the living room, pleased with how well he had handled the situation. He couldn't see Ellen behind him, or the expression on her face.

11
SUNDAY

"THE CARS ARE IN PLACE." Dupoulis rattled off the locations of three other police cars as he deftly steered through the center of town. He went on with details about who was where, how long they'd been in place, what they had seen. Only the departure of Ellen Mattson on Saturday evening interested Silva, and her arrival at a small but opulent summer house on the lake at the edge of town even more so. According to the officer in charge, she had remained the night, opening up the cottage by turning on every light, pulling sheets off all the furniture, and playing classical CDs alternating with rock music until almost three in the morning. Since no one else was staying in any of the other homes in the area, the police received no complaints.

"She built a fire in the living room as soon as she got there," Dupoulis said, "and seems to have spent the night in front of it." Silva nodded. He didn't need the details, not now. He had the ones he needed, the ones that would convict. What he wanted now was a witness intelligent enough to see that and to admit to what he already knew, what he had pieced together from the bits of a report or an interrogation that hung in the background like cobwebs. He had the truth, and he only had to convince a murderer of that, with or without a supporting witness.

Sergeant Dupoulis was still talking, about his briefing of the other officers, getting the warrant, going over the evidence. He was excited, tense. He was young, Silva finally thought, and not in years. Silva shifted in his seat, resting his arm on the open window. He had made too many arrests in his career to be excited, for he no longer felt exultant at the achievement, only relieved. He never felt the driving need to get a kid who seemed too free, too happy in the discovery of his own being, too careless to stop at every stop sign. He left those kids alone, to be nudged onto a narrow path of responsible behavior, not to be pushed into alienation from police and community by a resentful, small-minded cop.

Exultation was saved for the arrest of the career criminal, the man or woman who delighted in poisoning a life, injuring the harmless, the pathetic, the defenseless. There were, in his view, people placed in the world with the goal of hurting other people. Building a case against someone like that incited in him an intelligence and a tenacity that always surprised him. In years past, arresting one of those, people he considered evil—though he was reluctant to use that word among his fellow officers—was cause for celebration and congratulations. And he exulted. What he had to do today was different.

Dupoulis turned onto a quiet street and Silva felt the moment of decision coming closer. Today he would end the freedom of a decent if imperfect life, of an ordinary person trying to live out an ordinary destiny to whom fate had given a twisted path. This was the kind of arrest that unsettled him. Murder was a crime with no forgiveness, but he would be inhuman if he did not understand the grief and longing that drove a man or woman to kill. Desperate, confused, scared, one person destroyed another; now, methodical, unfeeling, relentless, the state would destroy one too.

A college professor once told him about a small tribe in Asia in which murder and other violent crimes were unknown. The anthropologist attributed this remarkable state of affairs to the tribal practice of analyzing dreams every morning. Silva, even then, attributed it to their small number and isolation, which gave them the opportunity to deflect or moderate deeply embedded traits of human nature. He wondered how the tribe was faring, now that outsiders had found it and penetrated it enough to identify and study the practice of dream analysis. Silva estimated one murder every fifteen years; no, he corrected himself, that probably wasn't right statistically. It depended, in his view, on how deeply outsiders penetrated the culture. It was Silva's theory that those least willing or able to tolerate change in their lives were the most likely to lash out in some way: the lawyer who embezzles, the uprooted wife who turns to affairs, the son who chooses drugs, the daughter who gets pregnant, all because they cannot adapt to change.

Dupoulis pulled onto a dirt road and Silva touched his pocket to check for his notebook, then looked across at his sergeant's pocket. How would the townspeople feel when they discovered that someone they considered one of their own was guilty of murder? How long would it take them to repudiate the criminal?

■ ■ ■

Ed Correll parked his car on the edge of the driveway and looked up at the modern house. This was what he had always wanted, not this house per se, but life on this scale, life on a scale that embraced all the world as he knew it, life as his brother, Joey, had meant to live it. He always intended to follow his big brother, work for him, learn from him, grow with him, but then Joey married Ellen, and Ellen had a different dream, one that didn't include younger brothers. He wondered if he would have acted so quickly if Ellen had treated him differently while Joey was still alive.

Late Thursday night Ed Correll got the news that for a few glorious hours had changed his life: Ellen was already married when she married Joey. Ed's mind did not linger to speculate on Ellen's character—her motives or moral failings or oddities, or even on whether or not Joey had been happy—for more than a few seconds; rather, his thoughts leapt instantly to the implications of an undissolved first marriage. He didn't stop to call his lawyer first. The opportunity seemed so obvious that he instantly made up his mind, and his call to Preston on Friday morning was just confirmation. In Ed's view, when Joey died without a will—and without a legal wife—his estate belonged to his parents, and since their death, to him. As Joey's only living close relative, Ed was entitled to everything Joey had, or so he told himself.

This line of reasoning sounded solid, unassailable, true, and he placed it before his lawyer, a friend who had once done some legal work for Joey. Bill was cautious, serious, and Ed was sure he could win him over in time, but he was wrong. Bill frowned and mumbled about the amount of time that had passed and seals on records, the difficulty in proving intent to defraud on Ellen's part as well as Joey's ignorance (who is to say what she told him about Hank?), all the time squirming in his chair. It wasn't what Ed had expected from someone who was almost a friend, and it took him half an hour before he understood that Bill wanted nothing to do with the idea for strictly practical reasons. Ed almost kicked the teak desk in front of him. It had been so easy for Joey and so hard for him, and he had almost managed to change that.

Ed slammed the door of his compact car and walked up to Preston's front door. He knew now, after several surreptitious phone calls to friends and friends of friends, that at least one-quarter of the house belonged to Preston, his contribution after he sold his own modest Cape and sunk the profits, along with Ellen's from the sale of her house, into what he considered the perfect home for an artist: an architectural wonder with a cantilevered roof on one part. The solid redwood facade, with its tiny upper-story windows, concealed sweeping walls of glass on two ends that came together like the stern and the prow of a ship dipping low to cut through the ocean of pines ahead.

Never before had he come so close to so much—almost two million dollars in real estate and unemployment on an equally grand scale, all in forty-eight hours. In his eagerness to embrace his dream, he had almost quit his job; he shuddered to think where that would have left him. Ed pressed the doorbell a second time. Just twelve hours ago, at 9:30, as he opened another beer and finished a sandwich, his spirits sinking with the day, Ed understood what Bill had been telling him. There was no way in the world he could wrest Joey's wealth, as Ed regarded it, from Ellen. That was his attorney's position, but Ed still harbored one last hope.

Ed leaned on the buzzer, wondering if Ellen and Preston were already busy at 9:30 in the morning. He stepped back to get a look at the garage, but both doors were shut. He'd forgotten what it was like to sleep late on the weekend, something he'd loved to do before he got married, and yet even when he thought for sure he would have all that had been Joey's, it didn't occur to him to plan for a housekeeper. All he imagined was himself lifted out of his world and planted in another. Now he'd be happy to settle back into his own life with as little fuss as possible. He'd had an awkward time as it was explaining to his wife why he had to see Preston Mattson at 9:30 on Sunday morning. This was "her time," she insisted, her time to do something other than child care, and "his time" to be a father. He refused to think about what he had promised her to get away. On Monday he had to face even worse at work. At that instant, he heard his brother Joey once more, the one who was going to take him higher than he could get on his own. How could he have forgotten his advice: Never brag; it attracts the wrong kind of attention.

Ed banged on the door and started when it opened almost instantly. Preston stood in the doorway in his pajamas and robe, scowling. Ed knew he had to make his pitch work in less than two minutes, and he hadn't counted on Preston being in a bad mood. Ed followed Preston inside, listening for the right opening. He complimented Preston on the coffee, declined an offer of toast, and exhibited an interest in the artwork on the walls. This last effort, however, produced unexpectedly little warmth in Preston, so Ed immediately dropped it and got down to business.

"First, I want you to know how very sorry my wife and I are about how difficult things have been for you during the last couple of weeks." Ed smiled. This wasn't sounding as warm as he wanted it to. He tried again. "Personally, as far as we're concerned, you and Ellen are legitimately married, no matter what anyone might say." That seemed better, to Ed's ear at least, and he hoped it sounded as pleasant to Preston. He waited for Preston's acknowledgment. Preston scowled.

"So," Ed went on, "I've decided to forget about the lawsuit." He shrugged his shoulders and lifted his hands, as if to dismiss the whole affair as a fluke, an absurd aberration. "We've known each other too long, eh?" He smiled even more but Preston's continuing silence was starting to worry him. He had counted on some reaction from the other man by now.

"Really?" Preston raised his eyebrows.

"Really. Hey, we're—"

"Why?" Preston asked bluntly. He stared back at Ed, who couldn't think of any other time when Preston had asked a direct question.

"Well, we've been friends for so long. I just don't want to sue." Ed laughed, keeping a friendly open look on his face. This was not the Preston Mattson he had known for so many years, the man without a savvy bone in his body, the man who could be led to admire the sorriest middle-aged washout just by an apparently admiring reference to the fellow's clothes. This was the one who was now proving to be impervious to Ed's maneuverings.

"What do you want?" Preston now regarded him with

open hostility and suspicion, but this sounded to Ed like an opportunity not to be missed.

"I'd like to see us go on as we were," Ed said. "We can reach a nominal agreement and let it go at that." The lawyer's words came back to Ed, and he felt a glimmer of satisfaction when he began to think he might get more from Preston than Bill thought possible.

"Nominal? What's nominal?"

"Nominal, just nominal," Ed said, still smiling and nodding reassuringly, every syllable modulated to end on a comforting downward note.

Preston watched him. "I'm glad you've come to see things reasonably." Preston began to assume his old personality, but still something about him was different. "I'm sure we can work something out. But we do have to be specific, don't we?"

"Yes, right, good, yes, good." Ed wasn't quite sure where he had taken the conversation even though it sounded like he had won a point. "I suppose I could come up with a percentage. How does that sound?"

"A percentage of—" Preston left the sentence unfinished and vaguely waved his hand in the air as though groping for the precise amount, a caricature of his usual self. Then his eyes hardened. Ed gulped.

"Well, of what Ellen held jointly with Joey when he died. The part that would have gone to his parents and then me." Preston didn't blink at that, and Ed grew more confident, watching for Preston's reaction; he knew the other man could fall on either side of the offer, backing away or accepting with a handshake, but Ed was sure he had him now.

"The rest—" Preston said softly.

"Whatever she held in just her name, I know, is fully hers, no matter what. Besides, Joey loved her." Bill had been adamant about that. If Joey chose to put his considerable profits into Ellen's name, then it was hers unless Ed could prove fraud. His only hope—and it was a slim one Bill wanted nothing to do with—was to seek a settlement on what Ellen and Joey owned in common. Ed, therefore, tried to sound as though he were willing to accept less than he knew he could get. It might make things move more smoothly, Ed thought, if he sounded generous and understanding, proving that he had no hard feelings for Ellen, and therefore for Preston. That seemed a nice touch, he thought. He tried not to think of Bill.

"Quite," said Preston.

"But I think a percentage of what was held jointly at the time of Joey's death would be fair," Ed said, hoping he still had the initiative. He found it easier to smile now. No matter what Bill said, however, Ed felt aggrieved and always would. He watched Preston, but instead of seeing a man coming to agreement, he saw a man whose eyes grew harder, like black pellets falling deep into a rifle barrel. This reaction was so unexpected that Ed felt momentarily off balance. He had expected some resistance, and was prepared to discuss the many advantages of reaching a settlement of this sort. Concerned that Preston's eccentric response might mean that Ed was losing his attention, he began to go through his arguments one by one, watching Preston for some sign that he was impressed by one or another of them. Instead, Preston's icy cold eyes stared back at him.

Just as Ed approached the final, most persuasive point, Preston said, "Fine. I'll think about it." He stood up and moved to the front door, forcing Ed to follow him. "I'll be in touch." Preston pushed Ed out the door and ran to the telephone in his study.

■ ■ ■

Chief Silva stepped past Ellen Mattson into a stone-and-wood entry hall. When he turned to speak to her, she was just leaning out the door. She couldn't fail to see Sergeant Dupoulis at the wheel of the police car. Frowning, she swung the heavy wooden door shut and preceded Silva into a living room of cream-colored sofas and chairs. The fire in the stone fireplace crackled and dirty plates and glasses, pillows and blankets, were scattered around the room. The silk-clad hostess looked out of place in her own living room, though she had told him during one of her many digressions that she had decorated the lake house herself and considered it her favorite refuge for the summer. Though supposedly closed up for the season weeks ago, it hadn't taken her long, Silva noticed, to give the place a lived-in feeling. He kept his eyes on her face when she turned to him, but all he saw was a wariness and perhaps some surprise, a sign, he hoped, of her not having anticipated his arrival.

When she motioned him to a seat, he looked for one that might have more firmness to it than the deep sofas and chairs. This might have been an old hunting lodge at one time, but it was now only slightly less luxurious than her other home in Mellingham. He pulled a straight-backed chair from next to the fireplace and drew out his notebook.

"I want to hear from you one more time, Mrs. Mattson, exactly what Hank Vinnio said to you when you saw him in the painting studio on Saturday afternoon." He flipped through his notebook as nonchalantly as possible, trying to convey to her the relatively minor importance this interview had for him. He had calculated that this approach would calm her, free her to remember and to talk. If he was wrong, he was in trouble.

"I told you everything I can remember." She was stiff in defense against his questions.

"I just want to get a sense of the afternoon, of what he was like. I've read your statement, and it covers your actions perfectly. This time I just want to learn anything I can about Hank, not about you." Silva waited, praying this ploy would work. Ellen studied him.

"Well," she said, considering this new purpose of the interview.

"He said hello," Silva began.

"No, no, he didn't. He called me by name." She crossed her arms across her chest, angry but also pouting. "He was showing me he knew who I was."

"And then what?"

She glanced around the room, frowned, screwed up her face. "He said he knew I remembered him, something like that." She made no pretense of politeness, letting her irritation show. "I told you all this and you wrote it down and I signed it. I don't have to go through this again." She stood up.

"He remembered you, Mrs. Mattson." Silva leaned back slightly, keeping his voice calm, even, bland. "I don't see what the problem is. You can admit to that. I'm only interested in what Hank was like. So, now, he remembered you, he threatened you."

"No, no, he didn't. He didn't do anything like that." She snapped her mouth shut, twisting her hands together.

"He walked up to you and surprised you," Silva persisted.

"No. I told him so." She sat down abruptly and leaned toward the chief. "He thought he'd surprised me. He really did, but he hadn't. I told him. I told him I wasn't surprised. Of course, he couldn't accept that. He didn't believe me. 'Surprised to see me, honey? You aren't the only one.'" She sneered as she mimicked him.

"He was moving closer. He was trying to scare you."

"I don't know. I don't know if he was trying to or not, but I was scared anyway." She looked up at him. For the first time, Silva thought, she was without a façade, telling the truth.

"Go on from there. What happened after that?"

"He badgered me—about being married to Preston, about having been married to Joey. He knew all about Joey, how he was starting to make a lot of money. He hinted at how well-off I was." She twisted sideways on the sofa.

"Go on," Silva urged her.

"He just hinted about money," she said, looking away.

"What kind of hints?"

"He was alive when I left." She grew tense, ignoring his question.

"I know he was," Silva agreed. "I know he was."

"Well, if you know that, why are you still questioning me?"

"Because I think something else happened." He waited. "Something did happen, didn't it?" She hunched over as he spoke, her hands gripping the sofa, her shoulders tight. "There's something else about that afternoon that's important, something you saw or heard. You have to tell me everything you can remember. I don't think you killed him; I just think there is something you know that will help me." This admission from the chief of police so surprised her that Ellen leaned back and stared at him.

"Well." She glanced up and down as if trying to come to a decision. "It was awful. I was so scared." She let the fear come back, washing over her as she looked down at the white carpet beneath her bare feet. "He had brown sneakers on and he had a drop of red paint on one toe and green paint on the other. I kept thinking it looked just like Christmas on his sneakers and that was crazy and I should get out of there. I should run away. But I couldn't. It was like I was stuck to the ground. And then I had to. I knew I had to get out of there and I just reached out and pushed him. He fell and hit the crates stacked along the wall. I didn't mean that to happen. It made him angry. He started to come at me again and I pushed myself away; I pushed a stack of crates at him and ran." She stopped speaking and the house was still, except for the fire whistling and gasping nearby. "I could hear them falling when I was running down the hall."

Silva waited. He knew it wasn't over yet. He had heard too many confessions to think they stopped with the escape.

She took a deep breath; it shuddered down to her lungs. "When I heard that Hank had died from a cut throat, I thought he had died in some kind of freak accident, so I thought it didn't really matter about the boxes and crates because they hadn't killed him. So I didn't say anything. Then when I heard that he'd been murdered, that it wasn't an accident, well, it seemed too late. So I didn't think about it anymore." She leaned back, pouting.

No, he thought, you certainly didn't. But at least you have now.

■ ■ ■

"Well, thank you anyway." Preston hung up the telephone. He crossed a name off the list in front of him and flipped the pages of the telephone directory. A light oily film had formed over the remaining coffee in his cup, and his toast sat cooled and uneaten beneath the travel section of the Sunday paper. He was getting hungry again; it must be close to lunchtime. He pulled his watch from his bathrobe pocket. It said 3:30, but that could hardly be. He shook the watch, then held it to his ear, forgetting that a quartz watch made no sound, no comforting ticking like another heart when he was alone. The golden second hand spurted rhythmically on its circle, ignoring Preston's frantic shakings. It was indeed 3:30. He had been dialing the telephone for almost six hours. He flexed his index finger; it felt stiff.

Preston dropped his head into his hands, which brought fragments of his forgotten breakfast into sight; he pushed the scraps of toast into the wastebasket. In less than five minutes this morning Ed Correll had, for the second time, thrown Preston's life into turmoil. He wanted to strangle him, to lock his hands around Ed's throat and squeeze, looking into the eyes that never looked at him. He wanted to stomp on him, crush him with his foot, break the arms that never broke in a golf swing, from the first tee to the last. A man to whom Preston had always been courteous, considerate, even deferential on occasion, had threatened to sue him, thrown his personal and professional life into disarray, then come back to say it was all a mistake. That was fine. Preston could forgive; he was generous. But what about Ellen?

The mere sound of Ellen's name in his head jolted Preston and he reached for the address book again. He was down to the letter *R*. He had to reach Ellen before anyone else did, especially Ed. It would be just like him to seek her out and set things right for himself before Preston had a chance to get things sorted out with her first. He should never have taken Ed seriously in the first place. The guy was nothing but a small-town, small-time loan officer at a tiny bank, and he'd had the nerve to threaten Preston. Preston had a good mind to sue.

This thought sobered him at once. The last thing he wanted was a court action for any reason. That's what had gotten him into this mess in the first place. He wiped his hand across his forehead and groaned. He was hungry, his mouth tasted like the bottom of a garbage can, and he needed a shower. He almost called for Ellen, then stopped himself. He had to find her. He put his finger on the first name under *R*—Rabkin. Surely Ellen wouldn't have gone to stay with Mike Rabkin? He rocked back and forth in his chair, but, he admitted to himself, he had called stranger prospects today. He dialed Rabkin's number, practicing his spiel while he waited for someone to answer.

In the six hours since Preston had pushed Ed Correll out the door, he had adopted at least six speeches to give to Ellen. Each one had been discarded as Preston's mood grew increasingly frantic. At first he had opened with a genial inquiry about how she felt, progressing to an exchange of casual information he had forgotten to give her the day before, and moved, seemingly for lack of anything else to say, to a mild offer to have her back, but as his phone calls produced no response, confused disclaimers, or outright hostility, his intended overtures grew more inviting until the last one was downright imploring. Unfortunately, he had no opportunity to deliver it, even though he was now resigned to abject contrition.

Mike Rabkin didn't answer the phone, and to be certain

he hadn't dialed a wrong number, Preston dialed again. This time he let it ring only twelve times before he slammed down the receiver. It wasn't fair. He pushed the phone away. He had only done what any reasonable man would have done and now his life was going to be ruined because he, a reasonable man, had listened to Ed Correll. No matter how Preston looked at the situation, Ed was guilty. If he could just locate Ellen before too much time elapsed, she would see that too. No man could be expected to stand idly by while problems entirely of his wife's own making threatened to engulf him; he had done only what was prudent. If only others were as reasonable as he was. He turned to the next number and dialed. No one answered.

There was one other possibility that had seemed remote until now, but Preston began to think it rather a good one. Tonight was the opening of a new exhibit in the school gallery. He and Ellen always went to the openings; he was, after all, chairman of the painting department. A sudden rush of warmth for who he was in his professional life came over him, momentarily pushing aside a cold reality. He thought of his office, his command of students, and the school staff. The more he thought about it, the more likely it seemed that Ellen would expect to meet him there; they had never missed an opening, after all.

Comforted with this thought, Preston took his breakfast plate into the kitchen and made himself a cheese sandwich. Life looked a bit better as he soothed himself with reassurances and rationales. As dismaying as the last few days had been, life would go on as it always had. Preston eyed the clock. It was 3:55. He had three hours before the opening, just enough time to finish the address book.

■ ■ ■

The longer the day got, the closer Chief Silva drew to his goal, but that didn't make the whole thing any easier. It was past four o'clock, he was tired, and Sergeant Dupoulis was watching him as much as the suspects. Silva would be glad when this case was over. He looked around the neat and modestly furnished living room while the door closed behind him and the sergeant. The Sunday newspaper, each section neatly folded, sat piled at one end of the sofa. A tray holding an empty cup and saucer and a sandwich plate with a few crumbs sat on the coffee table. Betty Lane walked over to the radio in a cabinet and shut off the light opera filling the room.

"Please." Betty motioned the two men to seats and sat down in an old wing chair, reiterating her willingness to help in any way she could. "Though I do think I told you everything I know already."

Chief Silva went through the niceties again. "Some points we've uncovered have left a few questions. I just want to get a few things sorted out."

"I'm glad to help, Chief." It was obvious to Silva that she meant it, and he was once again reminded of her importance to the college. She might not be loved by everyone, but she was admired, respected, and trusted. Definitely trusted. Students and faculty alike relied on her and she had been eager to push and prod them through real life. In some ways, particularly her lack of personal feeling for her charges, she reminded Silva of his elementary school teachers, women who might like a few of the children in the class but never let it go any further than that. Betty Lane had no regard for the individual creative artist; her mission was strictly business—to keep artists in touch with the exigencies of reality—and she did it well. Silva thought of all the accolades he had heard about her over the last few days. He thanked her again for seeing them on the weekend. She smiled. Dupoulis had his pencil poised over his open notebook.

Silva led her through information that, he suspected, everyone at the college now knew better than most of the men on the force; she nodded, added a detail, a comment, fully relaxed.

"What about Mrs. Mattson?"

"What about her?" Betty was perplexed.

"Had you ever seen her before she started taking painting classes?"

"She only started doing that when she married Professor Mattson a few years ago. Before that I don't know what she did. Why do you ask?"

"I got the impression that you might have known her before. She comes from your hometown."

"Really?" She shook her head, and Silva was convinced she spoke without pretense. "I had no idea, but then we never spoke socially. I only see her in the office once in a while, when she's meeting her husband." Silva believed her, and wondered how things might have been different if the two women had recognized each other three years ago.

"We now know that someone left the college building at approximately four o'clock, right after encountering Hank Vinnio in the painting studio. We know that person had a disagreement with Vinnio and ran out, after leaving Vinnio injured." Silva paused. Betty struggled to absorb this new information; it was obviously a surprise to her, but Silva wasn't sure which part of his statement surprised her.

"Well, then you have the murderer, haven't you?" She clasped her hands. When Silva didn't respond, she said, "He got into a fight and died. Isn't that what you just said?"

"No, Miss Lane, not quite." Silva continued. "When this person left, Vinnio was injured, lying on the studio floor amid crates of paint and broken jars and the other paraphernalia of the art school. He was lying there, unconscious probably, when someone else came in, someone who hadn't planned to. Maybe this person saw the lights on. They would be on in at least the painting studio. Or maybe this person heard the crates falling. They must have made quite a racket. The sound of the falling crates and jars and the rest of it must have been loud enough for someone outside the building to hear." Silva tipped his head to one side, looking thoughtfully at Betty. "But I think you said something like that, didn't you? About what a racket the crates must have made when they fell? Anyone in the parking lot or in the offices would have heard them falling."

"I don't remember, Chief. I might have said something like that. I mean, it would have been obvious from the mess, don't you think?" She took a deep breath. "Anyway, I wouldn't know. I went shopping with my friends. We often do that. We spent the day in New Hampshire."

"When did you see what a mess it was?" Silva asked.

Betty stared at him, her face paling. "I'm just surmising. It must have been a mess. Buddy said he had a lot to clean up." She looked hard at him now. "But I never saw it. I told you when we got back. It was well after five o'clock. I just picked up my car and drove home."

"It was four o'clock, by your own admission." He noted the startled look on her face as she turned away to think.

"That's nonsense," she said. "It was five o'clock. The store prices were on." She smiled the smile of victory.

"The prices you and your friends heard on the radio ran at four. You were listening to the previews." Silva spoke calmly. He had decided earlier in the day that he would approach her differently, obliquely, by showing her what minor, apparently unimportant details he had and letting her see for herself where he stood. The soft reproach that he was deferring to her gender, because he disliked seeing women involved in violent crime, never left him over time. He could see the light of awareness creeping into her eyes, and he wondered why he had thought this would be easier than confrontation. He was glad he had cautioned her at the outset.

"What was the last store you visited?" She named a store only an hour's drive away. "Did you buy anything?"

"No, but one of the others did." She spoke firmly, more confident now that the questioning had moved to her alibi.

"I've been there. Their receipts come from a computer that records both day and time." Silva waited while Betty assimilated this information. "Most people only look at the total and their change, or at the total and their signature. Receipts have changed in the last few years; they have a lot more on them now. Your friend's receipt is punched two forty-three. You drove straight back from there. It's only an hour." Betty was silent, leaning back in her chair.

"You arrived back at the college a few minutes before four, driving around to the back parking lot. You sorted through your packages and your friends drove away. You heard a crash and went in to investigate. You must have wondered why the door was unlocked, with only one car out front and one in the back, but you knew students sometimes worked on Saturday. Were you worried they might have done some damage?" Betty stared at him. "The truck out back belonged to Vinnio. The car out front belonged to Mrs. Mattson, but she was driving away by the time you entered the rear door.

"You went from room to room, looking around for what might have caused the noise, and found Hank Vinnio lying on the floor, unconscious. At your feet, vulnerable for the first time since his arrival at the college, was the one man who could hurt you in any way. Unconscious, possibly injured, he was at your mercy. This was an opportunity you hadn't sought, and it must have felt like fate giving you a second—no, a third—chance. Near you on the floor was a shard from a broken jar. You picked it up and went over to Vinnio." Silva paused, expecting Betty to interrupt him with protests and denials, but she didn't.

"Don't be squeamish, Chief," she said. "He was an odious man. You're wasting your finer feelings on a rodent."

Silva was stalled; it came so quickly, so easily, this flash of truth among the murmurings. "You cut him, a neat cut across his throat. But still pretty bloody, despite how carefully it was done."

She raised an eyebrow. "Was it?" she asked with a smirk.

"We found the shard with his blood on it. He bled to death."

"Really, Chief Silva. Are you trying to make me feel sorry for the man?" Betty said, her eyes cold. She adjusted her legs so that her feet were exactly parallel. "I don't think you quite understand what happened."

"Tell me where I'm wrong so far." She didn't answer. "You cleaned off your hands with a tissue," Silva went on, "and threw the glass onto the floor and the paper into the wastebasket. Did you decide to check the rest of the building, just to be safe? Did you want something in your office? It doesn't matter. You went in there, to your desk. You wiped your hands once more, leaving—"

"For all your investigative powers you don't seem to be able to get even basic information correct." She sniffed with disdain and Silva decided she no longer understood the seriousness of her comments. "My leg," Betty said sarcastically.

"You left the tissue in the wastebasket there, locked the office and left." Again he waited for her to comment, then continued. "You locked the back door, then left one more tissue in the trash bin behind the school, on the edge of the parking space. Buddy found it a few days later."

"One of my shoes," she said, growing angry at his failure to draw the correct conclusions.

"Of course, your shoes." Silva thought of the search warrant in his pocket and the evidence waiting for him in the next room. He was deeply relieved. "The blood on all three tissues matches Vinnio's." Her lips drew into a tight circle of disapproval. "You didn't reset the alarm, just locked the building, front and back. Would setting the alarm have been too obvious? Or were you too upset?"

"Upset?" she asked indignantly. "Over him? I don't think you've quite caught on yet, Chief. As for the alarm. Well, it's not my job to set alarms."

"I see." This wasn't going at all as he'd planned, but he could hardly complain. "So you just left it. Well, Vinnio was dead by four-thirty. It took him some time to die."

"Typical of him," she said. "He would have to make as much of a mess as he could. I didn't want to touch him, but he certainly had made a mess, knocking all those crates down. I'm sure he meant to do worse. You have no idea what kind of person he was. The way he behaved towards me. The idea! The very idea! With the school counting on me and that, that, well, there's nothing decent to call someone like that." She tugged at her skirt, pulling out an imagined crease.

"I think I understand," Silva said.

"Well, I should hope so."

"He recognized you," Silva said.

"He said he recognized me right off, the very first day, as though that were a sign of intelligence." She snorted and curled her lip.

"When did he tell you that?"

"Just a couple of weeks ago." She closed her eyes as though she could erase the memory. "He had the nerve to come into my office and insinuate." She opened her eyes and lifted her chin. "He had no business being there at the school. And trying to make trouble for me, as though I were just a secretary, someone to intimidate. The nerve!"

"He must have been just a boy when you saw him last. He would have changed a lot over the years. But you were already an adult."

"He was always worthless, but, yes, he was all of ten or twelve. I don't know how he remembered me. I don't look at all the same." She patted her hair. "Maybe he didn't. Maybe it was just a lucky guess. His mother was a friend of . . . of the other Betty Lane." Silva nodded. He had guessed most of it. "She let me stay with her for a few months. I left my husband; he was going nowhere except into trouble." Poised and confi- dent in her own living room, Betty looked thoroughly unfamiliar with failure. "I knew it would be like that for the rest of my life unless I got out. So I did. I left him and went to stay with Betty. She took me in." She spoke without feeling, as though the event had had no importance for anyone.

"And then the fire," Silva prompted.

"Yes," she said. "The fire. The fire." She paused. "The whole place went up while I was out. The landlord was not safety conscious, not at all. He was careless about all sorts of things. No one was there except Betty, only I didn't know that until it was all over. There was nothing left. It was just a little place." There were three apartments in the building, Silva knew, tiny ones, but three homes. One apartment was empty and a couple lived in the third one. They were out too when it happened.

"Betty Lane died in the fire," Silva said, wondering how close she could come to that memory.

"Some things are just meant to be, I guess." With these words, the woman on the sofa dismissed the life of another, one who had been a friend. "The Red Cross found me a place to stay, in another town. They were not organized," she said, looking knowingly at him. "It took hours to set it up. They helped me fill out forms about what was lost," she said and paused. "They really weren't very competent. They seemed so efficient, with all their papers, but it really was confusion masking chaos. Then a man came to see me and look over the building, or what was left of it, which wasn't much. He called me Miss Lane. That's how disorganized they were. When the check came, I knew what had happened. He was young, in a hurry, honest but careless. He obviously wasn't very well trained. I kept the check. Not for the money. It was only a couple hundred dollars. Betty didn't own much, some furniture and her clothes. She'd just sold her car so she could buy a new one. She didn't have a checking account. She didn't make much money as a clerk. Really, after everything she'd been through, all they were offering was that tiny check. Well, it made me mad, I can tell you." She snapped her mouth shut in a disapproving line, and Silva saw again the face of the woman she had been for so many years.

"What about her friends? Her job? The insurance company?" Silva knew strange things happened every day, but he marveled at how this woman had carried out a major fraud year after year.

Betty laughed contemptuously. "The firemen made a mistake in their reports and I never said anything. The insurance company canceled her policy right away. I called the place where she worked and told them I was a friend of hers and she was quitting because the fire had upset her so bad. And I told her friends that she was going to visit distant relatives—she had no close family—to help her recover. When you move away, Chief, people who once said they would die for you forget you in two weeks." She spoke without resentment, merely reciting a series of practical steps and her own reasoning.

"I did what I had to do, and I think if you ask anyone at the college they will inform you of just how well I have served that school. Half those students wouldn't graduate if it weren't for me just because they wouldn't be able to tell when they'd finished all their requirements. I wasn't going to allow someone like Hank Vinnio to interfere in my life. A man with no decency whatsoever? I'd have to be mad."

■ ■ ■

At precisely 7:30 Preston Mattson surveyed the crowded gallery and worked his way through guests mingling in the doorway. He liked to wait until a large crowd had gathered before arriving himself, to avoid the awkwardness of standing around with no one to talk to or little to talk about, a hazard for all early arrivals. Although this had been his practice for years, he still spent time calculating the time of his arrival before every event. Today had been no different, even though at first his mind had been preoccupied with finding Ellen. He had put that concern aside, convinced that since Ed Correll had dropped his threat of a suit, all would get back to normal. It was just a matter of time. Ellen must know that, although if asked why he thought so, he could not have said. He turned sideways to work his way through the crowd.

He encountered a group of his painting students, but since they seemed to be inordinately absorbed in one of the works in the exhibit, he moved past them, smiling and nodding. No sooner had he reached the interior of the room than one of the freshman painting students swung around in front of him. The young woman tugged at her father's arm, turning him to face her painting teacher. Her shy but sincere praise flowed forth. Preston relished such recognition and knew all the tricks for drawing out a compliment. He moved graciously from parent to parent, so absorbed in his own pleasure that he forgot his earlier worries.

Chief Silva saw only the crowd in the doorway as he stood outside the administrative offices. At the far end of the hall, outside the last classroom, Buddy waved before he turned toward the stairs. A few students with their parents were exploring the rest of the building, which had been cleaned up for the occasion. Whenever one of the fathers glanced at him in an effort to identify him, Silva had to remind himself he was in mufti. After all these years, he was now more self-conscious in street clothes than his uniform no matter where he was. In another moment Evan Goldman, dean of the faculty, came striding down the hall from the gallery.

"So sorry I wasn't here when you called. Come on in." The other man hustled Silva into his office and into a chair. "It must be important to bring you out here now." From anyone else the comment would have sounded like a reproach, a mild or stern reproof, but from Professor Goldman it was genuine. He was ready to help and his face was eager and warm.

"We've made an arrest and I thought someone at the college might want to know before the news hits the streets or the newspapers. Your president is out of town, I understand."

Goldman nodded and Silva reported the arrest of the woman he had known as Betty Lane. After recovering from the shock, the dean reacted charitably, much as the chief expected him to, testimony to the woman's year's of dedication and hard-won respect.

"You must stay," the dean insisted at the end of a brief discussion about what would happen next. Goldman overrode Silva's protests. "We're a good little college. I want you to know us at our best. You've seen us at our worst. Now give us a chance to balance the scales. This is one of our best exhibits, and I noticed some of your men are here. Please enjoy the exhibit as our guest." It was a fair request, Silva agreed, and walked back to the gallery with the dean.

■ ■ ■

Preston Mattson was also pleased with the opening. He turned to the dean of faculty, and said, "Well, Evan, a very good turnout. You must be pleased. The biggest in all your years here, I believe."

"I would say so, Preston. Just one sign of how much the school has grown."

"Yes, indeed, it has." He repeated this phrase in a soothing murmur several times. "Of course, it will always be a small school, there's no doubt about that. I think it's very important that we maintain a manageable size, don't you?" Preston asked this question of the dean, but since he was also looking out into the crowd he didn't see the side glance the dean gave him.

"A favorite topic of mine," the dean said. "A school can grow either in size or in quality, but not both at once under the same plan. It's one or the other, in my view."

"Indeed," said Preston, only half listening to him. "I agree."

"Good, I'm glad to hear it. And I, as you know, have always wanted us to grow in quality." The dean paused while Preston again mindlessly agreed. He went on in a different tone of voice, one that finally caught Preston's attention. "I've been having some interesting talks with some of the students, Preston. They've made several suggestions for improving the painting program." The dean stopped speaking while Preston turned to look at him. "Perhaps you'd be interested in hearing them sometime?"

"Ah, yes, thank you, Evan, thank you. I'm sure they'd be most interesting."

"Some other students have come up with an excellent idea for a spring show," the dean continued. "They're going to put on a special exhibit of the work of students who have graduated in the last five years. It seems their first idea was too big for them and they've asked permission to change it. I said we had to discuss it, but I think they've made a sound decision."

"Really?" said Preston as he stared at the dean. "The spring show, but—"

"Yes. They convinced me that we should be focusing on our graduates out in the community rather than on ourselves, the teachers."

"Did they?" Preston was not pleased with this; it was a betrayal, a dismissal of all his time and effort to help them get his show ready. He had spent time, time, time, preparing for this. He was planning on it.

"Yes." The dean looked away from Preston, nodding to an older couple nearby.

"Well, I'm sure that's an excellent idea." Preston managed a mild if forced enthusiasm. They were, after all, only students. He would explain to them later the protocol for shows such as these, and his.

"Good, good," the dean said, still looking at the crowd. His voice changed again. "Hard to believe that some of these younger couples are actually parents of our students, isn't it?"

Preston nodded. This was all very irritating, to have his

plans disrupted without even a single student consulting him first. And on top of all that to have to make small talk about the students' parents was too absurd.

"Makes me think about retiring," the dean said. "How about you, Preston? Have you started to think about retiring? Or moving on to other things? You must be giving it some thought these days, eh, Preston?" Their eyes met, and the dean nodded before turning away.

Preston was stunned. The dean was being absurd, ridiculous, just running off at the mouth because he couldn't think of anything else to say. Preston had far too much to do right now at the school to think about anything else. He'd barely been able to fit in the spring show and had only agreed when he'd thought the students wouldn't take no for an answer. Right now he had all that artists' health hazards material to disseminate. He certainly couldn't leave it to Betty Lane to handle on her own.

He glanced around the room, searching for the prim figure of the school secretary. That's just like her, he fumed to himself, to let me down now. She's never around when I need her.

■ ■ ■

Professor Goldman made a point of introducing Chief Silva to several other guests, then left him to enjoy himself. Through the crowd Silva could see Ken Dupoulis casting doubtful glances first at the paintings, then at a young woman who seemed to be his companion; she, for her part, was entranced by the artwork. Amused by these and other viewers, Silva was glad enough to browse alone. He readily admitted a lack of artistic knowledge, but not of curiosity, and he was now and again delighted by the apparent incongruity between title and work. This was, to his mind, one of the most entertaining features of modern art and he gave his mind up to the full enjoyment of it. He was standing in front of a black linen collage with a French title when Karen Meghan joined him.

"It's for sale, Chief. You could hang it in the station."

"I'd probably have to get approval from the board of selectmen and a vote of town meeting," Silva said, "and that might take a while. Besides, it's not quite my taste." She pointed to another painting of the back of an alley seen from a fire escape.

"How about this?"

"Pretty good," Silva said admiringly.

"So you're fond of the Ash Can School." The soft Scottish lilt lifted over his shoulders, and Silva and Karen turned to see Gregory Stewart. And Lisa Hunt. Silva's hand went to straighten his tie unconsciously as they greeted each other. He missed the rest of Stewart's comment as the Scotsman leaned toward the painting to point out something to Lisa. Silva scrounged through his memory but he had no recollection of Stewart and Lisa being friends. Even after interviewing both of them about Hank Vinnio and what they knew about the school and the day of the murder, he never picked up any hint that Stewart and Lisa were such good friends. It bothered him. He had the unreasonable feeling that one or the other should have told him about this relationship.

Only Karen's gurgling laugh nearby brought Silva back to the present. Lisa and Stewart moved off, and Silva turned back to the painting, feeling a trifle insulted as well as unsettled. He didn't think the painting was the least bit trashy. It was certainly realistic, but that was what Silva liked. His mother had collected copies of the work of Domingos Rebelo over the years, ensuring that her children would grow up knowing what life in the Azores looked like even if they never went there. For a long time this was as close to serious art as Silva got. He had little opportunity to visit museums, but he had once seen a book of paintings by a man who painted street corners and diners in the Midwest. He liked those. This painting reminded him of them. He watched Stewart across the floor, knowing that the revision the man's character was undergoing in his mind was unfair, small-minded, and temporary. He turned to the next painting, nodded to Karen and her friend as they disappeared into the crowd, and thought once again of his mother's lament. She was right; he was going to have to move faster.

"Did I hear you say you liked that painting of the alley?" Chickie Morelli stood beside Chief Silva, his dark hair brushed to the side, his usually somber and thoughtful face animated. Silva allowed as how he did, comforting himself with the knowledge that someone else must like the trashy paintings, since there were several included in the exhibit.

"I do too. I think John Sloan and the Ash Can School produced some of our country's best work." Silva's brain did a quantum leap to catch up with Chickie.

"Really?" Yes, really, Chickie said, and proceeded to tell the chief exactly why he thought so. When the young student started to explain the work of Edward Hopper, he made a convert to the world of art and a friend for life. Silva felt redeemed and not a little smug.

"Well, it's obvious you chose the right path." Silva offered the compliment with feeling, and was surprised when Chickie shook his head. "No?"

"No. I've just discovered my mistake." For a second, the dark hair fell down over his eyes, and Silva felt himself looking once again at a stranger, then Chickie brushed his hair out of his face. "I have a degree from a community college in California," Chickie said, "and I thought getting an MFA would help my career but that's all wrong. I'm good enough to be working on my own, painting and selling, if I can. If I go to school for another degree, then I'll be qualified to teach painting in school but I won't for sure be a better painter. I've had trouble seeing the difference between a career and a job."

"I think you lost me." Silva was stumped by the once-laconic student's sudden outpouring.

"I went to college to be able to get a job so I could paint, and I was turning into a bum, just like Hank." Once again Chickie was lost behind a screen of black hair.

"That's a bit harsh."

"Maybe." Chickie flushed. "I need to paint, but I don't need to be taking classes and getting approval from other people. If I need to work on technique, I can work for a while with a senior artist. Mr. Muir is right."

"Mr. Muir?" The name of Mellingham's famous sculptor as well as infamous gadfly instantly caught Silva's attention. The chief began to hope he might actually learn something before Gordon Davis did. "What has Henry Muir got to do with it?"

"He's giving me a job, sort of an apprenticeship." Chickie spoke matter-of-factly, as though a job with Henry Muir were as easy to come by as sand on a beach. Now Silva finally understood what had prompted Muir to wind up his battle with his neighbors.

"Let me see if I can guess," Silva began, but stopped when he saw the familiar hoary head and melanous brows. Henry Muir winked at the chief.

"I'm going to be working in part of the gallery, doing my art and helping with exhibits and stuff like that." The young man, once more boyish in his excitement, smiled at his new employer and proceeded to explain to Silva the schedule that would leave him time to paint every day. It was an ideal partnership. Chickie moved off to the refreshments table and Henry Muir turned to the crowd, ready to slip away. For a second he turned back to the chief and whispered, "He will be great." The crowd absorbed him so fast that Silva wondered if he had really heard him. But he knew he had.

Feeling happier that his last mystery was solved, Silva moved on around the room, working his way from one painting to the next. On the opposite side of the room, Gregory Stewart and Lisa Hunt were discussing a large picture of an automobile. He touched her arm and drew her attention to a detail. Somehow it seemed right, even to Silva.